Lindos Eros
and
Hades

John Wilton

PublishNation

www.publishnation.co.uk

Acknowledgements:

I would like to say another huge thank you to all my friends in beautiful Lindos. My warm thanks go to my good friends Jack Koliais and Janis Woodward Bowles, both of whom encouraged me greatly to get on and write all my Lindos novels. My thanks also go to everyone in Lindos and beyond, including the many regular Lindos visitors, who have said and written such nice things about all my previous novels. Finally, my boundless gratitude and admiration goes once again to Fiona Ensor for her tireless proof-reading efforts in identifying my errors. Any that remain are entirely my responsibility.

Needless to say, this story is total fiction, some of which is set in the period in 2020 of the Coronavirus lockdown across Rhodes and Greece in general. During those, and the subsequent difficult times of the global pandemic, I wish my friends and all the people of Lindos a safe and healthy life. I hope that life and tourism for all in the village will soon be able to return to the normal usual bright and sunny Lindos times. Without the magical village of Lindos, and the people in it, this novel could never have been written. For that reason, as with all my previous Lindos novels, I will always be eternally grateful to the people there, my friends in that magical paradise.

Author's website: www.johnwilton.yolasite.com

Previous novels by John (available on Amazon and Kindle):

The Hope (2014)

Lindos Retribution (2015)

Lindos Aletheia (2016)

Lindian Summers (2018)

Lindos Affairs (2019)

Lindian Odyssey (2020)

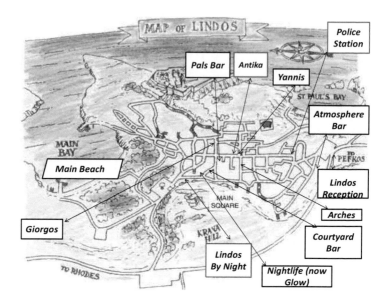

MAP OF LINDOS

Police Station

Pals Bar

Antika

Yannis

ST PAUL'S BAY

Atmosphere Bar

MAIN BAY

Main Beach

TO PEFKOS

Lindos Reception

MAIN SQUARE

Arches

Giorgos

KRANA HILL

Courtyard Bar

TO RHODES

Lindos By Night

Nightlife (now Glow)

The Pythagoras Cup

This is a story based on the philosophy of the Greek Pythagoras cup, and the principle of behaviour embodied within it. Pythagoras of Samos was an Ionian Ancient Greek philosopher. A Pythagorean cup looks like a normal drinking cup or beaker, except that the bowl has a central column in it and a line marked a short distance below the rim. The column inside the cup has a small hole at the bottom of it. Inside the column there is a u-shaped pathway which loops up and then straight down through the stem of the cup, culminating with a hole at the base of the cup. When liquid is poured into the cup the u-shape fills up at an equal level. Once the liquid goes over the column, and therefore the top of u-shaped pathway, the liquid is siphoned out of the bottom of the cup and doesn't stop until it is empty. The siphoning works by gravity and hydraulic pressure.

Consequently, if the cup is overfilled beyond the line, for instance with wine, all of the wine will drain out of the bottom of the cup. The philosophy of the cup relates to morality and greed. Don't want or seek more and more than you have, because if you do, in the end you'll end up with the accidental disaster of nothing. For a man and a woman in this story that is the dilemma they faced; a dilemma lingering between Eros, the Greek God of Love, and Hades, the Greek God of Hell and Death. Initially, it was about the possibility of taking a chance, making the leap by expressing their love for each other, but that might simply result in the hell of rejection and disappointment, and the death of any hope of lasting love between them. Eventually however, the man is forced to acknowledge that even greater danger loomed for both of them from overfilling the Pythagoras Cup by seeking more between them, seeking to live a life together – the danger of Hades and death.

Part One: The two of them

1

The attraction

"How long are you here for? One week or two?" she asked, having taken his order.

"All summer, I'm here all summer."

"Oh, really? Are you working on the beach?"

That confused him. Why would she think he was working on the beach? Strange. He wasn't exactly young, at least not that young. Not like someone who looked like he was on a gap year before university or even between years there, and had come out to Lindos for the summer and took a job on the beach selling sunbeds or even renting out pedalos or kayaks. He might wish he was that young, but he definitely wasn't. Those days were long gone. Not that he'd ever actually taken a gap year, or had the opportunity to as a teenager, as his teenage years were gone by the time he went to university.

He couldn't help but smile slightly over his amusing confusion before replying, "No, not on the beach. I suppose you could say I'm working here, but not in that way anyway. I'm a writer. Here for the summer to finish a novel, hopefully. Why the beach? Why did you think I'd be working on the beach? Do you think I look like a beach bum then, here for the summer?"

He was rattling off questions, deliberately trying to engage her further in conversation.

She never reacted in the way he'd hoped though, or explained her reason for thinking that. Instead, she just told him quite coldly, "Oh, okay, I'd better get your food order into the kitchen."

Then she made off, order notebook in hand, towards the door to the restaurant kitchen on one side of the upstairs terrace.

Maybe it was his amusement at her "Are you working on the beach" question, amongst a few other things, but she'd definitely had some sort of immediate interesting effect on him. Something he hadn't reckoned on happening at all when he merely chose a random restaurant for dinner on his first night of that summer in Lindos; the first night of his long summer of 2019. There were plenty to choose from and they all looked good. This particular one was pretty busy considering it was early in the season. Like most of the others its main dining area was on an upstairs terrace in the warm evening air, and all the tables were occupied, except for one.

It was a summer that was to precede global events the following spring that made Lindians and their tourist visitors wonder and doubt if things could ever be the same again as they were in the summer of 2019 in the little village, as well as in all those previous summers over the past forty years or so. It was to be a summer that made him wonder if things could ever be the same for him too. He wasn't intending to eat out at restaurants every night, but for the first night he'd decided not to cook in his small flat, but treat himself instead.

As soon as he saw her, set eyes on her that first time, there was something about her that instantly appealed to him. An edge he called it. She had an edge. How to describe that to anyone? Not easy, but it was definitely something, something obvious to him. Something that immediately struck him, registered with him instantly as very attractive. An attitude? A self- assurance? Sort of, yes it was all of that and more, and yet as he was to find out over time, somewhere in that unfathomable personality mixture there was also an insecurity that surfaced and suppressed all the other elements on occasions. Yes, there was also anger, always bubbling below the surface, liberated by her often simply to fight the insecurity.

Yet it was that edge of hers, comprised of all those emotions, that defied description which made her most attractive, for him at least. Maybe that's the way it always is between a man and a woman. Those that are most attracted to

3

one another. Maybe it should be, and should always remain, indescribable, an attraction beyond description. Maybe, in reality, that was the essence of the attraction, the struggle to put it into words? Maybe that merely enhanced its appeal. Not merely at first, with the instant initial attraction, but as an enduring one over time, for as long as the edge doesn't fade. Perhaps that was what he liked about her most of all, the sum of the parts of her character that defied description. He made his living through the use of words, hopefully now through his writing. Yet he couldn't quite find the words to completely describe this enigma of a woman who he'd stumbled across purely by chance that evening. Nor could he completely find the words to describe and determine the instant effect she had on him.

It was crazy. They had barely exchanged a few sentences, most of which were about his order, but it seemed he wouldn't be able to get her out of his mind that evening or for most of the summer. Can anyone really have such an instant dramatic effect on someone from such a fleeting initial meeting? It had never happened to him before. He'd known and met many women over the years, but none of them had such an immediate effect on him, not even his ex-wife. Of course there was her looks. The way she looked, dressed, laughed and smiled. But that wasn't all of it, by any means. There was much more to it. She definitely wasn't bad looking, but not what could be described as stunning. He'd met better looking women than her, stunning even. Although her looks did attract him it was the rest of her, what he immediately experienced from her character that had the greatest effect on him, even in so brief an encounter. As it turned out, her attraction, and that effect on him, would only constantly increase throughout that summer. That wasn't what was supposed to happen. It wasn't what he came to Lindos to do. It wasn't the reason he came to the picturesque little tourist village to spend the whole summer. That was something else altogether, something totally different. The two things – his attraction to her and the reason he came to Lindos – were not connected in any way. At least, that is what he thought at the time.

Was she sexy? Did she exude and radiate sex appeal? Not in an obvious sort of way, anyway not for him. There was definitely something though, definitely something for him, some sort of sexiness which attracted him to her strongly. Something deeper, a deeper type of sexy, if there was such a thing. Something that felt deeper than a blatant, obvious superficial sex appeal.

There had been others of course, other women in his past. A few, in fact, but none like her, none that were anything like her in any way. Certainly none that had the instant effect on him that she did. The question that went through his brain was what was his impact on her? Was she thinking he was worth a second look? He had the whole summer ahead of him to find out and to explore that possibility.

2

Him

David Alexander was in his late thirties, just turned thirty-nine to be exact. He'd been divorced for ten years, having been married for eight years prior to that, and had three children, two boys and a girl. They were all teenagers now and living with his ex-wife, except when the eldest boy was away during his first year studying Law at Manchester University. He was quite tall, around six feet, with light brown shortish hair, and a relatively slim figure. Although not exactly well built he had so far managed to stave off the seemingly obligatory paunch, or even larger stomachs and beer bellies so proudly displayed by some British tourists he'd encountered on his previous holiday visits to Lindos.

His quite long, thin face, with its striking jaw line, wasn't yet displaying any of the creases of middle age, although he was starting to think when they might begin to appear, especially with the effect of the Greek sun during his present extended Lindos stay for the whole summer. At one point he had briefly tried to cultivate the standard academic beard. Very suitable for a lecturer in Russian Literature perhaps. However, he quickly abandoned that idea, not least because he reckoned it made him look more like Rasputin than Chekhov. Resembling a mad Russian mystic wasn't really a good look for a university lecturer. So, he was clean shaven, although he did wonder if during his six months sojourn on that particular Greek island he would try the beard and bohemian writer look once again, if only from laziness of not being bothered to shave. In fact, he was soon to realise and experience that beards are not particularly comfortable at all during the heat of the Rhodian summer, even if some Greek men did favour them.

David had taught Russian literature for thirteen years at Bristol University. In more recent years that had strayed over into also teaching contemporary Russian foreign policy, not least because the two subjects were historically linked. Whenever anyone asked him what he taught though he just told them about the Russian literature, and never mentioned the foreign policy stuff. He decided that as a subject of conversation that was a bit of a minefield in the current political climate.

As forty came charging towards him he'd decided to deal with what his ex-wife described as his own particular mid-life crisis by impulsively quitting his well-paid Senior Lecturer post and do what he had wanted to do for years. Instead of reading and teaching famous Russian writers such as Tolstoy, Dostoyevsky, Turgenev and others, he would become a practitioner rather than an observer and attempt to write his own great novel. Where better to try and find the peace and unhindered solace than the picturesque village of Lindos on the island of Rhodes. At least that was the thought he set out with at the start of that summer, even if it didn't quite work out that way. David had been there quite a few times before for holidays of one or two weeks. However, this time his stay would be for the whole summer, from early May to late October if necessary. From his past holidays there he knew quite a few of the Greek locals, as well as some of the Brit ex-pats living and working in and around the village.

His new life would be filled with writing. The aim wasn't quite to be the bohemian writer's lifestyle in Paris. Instead, his initial intention was to embrace and enjoy the rootless drifting life between places such as Barcelona, Havana, or Prague and Vienna, much like some of his Russian novelist heroes or the likes of Hemingway. He would travel between those places as and when he wanted. In the end he'd settled simply for Lindos, at least for that first summer. It didn't exactly fit in with those other literary and author associated cities, not anywhere near the same impact or importance. But it was a start, a safe start in a place he was familiar with and amongst people there he knew quite well.

He'd rented a small flat right in the centre of the village, just behind a couple of the popular bars, Yannis and Bar404. It was probably best described as functional, with a double bedroom, a basically furnished lounge, a small kitchen, including a required washing machine, and the usual Greek shower room plus toilet. It was one of two flats in a courtyard which pleasantly got the warm, sometimes very hot, Rhodian sun for most of the day. The flat's greatest attribute in the middle of the hot summer, however, was undoubtedly its much needed, perfectly functioning air conditioning unit. When the owner showed him around he flat he instantly thought it would be perfect. It was central in the village, simply furnished, and low maintenance in terms of keeping it clean. The shutters on one side of the bedroom opposite a small desk opened onto the alley outside, allowing the sun to stream through most of the day. That would provide the perfect setting for sitting and writing his great novel. In the grand scheme of things, and of holiday lets of one or two weeks in the village, the flat wasn't that expensive, as long as he agreed to rent it for the whole six month period.

It was indeed more than adequate for what he intended to achieve through that summer of 2019, writing and completing the first draft of his novel. Any sort of meeting or relationship with a woman was furthest from his mind, at least until that first encounter with the waitress at the Lindos restaurant. Instead, his intention was to focus and concentrate on his writing. Providing all went well with his writing in the mornings he would reward himself with a quick baguette lunch and a cappuccino at Café Melia in the Amphitheatre square just around the corner from his flat, or at Giorgos café bar on his way to the beach, mostly Pallas Beach, for a deserved swim in the clear blue Lindos Bay cooling sea. Very virtuous.

Anyway, his recent track record with women and relationships wasn't exactly studded with success. Given what happened in some of those after his divorce, some of his male friends found it hard to accept that in his teens, even his late teens, he was very shy where women were concerned, as he told them. Not at all confident in approaching them. To some degree elements of that lack of confidence lingered even now.

He found himself occasionally briefly wondering if all of that - his lack of confidence and his relatively poor track record of relationships with women - was in any way connected to the final years of his relationship with his mother. A psychologist would no doubt readily dig around in that particular abyss given the opportunity.

He never spoke to his mother for seven years after she left his father when he was in his late teens. On occasions he even walked past her in the street without exchanging a word. When he recalled those times now it ripped his heart out. That was an indescribable feeling over stupid self-centred actions at a particular time in his life. Only when he heard that his mother was dying of cancer in hospital did he visit her, talk with her, and try to convey his sorrow over his actions in response to her leaving. His only consolation was the smile on her dying face when she saw him arrive at her hospital bedside. By then his mother and father had divorced, but he even managed to persuade his father to visit her in the hospital with him at that time. Why do people react in such stupid idiotic ways over people they loved? He always regretted the way he reacted, but was glad that at least he managed to see his mother before she died a week later.

He never really knew the reason why his own marriage eventually ended in divorce. All he knew for certain was that it wasn't his choice. One of his cousins even told him some years later that she felt he never really fought hard enough to save the marriage. There was no infidelity involved by either him or his wife, definitely not on his part, and as far as he knew not on her part either. She simply told him one Sunday evening that she was unhappy and wanted them to separate. He had no clue at all that was coming. Looking back on it perhaps the fact that he didn't have a clue that she was so unhappy, and felt the need to say what she did when she did, said it all. Anyway after living apart for almost two years she filed for divorce when he did eventually start seeing other women.

In the middle of David's divorce his father died of a heart attack. It was only after he'd gone that David realised that they'd never really talked about important things, such as when

9

his mother left, not about feelings. Perhaps it was a generation thing. His father's generation never opened up and talked about things like that, their feelings. David was the oldest, but his parents had lost three other children. Neither his father nor his mother had ever talked to him about his brother's or his two sisters' deaths. He knew how they died, of course. His brother was killed in a road accident on a bicycle at fifteen. One of his sisters died when she was just a year old and the other when she was only four months old.

Now he was older David thought he understood much better what affect those deaths must have had on his parents, particularly his mother. His brother was killed less than a year before his mother left his father. Perhaps that had an effect on her decision to leave?

Grief grows inside you. It never goes away. It gnaws away and even after a long time, after many years, just when you think it has finally gone away it comes hurtling back into your mind over the smallest thing. That was the case for him.

He often wondered if all that – what happened with his parents and with his own marriage and divorce - had an effect on his later relationships with women? After his divorce there were, indeed, a few other women and relationships, not entirely successful, or even in some cases remotely so. The longest relationship of those that he'd had was for four years, until the woman went off for a fling with a French guy for six months. Following that there was almost two years of pain after she eventually came back to him. He always thought he would never be able to handle what had happened between her and the French guy if she did ever want to come back to him. However, when she told him she wanted to he changed his mind and convinced himself that he could. So, they got back together. It wasn't the same. Not least because it always seemed that actually it was her who found it much more difficult to handle what she had done than he did. Finally, the madness of the situation got worse and worse. It culminated with her bizarre suggestion that he should have sex with one of her best friends. In an almost matter of fact way one evening over dinner she told him that would even up their infidelity. Equally amazing was that, according to her, her friend had agreed to it. All that knocked him sideways at the time, and that is when he realised there was no future between them and ended the relationship. Although he didn't at the time, looking back on it now from some distance he could at least take a more light-hearted view, often remarking when he recounted the story to his friends that he'd surprised himself with his reluctance to take up the offer as her friend was very attractive, lovely. In reality, it was another disaster, a loss in his realm of relationships, if that is what most of them could be called.

The worst and lowest moment for him of that disastrous relationship was when he quite literally curled up in despair and went to sleep on the grass on a hill nearby where they were living after she came back to him. He was totally lost, not knowing quite how to deal any longer with all the craziness coming from her towards him. Despite her infidelity, for some unfathomable reason at that point she clearly never trusted him. Whether that was a reflection of her being unable to deal with her own guilt or not he had no idea, but she was by then regularly going through his phone and his work diary. He actually had nothing to hide, as he consistently told her. He was being completely faithful. Given his later string of subsequent relationships that was something some people found hard to believe, but at least he knew it was the truth.

Then there were the two Czech women he met at an academic conference near Vienna about six months later, who were best friends. The conference was held in the autumn in the small town of Baden bei Wien, near Vienna. The narrow atmospheric streets were bordered on either side by beautiful perfect examples of the architecture of the Habsburg Empire. The buildings definitely added to the romance of the place. In his mind he could easily picture the musical masters Beethoven and Mozart hurrying down the narrow streets while the sounds of magical symphonies were incubating in their heads. Beethoven had a house there where he stayed for some summers, away from the stifling heat and dust of the city of Vienna. He stayed there during the summer months and used the mineral baths in the spa town in an attempt to cure his many ailments. It was whilst there in the summers of 1821, 1823 and 1824 that Beethoven composed large sections of his famous Ninth Symphony.

In the park near the hotel in which the conference was being held the strikingly coloured autumn falling leaves had already begun to cover the paths that the three of them, David and the two Czech women, walked together in the chill early evening air. The crisp leaves crunched beneath his shoes and the women's leather ankle boots. No doubt influenced by the romantic surroundings, and the historic atmosphere of the place, he found himself initially attracted to one of the women. Eventually though, a few months later, he realised that he was, in fact, far more attracted to the other woman, who was her best friend. By the time he recognised that, however, it was too late. After the conference he started an affair, or more accurately some sort of relationship, with the first woman, all be it a long distance one between Bristol and Prague, where the two women lived. For a few more months he grappled with all the extremes of emotion one way and another over both of them and how he felt. Almost inevitably, of course, he messed it up and fell between the two. He hurt one of them, the first one he was attracted to, when he finished his affair with her. By which time it was obviously too late for him to tell the other one how he felt, her best friend, and definitely by then far too delicate and insensitive.

Most of the other women after that were more or less simply a string of dates. The most amusing of which was the blind date his friend fixed him up with in Bristol. All went well over dinner that evening in an Italian restaurant. No awkwardness or long silences. At the end, when she said she needed to go off to the toilet, he told her that he would get the bill. She responded by suggesting they shared it, but he told her he would pay it and she could pay next time. He said that with a smile, trying to make it as light-hearted as possible, but she responded with, "How do you know there will be a next time?" He was a little taken aback, but assumed that the smile she accompanied that with was encouraging, not discouraging. When she returned from the toilet, however, and he'd paid the bill, she had a very surprising question for him.

"Before I agree to meet again I need to ask what you think of Doctor Who?"

"Err … I don't really watch it," he began to reply. "But I do like David Tennant. Is he still playing the Doctor?"

"No, no, what do you think of the Doctor?" she pressed him.

He was bewildered. With a bemused look on his face he told her, "You mean the fictional character?"

"No, no, no he isn't. Of course he isn't fictional. He definitely isn't," she snapped back at him aggressively.

"But he-" he tried to respond as gently as possible.

"No, he isn't," she interrupted, still aggressively, adding, much to his surprise, "If you don't believe the Doctor is real I certainly don't think we can meet again. There would be no future in any relationship between us."

"Oh, I … I … I see," was all he could say while she immediately got up and left, without even a goodbye. He did though allow himself a slight smile as he muttered, "Perhaps she has a Tardis waiting."

He could chuckle about it for years later. Not least, because when he relayed the story to his friend who had set up the blind date his response, with a laugh, was, "Oh dear, David, I'm guessing that was just her way of politely telling you she didn't want to see you again."

Then there was the woman he dated four times who lived in Southend in Essex, who was determined not to tell him where she actually lived, and insisted one evening when they were on a date that he change into a shirt she had bought him that day. She had bought it because she thought it would suit him and was desperate to see him wear it. The problem was they were in his car in Leigh-On-Sea, near Southend, when she handed the wrapped shirt to him and insisted that he go into a closed shop doorway to change into it. Unbelievably, he did. That was when he knew there was no future in that relationship.

Finally, in that period of disastrous dates after his relationship with the Czech woman ended there was the Botox heavy drinker. Another who lived near Southend, another blind date from a friend, and another disaster. Maybe by then he should have realised that there was, indeed, a pattern emerging. She was a very smartly dressed woman in her mid-thirties and divorced for two years. He telephoned her at the request of his friend and arranged to take her to dinner, telling her he could pick her up, to which she readily agreed. When he turned up at her house and rang the doorbell she opened the door with a very large glass of white wine in her hand. It clearly wasn't her first, and later she proceeded to consume most of the bottle of wine he ordered over dinner. Not that she really gave him much chance for anything more, but he only had half a glass himself as he was driving. By the time his car pulled up outside her house later she was barely conscious. Consequently, he declined her slurred invitation to go in for coffee and simply bid her goodnight, without even attempting a kiss. When David recounted the evening his friend who had set up the blind date argued that she was probably simply nervous and that is why she drank too much, begging him to, "Give her another chance."

Unbelievably he did, but the circumstances were just the same. She was quite drunk once again when he picked her up. Against his better judgement, and much to his own bewilderment, he agreed to see her for dinner once more, a third time, again at his friend's pleading request. In fact, David's friend was dating the woman's best friend and it was she who was bending his ear to persuade David to give the woman one more chance.

Much to his pleasure and surprise, when David turned up to pick the woman up that third time she opened the door to her house completely sober, with no sign of any glass of white wine. She wanted to go for dinner at the Casino Restaurant at Southend, and he readily agreed.

Five minutes after they drove away from her house she turned to him and said, "Look, he's marked me today." As she spoke she pointed to a very small mark on the right side of her head, near to her eye.

"Sorry, what do you mean 'marked'?" he asked. "Who has, who's marked you?"

"Botox, my Botox injection. The idiot doing it today has marked me. Look." Again she pointed to a very small mark on the side of her head.

He frowned and glanced sideways at her briefly, but couldn't really see much, and simply told her, "I'd better just keep my eyes on the road."

It seemed a very odd thing to tell him, especially after the disasters of the previous two dates. Maybe she thought those went well or maybe she was so drunk on each of them that she couldn't really remember much. Either way, if not a 'red flag' warning sign, her Botox comment was definitely a 'yellow flag', proceed with caution warning. Not only did she seem somewhat young to be indulging in Botox, but it was surely more than unusual for women to tell a man about it, even on a third date, especially given the disasters of the first two.

The rest of the evening, and the dinner, seemed to go well. She only had a couple of glasses of wine and by the time his car pulled up back at her house she was definitely sober. So much so that when she invited him in for coffee this time he agreed. In effect though, he was simply being lulled into a false sense of security.

She brought the coffee – a surprise in itself as the thought crossed his mind that she would now appear with a bottle of wine – and placed it on the coffee table in front of the settee on which she joined him. As he reached to pick up his cup from the table she threw another conversation grenade his way.

"You know last year I was very ill."

"Oh, really, sorry to-"

She never let him complete his consoling sentence.

"Yes, I started bleeding from … well, you can guess where."

Now a rather large red flag was waving backwards and forwards rapidly across his brain. Where the hell was she going with this? He placed his coffee cup back on the table, just in case what she was about to tell him would shock him so much he might drop it. He certainly wasn't going to take the chance at the moment of taking a mouthful of coffee in case what she was about to say would cause him to choke on it. He was sure that

15

whatever it was wouldn't exactly be appropriate to unload on someone, even on a third date.

"Err …," was all he could manage to say hesitantly.

He didn't have long to "guess where" as she assisted him by pointing to the lower part of her body and telling him, "Down there."

He didn't really know how to react, let alone what to say. He needn't have worried. She wasn't about to give him the chance.

"They rushed me to hospital."

He stared straight ahead away from her and across the expensively, well-furnished room in total bewilderment and disbelief. She wasn't stopping though, and was in full flow.

"And do you know what I thought, David, on that hospital trolley as they rushed me down the corridors towards the operating theatre?"

He continued to sit in uncomfortable silence staring into mind-numbing space.

"I thought that I was going to die. But then I thought that at least if I did I'd have the consolation of knowing that I'd never shagged an ugly man."

Now he was definitely glad he'd put his coffee cup down and didn't have a mouthful of coffee. Not only was the red flag waving furiously, warning sirens were screaming loudly in his head. All he could hear above those was a voice in his brain saying, "Leave, leave now."

He visibly took a deep breath, puffed out his cheeks and then managed to reply, "Really, that must have been difficult and worrying, thinking that you were going to die."

He was clearly flustered, but she didn't seem to notice at all. She seemed totally oblivious to his discomfort and merely continued to take sips of her coffee. No doubt what she had just told him all seemed perfectly normal to her.

Without allowing her to add any further startling revelations he quickly glanced at his watch and told her, "Well, it's getting late. I'd better get off. This has been very nice. Thank you for the coffee."

She seemed surprised. "So, soon, I thought perhaps-"

He didn't allow her to tell him what she thought. He really didn't want to know. Maybe she thought he wasn't "an ugly man" and was about to suggest a shag, as she put it, but he definitely now wasn't about to take up that offer if she was.

He got up from the sofa, telling her, "No, I really should get off," adding, "We should do this again. I'll call you and we can arrange something," even though he certainly didn't mean it.

She showed him to the door, gave him the peck of a kiss on his cheek, and within half a minute of getting up from her settee he was driving away from her house shaking his head from side to side.

The next day his friend called again to ask how it went. When David told him the, "Never shagged an ugly man," comment his friend burst out laughing. Then he told David with a snigger, "So, you never got a shag then, ugly man."

That was probably the point at which David Alexander decided to give up the chasing and the dating game, and concentrate on his academic work life. Unfortunately though, that was soon also to be bedevilled with turmoil and craziness. In fact, that, together with the disasters of his dating and relationships experiences, led him eventually to decide to take a pay off from his university post and make plans to go to Lindos for the summer to write his great novel. He'd been saying that was what he wanted to do for the past five years at least. Now circumstances had contrived to push him to actually do it.

He was to be in Lindos for the whole of the summer of 2019. The plan, the aim, was to get on with his writing. That definitely didn't include any relationships with women. At least that is what he thought and intended until the Lindos waitress crossed his path.

3

Her

Alice Palmer's character was far from easy to describe. It was a complex mixture. Sometimes she could exhibit a soaring, sparkling self-confidence based on an easy charm and a friendly nature as she spoke with customers at work in the Lindos restaurant. At other times, outside that environment and those work surroundings, she could also display a mountain of self-doubt bordering on self-deprecation, which could easily spill over in some moments to manifest itself in self-defensive aggression. It quickly became apparent to David during that summer that she was, in fact, much smarter than she thought, or chose to believe, even though it was never easy to convince her of that fact.

He soon learned a number of things about her character; a character with many sides and many personalities. Sometimes she displayed a bravado bordering on aggression. However, it soon became apparent to him that often that was just to cover up insecurity beneath the surface. Her aggression was a shield she allowed herself to employ to cover and disguise her lack of confidence at times. It was almost a reflex response. Her external uber confidence at times merely sometimes masked her inner self-doubt. She had her ups, "living the dream," as she was fond of saying. She had her downs, her blue times, times when she was down, not bubbly at all. Her mood swings. Even living in such a beautiful place as Lindos it wasn't all up times and, "living the dream." Although, even her blue times, her down times, still seemed to find a way to surface within a glow of her personality. That's what it felt like to him.

Alice was in her mid-thirties. She had a slim figure, no doubt kept like that now through working as a waitress in the Lindos restaurant, and continuously climbing back and forth every evening up and down the staircase to the various rooftop terraces to serve the customers. Her figure had never been challenged by the ravages of child birth. She'd been married for a relatively brief five years from when she was twenty-three and was now divorced, but there had been no children. She was medium height; around five foot six in her flat waitress shoes or the practical flat sandals most of the waitresses wore around the village when not in work. Her thick long dark black hair could reach down to the middle of her back when she allowed it, although at work she always wore it up, either in a pony-tail or piled up and pinned on the top of her head. Pinned on the top of her head was how she was wearing it the night David met her in the restaurant, fully exposing and highlighting every feature of her attractive thin face and slender neck, as well as her sparkling brown eyes.

Whether in work in the restaurant or in the rest of her daily life Alice was always a busy character, seemingly restlessly so. She wasn't content unless she was doing something. It was as if actually relaxing just nagged away constantly at her conscience. Even though sometimes in her down periods she could make a willow weep in frustration she still had a style, an irresistible style of her own that appealed to him throughout that summer, and drew him in to her. Although she never really actually let anyone in, not in completely. It was like there was a part of her that could never be really fully reached. A part of her that she would never let him into, or anyone it seemed.

One time in the office where she'd worked in Sheffield before her Lindos years her boss told her, "You're not really a team player."

"What? What's that? A bloody team player? What's that supposed to mean, and how's that relevant?" she snapped back at him aggressively.

"Look, everyone else in this department works together, even socialises together. But that's obviously beneath you," he told her with an aggressive tone now clearly also evident in his voice.

"Yep, but not obviously beneath them," she replied contemptuously.

19

As was her way, she wasn't backing down an inch. She could do that, often almost automatically. Respond with an answer that defied an argument or facilitated any further response. Her boss merely turned and walked away shaking his head. Was it sheer arrogance? Was she an arrogant person? She certainly could appear so when she chose to. David definitely saw that in her quite a few times during that summer of 2019. But perhaps it was merely her insecure self-defence mechanism which kicked in automatically; a reflex reaction from a lack of self-confidence deep within her.

Whichever it was, that particular confrontation with her boss was probably the trigger moment when she realised that she felt imprisoned in her job and in her life. The one moment, if there was just one, when she decided she wanted to change things, go to Lindos, and, "live the dream."

In Lindos Alice didn't appear to have any really close or true friends, although plenty of acquaintances - tourists through her work, other ex-pat workers or Greeks in the village. Not that she appeared either to have any enemies in the village. Somewhere deep inside her, however, there existed a place that she would never let him reach. Was that her soul? Maybe? But did she actually have one? She could turn her mood on and off just like turning a tap on and off. It wasn't an accidental response. It never appeared really completely calculated either. It was just a sort of reflex alarm and barrier inside her which kicked in whenever she got to the point that she felt was a dangerous area in any personal interaction. Then she would react instantaneously and detach herself from the person – him that summer - physically and mentally. At least that is what it seemed like to David.

Alice was a soul of the dark night in the little tourist village. She, and her world, only came alive once the sun had disappeared from the Lindos sky and the stars began to twinkle above alongside the large clear moon. She usually worked from early evening to one or one-thirty at night. Then she'd regularly go and party in the bars and the clubs, often until five or six in the morning, just like many of the other summer season workers - Brits, Albanians, Greeks and a few from other nationalities. Sometimes, on Fridays and Saturday in the middle of the summer that would be even later, literally until the sun came up. That would be in the open air Arches Plus club down by the main beach or in the Amphitheatre club on the hill just outside the village. Then it was bed and sleep under the air-conditioning until one, or two, sometimes later, in the afternoon, some food, a shower, and back to work by six or six-thirty. She only very rarely managed to visit the beach or swim in the clear blue warm sea. Living the dream didn't really include living in the sun or days of living on the beach much. Just like many of the other bar and restaurant workers, including many other Brit ex-pats living the dream, the nocturnal structure to her life began from mid-May and eventually exhaustingly petered out towards the end of October as the season ran down. By then she was completely knackered, not to mention the serious assault on her liver from the summer's alcohol consumption.

It was the way of life of many of the Lindos summer season bar and restaurant workers. It always started with excitement and enthusiasm for a new season in May and early June. Their energy began to drain and slowly slip away during the mid-summer July and August soaring temperatures, with the accompanying spiralling humidity. Relief arrived with the cooler, more manageable September temperatures, but by late September and early October the workers displayed total weariness. Despite that the majority of them loved it. Many of them returned summer after summer, like it was some sort of harmful drug that they simply couldn't resist, were addicted to. The ones that finally kicked the habit largely did so because they met someone, usually in Lindos, and either stayed together in the village for all time, or returned home to live with them. Quite a few Brit ex-pat women who came to work in Lindos for the summer met Greeks, stayed, married and had their families in the Lindos paradise. Alice was determined that she wasn't going to be one of those though. That definitely wasn't for Alice Palmer. She'd been married, not to a Greek, and was now divorced.

21

"Done that, got the t-shirt, no more thanks," she eventually told David late into one night while they were drinking together. She wasn't an easy person to get anything out of, particularly anything about herself and her past. Although at least he'd managed to eventually prise that out of her after a few drinks, along with the fact that she had no children or brothers and sisters, and that her parents were both still alive and lived in Hallam in Sheffield.

That was pretty much all he did get out of her initially about herself and her past, with the exception that she'd decided at the start of the summer of 2016 to give up her job in Sheffield, where she was from, and take the plunge to come to, "live the dream," working and living in Lindos. This was her fourth summer season, although unlike many of the Brit workers in the village she had also stayed through the intervening winters.

So, she wasn't one to talk about her past or her family easily, if at all. Not that he managed to get it out of her, get her to tell him about it initially, but her divorce had been messy. She actually met her ex-husband, Colin, in Lindos while on holiday with some women friends in 2006 and a year later they were married. They came back to Lindos a few times for holidays after, three times in all. He had a good job, working as a manager for a car rental company. Her job was as a computer data processor and programmer for a large engineering company. It wasn't the most exciting work in the world, but the pay was good. They bought a small house on the edge of Sheffield and had decided to wait a few years before considering having kids. She'd fallen in love with Lindos that first summer she came on holiday, the same summer she fell in love with Colin when they kept in touch after the holiday. She lived on the northern edge of Sheffield and he lived in Wakefield at the time they met, so meeting up after the holiday wasn't a problem. When that quickly developed into them spending every weekend together, either at his place or hers, the almost natural progression took place. They moved in together and married soon after.

At that point it appeared her life was fully planned out ahead of her. That is until she discovered by chance that her husband had been having an affair with her best friend for a year. He'd told her he was at a work national conference in Birmingham for a week. A couple of days after he got back from the conference she had a work suit of hers that she wanted to put in the dry cleaners. They had a two for one offer and so she thought it would be a good idea to take advantage of that and put the suit he'd taken for his conference in Birmingham into the cleaners as well. When she checked the pockets of his jacket for any rubbish before she put it into the cleaners she found a receipt for a double room in a hotel in Manchester for the week that he was supposed to be at the Birmingham conference. She had been suspicious of some of his actions for a few weeks, including his increasingly late work nights. Consequently, she took a chance and rang the hotel telling them she was the woman who had stayed there the previous week with him and required a duplicate of the bill. The hotel receptionist responded with, "Oh, yes, Miss Simmons, if you give me your email I-"

She rang off immediately. Her best friend, Carol, had even used her real name, or rather Alice's husband had used Carol's real name. She was shocked and stunned. When she confronted him he eventually admitted they had been having an affair for the past year, ever since Carol's own divorce. That was the end of her marriage and of her friendship with Carol. She lost a husband and her best friend. After she confronted her husband Alice got some satisfaction from confronting Carol physically. The result of which was a nasty looking black eye from just the one blow. Real friendship, as well as any real meaningful relationship, didn't come easily to Alice after that.

Alice Palmer was not someone to mess with, as Carol and her ex-husband discovered, physically on Carol's part and financially as far as Colin was concerned. The divorce was messy and Alice's solicitor managed to secure the largest part of the equity in their house for her. In fact, her part of the divorce settlement was seriously enhanced by the fact that her solicitor discovered that her ex-husband owned another rather large house besides the one that he owned with Alice and that they were living in. He'd owned it for five years and rented it out through an agent. She had no idea. That gave her some small satisfaction, together with the damage she inflicted on the major part of his wardrobe, taking scissors to his clothes the night that she discovered his affair.

The whole episode left a mark on Alice that she found hard to shake off. It made her a harder person, often appearing detached and cold. Devoid of any emotion, she wasn't easily going to let herself fall into that trap again, if at all. Trusting any man again in the way she'd trusted her ex-husband was alien to her now, completely out of her mind. She was determined that wasn't going to happen again. She had relented a couple of times and gone on dates with men her work friends had recommended and were determined to fix her up with. However, it never felt right. She never felt comfortable. It wasn't that they were unattractive, just that she couldn't get past the trust issue. Consequently, she hadn't had anything that could even remotely be referred to as a relationship since her divorce.

So, there were certainly a couple, or even more than a couple, Alice Palmer's. She was different characters in different surroundings, and in different circumstances. The Alice who was the waitress working in the Lindos restaurant was friendly and chatty with the customers, the tourists. She was very good at that, and not only in the restaurant, but also when she encountered any of them after work in the late bars or the clubs. Then there was the aggressive, self-preserving, and simultaneously defensive Alice. That Alice occasionally surfaced when she encountered other Brit ex-pats in Lindos, as well as, at times through that summer, David. Often there didn't appear to be any reason or explanation for the contrast in her character, or indeed, the timing of it. Equally though, the chatty, friendly Alice could also unexpectedly re-emerge when talking to some Brit ex-pats, and even with David. When that happened with him, and she was much friendlier, he put the difference down to something developing between them. That's what he wanted to think of course, convince himself that was the case. Not that he knew for certain, but her defensive aggression he rightly or wrongly put down to the fact that she'd obviously been hurt in her past, probably by a man. Now she appeared determined not to let her guard down again in that respect, not let that happen again. He was right about that.

The two of them, Alice Palmer and David Alexander, were clearly both deeply scarred by the disasters of past relationships. They were two damaged people emotionally. With that constantly in the background could anything between them really succeed during that summer of 2019 in Lindos?

Part Two: Lindos, Summer 2019

4

Mid-May and the beginning

Many regular Lindos visitors say May and September are the best months. In those months the weather is great, warm but not too hot and humid, and the village is less crowded, with not so many tourists. By the middle of May the season starts to open up. The owners and staff of the bars and restaurants begin the long hot six months of sunny days ahead, stretching almost to the end of October.

The May days of sun are often accompanied with a very pleasant welcome cooling breeze. Occasionally, very occasionally, there might be the odd short rainstorm. The final voice of winter issuing a very brief protest as it bows out, giving way to another roasting hot summer.

September, more than May, was David Alexander's favourite Lindos month. The workers were beginning to display weariness after the 'dog days' of August as the searing heat had taken its toll. However, overall in September it felt like there was a soothing relaxed calmness in the village. Maybe it was merely a sense of relief amongst the locals over the slight drop in temperatures, along with the accompanying fall in humidity levels. Whatever it was, it always felt much more relaxing for David.

In September there were more tourists than in May, but the village never experienced the hustle and bustle of August, when hordes of Italian tourists descended on it during Italy's two weeks of traditional summer holidays.

Although David had been many times before to Lindos in both months, May and September, this was the first time that he planned to spend the whole summer staying in the village, even enduring the August heat.

So, it all started between him and Alice Palmer in May, just after that first meeting in the restaurant where she worked. It started in a similar way to how the season starts in Lindos; calm, careful and yet full of expectations of what was to come. Expectations of what might develop between them through the rest of that summer of 2019, what he wanted to develop. He was sure right from that first restaurant meeting that there was something between them, an awkward, but electrifying dynamic. Individually they were undoubtedly different. Through that summer they both came to realise that when they were together they were each different from what they were like individually, alone. It was as though the obvious dynamic between them produced something that made them both different people, different personalities from when they were alone. Their personalities changed as soon as they were in each other's company, even also when in the company of other people. Yes, at first it was awkward, but that awkwardness only betrayed their obvious attraction towards each other.

The next time their paths crossed was a couple of nights after their initial restaurant meeting, late in Jack Constantino's Courtyard Bar. It was approaching two a.m. As well as David there were half a dozen others enjoying a late drink, mostly restaurant workers, some Greeks and a couple of young British girls in their late teens that were in Lindos for the summer working.

The Courtyard Bar was a popular spot for British couples and families who returned to Lindos year on year, in some cases more than once each summer. It tended to mainly attract a more middle-aged clientele, many of whom enjoyed their evening cocktails seated at the tables and chairs outside in the courtyard that gave the bar its name, or up on the roof terrace with its fine views of the illuminated Acropolis. Inside the bar was traditional old style Lindian décor with its usual fair share of dark polished wood. The bar itself ran all along the length of the back wall, except for a few feet at the end where there was a doorway and a set of narrow steps down to the toilets. At the opposite end was the music console, together with a larger and wider area with some tables and chairs and room for dancing, with stairs up to the open terrace.

Jack Constantino was a very convivial bar owner and host. Some evenings there was live Greek music and dancing in the bar as Jack himself entertained the customers with his considerable various musical instrumental skills. He was a stocky, dark-haired, quite tall man in his early-fifties. Born and bred in Lindos he could relate many stories from his youth in the village in entertaining his customers, especially late at night. He'd also spent some time in America a few years before he married back in Lindos. Besides his bar, or maybe as well as is a better way of putting it, his passion was his music and he was a great fan of Cat Stevens, or Yusuf Islam as he now called himself. Jack would regularly entertain his customers with renditions on his guitar or bouzouki of the songs of his favourite musician.

The Courtyard was one of the bars popular with workers to congregate for a late drink in order to wind down after work. That was precisely what happened the night that David met Alice the second time. She came breezing in, although looking slightly weary and a bit frazzled, but had clearly gone back to her apartment after she finished work for a quick shower and a change of clothes from her restaurant t-shirt and short skirt. She'd opted for a plain black sleeveless dress, a bit longer than her restaurant short skirt, but still just above the knee. Frazzled or not, to him she still looked good in her simple dress and obligatory flat Lindos sandals, standard footwear given the uneven, and in places shiny, alleyway footpaths.

He was sitting at one end of the bar nursing his Mythos Greek beer and trying to decide if it was time for bed or whether he should have another drink of something stronger. As soon as she'd said 'Hi' to Jack and ordered a vodka and coke she scanned the bar and spotted David. There was an exchange of the briefest of smiles between them and then she quickly made her way to his end of the bar and sat on the stool next to him while Jack made her drink.

"We meet again," she commented as Jack put her drink down on the bar in front of her. Despite her work weariness there was now a bounce and bubbliness in her voice, as well as her body as she'd hoisted herself onto the bar stool. It was as if she'd been freed of her work chains and a much more relaxed mood was starting to surface.

"Well, it is a village, so it was always likely wasn't it, even if I never came back to your restaurant again this summer."

It was an awkward, clunky response and he realised that straightaway. Maybe even a nervous one, hopefully not too obvious though. She, on the other hand, now seemed completely at ease, not missing the chance to take advantage of his apparent discomfort.

"Was the service that bad then?" She allowed a slight grin to spread slowly across her lips as she teased him with that comment.

"No, no, I didn't mean that. Of course not, just that ..."

He stopped as he saw her cheeky grin, and changed the subject.

"Busy night?" He tried to eradicate his awkwardness.

"Very, and it's only mid-May. Bloody crazy, manic, I can't imagine what it's going to be like in July and August. But I said that last year, and the year before, and the year before that, so somehow I expect I'll survive."

"This is your fourth season then? You must like it really," he suggested.

That was when he first heard her use the phrase he got very used to hearing from her many more times that summer.

"Living the dream, at least that's what I tell myself to keep going."

She ended with a smile, a bright radiant one that instantly hid all trace of her weariness, and then reached to take a drink of her vodka and coke.

"Phew, I needed that. When you've been working since six there's no chance for any alcohol intake. That would be stupid, especially with all the bloody stairs you have to keep chasing up and down to the rooftop terrace with customer's meals, and the heat of course."

"Must keep you fit though," he told her. He started to add, "And it certainly looks like ..."

He stopped, mainly because she gave him a sideways glance and her pleasant facial expression had disappeared, to be replaced with what looked to him like a bit of a wary scowl.

That was the first time he saw and learned what was to become very clear to him throughout the rest of that summer. Alice Palmer didn't take compliments easily, actually not at all really.

He decided to back off and change the subject quickly, to try to lighten her mood again.

"Is this your regular after work watering hole then?"

"Here, and sometimes LBN, Lindos By Night."

"Yep, I know LBN." He felt awkward again, and that wasn't eased by her next response.

"Why, you gonna check up on me then? You're not gonna stalk me are you?"

He was hoping to see a hint of a grin on her face as she finished saying that, but he couldn't really detect one. That unnerved him. This wasn't going well. Eventually he would learn through that summer that she liked to unnerve people with comments like that, especially men if she thought they were trying to come on to her. Throughout that summer he would see her do it to a few guys who tried to do that. At this point though, he didn't know that. She had the upper hand and appeared to enjoy his obvious discomfort.

"No ... err ... stalk ... no, of course not." He was stammering and hesitating, but following a few long seconds she put him out of his misery after taking another swig of her drink.

"It's okay. You definitely don't look like a stalker. Although I can't really say I know what a stalker looks like, if there is a stalker look. Never had one thankfully."

Now at least she did offer him another grin as she finished telling him that.

30

To make things more relaxed for him she quickly added, "I just come in here or LBN for a drink or two after work, like many of the restaurant workers here, and even some of the workers from the bars that close earlier, as well as those working in the crepe shops. When you've been working solid for hours sometimes, most times, it's impossible to wind down and get straight to sleep. So, a drink or two for an hour or two, sometimes more if I go to one of the clubs, Arches or Glow, helps. Only problem with going to the clubs is sometimes it's gone six before I get to bed and then I wake up with a hangover. Not exactly, 'living the dream', more 'the nightmare'."

She chuckled as she finished, which he took as a good sign, a better sign at least.

When she turned her head to look straight into his eyes and added, "I'm Alice, by the way, we never introduced ourselves the other night in the restaurant," he definitely thought it was a better sign.

"David, David Alexander," he responded.

"Very formal David Alexander," she told him. Now she was clearly teasing him and trying to make him feel uneasy again. "In that case, it's Alice Palmer," she added with another smile, accompanied by, "But you can just call me Alice."

"So, this novel you're here to write. What's it about?" she asked.

He was surprised by her question, but pleasantly so in that she'd actually remembered he'd told her that was why he was spending the summer in Lindos when they met in the restaurant.

"Relationships, it's about relationships." He hesitated. Definitely a tricky subject, but he'd blurted it out without thinking.

She filled his silent hesitation with, "Hmm … sounds interesting, yours?"

Not a hole he wanted to go down. "What?"

"Yours, your relationships? Is it based on your relationships?" she added. She wasn't letting him off.

"No, no, it's a novel, all fiction." He tried to clamber out of the hole.

31

"Yeah, but I bet some of it will be based on you, your relationships? Don't they say that all writers have something of themselves in the characters?"

She raised her eyebrows slightly at him. She could sense his slight discomfort. It was almost as if she was enjoying it while she waited for his response.

"Well, yes they do, but-"

She didn't let him finish. "Tolstoy, now there's a prime example. Levin in Anna Karenina, everyone says it's Tolstoy."

That surprised him. Not just a waitress then, but someone with hidden depths, and some that were especially appealing to a former lecturer in Russian literature.

"You like Russian literature then?" He decided to explore on what he hoped would be safer ground than any talk of his past relationships.

"Love it, when I get the chance to read and get my hands on any books out here. Not easy, although sometimes the tourists leave them for me. Also they have some books up at Lindos Reception which tourists have left on their way home. Not exactly many Russian novels though. Sometimes I come across one. Not that I like them all. Tolstoy, yes, Turgenev and Chekhov are okay, although they can be a bit wishy-washy. All that idyllic Russian nineteenth-century countryside liberal stuff is a bit crap. It wasn't like that at all for most of the peasants and the serfs. Was bloody grotty and grimy."

She took another gulp of her drink and turned her head to face him. He was grinning from ear to ear. As she frowned, thinking he was laughing at her, he explained. "That was what I did for thirteen years at Bristol Uni, taught Russian literature, as well as some other Russian stuff."

"Oh, I see, so that's why you were grinning while I was rattling on. Well, I guess you'd know all that. You should have stopped me instead of letting me ramble on and make a prat of myself."

"No, no, I'm always interested to hear what people think about it." He was determined to put her at ease again.

"Like I said, I don't like them all of course, the Russian writers. Dostoyevsky, for instance, does my head in. Jesus, all that dark inner soul self-guilt stuff. No thanks," she told him.

"Yes, Dostoevsky, very bloody dark and soul searching, I'm just a bit surprised to come across someone here who likes Russian literature, that's all. Not the usual conversation I've had in Lindos bars late at night."

"My father got me into it in my teens. He was a great reader and loved all that Russian stuff, Russia too really."

She hesitated for a few seconds, staring at the back of the bar and the row of bottles.

He decided to let the moment last while she obviously thought about her father.

"Anyway, that's how I got into it." Her mood lightened again as she turned her head back towards him to ask, "So, come on then, who's your favourite, Mr Russian literature lecturer?"

He felt better with that change in her. More relaxed. Although he didn't really think reeling off the names of some serious nineteenth century Russian writers was exactly going to contribute to the continuation of what was now a much lighter atmosphere between them. That showed in the slight hesitation of his response.

"Err … hmm … well … let me see, I guess that would be Gogol and Sholokhov, although Sholokhov wasn't writing in the nineteenth century. Gogol's most famous novel was 'Dead Souls'. It's about the buying and selling of the souls of dead serfs in nineteenth century Russia, to make the landowners appear more important amongst the rich. The more you owned the more important you were. It's generally accepted as being a key contribution to the abolition of serfdom in Russia in 1861. Sholokhov's first novel, And Quiet Flows the Don, was published in 1929."

No doubt because his nervousness had resurfaced he really was now sounding like a lecturer, and as though he was giving her a lecture. Far too serious a response, as well as much too much pedantic detail, was what was rushing through his brain. He desperately didn't want to kill her lightened mood again because of that, but was searching his mind to find something much less serious to add, without any success. There were plenty of subjects much lighter than Russian literature, but his mind had gone completely blank.

He needn't have worried. She helped him.

"Hmm ... I've not heard of either of them. Have you ever been? To Russia, I mean?"

"Yes, three times, for work, university work, academic research stuff, to Moscow and St. Petersburg, and to Smolensk."

"Where's that?"

"It's a small city in western Russia, towards the border with Belarus. There was a famous battle there in 1812 during the war with Napoleon. It was the first battle of his invasion of Russia. I went there for a few days because there was a very good book called "Smolensk under Soviet Rule" written by an American academic, Merle Fainsod, that was part of my research and one of my courses at the uni. Smolensk is actually a very nice city in parts, especially inside the old city wall."

"Really?"

He glanced sideways at her and could see he was losing her interest, or so he thought. Far too serious a conversation.

"Not as lovely as St. Petersburg though," he quickly added.

That did the trick.

"I'd love to go there." She perked up and the sparkle of interest was back in her eyes again.

"Always wanted to go."

"Yep, it's really beautiful. Maybe I'll take you."

As soon as that came out of his mouth he realised it was far too bold a statement to make to her, someone he'd virtually only just met. He immediately tried to play it down by adding a wide grin.

"Sure you will. I'll look forward to it." Thankfully she took it as just a flippant remark.

Any possible further awkwardness at his crazy invitation was thankfully relieved by Jack appearing at their end of the bar and asking, "More drinks for you two?"

34

While he brought them another drink each she never returned the conversation to Russia, or his invitation, thankfully. Also, she had obviously long forgotten what she had asked his novel was about. Instead they did the, "Have you ever been married," and "What about kids?" bits.

He instigated it by asking her about the married bit first, but he noticed straightaway that she didn't really reveal that much to him on that subject at all. She seemed reluctant to talk about that part of her life. Instead, she appeared very adept at turning the conversation on to him and his past. So, he decided not to pursue it, the "Have you been married?" stuff, and instead ask her, "Why here, why Lindos?"

"Hi, Alice, busy night?"

Before she could answer David's question about why Lindos a voice appeared on her left shoulder. It belonged to a young, early twenties at most, guy, who David took to be Greek.

She half turned on her stool.

"Oh, hi, Marco, yep, crazy, and it's only May."

"Same in our restaurant too. Looks like it will be a good season if this keeps up," the guy told her.

It felt awkward again. David really wanted to continue with their conversation, but now this guy, Marco, had appeared. Thankfully, it seemed that Alice wanted that too. She never bothered to introduce David to Marco, and after a few seconds of uncomfortable silence Marco took the hint and told Alice, "Okay, see you around. Maybe Glow later?"

"Probably not tonight, I'm too knackered. I need some sleep. See you around," she replied.

As she turned back to face him and Marco walked off to join a couple of Greek guys at the other end of the bar David asked, "I guess you know a lot of the Greek workers in the village then?"

"Marco's not Greek. He's Albanian. He's been working here in restaurants for quite a few years now, like quite a lot of Albanians. I met him six years ago when I came here on holiday with some friends."

"Is that why you chose here to come and live and work then, because you'd been here a few times on holiday?"

"I met my ex here, my ex-husband, thirteen years ago while I was on holiday."

Now they were back onto the "Have you been married stuff".

"What happened?" he asked. "I don't mean when you met. What happened to your marriage?"

She wasn't going to expand on that.

"Long story. It just never worked out I guess. Lasted five years."

"No kids then?"

"No, no kids," she looked thoughtful as she reached to take another drink of her vodka and coke. As she placed the glass back on the bar she shook her head slightly and added again, "No, no kids," in a soft, barely audible voice.

"Three, I've got three, two boys and a girl," he volunteered. But she didn't seem very interested. Family stuff definitely didn't appear to be her thing.

All she replied was, "Nice," quickly followed by a change of subject. "What about you? Why did you choose Lindos to come and write your great novel?"

"I think that may be overstating it somewhat, calling it a great novel," he started to tell her with a small ironic smile. I've been to Lindos quite a few times on holidays. So, I decided this was as good a place as any to come and try to write, especially as I knew it quite well."

As he told her that she seemed distracted, constantly looking around the bar like she was looking for someone or at least someone else to talk to. He took a quick look past her towards the other end of the bar, then decided to just plough on, hoping that she wasn't periodically looking around out of boredom.

"What was it that made you decide to give up your job in England and come to work and live in Lindos then, Alice?"

She just stared at the back wall of the bar ahead of her for a long minute, as though she hadn't heard him ask that.

Her apparent disengagement was starting to make him feel uncomfortable again. He wasn't giving up though, so he asked her that again. As he did so, in order to regain her attention he reached to gently touch her hand with his left hand.

"What made you decide to give up your job in the U.K. and come out here to live and work?"

She turned her head towards him, startled, like she'd forgotten he was there, and quickly pulled her hand away from his. Finally, after a few more seconds, she explained.

"Oh, yes, sorry, I was miles away, Err, yes, well life was passing me by at home, or that's what I thought. That's what it felt like. So, I took the plunge and decided to come here to start living the dream. I'd been here a few times on holiday when I was married and a couple of times after my divorce. I told you I met my ex-husband here. I didn't have any kids to consider, so I thought why not. There are worse places to live and work. I thought about coming here to live straight after I split from my ex and the divorce, but just kept finding reasons to put it off I suppose. In the end I thought sod it, just go, So, I did. You must have felt something similar when you decided to come for the whole summer and write?"

As she finished she reached for her drink and took another hefty swig. Then she turned to look him in the face and added, "I have this belief you see, that sometimes things happen, often unexpected things that provoke us into changes in our lives, prompt us into changes. Sometimes they even help us make them. What's the word … umm?"

She hesitated, searching through her mind for the right word while she turned and fiddled with the half empty glass in front of her. Eventually he helped her.

"Facilitate?"

"Yes, that'll do, facilitate. Help us make the leap, the jump into the changes we keep thinking about. Anyway, that's what happened to me, I guess."

She took another gulp of her drink and then added as she turned back to face him, "Serendipity, yes serendipity, that's the word I was actually searching for."

"That means good things though," he told her.

"Does it?"

"Yes, serendipity, to be precise it means the occurrence and development of events by chance in a happy or beneficial way, as in a fortunate stroke of serendipity."

37

She smiled at him again as she replied, "Maybe it will be then. Lindos, coming here, will be, what was it?"

He returned her smile, "Your fortunate stroke of serendipity."

There was what was becoming an awkward silence between them as they briefly gazed into each other's eyes for a moment. Eventually he swallowed slightly, then reached to take another sip of his beer before he told her, "That's an interesting way of looking at things," nodding his head a little as he did so. "That's sort of what happened to me I suppose. Not sure if you could call it serendipity, but it was circumstances that led me to decide to change things, change my life, leave my job, leave England and come here."

"A failed relationship or just your divorce?" she asked, once again turning to look at his face. She had turned the conversation away from her relationships and back once more to his.

"Did I tell you I was divorced? I don't remember that, maybe I did?"

She shrugged her shoulders and nonchalantly replied, "Can't remember, but you've got it written all over you anyway."

"Really? You can tell?"

"Yep, see plenty of them here, middle-aged divorced men on holiday."

He never responded. He just pulled a bit of a face and looked ahead.

Her comment was deliberately flippant. Her next one was more serious, as the change in the tone of her voice betrayed.

"Do you think there's just one person, one right person for everybody?"

He turned to look at her for a few seconds, although she continued to gaze ahead at the bottles of spirits at the back of the bar. Her question and the change of tone surprised him.

"No, no, I don't think so," he finally replied, adding, "Do you?"

"I used to, but now ... I'm not so sure."

She took another sip of her drink, then let out a bit of a weary sigh, before she returned to, "So, your serendipity that changed your life and brought you out here for the summer? Was it your divorce?"

His answer wasn't entirely what she expected.

"Well, some of that, relationship and divorce, in the past of course, but more recently the crap of academia, my work and academic life I mean, or more accurately some of the bloody corrupt academics and their frauds I came across. Prats who worked in the same university, the same department as me."

Now he looked angry. She'd clearly touched a nerve.

Her eyes widened and brightened as she said in surprise, "Wow! That's quite a reaction. There's a lot of anger in that statement. Obviously a touchy subject?"

He took a deep breath and then replied, "Yes, sorry, I still get mad over it, over all the shit those pompous prats tried to pile on me."

"What, you mean the university?" As soon as she asked that she wasn't at all sure if it was a good thing to do. She had a feeling it would lead to more anger spilling out of him. She was right. It did.

"No, I wasn't talking about the university as such. I don't have any evidence of their involvement of course, but I wouldn't be surprised at all if there was plenty of corruption going on at the university-wide level. I meant a couple of lazy, useless, corrupt Professors in the same Faculty that I worked in."

"How so?" she asked, as he reached to finish his beer and then indicate to Jack at the other end of the bar for another, as well as another Vodka and coke for her.

He turned back towards her as he asked, "How so what?"

"Corrupt, how were they corrupt exactly."

"It's a long story. I'm not sure that-"

She interrupted before he finished. "That I'd want to know? It sounds even more interesting if it's a long story, and involves corruption. And I'm not going anywhere now Jack's bringing me another drink."

As she finished telling him that she gave him another small smile.

"Okay, but one drink is not going to last the full long story, so I'll shorten it and give you the important bits. Some of it is really the nitty gritty of the academic world and I still don't think you'll be very interested."

He shook his head slightly as he finished speaking, and then hesitated for a moment gathering his thoughts before continuing.

"In academia there is a lot of kudos put on getting academic papers, articles, and books published, plus getting grants from various research institutions for research projects in producing those publications. Getting the research grants, and producing subsequent publications, is supposed to help the individual's career prospects, to rise up the academic ladder so to speak. The research grants can run into hundreds of thousands of pounds. Initially the grants are paid to the university, who has to administer them on behalf of the academics awarded them. It's sort of part of the deal with the organisations who give out the grants. The academic or academics awarded the grants can then claim from the university from the research grant fund for travel and accommodation, as well as, in some instances, for employing people short-term for research for the project."

He stopped as Jack brought their drinks and took a sip from his fresh beer.

"You bored already?" he asked as he placed his beer back on the counter.

"No, no, go on, I want you to get to the juicy bit, the corruption. Tales of academic corruption are not the usual late night stories you hear in a bar in Lindos."

She allowed a small smile to creep across her lips once again as she finished and then reached to take a drink from her new Vodka and coke.

He let out a slight chuckle. "No, I'm guessing definitely not. But in a way there's a link between the academic corruption and what you thought I meant earlier, relationships. Although, it wasn't a relationship at all really. Far from it, just a complete fabrication."

40

He was rambling a bit and his voice got softer, then tailed off, leaving a few seconds of bewildering silence for her as he reached for his beer once again.

"And?" she asked. "You can't stop there. I'm even more intrigued now; corruption and relationships, even fabricated ones. I hope this novel you're here to write is going to be as intriguing as this." She gave him another grin.

"Doubt it. You couldn't make this shit up," he replied firmly. The anger was back in his voice.

"And? Come on," she urged him.

"Okay, well, I never had much time for the two Professors I mentioned before anyway. All they were interested in was getting their hands on as many of the bloody research grants as they could, and eventually I stumbled across the reason why. I didn't have much time for them because they didn't care a sod about the students. At the most they taught an hour's lecture a week, and even then moaned about that. In effect, of course, the students were paying their hefty salaries through their student fees. Basically, I didn't like them, and they didn't like me, because I was much too straightforward for a couple of slippery Professors like them. What's more, all three of us knew there was a mutual dislike."

"So, what happened," she asked, trying to gently urge him to get to the heart of the story.

"I had a grant too for some research I was doing on what happened in East and Central Europe in 1989, the Russian involvement in it, Gorbachev and the rest when the Berlin Wall came down. It was just a small one, nowhere near as big as the one the two Professors had, which was over a hundred thousand pounds. Mine was less than ten thousand. As I said before, the funds were administered by the university Finance Office, but all the claims against the grants and the necessary receipts were kept by the individual Faculty Office Administration, the Faculty our department was in. So, periodically I could go into the office and check the balance left on my grant. As I also said before, what was also allowed in the research grant conditions, if the grant was large enough, was to employ a temporary research assistant to process data and research surveys, for instance. As long as you included that in the original bid for the grant that was okay, and it was usual to employ a Ph. D student, for example, as a temporary research assistant for three months or so, which would also help them with their living costs."

He looked towards her by his side and added, "You still with me? Not bored yet?"

"No, no, go on, get to the best bit." She squeezed his arm as she told him that, which he took as a sign of encouragement, and not only for his story perhaps?

"Well, one day I went into the Faculty Office to ask to see the file for my research grant as I wanted to check the balance as I thought all of it had almost been spent and I wanted to make one final trip for some more research on the project. But the admin woman who dealt with the research grants wasn't in that day, so her assistant, a new woman who had only been working there a week, gave me the wrong research file. It was the expenditure file for the two Professors' grant. Of course, I couldn't resist having a quick look. When I scanned their expenditure I saw that they were, indeed, employing two research assistants short-term, but paying them handsomely, way over the going rate for research assistants. One was the wife of one of the Professors and the other research assistant was the other Professor's daughter, who I happened to know was fifteen years old and still at school. Basically, the employment of the supposed research assistants was a scam for the two Professors to siphon off money from the grant into their own pockets. The wife and the daughter were not even doing any work at all."

"What did you do?" Alice asked.

"Nothing for a day or two, I just tried to figure out the best thing to do, try to expose them or stay silent. I eventually told another lecturer in my department, who was a good friend and who I knew I could trust. It was obviously fraud and embezzlement, and he told me I had to report it to the Dean of the Faculty, in effect our boss. My friend pointed out that if I didn't and it all came out later, including that I knew, then I'd be seen as an accessory to the embezzlement and fraud."

He shook his head slightly and bit the inside of his mouth before continuing as she sat listening in silence, occasionally taking a sip of her drink.

"I had no choice really, so that's what I did. I should have realised though that the higher up the academic ladder you go the more they stick together, like an 'old boys club'."

"Why, what happened then?" she asked, with much more curiosity evident in her voice.

"They did just that, stuck together, tried to hush it up, and then the Dean turned on me, along with the two Professors of course. It all became pretty ugly, nasty. Basically, the university and the Faculty got ten per cent from every grant its staff received, and the two Professors were quite successful at getting joint grants between them due to their own particular 'old boys network' with the other academics deciding if they should be awarded the grants. Other academic mates of theirs evaluated grant applications for various research funding institutions, and vice-versa. It's a sort of 'you scratch my back, and I'll scratch yours' situation for some of them. I was never in that circle as any research grants I got were nowhere near that big. So, it quickly became pretty clear that the Dean of the Faculty and the university weren't going to expose the scandal and the fraud as it would mean the institution losing thousands of pounds from what was known as their top slice ten per cent of the grants the two Professors were being awarded. No one in authority at the university wanted to rock the boat, not least because it would hardly do much for the reputation of the university, including its failure to administer and audit grants properly, as well as impact on student recruitment."

As he stopped to take another drink of his beer she asked, "So, how did it get ugly, nasty you said. What did they do?"

"At first the Dean tried to hush me up, told me that he'd spoken to the two Professors and it was obviously all a misunderstanding, so I should forget it. But how could I? As I said before, if it all eventually came out at some later date, and that I knew about it, I would be implicated. At first, when he was trying to persuade me to forget it, the Dean, my boss, was all very nice, but when I pointed that out to him and that I couldn't do that, he turned nasty, along with the two Professors. The whole thing was corrupt, all of them."

"Sounds like it, but what's that got to do with relationships, although I think you said it was far from it?" She stared into his eyes and frowned as she asked him that, looking confused.

He let out a small chuckle.

"That's when it got really bizarre. Shortly after all that I was in a bar in the city one Friday night with a mate of mine, Daniel, who's not an academic, and out of the blue the wife of one of the Professors approached us and started being very chatty and friendly. She was the one who had been supposedly employed as a research assistant in the research grant. She just went on talking to us like nothing had happened. Even Daniel, who I'd told all about the grant fraud, thought it was weird. I could see that from his face and he kept raising his eyebrows at things she said, especially when at one point she grabbed hold of my hand and another time my arm."

Now Alice was wide-eyed and listening intently. This was definitely the most interesting part, as far as she was concerned.

"Then Daniel, who was obviously feeling uncomfortable, just like me, went off to the toilet. Before he left us though he virtually signalled to me with his eyes, and then said, 'We should go soon. Don't forget we arranged to meet some friends in that other bar'. We hadn't, of course, but I got what he meant. We obviously both wanted to get away from the Professor's wife. She wasn't taking the hint though, and definitely didn't want us to leave. Well, not both of us anyway, Daniel and me. She grabbed my arm again, stared straight into my eyes, and then said, 'Let's go, now, let's go. I'm sure we can find somewhere more private, like your place'. I was stunned, like a rabbit caught in headlights."

Now Alice was open mouthed as all she could utter was, "Wow!"

"Yep, you can imagine. I was shocked, not just at the obvious invitation to have sex with her, but also in trying to figure out what weird twist this was in the whole situation. I sensibly politely declined, of course, telling her that really wasn't a good idea at all. Daniel returned from the toilet just at the point where she was angrily telling me that she'd told her Professor husband that it wasn't a good idea, but he had been insistent that she do it to protect herself from any involvement in possible fraud allegations."

At that point Alice let out another, "Wow!" She followed that with, "Incredible! What a strange couple. Now this really would make a good novel," and then another smile accompanied her wide open eyes.

"Maybe, but I think it's even too bizarre for that," David responded. The two of them, the Professor and his wife, were sick. Apparently, Daniel told me that he'd heard somehow that they had some unusual marriage arrangement, and that she slept around. The only thing I could think of at the time in trying to figure out why she offered to sleep with me was that it was in order to try and undermine my allegation of their fraud with the research grant, and show me as unreliable and not to be trusted. That conclusion was only reinforced when the following Monday the Dean asked to see me and said he had been told I had been sleeping with the Professor's wife, and that I obviously had some sort of grudge against him. That never made sense at all, as I pointed out to the Dean when I denied it. The woman had apparently claimed that we had sex together and had been sleeping together for weeks. So, as I said, not a relationship at all, only one in the woman and her husband's twisted minds."

"I see what you meant now," Alice told him. "What happened after that?"

"Firstly, the Dean suggested that maybe it would be better if I moved on, get a job at another university, so that the whole business could be left to die. Not in so many words, but he was clearly intimating that I should find another job, a post at another university. He even told me he would, of course, give me a good reference. I told him quite plainly 'no' and 'why should I? I hadn't done anything wrong. Because I'd discovered a fraud there had been a web of lies concocted against me. Overall, it was a complete shit storm, and I was angry, bloody angry. All I wanted to do at that point was confront the two bloody Professors and tell them what I thought of them, but my union rep, who I'd consulted on it all, told me that I definitely shouldn't do that as they'd probably claim I'd assaulted them or something. Something I obviously wouldn't have done. But beating people up, or getting other people to do it for them, clearly wasn't beneath the two Professors. Firstly, I heard that the one of them whose wife tried to sleep with me had beaten her up. My friend Daniel told me he'd heard that, and that it was over the Professor's fear that the grant fraud was all going to come out and be made public."

"Nasty," Alice interjected.

"Very, Alice, bloody nasty crook basically, which was even more substantiated when what was clearly one of his rather large 'associates' turned up on the doorstep of my house one night threatening to beat me up, telling me that, 'If I knew what was good for me I'd leave my job at the university and the city'."

Alice just stared into his face in disbelief. This certainly wasn't the story she'd anticipated when she'd asked him about it, and not one she'd expected to hear from someone she had only just met for the second time.

"Anyway, I'd had enough by then. I was always planning to eventually give up my job and come away somewhere to write. So, when the Dean of the Faculty offered a way out for everybody by making me an offer of a substantial supposed redundancy pay off from the University, even though I haggled over it a bit, helped by my union, and managed to push it up considerably, I eventually took it and moved house. A year later I decided to come here for the summer."

"Phew!" was all she could say as she puffed out her cheeks.

"Sorry, I did tell you it was a long story," he apologised.

"No, no need, I did ask, and it's somewhat different from my, what was it, my serendipity of events," she told him and reached to squeeze his lower arm again as she did so. She was also well aware that she hadn't actually told him the details of what they were - her serendipity of events - especially in terms of her divorce and the circumstances that brought that about.

She wasn't about to do that now though, if ever. His thought that the squeezing of his arm was a promising sign was

46

instantly eradicated though when she told him quite abruptly as she finished her drink, "I think I'm going to call it a night now. It was a busy night in the restaurant and I'm quite tired."

"Oh, okay, hope my story hasn't done that, made you tired?" There was clear disappointment evident in his voice.

"No, not at all, just tired from work," she told him as she lowered herself off the bar stool.

"I thought we could maybe go on to Arches or Glow for another drink," he tried to persuade her, without success.

"Maybe another night, when I'm not so tired."

She leaned in to give him a small kiss on the cheek, adding, "Night, see you around." Then she was gone, saying a quick, "Goodnight," to Jack as she left the bar.

Jack Constantino made his way along the bar towards where David was left sitting alone and asked if he wanted another beer.

"No, no thanks, Jack. It's almost three, time for bed for me I think. I did think Alice was up for going to Glow or Arches, but obviously I was wrong."

He consoled himself with the thought that things had seemingly gone well between him and Alice, even though his university story may have been a bit long and boring. She seemed okay with it though, so ...

Jack offered him a broad, knowing smile, telling him, "That's Alice for you. You'll get used to that. She changes instantly, like the wind."

As David lowered himself off his stool, Jack added, "Night."

5

The third meeting

June came in with its usual increasing heat and almost two weeks went by without their paths crossing. That was certainly not normal in a small village like Lindos. Although he went to all the usual late night bars and the clubs - Glow and Arches - she was nowhere to be seen. Even on the couple of times he went to Giorgos café bar to treat himself to a late breakfast he never ran into her. Prior to their second meeting that night in the Courtyard Bar he'd often noticed her there on his way to Pallas beach in the early afternoon. She never ever noticed him, busy as she was refuelling with a good Tsamis cooked breakfast or a burger and chips. He never stopped to say, "Hello." At that point he'd only met her once, when she'd served him in the restaurant. He wanted to stop and talk to her, but always hesitated to do so. By the time he'd thought it through he'd passed Giorgos.

When he never ran into her during getting on for two weeks he began to wonder perhaps she was sick. If she was she obviously wouldn't be working in the restaurant. He thought about going there one night for dinner as then he could check out if she was working or not, maybe ask one of the other waitresses what was up with her if she wasn't there? He quickly dismissed that idea, however, when he remembered the jokey comment she had made to him in the Courtyard about stalking her. What would it look like if she wasn't sick, and was just working as usual? Giving the impression that he was actually stalking her definitely wasn't a good idea at all.

Eventually his dilemma was resolved for him. Two nights later he bumped into her around three o'clock coming out of the Arches club through the sound-proofed door system. Arches was right in the centre of the village and the system was designed to prevent the loud music being heard in the village through the night. The system worked through a member of staff operating each of two doors, one leading to the inside of the club and the other opening onto the outside courtyard. Neither of the doors was opened by the staff member until the other was closed. So, people going into the club had to wait until the inner door was closed and the people leaving were in the space between the two doors before the outer one was opened and they were able to exit to the courtyard. The local village by-law decreed that all music in the bars had to be turned off at one a.m. This system in Arches enabled music to continue to around six in the morning sometimes. The interior of Arches was a long rectangular single room with a high ceiling and a couple of bars, one immediately opposite the inner entrance door and one at the far end of the club, running along a side wall into the corner and then round to the DJ stand and consul. Like most, if not all, clubs it was pretty dimly lit, with occasional strobe lights, which disguised the inner natural brickwork.

David was waiting in the courtyard along with a couple of other people for the staff member to open the outer door to let them into the sound vacuum between the two doors and then into the club. That was when she appeared. As the outer door was opened four people came out, and Alice was one of them. This time he didn't get bogged down with thinking it through and instantly simply said, "Hello."

The staff member operating the door motioned to him to join the other two people and go through before the inner door could be opened, but David indicated to him it was okay as Alice returned his, "Hello." She sensed his awkwardness, as her accompanying grin indicated.

"Err … you're not leaving are you?" he blurted out, not exactly feeling comfortable or at ease.

"Toilet."

"What," he asked, looking confused?

"No, I'm not leaving I'm going to the toilet, over there."

She pointed to the corner of the courtyard and the women's toilet entrance.

"Oh, I see, I just haven't seen you around for a couple of weeks. You been sick?"

"What? No. Why do you think that?"

Now it was Alice who was looking confused.

This wasn't going at all well. That last comment from him about not seeing her around was definitely beginning to sound like stalking. She helped him out though, at least temporarily.

"Sorry, I really need to get to the toilet now. I'll catch you back inside later."

With that she turned away and headed towards the corner of the courtyard and the toilet.

As he turned back to join the queue of three more people waiting for the outer door to be opened he couldn't help notice Valasi, the owner, and Chris, who worked for him as a sort of 'front of house' guy on the entrance arch from the alley to the club's courtyard, tilting their heads to one side and grinning broadly over at him. David knew them both quite well from his previous Lindos holidays and they had obviously enjoyed his awkward discomfort of the last few minutes talking to Alice. He just slowly shook his head from side to side back at them as the outer door was finally opened and he entered the club.

Inside he headed for one of the few empty spots in the corner at one end of the bar directly opposite the inner entrance door. One of the bar staff he also knew, a tall young English guy, Pete, spotted him and straightaway placed a bottle of Greek Alfa beer on the bar in front of him. David stood in the corner, intermittently glancing over towards the entrance door checking for Alice's return and in between looking down the length of the club through the crowds towards the far end and the other bar.

He'd barely taken a sip of his beer when two rather large middle-aged, badly dressed women appeared at the bar alongside him. From their accents he realised immediately that they were Scottish. Rather than moving away from the bar once they had got their drinks from Pete though, one of them, who had turned her broad back and naked shoulders to him, seemed to be gradually moving herself backwards, increasingly invading his personal space and trapping him more and more

50

into the corner. As David flashed a glance over at him Pete was grinning at what was happening and then tilted his head slightly to one side while simultaneously widening his eyes and raising his eyebrows. By now David was almost totally penned in the corner by the woman's back, and not feeling very comfortable about the situation at all. As a result the thought of constantly checking the inner entrance door for Alice's return had vanished from his mind. However, just as he was on the point of summoning up enough courage to tap the woman on the back and ask her to move away a little a hand came through the crowd and grasped his firmly. To his relief it belonged to Alice. As she extricated him from his corner prison and led him by the hand through the crowd to a much less populated, almost empty, spot in the club she told him with a smile across her soft pink lips, "Come on, come and dance with me."

She clearly loved to dance. She was dancing as if she didn't have a care in the world and loved life. Life was good, very good, for her at that particular moment in time. She was indeed living the dream.

He couldn't help thinking that her movements were worthy of the description of Natasha's dance in War and Peace, Tolstoy's portrayal of the young and beautiful Countess Natasha Rostov's instinctive dance and movements upon hearing the peasant rhythm of a popular Russian melody. As Alice's hips swayed rhythmically and gyrated smoothly to the music that night in Arches she looked even trimmer than he remembered from their previous two meetings. Working the long hours and constantly climbing the stairs to the upper terrace in the restaurant may have been hard work, but it obviously also kept her fit. She moved effortlessly in time with the music, just like the Russian Countess. Although, instead of a peasant rhythm it was 'Moves Like Jagger' that was blasting out over the club's sounds system.

She was wearing a short black skirt that highlighted her finely shaped legs and a tight fitting black shirt, come blouse, as well as flat sandals with sparkly bits on the straps. The shirt showed off her figure perfectly, unbuttoned as it was down to the top of her cleavage, and her long dark black hair was hanging loose half way down her back. As usual she'd gone back to her flat after work to change out of her restaurant clothes.

Just before he was pinned into the corner by the large Scottish woman he began to wonder if Alice would actually come over to him even if she did come back into the club. Perhaps he should simply go over to wherever she headed in the club if she didn't. He thought he recognised a couple of other waitresses from her restaurant at the far end of the club, near the bar at that end. Perhaps she came to Arches with them after work.

As it turned out he needn't have worried, although he never bargained at all for what she actually did when she did come back in. It was certainly an interesting ice-breaker, although definitely not one he was expecting. He enjoyed a dance, but wouldn't claim to be an expert by any means, and certainly didn't move like Jagger.

From the way she moved she clearly enjoyed dancing a lot. At least she kept smiling at him, which he took as a good sign, although he quite quickly figured out that she was probably just basically sizing him up character-wise. Seeing if he was just some stuffy university lecturer, or whether he could relax, enjoy himself and let his guard down.

Then just as quickly she stopped, took hold of his hand once again and told him, "Yes, I will, thanks."

"Will what," he asked?

"Will have a drink, Vodka and coke please. That's what you were about to ask wasn't it?"

She was grinning once again.

He smiled back and took her hand this time to lead her through the groups of people to the bar to order her drink and take a swig of his beer. After he attracted the attention of Pete and ordered her drink he told her, "You're a good dancer."

"Thanks, you're not."

She obviously spotted that he was no Jagger. There was that edge to her again in that remark, even though she couldn't suppress the barest grin.

At least it felt more relaxed between them.

"So, you've not been ill then? Just not seen you around in the village, in Jack's bar late on, or anywhere. Thought I might have bumped into you again, after all the place is not that big."

Pete brought her drink and while David paid him Alice took a drink of it through the straw.

As she placed it back on the bar, rather than answer his question she asked, "Aren't you going to thank me for saving you?"

"Saving me? From what?"

"The fearsome looking woman who had you penned in the corner, of course. You looked terrified." This time she let out a small chuckle as she finished.

"Oh, her, yes, she did seem a bit fearsome, and I didn't really want to say anything to her as she might take that as me wanting to engage her in conversation. She just kept slowly moving backwards into me, pinning me in the corner."

That drew another chuckle from Alice as she placed her drink back on the bar.

"Well, the fear was all over your face," she told him with another grin. "But you must have liked it. You could easily have moved. You obviously have a thing for large women."

He was about to firmly put her straight on that, but she never gave him the chance. Instead she let him off the hook by changing the subject.

"But no, as I said outside, I've not been ill, just been really busy at work and most of the time was too knackered to even go for a drink after. Went to LBN a couple of times after work with a couple of the other girls, but no, not been to Jack's."

He continued to think it odd that he hadn't bumped into her. In the Courtyard Bar he'd asked Jack Constantino a couple of times if he'd seen her, if she'd been in for a late drink. Jack just told him no. He'd been to LBN himself late on a couple of nights, at gone one-thirty. That was only thirty metres or so along the top alley in the village behind the Courtyard Bar. So, it was easy to nip along there and check if she was around once he'd checked Jack's. The entrance to Lindos By Night was up an initial flight of around a dozen steps It had two bars. There was a long narrow bar to the left at the top of that first flight of steps, with an area full of tables and chairs outside to the right. Further up another flight of stairs was another open seating area with tables and chairs and a small bar to the far side up against the rock face. A key attraction of the top bar was its wonderful view of the illuminated Lindos Acropolis.

She wasn't to be seen in either of the LBN bars though. He asked the bar staff in the top bar the same question as he'd asked Jack, but they hadn't seen her either. However, to David's surprise one of the late drinking customers piped up somewhat aggressively with, "Yeah, she's been in a few times, Alice. Had a few drinks with her. Who wants to know?"

David had seen the guy around in the village a couple of times. He assumed he wasn't a tourist, but was a Brit, maybe an ex-pat living in Lindos or perhaps working or staying in the village for the summer like David. Whichever it was, the guy had clearly had quite a few drinks that night, although David couldn't quite fathom out why he had immediately been so aggressive. He put it down to maybe it was just the drink in him talking.

"David, David Alexander-"

He intended that to be an invitation for the guy to identify himself in return. But as the guy interrupted him it was plain that he wasn't about to do that. He snapped back, "Why? Why are you so interested? Why you so interested in Alice?"

As he asked that he moved a little away from leaning on the bar and his body swayed slightly. David had no idea whatsoever why the guy was rattling off his questions in such an antagonistic manner. He decided not to react, but instead simply try to take the obvious heat out of the situation. Calm the guy down.

"No reason, I had a meal at the restaurant she works at here a week or two ago and she told me she sometimes comes up here to LBN for a late drink after work, if I ever wanted one. You-"

"So, do you?" the guy interrupted once again.

"Do I what?"

The guy let out a small patronising chuckle and shook his head slightly at the two young Greek guys behind the bar.

"Want a drink? Do you want a drink? I'll get you one."

"Err … thanks, very kind of you but no thanks. Think I'll call it a night."

There was no way David was going to waste even a few minutes of part of his new Lindos life indulging in a drinking session with what appeared to be a drunken, quite obnoxious and hostile guy. Indeed, he was somewhat puzzled that Alice Palmer could have actually, "Had a few drinks," with him, as he suggested. Perhaps there was more to Alice than met the eye.

The guy wasn't taking no for an answer though.

"My money not good enough for you then, David? What was it, David Alexander? Not good enough for you to drink with me?"

He spat the words out rapidly, aggressively, like they were bullets from a machine gun. He clearly hadn't calmed down and the hostile tone in his voice was still evident. David glanced across at the two barmen, both in their early twenties. They were both wide-eyed, looking a little apprehensive at the guy's persistence. Besides anything else they obviously just wanted to get rid of him. There were no other customers on the terrace, so they clearly just wanted to close up and maybe get off to one of the clubs full of female tourists.

"No, of course it is, your money, good enough I mean. Sorry, I didn't get your name? Do you live here?"

"Simon Chapel. I'm here for all the summer. Been here regularly for quite a few summers. I'll get you a beer, or perhaps you'd prefer a shot? Tequila?"

He clearly wasn't giving up, and David decided that it was going to be easier to humour him and have one drink. Besides which he didn't want the guy – his 'new friend' Simon - getting any more aggressive. He was drunk, but he was solidly built. He looked around forty, was tall, with short light brown hair, and had a slight beer belly, but generally he looked like he had a well-built body. The muscles towards the top of his arms bulging out of his black t-shirt suggested he had done some weights at some point in his life, and maybe quite recently.

So, the last thing David wanted, or needed, early on in his Lindos summer, or at any time for that matter, was to get into an argument or definitely not a physical confrontation. Instead, trying to sound as enthusiastic as possible as he replied, "Yep, why not, yes, Tequila thanks." He'd down that in one and then disappear was what he thought. Simon had other ideas though.

"Same again?" But instead of waiting for David's answer he nodded an indication to one of the young Greek barmen.

Before he could pour two more Tequilas though David stopped him, saying, "No, one's enough for me thanks. I need to get up fairly early in the morning to do some writing."

As soon as he said that he thought he might regret it. It might not be the right thing to say at all. He certainly didn't want to give Simon the opening to start asking all about what David did, writing what?

He needn't have worried, however. Simon Chapel wasn't the sort of person generally remotely interested in hearing about what other people did, at least not men. Women maybe, but only if he was trying to get in their knickers. He was only interested usually in blowing his own trumpet, going on and on about what he did and trying to impress anyone who would listen.

"You're no fun then," he told David. "Not coming to Glow or Arches then for a nightcap?"

Not tonight David thought, and definitely not with you. He'd quickly sized up Simon's character and there was no way he was going to be in one of the clubs with him in his drunken aggressive state. The clubs in Lindos very, very rarely had any trouble in them, but he wasn't going to take the chance with Simon that night or any other. It was what Simon threw out of his mouth as David was leaving though that he remembered and threw him a little.

David told him, "No, no clubs tonight, thanks for the drink, night," and he turned to quickly make his way to the stairs from the rooftop bar. From behind him he heard Simon's slurred voice shouting, "You're no fun. Alice is much more fun than you. Don't worry she'll be here soon. She'll drink with me. She's always is happy to."

David decided to ignore that, carried on down the stairs and out into the alley. He dismissed it simply as the ramblings of a drunken man.

Anyway, now he was with her a few days later in Arches, and thankfully he hadn't come across his 'new friend' Simon since. However, that didn't last very long. She did seem pleased to see him, touching his arm a couple of times and smiling quite a lot. But after she finished her one drink she said she was off, told him goodnight and added, "Watch out for those large fearsome women. Make sure you stay away from them."

Then, once again, she left abruptly. The one positive sign was that when she warned him about watching out for the fearsome women she did so by telling him it into his ear over the loud music, and then placed an arm around his neck and kissed him on the cheek.

Was she really that rude, or just scared of getting into anything with him? Whatever it was that seemed to spook her, it certainly was bloody frustrating for him. He'd spent a couple of weeks looking out for her night after night, deliberately resisted going to the restaurant where she worked, and then within half-an-hour of finally catching up with her that night she disappeared again. Jack said to him the second time he met her and she left abruptly that she, "Changes instantly, like the wind," and that was the way she was. So, perhaps it wasn't really anything to do with him, or his character, at all. Plus, she had made a point of telling him to watch out for and stay away from the fearsome women. So, on the positive side, maybe that was a good thing, if she meant it and wasn't just joking.

As it turned out, that night he bumped into her at Arches was really the true beginning of it, the two of them and that summer of 2019. They were to meet like that on many more late nights in the Courtyard Bar, LBN, or in the clubs, Arches and Glow over the coming months. On those subsequent times, however, she never rushed off. Instead they spent many long nights together drinking and talking.

6

End of June and into July

The Lindian summer wore on, bringing its increasing level of heat and humidity. The relatively pleasant coolness of May disappeared, overwhelmed and replaced through June and into July by the unrelenting long sunny days. Similarly, it seemed to David that Alice's coolness towards him eventually appeared to be changing. She wasn't exactly exhibiting anything towards him that could be described as rivalling the heat of late June and early July, but generally she did appear to be warming to him.

There were still occasions when she would abruptly end their late night drinking for seemingly no reason and leave to go off to bed. In that respect her unpredictable actions mirrored perfectly the relieving warm low breezes that periodically on some evenings, and equally unpredictably, swept through the narrow white walled alleys of the village.

By mid-June though, on most nights not a breath of air stirred in the Lindos alleyways to disturb the late evening mid-summer humidity. During the long sunny days the heat bounced of the bright white walls, providing the tourists with plenty of opportunities for photos of some of those alleyways which were framed with beautiful striking reddish pink flowering hanging Bougainvillea.

Within a month of their initial meetings, and the confusion over the myriad of feelings about her it brought into his life, the rhythm of David's first full Lindos summer started to settle down much more and take shape. If not exactly regimented, it certainly became more ordered, some would say more predictable, although he was convinced that was not exactly a bad thing. It was what he sought when he'd decided to come away for the whole summer, what he needed after the traumas of the end of his academic career. And most of the time Lindos was definitely calmer and more relaxed. That wasn't hard given the almost idyllic surroundings and the endless hot Rhodian summer days. Even though he'd been there on holiday plenty of times in the past, everything about the place and being there for a whole summer of bordering on five months just became more and more appealing as everyday went by and the hot sun rose in the clear blue, cloudless sky.

Even the unusual surprising evening rainstorm at the end of the second week of June didn't dampen his enthusiasm. He had been in Lindos before when a torrential rainstorm had struck the village, but it was not a usual occurrence in June, more so in late September or in October. Anyway, it only lasted for fifteen minutes. That was enough to flood the alleys, however, as torrents of water a foot deep in places swept through the village down the slopes of the alleys and paths from the top of it to the bottom towards the Main Square. The rainstorms and torrents of water gushing through the village alleyways were always quite a spectacle. In less than an hour though, the water from the storm, as well as the wind and rain had gone. The Lindos air was still once again and the humidity began to return. However, the peculiar damp smell throughout the village lingered through the night, all the way until the returning heat of the next morning. Although the paths were completely dry a couple of hours after the rainstorm, which was just as well as the paths could be tricky in parts even when dry, and more so when wet. The flagstones were worn shiny in places from the millions of tourist footsteps over the years.

David eventually settled easily into the slower tempo of Lindos village life, got to know more and more people, and his late night discussions over drinks with Alice Palmer became more and more frequent. Sometimes, of course, that disrupted the predictable rhythm and timings of his Lindos days when their late night talking and drinking stretched into daylight and the rise of the Rhodian sun. However, those increasingly frequent occasions could hardly be described as unpleasant diversions. He loved the surroundings and the whole environment, the atmospheric effect of the cooler clear night sky with its myriad of bright stars overhead and the often strong silvery light of the almost full moon above them.

He grew more and more to love the fact that he was sometimes experiencing all that with her. Something he definitely hadn't bargained for when he had decided to come to spend the summer in Lindos. However, what he could never figure out now was whether she was feeling the same way. No sooner did he begin to feel more relaxed around her than she would put a very sudden brake on whatever he thought was developing between them. Two steps forward in that respect would dramatically be brought to an abrupt shuddering halt by her, usually by her doing her immediate Houdini act and disappearing back to her flat for bed. So, two steps forward in those early couple of months was always halted with one step back, or more accurately, actually three steps back as a week or more would go by again without their paths crossing.

When they did meet up again a few days or more later following one of her disappearing acts the nervousness he had initially felt around her returned. He would feel like he just wasn't acting naturally, being relaxed, being himself. He tried to quickly shake it off, but that was the effect she had on him. He wasn't his normal self. Sometimes when he sat talking with her on those late nights, early morning, drinking and clubbing sessions his lips would betray the sceptical and yet ready smile of a man who never really knew what he would hear next from her, what she would say or tell him next. At those times, as he gazed attentively into her face it appeared it expressed everything, everything he was seeking. In reality though, even at those times she expressed nothing behind her deep brown eyes, gave nothing away when she chose not to. She was very good at that, very practiced in that skill. Yet somehow, and for some unfathomable and totally irrational reason, he even came to find that appealing and attractive in her.

His academic life had instilled a sense of order in him in terms of planning his time. He had started the summer, or rather before he even arrived in Lindos, with a clear plan of how his days would look through that summer. He would spend his mornings writing his 'great novel' in the flat he had rented. The sun would be streaming through the open windows and shutters, and he would have classical music or opera, probably Puccini or Verdi, playing in the background. That would take care of his mornings. Then there would be a light lunch of a filled baguette or Greek feta pie from Café Melia just around the corner from the flat, followed by the beach and some swims. He would alternate between Pallas beach, the Main beach, or St. Paul's bay, depending on how the mood took him that day. Even then though, he would have a pen and a pad with him, just in case some blinding plot inspiration came to him on a sunbed at one of those.

That was to be his relaxing, pleasant Lindos life for five months. Alice Palmer had disrupted that plan, however, or at least thoughts of her had for the first four weeks or so. In addition, what he hadn't factored into the equation of his Lindos summer was the village nightlife. Most nights the many bars were bustling with tourists, as well as some Brit ex-pats who lived in the village or nearby. In the bars there was the constant hum of conversations over the music, along with the clinking of glasses of alcohol. Because of the local by-law the music stopped in the bars at one a.m. of course, but even so there was always a late drink to be had in the Courtyard Bar, Lindos By Night, Bar404, Antika, Apollo or many of the other bars. When they had finished and closed there was always the clubs, Arches and Glow, where music could be heard and drinks taken until five or six in the morning. Friday and Saturday nights were particular long nights though in that summer of 2019, with regular visits for him with locals and friends to the Arches Plus open air night club down by the Main beach. He saw quite a few stunning, but blindingly bright, Lindos sunrises as he left there at six or even seven some Saturday or Sunday mornings. Quite a few times that was with Alice, both of them intoxicated by a mixture of alcohol and a lack of sleep.

So, although she played her part at times, it wasn't just Alice Palmer who disrupted his meticulous plan, especially his writing. The late nights and early mornings of the Lindos bars and clubs played their part fully, including the alcohol he consumed in them. Some mornings simply disappeared completely when he never surfaced until one or two in the afternoon, grabbed an excellent late breakfast at Giorgos café bar, and headed for a revitalising swim on Pallas beach or at St. Paul's bay.

Giorgos was a popular spot for lunch for the day trippers for Rhodes Town, as well as for coffee or more for some of the Brit summer season workers and ex-pats. It was in the heart of the village on the main thoroughfare up from Pallas Beach where the day boats from Rhodes Town moored at the small jetty. For the daytime coffee or small beer drinking summer season workers and ex-pats it was a great place to sit, chat, catch up on the village gossip, and watch the world go by from the small tables outside. On more than one occasion that summer that pastime proved an easy distraction from his writing for David too. In the evenings Giorgos transformed itself into more of a bar and was very popular with many of the regular returning Brit couples and family groups. In addition to its fine selection of cocktails, the bar's added attraction for many was its full complement of regular live sport on the multiple televisions, along with its very friendly owner Tsamis. Inside the bar was furnished with bright modern style tables, chairs and bar stools, with an impressive range of bottles of spirits and liqueurs on the shelves stretching almost up to the ceiling behind the bar.

On a couple of nights David did resolve to have, or try to have, a relatively early night. He was in his bed by one o'clock, trying to read. By one-thirty he attempted to sleep. The problem was that after so many late nights that turned into early mornings over the first three weeks or so he couldn't get to sleep that early. His body clock had become accustomed to a different Lindos rhythm.

As the summer wore on David's disappearing mornings increased in direct correlation with the decrease in his writing, as well as the increasing time he was spending with Alice Palmer. Not that he found that disagreeable or inconvenient whatsoever.

The regularity and rhythm of their late night meetings grew as the summer progressed through June, such that by early July it became almost inevitable that they would bump into each other late on in the Courtyard Bar or LBN, or even eventually in one of the clubs, Arches or Glow. There was definitely no calling by him to arrange to meet, although on a few odd occasions she did text him as she finished work in the restaurant asking where he was and did he want to go for a late night drink now. Of course he readily agreed every time. She would always want to go back to her flat before they actually met so she could shower and change out of her waitress uniform. Consequently, she would text back saying just that and that she would see him in half-an-hour or so.

Did that mean she would specifically choose clothes to wear after work when she knew she wanted to meet up with him? Mostly they were a combination of short skirts, mainly black or dark blue, and t-shirts. Occasionally these were interspersed with sleeveless short dresses, predominantly black. Occasionally the t-shirt would be replaced by a white or coloured shirt or blouse tied above her waist to expose and display her flat stomach, and always there was the flat black dressy sandals, obligatory for negotiating the worn flagstones of the Lindos alleyways.

One time he was in the Apollo bar nursing his late drink when she texted. It wasn't one of her regular or favourite haunts. When she eventually turned up she didn't seem quite so comfortable and relaxed there as in the other bars. Apollo had a long, quite narrow, bar inside, and a couple of terraces outside with tables and chairs. It was on one of the alleys beneath the Acropolis, and so slightly off the main alleyways in the village. It was another bar where some workers at the village restaurants went for a late drink after work, and was also popular for a late drink with some of the more regular returning tourists to Lindos. He was sat on one of the bar stools at the far end of the bar when she arrived. Initially, she appeared anxious and tired, telling him how, "Bloody busy," the restaurant had been that evening and even asking him why he'd decided to come to that bar, the Apollo?

As was her way her mood and demeanour changed instantly when, before he could answer, a woman's voice from behind

Alice said, "Hi, you served us in the restaurant earlier tonight, remember?"

As she spun around on her bar stool to face the woman she allowed a broad welcoming smile to spread across her lips. Instantly she was a different person from the one for whom David had just ordered a drink.

"Yes, yes, I remember, there were four of you, two couples," she replied.

David was shaking his head slightly at Alice's personality transformation as the woman pointed through one of the doorways of the bar to a terrace table and two middle-aged men and a woman.

"Yes, my husband, my sister and her husband are out there. The meal at the restaurant was really good, and we've just been having a couple of nightcaps before bed."

"Glad you enjoyed it," Alice replied, with another smile. "Your first time in Lindos?"

"Yes, and we love it, so I'm sure it won't be our last."

"Most people come back over and over again," Alice informed her.

This was now a much more relaxed and confident Alice Palmer. Clearly this was the environment in which she was most comfortable, chatting to tourists, customers at the restaurant where she worked. She was actually bloody good at it, obviously born for the hospitality trade. At least that was the clear impression David was now getting. That sort of encounter and conversation late at night in a bar with tourists who had previously been customers she had served in the restaurant occurred increasingly as the summer wore on. Alice never seemed to tire of it. Sometimes, as on that occasion in Apollo, she would be taken over to say hello the rest of the group of customers sat at a table outside the bar, or at the other end of the bar, and David would be left sipping his beer at the bar for five minutes or even sometimes ten or more. He was very patient however, and never complained or even mentioned it when Alice returned to join him at the bar. Little did he realise at those times that his patience was earning him 'brownie points' with Alice, as he found out later that summer in one of

64

their long late night drinking conversations. Completely out of the blue that night she told him, "You know what I like about you, David? When I go off to talk to people, customers from the restaurant, in Jack's or LBN, or even in Glow or Arches, you never give me grief when I return, no matter how long I've been off chatting."

He took that as a good sign, although if truth be told he did find it hard when she disappeared off to talk to people and sometimes it felt like she had completely forgotten about him. However, he certainly wasn't going to tell her that. He'd just bite his tongue and take the 'brownie points'. He realised quite quickly that summer that Alice Palmer wasn't someone to tell what she should or shouldn't be doing.

Anyway, it was obvious that Alice was a more relaxed and all round nicer person when she was interacting with customers, tourists, although once again that wasn't something he was going to tell her, at least not in those terms. Her mood did change momentarily though that night in Apollo when the woman asked Alice if David was her husband or even her boyfriend.

A frown stretched across her forehead as she quickly replied sharply, "God, no, David here is just a friend who's here for the summer. Sometimes we go for a drink after I finish work."

That was overly defensive of her he thought. Not exactly a good sign at all.

7

Early August and 'letting people in'

Over the rest of that summer of 2019 the occasions when the two of them sat and talked in the courtyards outside the Arches or Glow night club, or sat on the low white circular wall in the square by Nikos' pizza place in the emerging dayglow, multiplied. What started with them just meeting up a few times by chance in the clubs at one-thirty or two at night after she'd finished work, or even later, or while he was having a late night drink in Jack Constantino's Courtyard Bar, at the Apollo Bar, or in the bottom bar of Lindos By Night, became more and more regular. So much so that was soon usual for some of the bar staff in those places to remark to him that, "Alice will probably be in soon," without him even mentioning her. Whether it was Angelos in Lindos By Night, Apostolis behind the bar in Apollo or the waitress there, India, or Jack Constantino himself in the Courtyard Bar, they all grew to expect Alice Palmer to turn up in their various bars late at night to join David after she finished work.

So, their once or twice a week meetings turned into three or four nights, sometimes even more. Most times it was just the two of them, but at times they would end up in a group with the workers from the bars and restaurants, mostly Brits, as well as some tour reps. Their meetings weren't initially arranged as such, but Lindos was a small village with just the two clubs so it was always likely they'd bump into each other in one or other of them if they didn't do so in the late bars. Unless, of course, one of them had decided on the odd early night. After a couple of weeks in the early part of the summer they finally got around to exchanging phone numbers, although they only very rarely arranged by text where and when to meet late at night. It just never seemed necessary. Occasionally, when they managed to surface at an almost reasonable hour, they would bump into each other having a late breakfast outside Giorgos Café.

She liked to talk during those late nights, and seemed more than happy to talk to him, increasingly so over time. With the loud music in the clubs it wasn't easy. Consequently, often she would suggest they went outside to sit and talk in the courtyard of the club. She did like to talk, but not really about herself. She told him very little in that respect. There would be many times that they sat and talked, staying up to greet the sun as it came up to join them. At times it was after they'd had plenty to drink, maybe too many drinks. A couple of times, after they'd adjourned from the Arches courtyard to Nikos pizza place as the sun came up to munch their pizza strips and gulp down bottled water to try to negate the alcohol, he tried to find out more about her, about her family, her divorce. Much as he tried, and tried to press her, however, she gave away virtually nothing. He never even found out if she had brothers and sisters, or if her parents were still alive. When he raised those sorts of questions he always hit a brick wall. She either got agitated or tried to change the subject, even one time turning the question back on him and asking about his family. Even with her divorce she only told him the very minimum about what happened, that she found out her husband had been cheating on her with her best friend. When he tried to ask more about the detail of what happened she shut the conversation down by suddenly telling him she was tired and was off to bed. He began to think that was really odd. Did she have some deep, dark family secret she wanted to keep hidden perhaps? Or maybe it was just genuinely something she never wanted to talk about, not wanted to dwell on? In a way that certainly appeared to fit with her overall character and approach to life now. What she was determined to forget or ignore about her past was not important, especially anything that caused her pain and anguish. She shut it out of her mind, easily, and apparently quite coldly in a calculating fashion. Eventually he decided to confront her head on about what appeared to be her obsession with not revealing some of the things about her past or her family.

On yet another pizza eating, seeing daylight breaking time, sat together in the eerie strange unearthly early light on the circular low white wall after a good night's drinking in early August he suddenly broke the munching silence by telling her, "You don't let anyone in easily, do you?"

He took a chance with that remark, but he'd consumed a fair bit of alcohol and was definitely on the verge of being drunk. So, why not say what he thought.

"What? In? In what?" she wiped her pizza sauce covered lips with a serviette as she asked what he meant.

"In, into you, into the real you?"

She frowned. She knew precisely what he meant. Yet again she tried to bat it aside, at first with a small laugh..

"Ha ha! That's a bit deep after such a long night, not to mention the amount of alcohol, don't you think?"

However, he wasn't giving up.

"Maybe, maybe it is, but you always divert the conversation away from any talk of your family, your divorce, or even any friends. Don't you have any real friends, especially here after over three years? This is your fourth summer after all."

While he sat in silence waiting for her response, if there was to be one, she finished her pizza slices, wiped her hands on the tissue and reached down to the ground to pick up a small bottle of water and take a long swig to wash down the last piece of pizza. This time though at least she didn't make an excuse about being tired and leave abruptly to go off to bed.

She placed the bottle of water on the ground between her feet, slowly and deliberately turned her head towards him, and seemed to bite the inside of her cheek slightly as though she was mulling over what to tell him.

"Is that what you think, David, think about me?" she eventually told him. There was a trace of annoyance in her voice. It wasn't really the response he was hoping for. It looked to him as though her defensive, self-protecting nature was going to prevail, and continue to maintain a barrier between them.

He hesitated, unsure quite how to react. He didn't want to upset the apple cart and annoy her any more.

"Err ... well, I-"

He started to respond, although he wasn't sure at all what would actually emerge from his mouth. He needn't have worried. She interrupted him, and what she told him was at least a little more than he anticipated.

She visibly took a deep breath, breaking into something of a sigh of resignation, as though she knew she couldn't put off his enquiries about her, her background and her friends any longer.

"Of course, I have some, some friends here and back in the U.K."

She was now staring into his face intently as she continued.

"But I'm a quite private person. I don't like everyone to know my business, especially here. It is a village you know, and I'm sure you know what villages are like for rumour and gossip, even more so in a tourist village."

"But I wouldn't say-" He tried to reassure her, even momentarily taking hold of her left hand in his, which she quickly withdrew as she interrupted him.

"I'm not saying you would. I don't know for certain, of course, I've only known you a few months, but you don't seem like a person who would spread gossip."

He thought he detected that she offered him a slight reassuring grin as she finished telling him that.

"I wouldn't," he repeated, trying to reassure her further.

"Good, I thought not, that's good, but I like to protect myself. I don't give people information about myself, my background, easily. I find it difficult to let people get close to me, especially men. It's about trust, and they've always let me down, always. That's the way I am, and over the years since my divorce I've found that's the best way to be, protect myself, especially here, and there are things I'd prefer no one to know, thank you."

Any reassurance he gained with her explanation about being, "a quite private person," had been completely erased within him with her last comment. What on earth did she mean by that? Things she'd prefer no one to know. What things?

69

He decided that it wasn't the time or place to pursue that further, even if he remotely thought there was any likelihood whatsoever she would expand on it further. It would have to wait for another time. Instead, he tried something that he thought might be easier for her to answer.

"Friends, here, though? You said you had some friends here?"

That appeared to relax her more and remove any tension from the conversation.

"Oh … err … yes, well, plenty of what I suppose you might call acquaintances here rather than actual friends."

She brushed some strands of hair back off her face and tucked them behind her right ear before she continued.

"Although I don't think that's really exactly the right word, acquaintances. I guess some people here are more than that, but not actual friends, I suppose. Don't know the actual right word to describe them, but being here for the past three summers you are bound to get to know people here quite well; the Greek bar and restaurant owners, as well as some of the regular summer season staff."

She started to rub the back of her neck with her right hand as she finished telling him that. Obviously it was aching and tiredness was creeping up on her in what was now the broad daylight of almost seven in the morning. He thought he should ask just one more quick question while she was now in such an open mood. After that he reckoned that she would do her disappearing act off to her bed.

"So, not even one person you'd call a real friend here then?"

Tiredness was overwhelming her rapidly, reflected in the frown that spread over her face again.

"There's only really Dianne, Dianne Arnold. I introduced her to you in Glow earlier in the summer. She works at another one of the restaurants, the Village House, remember?"

He nodded without commenting, thinking it best to let her go on.

"She's been here six or seven years, I think. I got to know her in Glow one night when the owner, Michalis, introduced us while I was there with some of the other girls from our

70

restaurant early in the first summer I came to work here, 2016. She's probably the person I've met here who has the most similar outlook on life as me, if you know what I mean."

He nodded again.

"Anyway, we soon became drinking buddies. I suppose that's what you'd call it, and friends of sorts. If there was anyone here I'd tell things to, share things with, get advice from, it'd be Dianne. I soon realised I could trust her."

Tell her what things? Share what things with her and no one else, he was wondering. What exactly did Alice mean by that? It was the same sort of mystery comment she had made earlier about, "Things she'd prefer no one to know." Had she actually told Dianne that?

She was rubbing her neck again and now let out a yawn. Now was definitely obviously not the time to pursue some of the questions that were running through his brain about Alice Palmer and her past. They could wait for another time.

"You're tired," he told her. "We should go to bed."

She quickly turned her head towards him. There was a blank look on her face.

"Oh, I didn't mean, err … I meant you … and me, of course, but not together, no, not together of course."

He was rambling, trying to extricate himself and ensure she didn't get the wrong impression. He needn't have worried.

She liked his awkward embarrassment, and that he was worried she might get the wrong impression. It was something she liked about him.

She chuckled slightly, then told him, "Don't worry, I know what you mean, David. But, I think you need your bed too now. You're starting not to make much sense. I guess that's probably a combination of tiredness and too much alcohol. Didn't you say earlier that you intended to do some writing in the morning, this morning I guess it is now. Even if you do manage to surface before noon I reckon now you'll still be drunk."

She smiled at him as she finished.

"Write drunk and edit sober, that's what Hemingway always said," he replied.

71

She let out another small chuckle as she stood up from the low wall and then told him, "Good luck with that later, but you're no Hemingway."

She bent down to give him a quick kiss on the cheek and added, "Thanks for a lovely evening. See you soon, night."

Then she was gone. He watched her walk away, keeping his eyes firmly fixed on her back all the way down the alley between Yannis Bar and Bar 404. He sat there alone on the wall for a couple of minutes more watching the village waking up. It was morning, another morning in a picturesque Greek tourist village on a fresh, bright new lovely summer day. The shopkeepers were opening up and putting out the displays of their tourist goods on the walls in the sunlit alleys off of the small square. A few Greeks passed him by from up the alley Alice had left down and then crossed the square on the way to their jobs, offering him a pleasant, "Kaliméra." A couple of the waiters were setting up the tables outside Yannis Bar ready for their breakfast customers. The noise and bustle of Lindos people starting to go about their early morning daily summer work invaded the tranquillity of his thoughts and the scene before him. Above him the cloudless clear blue sky was already beaming down the rapidly rising sun's warm rays. It was a beautiful, shiny, unblemished scene, only intermittently shaded by the large tree in the centre of the white low circular wall, as well as by some of the vine foliage intertwined in the canopy structures of Yannis Bar's. Lindos was coming to life once more.

As he gazed at the developing waking Lindos scene before him quite suddenly he began to feel tiredness sweep over his whole body and mind. He felt lucky. He was contented in the lovely Lindos paradise. It had been a good day and a very good night. Hopefully, the rest of the summer would continue to be so with Alice Palmer, and things between them would go further, just as he wanted.

His good feeling about his night with her - a cocktail of optimism and tiredness – was immediately cooled though by negative thoughts reaching into his brain about the two of them. He knew relatively little about her, and in reality she gave away next to nothing of her past. From what little she had told him of her divorce and how her marriage ended, together with the disasters of his own past relationship experiences, he realised that they were both two damaged people. Could anything in terms of trust and a relationship between them really succeed?

8

St. Paul's Bay and "Friends, good friends, very good friends"

"Did I wake you?"

"Err … no, no," he rubbed his eyes with his spare hand. "I'm still in bed, but I wasn't sleeping. Just too lazy to get up and stir myself. Was actually just at the point of thinking I should. What time is it?"

"One, just gone one. Do you fancy getting some breakfast at Giorgos, and then maybe a couple of hours on St. Paul's?"

He was surprised, very pleasantly surprised. Alice Palmer had never actually called him before. They'd exchanged numbers, but if anything at all she only communicated with him by text on odd occasions to ask where he was after she finished work to meet for a drink. Now she was calling, and suggesting they went to the beach. Another thing she rarely did. He'd pushed her to do so with him a few times, but she always said she had things to do or had to go into work early.

"Aren't you working though?" David asked.

"Not till six-thirty tonight, so we could get two or three hours on St. Paul's if you got your arse out of bed sharpish and met me at Giorgos in half-an-hour or so. Don't be long though 'cos I'm starving."

She seemed full of life, even though at most she must have had only six hours sleep. He'd never heard her being this friendly with him. Perhaps what he thought was a good night they had together last night really had an effect on her. Whatever it was that had brought about her new mood he certainly wasn't going to pass up the chance of an afternoon on

74

the beach with her. It wasn't something that had happened before. Starting work in the restaurant at six, or sometimes six-thirty, didn't really leave much time for the beach after sleep following late night drinking that could sometimes stretch into early mornings. This time was apparently different, however, and she obviously wanted to make the effort.

"Sure, I'll move my arse now and see you at Giorgos in a bit."

She couldn't see it of course, but he was wearing a warm smile of satisfaction.

As he turned the corner towards the café bar just over thirty minutes later he spotted her sat at one of the outside tables clutching a coffee. As he came into view she placed the coffee cup on the table in front of her and gave him one of her radiant smiles. To him it was as bright as the blinding early afternoon sunshine. She had on a loose black plain t-shirt that exposed one of her shoulders, a pair of red tight fitting cotton shorts, and some black flip flops. Her dark hair was tied back off her face in a pony-tail. Despite the late night, or early morning, and a relatively short amount of sleep, she looked relaxed and fresh, although her no doubt weary eyes were protected by a pair of large dark sunglasses.

He had also opted for a t-shirt, light blue in his case, but instead of shorts he was already wearing his swimming shorts, of dark blue.

"Just over thirty minutes. Not bad," she teased him as he reached the table.

He leaned in to kiss her on the cheek. To his pleasure she never drew back.

At that time of day, just after one-thirty, the day-tripper tourists who had ventured to Lindos on the daily boat from Rhodes Town were beginning to make their way back down to Pallas Beach and the boat for its two-thirty departure. So, Giorgos was beginning to empty out of any groups of those who had stopped to grab one of the café's excellent bites to eat for lunch.

David still recognised some remaining French and German voices from the nearby outside tables. As he sat down across from her, removed his sunglasses and placed them on the table, Alice informed him, "I've already ordered a full English breakfast. I'm starving."

Giorgos' owner, Tsamis, appeared at their table as she told David that.

"Morning, David, English breakfast and coffee for you too?" he asked.

"Yes, thanks, Tsamis, but Cappuccino."

As the owner turned to go back inside David stopped him, adding with a smile, "Oh, and Tsamis, no salad remember."

The Greek returned his smile, then told him, "Yes, I remember, David, no salad."

"What was all that about?" Alice asked.

"Just a little joke between Tsamis and me. For some reason, I've no idea why, this summer they've started including salad on the same plate as the English breakfast."

"You're not a salad lover then?"

"Yes I am, but not with a cooked English breakfast surely. Some people might like it, but it's not for me with fried eggs, beans, sausage, bacon and the rest."

They had their late breakfasts, David's minus salad, and then made their way down the almost deserted alleyway immediately opposite Giorgios towards the square with the old Amphitheatre at one end of the village, avoiding the much busier alleyway with its gift shops and restaurants through the centre of the village. As they crossed the shade-less square the roasting sun was incessant, beating down on the two of them.

"Phew! This is my fourth full summer, but I'll never get used to the heat and humidity of the August sun," Alice commented.

"Yes, I know, can't wait to get into the cooling sea for a swim."

"Even the sea is not that cool at this time of year though is it?"

"No, that's true, it isn't, but it's got to be cooler than this. I can even feel the heat from the floor of the square coming through my flip flops," he told her.

That drew a smile from her aimed in his direction. Then she reached to gently briefly squeeze his hand.

As they reached the bottom of the slope by the Town Hall the first glimpse of the beautiful panorama of St. Paul's Bay came into view.

"The beauty of it, that first sight, never ceases to have a stunning effect on me," he said as they made their way along the top road above the bay towards the quite steep slope down to the beach and its picturesque little Greek Orthodox chapel overlooking it at one end. "It's the same effect, same feeling, that I get when I first arrive from the airport and round the corner of the road at the top of the hill and see the panorama of the village spread out far below with its pure white buildings."

"Breath-taking," was her simple reply. Anything more seemed superfluous.

As they reached the top of the slope she broke the silence with, "It looks busy. Hope we can find some sunbeds."

"Don't worry, I'm sure Ledi will find us a couple of empty ones," he reassured her.

Ledi was someone he knew quite well from his various Lindos visits over the past years. He was Albanian, but had worked in Lindos over a number of summers, and was in his late twenties or early thirties. Like many of the Albanian workers he literally kept himself busy working from morning to night, and sometimes long into the night working in the Amphitheatre Club on the top of the hill on the road out of Lindos, or partying in one of the clubs down in the village. During the day he worked on St. Paul's beach, as a sort of 'beachmaster', would be the best way to describe it. He literally ran the beach, with its sunbeds and parasols, for his employer, Panagiotis, who also owned the Tambakio Restaurant at the opposite end of the beach from the little chapel. A couple of hours after he finished on the beach Ledi would be running the bar in Antika, also owned by Panagiotis, in the middle of the village until gone one o'clock in the evening, and mixing his fine cocktails for the customers.

He did, indeed, find them a couple of recently vacated sunbeds, and in the front row right on the crystal clear water's

77

edge. Within a minute David had pulled off his t-shirt, kicked off his flip flops, and was wading into the cooler – though by no means chilly, but almost tepid from the days of hot sun – clear sea of the bay. He launched himself into it and swam a few strokes, then turned to float on his back and look towards the beach waiting for Alice to join him. She had pulled off her shorts and lifted her t-shirt over her head with her hair clipped up on top of it to reveal a very attractive red bikini. He liked what he saw through the sun's unrelenting glare reflecting and sparkling on the water of the bay between him and Alice on the beach.

"Come on, it's cooler in here," he shouted to her back on the shore edge. The beach wasn't exactly quiet. It was August, always busy. There were quite a few people trying to cool themselves in the sea around him, and talking or laughing, but she could just about hear him.

"Okay, okay, I'm coming, what's your rush?" She launched herself into the sea alongside him as she finished and turned to also float on her back.

"It's great isn't it," he told her. "One of the very good reasons to come here and spend the whole summer in Lindos, don't you think?"

As she let out a small laugh still floating on her back she almost swallowed some of the salty sea water.

"For you maybe, yes, of course, but for some of us who have to work all through, and every day, to stay here from May till October, it's not something we get to do very often."

"Not part of that dream you are living then, Alice?"

He spun over on to his front and swam a half a dozen strokes further out into the bay.

She swam after him. As she reached him and turned to join him floating on their backs once more she had one of those cheeky grins of hers that he found so attractive as she jokingly pretended to chide him with, "You taking the piss? Taking the piss out of my dream are you?"

Even in such a relaxed setting, and at such a pleasant relaxed moment, she knew precisely how to unsettle, unnerve him. Nearly three months after they first met he knew she could still do that to him, and so did she. He realised that most of the time she appeared to be only joking. But even then there was still some self-protective, self-preservative element that she just couldn't let go, present in whatever she said. It was like she never wanted him to completely relax with her, and certainly wasn't about to consistently let her guard down, relax, and be entirely comfortable in his company. She was determined to keep him on his toes.

This time the surroundings were far too lovely for him to bite, take the bait. He just grinned back at her, decided that on balance she really was just making a joke and teasing him, and stayed silent floating on his back.

They stayed there floating in the bay for a few more minutes until she told him, "Right, I need a drink," and then swam back to the shore and their sunbeds.

He joined her a few seconds later. As he settled on to his sunbed she told him, "Actually, this is only the third time I've been to the beach this summer. I only managed it about half-a-dozen times last summer too. Working here every night, and then partying through many of the nights after work catches up with you eventually, and there's the alcohol of course. After all that all you want to do is sleep and most of the time you can't be arsed to drag yourself out of bed to go to the beach in the hot sun, even if you know you should. That's not really part of living the dream, I guess."

Through her sunglasses she was staring out into the bay ahead of them from her sunbed as she told him that. She never turned her head towards him on the sunbed beside her at any point all through what she said. She was clearly directing that to herself, not him. Maybe she wasn't really quite so secure in herself as she liked to make out, or show, even to him.

At that point the lingering silence between them over what she'd said was broken by Ledi appearing and asking, "Everything okay, David, with the beds? Do you want some drinks?"

"Yes, thanks a couple of small bottles of water and I'll have an Alfa beer please."

He turned to Alice and she added, "Sod it, a vodka and coke please."

"Okay," Ledi told them, but as he went to walk away towards the bar by the Tambakio restaurant to get the drinks she told him, "No, wait a minute, that's stupid. I've got to work later. Just a glass of white wine with some ice instead, please."

"Didn't realise you were a wine drinker too," David told her as Ledi finally went off to get their drinks.

"Has been known, hidden depths, David, that's me. There's a lot you don't know about me you know."

He couldn't see the glint in her brown eyes through her sunglasses, but she was grinning again after she added, "Lots to find out."

He was thinking that was an encouraging thing to say. Then she quickly added with a slight tilt of her head, "Maybe?"

Was that a, "Maybe," that meant maybe he would want to find out lots about her or maybe that he wouldn't, or alternatively possibly even maybe she would or wouldn't want him to?

Indeed, she was an enigma, full of deeply hidden feelings and emotions. At times it seemed she knew she was and enjoyed being so; keeping people guessing, particularly him.

His deliberations over that were brought to an abrupt halt as Alice quietly pointed out something that clearly wasn't deeply hidden, or rather some things that weren't hidden at all.

As she began to rub some sun cream onto her arms and legs she asked him, do you want some of this?"

"It's okay, I put some P20 sun protection stuff on before I left the flat. It'll last all afternoon, so no thanks."

As she finished rubbing in the cream she told him with a slight giggle, "Look over there that guy just coming out of the sea. He really shouldn't wear swim shorts that small and that tight."

Ten yards or so away a guy sporting some rather unflattering tight white swim shorts, over which his large obvious beer belly hung, was making his way out of the sea and onto the edge of the shore. The shorts hid very little of the attributes of his lower body, particularly between his thighs, and in addition appeared to have developed a definite transparency from the sea water during his swim.

Now they both chuckled at the sight before them. As the man shouted something to his equally inadequately clothed large female companion laying on the sunbed nearby David recognised the language and told Alice, "Russian, they're Russian."

"Yes, there are a lot more of them here this year again. There were quite a lot of Russian tourists the first summer I was here working, then the last two summers a lot less, but they seem to be back in numbers again this year," she informed him.

Just then Ledi brought their drinks, with some nuts and crisps. As David reached for his rucksack to pay him Ledi told him, "No, that's okay, compliments of Panagiotis. He's up in the restaurant, says hello, and these are on him."

The Albanian heard the last part of what Alice had said as he arrived with their drinks. "Yes, Russians, more of them this year again and good for tips," he told them quietly, accompanied by a knowing nod.

She finished applying the rest of her sun cream and the two of them settled back on the comfortable sunbeds to enjoy the hot sun's rays.

David thought this was all going quite well. When she asked, "Have you ever been to the restaurant here, Tambakio?" he decided to take what he thought was an opportunity to try to move things on between them.

"No, never, I've heard it's very good though, and Panagiotis is always getting on to me that I should go. He said he'll do a special meal for me, and whoever I take."

He was fishing. She wasn't taking the bait though, so he pushed it a little further, even though his nervous hesitancy was clear in his voice.

"Well, we could ... we could go ... go if you fancy it one evening that is?"

There was that encouraging beguiling smile of hers again, followed by a much less encouraging, "Bit difficult for me, one evening, with work."

"Oh, yes, of course, well what about for lunch one day, unless you could get an evening off?" He shrugged his shoulders as he finished suggesting that.

"An evening off? Are you kidding? We don't get evenings off here in the summer, and definitely not in the height of the season in August. No chance, not even one."

She shook her head slightly in disbelief that he would even think that possible.

"Lunch then, maybe?" He wasn't giving in easily.

She took a deep breath, levered herself up slightly on the sunbed, and turned the top half of her bikini clad body to face him across on his sunbed. She looked a bit sceptical though as she told him, "Okay, lunch then."

She lay back down on the sunbed and then a few seconds later with her eyes firmly closed from the bright sun added, "Maybe, maybe."

Still an enigma, he thought. Was that another good, "Maybe, maybe"?

They both settled back down in silence to take in the sun's rays and try and top up their tans, or at least in Alice's case to add to what little tan she actually had as a result of her limited beach visits so far that summer.

The silence between them continued, but inside his head a thousand things were buzzing around, all of them thoughts about her and him, their relationship, if there was any such thing. How to try and actually get to the bottom of whether she thought there was one, a relationship? Was he just being stupid? After all, they hadn't even kissed properly. Was he merely acting like some lovesick teenager? He wasn't that though. He was a middle-aged man, a supposedly intelligent, well-educated one too. Then why was he so obviously nervous, ill at ease around her at times, and so timid. It was crazy. It was mid-August. He had been going round and round inside his head with this, over and over it, every detail of what happened between them, every detail of what was said between them, for almost three months. He needed to find out one way or another what it was between them, if anything. What it meant? He would try and find out for sure that afternoon.

He left it for a while, waited for around ten minutes, maybe a little more, while he lay on his back on the sunbed soaking up the hot sun's rays. Was he simply summoning up the courage to find out the truth. That's what he told himself, until eventually he couldn't put it off any longer. He propped himself up on his side, resting his right hand behind his head and his elbow on the sunbed as he gazed over at her lying on her back with her eyes still closed against the bright sunlight. Was she asleep now, dozing perhaps, or just resting with her eyes closed and also enjoying the rays of the sun?

He hesitated for a few seconds more, began to agonise over it once again, took a deep breath, and then finally started to tell her a little clumsily without any lead up to it, just blurted out, "I like you, you know."

He had no idea whether she was even awake and heard him say it. Perhaps in reality that is precisely what he wanted? Her to be asleep, not hear a word he said, but at least he would know he had said it. He would know he had, and if she never actually heard him say it then she couldn't respond in a negative way. He wouldn't have scared her off.

In fact, it was met with a mind-numbing silence. What to do next? Maybe nothing was the obvious thing to do. But he never did the obvious thing. He couldn't leave it. Instead he asked "So, what are we? Where are we? What is it between us?"

Without opening her eyes, without stirring in any way or moving any part of her body, or at the very least even turning her head towards him in any way or to any degree, she answered in a very monotone, matter of fact way, "Friends, good friends, very good friends, David."

And that was it, that was all she said.

It may not have been her complete intention, but the impression she gave was that she was not in the least bit interested in talking about it in any way. In a simple basic monotone phrase of seven words, one of which was his name, uttered without any trace of feeling or concern whatsoever, she effectively destroyed any illusions he might have had. He was shattered, disappointed, but tried desperately to hide it by sounding equally as matter of fact and resigned over her answer.

"Right, I see, yep very good friends, okay."

Now he was even more wary, frightened of exposing his feelings to her totally and making himself vulnerable. Inside though, there was some anger.

9

A kiss, and then another

A couple of days after their afternoon on St. Paul's beach his disappointment had diminished and dissipated somewhat over what she'd told him about being "friends, good friends, very good friends." He was feeling a little better, beginning to feel a little more optimistic again. He'd gone over and over what she'd said and what had been said between them on St. Paul's. He was dwelling on it once again on his way to Pallas Beach for the afternoon. He tried to console himself with the fact that at least it had been her idea for them to spend those couple of hours together on the beach.

He had spent a very productive morning writing in his flat for three hours. The novel was coming along nicely. It was a steaming hot mid-August early afternoon and he'd earned himself a relaxing time on the beach and a swim or two. By the time he turned off the main alleyway which the Lindos donkeys and their owners took back and forth down to Pallas Beach and into the side alley with its beautiful bright pink hanging bougainvillea small beads of sweat were laying on his forehead. As he stopped for a few seconds under the small area of shade from the lovely flowered hanging plant and the pleasant scent from it invaded his nostrils an English voice with what sounded like a Manchester accent asked from behind him, "Excuse me, does this alley lead down to the beach and the jetty for the boats from Rhodes?"

He turned around to see a man and woman, probably in their early fifties and both in shorts and t-shirts, looking equally hot, but also a little flustered.

"Yes, it's straight ahead. Keep going down the path and the steps and you'll come out onto the Main Beach. From there you can walk across to the smaller, Pallas Beach, on the right and the jetty. You'll see the boat as soon as you get on the Main beach. I'm heading that way, so I can take you if you like?"

"Thanks," the woman told him. As the three of them walked on down the narrow alley with its pristine white walls on either side she added, "We've never been here before. We came for the day on the boat and we're staying near Rhodes Town. It's a lovely place, Lindos, but you could get lost very easily I imagine, and there are no street names on the alleyways."

David smiled as he told her, "That's due to the pirates."

"Pirates, there are pirates here?"

She looked a bit concerned as she glanced sideways at the man's face.

"No, sorry, no, I didn't mean now, and actually to be accurate the lack of street names and all the alleyways looking similar wasn't so much due to the pirates many, many years ago, as due to a deliberate way by some of the villagers of deterring them from landing at Lindos."   .

"Well, they are definitely very similar, a lot of the alleyways," the man interjected.

"Yes, the village is a maze of narrow, very similar looking alleyways between white-washed houses and apartments," David continued as they approached the small archway at the end of the rough path to the Main Beach. "It's easy to lose your way, and yet eventually never be lost. That's part of the charm of the place, I think."

He looked across at them both briefly as they nodded their heads silently in agreement.

"It's said historically the similarity of the alleys was deliberate, so that any invading pirates would get lost. That's why I said it was due to the pirates that the alleys had no street names. Many of the larger houses in the village belonged in the past to Sea Captains. During the seventeenth century the ships' Captains became very wealthy and built themselves magnificent homes that were much larger than the traditional village homes. One is now a bar called the Captain's House. Originally many of the houses in the village were built with volcanic rock and stone, but were then painted white to reflect the heat of the sun and keep them cool inside. That's why everywhere is so sparkling white and why so many of the alleys look similar."

He stopped and stepped back to let the man and the woman through the archway first, and then told them, "There," as he pointed across at their Rhodes day-trip boat moored across the bay at the jetty from Pallas Beach.

"If we go to the right from here and through the beach café there is a path that will take us across to the other beach and your boat."

Five minutes later he was saying goodbye to the couple after they all reached the bottom of the small slope leading to Pallas Beach and they went off to make their way towards the jetty for their Rhodes Town bound boat.

A quick nip into Jack's Supermarket by the entrance to the beach to get a small bottle of ice cold water, pay the five euros for a sunbed and umbrella, and then he was desperate to get into the clear cooling sea of the bay. There was always a welcoming, "Hello," from Jack's son George, who now ran the supermarket and their part of the beach, as well as from his family, his wife and mother. David was partial to one of her homemade feta cheese and spinach pies on some days, or one of her other homemade Greek savoury pastries. Not today though, he'd already eaten a roll for lunch in his flat, or more accurately in the courtyard outside his flat. You could pretty much get everything in Jack's Supermarket, from lilos, beach towels, swim shorts and bikinis, to a whole array of food, drinks and ice creams.

Just like St. Paul's a couple of days before the beach was busy, most of the sunbeds with their shading umbrellas were taken. The girl working for Jack's supermarket looking after their part of the beach managed to find him an empty sunbed and umbrella though towards the back of the beach. The sea was just as busy, with its couples and groups of cooling bathers. Although quite a few groups were just standing talking, up to their chests in the clear water. It was August, which was always the busiest tourist month. A month when not only the Brits and the Germans descended on Lindos, but also many Italians during their usual summer vacation break over the two middle weeks of August. In the U.K. of course it was the height of the school holidays, so there was a fair smattering of families with young, and not so young, children on the beach and on the sea edge. Lindos wasn't exactly a prime place for families with children to holiday, but it still attracted its share and the regular Lindos returners of families, sometimes of three generations holidaying together.

He had his cooling swim and settled down on his sunbed for a relaxing afternoon, topping up his tan. The biggest decision he faced that afternoon was whether to carry on reading some of the book he'd been wading through since he arrived in Lindos – a Hilary Mantel historical fiction - or listen to the UK radio sports station on the internet on his phone. He plumped for the radio, figuring he was bound to doze off and it was easier to listen to some mindless radio broadcaster than try to keep awake reading. In any case, through his earphones the radio would drown out the low rumble of chatter and general sometimes louder noise of the late August holidaymakers around him and across the small beach, particularly the young Italians.

It was an extremely pleasant afternoon, one of those that made his decision to come and spend the whole summer in Lindos well worthwhile. The sun was shining hot and bright directly overhead, the sea was a clear blue matching the cloudless sky, and the view out over the bay from his beach sunbed was stunning, as always. The vista before him was certainly relaxing, unlike the nagging seeds of turmoil within him over Alice. That was a far from clear shining bright vision of what he should do. In contrast, it was cloudy and dark with uncertainty.

He was a person who predominantly craved certainty, a degree of order and an understanding of where his life, his future, was headed. The necessities of his academic background had attempted to instil that within him. Alice Palmer, however, was a completely different character. Due to circumstances her life was messy and unpredictable. It may have been different back in the U.K., more regimented and predictable, when she was married. That didn't seem to be the case now, even though she appeared to be becoming more settled once again, living and working in Lindos for the past few years. Nevertheless, she still had her quirks, her unpredictability, that would surface illogically and without warning from time to time.

He tried to put all that out of his mind for the afternoon as he dozed in and out of consciousness, sporadically stirring a little to pick up bits of the radio programme and a couple of times venturing back into the sea to cool down with a swim.

After six the August air got slightly cooler. Not a lot, but enough to notice the difference and make emerging from under the shade of the umbrella into the sunlight more bearable. The full round large red sun was slowly inching its way down towards the hill on the other side of the bay where it disappeared from sight on the beach each evening. By seven o'clock it was almost gone. All that lingered was the final defiant beautiful reddy orange aura of the edge of the dying sun. As that last vestige of another hot Lindos August day finally disappeared he stirred himself off the sunbed and reached for his flip flops beneath it, and then his t-shirt draped over the spokes supporting the umbrella above.

The sun had gone down, not exactly 'over the yardarm', but nevertheless it was definitely time for a beer to round off an excellent Lindos day of writing, sunbathing and swimming. He decided to call in to the Rainbird Bar for one on his way back up from the beach.

Minutes later he was wandering through the outer courtyard of the bar. As he anticipated, it was quite full. It was a popular spot at that time of day, particularly because of its amazing stunning view out over Lindos Bay. Through the outer archway the inner courtyard of the bar was a mixture of wooden and wrought iron trellis entwined with foliage and some vines. The floor was the traditional patterned pebble mosaic. Some of the seats were benches against the walls and wooden slatted double seats, covered in multi-coloured striped cushions, as well as white wooden typical Greek style high back chairs with similar cushions. They all surrounded quite small round black wrought iron tables. People, the regulars, never went to the Rainbird for the comfort of the furniture though. They went for the stunning

89

views, and the friendly greeting and service of Nikos, the main host of the place, with his dark long hair tied in a pony-tail. He always had a smile and a welcoming word, always remembered a name, and today was no exception.

"Beer, David?" Nikos asked as David took a seat at the only empty table.

"Just a small one, my friend. It's still a bit early for anything larger."

While Nikos went off to get his beer David enjoyed the view out over the bay and discreetly surveyed his fellow early drinkers. They were all couples, middle-aged and over. From what he could make out, and from overhearing their occasional comments in conversation with Nikos as he made his way to the seat a few minutes before, he figured that most of them were English, although he thought he detected a slight American accent emanating from one couple.

It was seven-thirty, the air was still warm, and the view and the surroundings were great. So, all was right with David Alexander's world. There were worse places to be in the summer of 2019, and hopefully many more subsequent summers. He'd decided that would certainly be the case for him with many more long Lindian summers.

Nikos brought his beer, along with a small dish of peanuts. After they chatted for a minute or so about how business was, and had been that summer, the Greek left David to his own thoughts.

For a few seconds as he gazed out over the bay he thought about the dulling heat and then eventually the fading sunlight on the beach. One minute it was bright and sparkling, the next it was gone. Much like Alice Palmer's moods perhaps? He didn't seem to be able get her out of his mind. Maybe it was looking around at the couples on the terrace of the bar, chatting, laughing and smiling at the view together that made him think of her. Whatever it was he was still dwelling on her, and what she'd told him so coldly in the heat of St. Paul's beach. Yet he had not even kissed her, and definitely not been anywhere near the prospect of sleeping with her. What would that be like? The nearest he'd seen her naked was in that red bikini on St. Paul's beach. His mind was wandering. His thoughts were veering off in many different strange directions.

Would sex with her be as aggressive as her character and responses sometimes were? Or would she be much more passive? Could she really be that passive though? He was curious, and now more than ever, eager to find out. It intrigued him. Quite a conundrum to be pondering over on a lovely relaxing early evening on a Greek island. Yet for some strange reason, some strange feeling really, the thought of actual sex with her, making love with her, felt almost too perfect. The thought of it was too perfect to disturb, too perfect to disturb the anticipation of it and his desire for it. To him she was beautiful, beautiful perfection in body and mind, even with her mood swings, her aggression and her determination at times not to take any shit from anyone. That was very much part of what attracted him, her unpredictable bouts of anger. Was that odd, strange, bizarre? It was definitely the case though that her character, even with all its obvious flaws, attracted him as much as, no in fact more than, her body. That's not to say that her body wasn't attractive to him, even were it to display the growing imperfections of time. Not that he would ever even briefly think of telling her that. If he wanted to see her angry side that was one sure way of producing it.

His meandering thoughts about Alice were brought to an end with Nikos asking, "How much longer are you here for?"

"October, till October, maybe the start or maybe I'll stick around till the end of that month and the end of the season. It depends on if I have to go back to London for some things at the start, some meetings. Never want to leave here, of course. Why would anybody?"

Nikos nodded as he agreed, "Nobody ever wants to leave," then asked, "Do you want another beer?"

"No thanks, time to go to the supermarket and find something to cook for dinner."

"We do good food here you know," Nikos responded.

"Yes, I heard it's good. Maybe another time. Don't worry; I'll give it a try. I'm sure it'll be good. With this setting and view how could it not be?"

He paid for his beer. Then gathered up his small beach rucksack and made his way through the courtyard and up the few steps to the path with the panoramic view of the Main Beach below. The lights of the restaurants at the back of the beach were already beginning to twinkle in the fading light. The whitewashed walls of the village alleys managed to hold on to a little of the light of the fading dying sun of the parting day for a short while, but it was a struggle they always eventually soon lost.

Twenty yards from the Rainbird exit he arrived at what was known to many regular Lindos visitors as 'cat's corner'. Six cats of various colours and hues were lounging spaced out on the lingering heat of the concrete of the path at the bottom of the steps. Nothing seemed to faze them by that time of day, no passer-by, many of whom stopped to stroke one or two of them without any of them stirring. They had probably been like that in that perfect relaxed stretched out position since mid-day and for most of the hot afternoon. Their only movement being to occasionally seek out some shade before resuming their stretched out pose. Lucky cats, nine lives and lazing between the sun and the shade all day in Lindos David thought as he passed them by and smiled at their obvious relaxed comfort.

A few minutes after that he was walking down the main alley through the centre of the village making his way towards the little supermarket by Yannis Bar on the way to his flat. The alleys were starting to get busy, filling up with tourists making for an early evening drink at one of the bars before dinner at one of the restaurants with their rooftop panoramas over the village. He didn't consciously choose to go that way through the village on the way to the supermarket. It was merely the shortest way from the Rainbird. Although he was well aware that his route would inevitably take him past the restaurant where Alice worked. He hadn't seen her for a few nights, getting on for a week. But now there she was, standing at the open doorway to the restaurant, hopefully encouraging early evening customers, and greeting him with a broad warm smile.

"You coming in later?" she asked. "We've got some good, fresh Tuna. I'll save you a piece."

He stopped walking, returned her smile, and told her, "Why not? Probably be after nine though I guess."

He had instantaneously easily abandoned any thought of the supermarket and cooking something.

"Good, I'll look forward to it," she replied encouragingly, although the slight smile on her lips indicated just a hint of easy sarcasm.

He couldn't resist an equally sarcastic, "Hope the service is as good as the Tuna though," as he walked on.

Behind him he heard her short, sharp, "F-off," although admittedly said in an obvious light hearted voice.

Even after what she'd told him on St. Paul's beach about being, "very good friends," it still constantly nagged away at him that from that night when they first met when she served him in the restaurant at the start of that summer of season of 2019 nothing had happened between them. Somehow he couldn't put it out of his mind, let it drop. It just kept popping into his brain. Nothing close between them had occurred, except some sort of growing friendship. Was that really all there was to it? Were they simply new friends who would occasionally meet up after she'd finished work and go out to drink together in the bars and clubs of Lindos; just drinking friends?

As time passed that summer he tried more and more to put the thought out of his mind of anything sexual and more developing between them. However, that was easier said than done. There were always triggers, things she said, and occasionally, very occasionally did, that re-ignited the thought in his head. Got him thinking about it, and pondering over it all once again. At times like that he actually wondered if she was doing it deliberately. Was she enjoying it, keeping him dangling and keeping his attention just whenever she decided she wanted it? Perhaps it was simply when there was no one else around to give her attention? No other man?

That night of a Tuna dinner in her restaurant, and what happened after, what she did later, was yet another of those instances. Even asking as he passed by if he was coming into the restaurant later, and telling him they had fresh Tuna that night, was one of those triggers that started him thinking more positively. Perhaps it wasn't a deliberate thing by her, and instead, merely a chance to get another customer that evening? However, what happened later that night after she finished work made him think there was more to it than him simply being another customer.

It started with what seemed an insignificant gesture by her. As they had done many times previously that summer, they were making their way from Jack Constantino's Courtyard Bar to the Arches club. It was just gone two-thirty and the alleys were mostly eerily deserted. It was that strange time when the usually busy alleyways were empty. The shops and restaurants in them were boarded up, and most of the owners had long gone to their beds. Only the bright full moon above lit up the large, well-worn slabbed paths between the buildings. The fierce heat of the August day had penetrated the alleyways for hours on end, producing its legacy only a few degrees lower well into the night accompanied by a high level of humidity. In the heat and humidity locals and tourists alike were longing for a wind, or at least a breeze. Even on the odd occasions it arrived, however, it was a warm one.

Alice turned up in Jack's bar slightly before a quarter to two, as was often her way. David was there nursing his Mythos beer, his fifth or six of the evening, and wondering whether he could drink another, should go on to a vodka and coke, or just push off to a club or to bed. As he left her restaurant earlier Alice had made a point of kissing him on the cheek and telling him, "See you later, probably in Jack's?" He just nodded, although even then he wondered why she had said, "probably in Jack's," rather than a more definite, "see you in Jack's". There was always a doubt. She always left him with a doubt. It was deliberate.

Just before she actually turned up he was starting to wonder just how futile this all was, and that perhaps he should just go off to his bed. Her initial abrasive attitude when she did turn up didn't exactly persuade him otherwise.

"Nice dress, not seen you in red before, mostly black," he straightaway attempted to pay her a compliment. However, he clearly had forgotten momentarily one of the few things he knew for sure about Alice Palmer. Compliments didn't sit easily with her, if at all.

She never actually said anything as she sat down on the bar stool next to him. She didn't have to. Instead, she gave him a sideways glance accompanied by a frown that spoke for itself, which he took to mean, "Why are you saying that?"

Not a good start to the evening, but he chose to ignore it, putting it down to the fact that she'd probably had a heavy night at work in the restaurant. Instead, he just ordered her a drink. She only had the one vodka and coke and then suggested they went to Arches.

Things certainly picked up after that as far as David was concerned, initially at least. No sooner had they said goodnight to Jack and his head barman, Dimitris, and navigated their way down the few rough steps nearby onto the flat alley path, than she tucked her bare arm into his, clearly squeezed it a little, and briefly looked up into his eyes. It was an obvious and deliberate sign. He thought about kissing her there and then, but his caution arising from previous experiences with her throughout the summer caused him to hesitate. So, they walked on arm in arm through the village to Arches.

In effect, it wasn't really much, tucking her arm in his and squeezing it a little. However, it stirred something inside him again, re-ignited something; another deliberate trigger perhaps? Later that evening he knew that he should just have kissed her at that moment. When they got into Arches she decided they should have Tequila shots, and headed straight to the bar to order them. The club was fairly busy, but by no means packed. It was a Wednesday night. Along with Saturdays that was one of the nights of a traditional Lindos changeover day, when new arrivals would be on the first night of their holiday. Many would have arrived late that night or simply be too tired from travelling to go out straightaway for a long night's drinking and clubbing. A couple of drinks and bed ready for the start of their holiday the next day was the routine of the majority of new arrivals. Thursday and Sunday nights were much busier, not just in the clubs, but in the bars and restaurants in the village in general – the first real night of people's holidays.

The clientele in Arches that Wednesday night was mostly workers from the bars and restaurants, and fairly young. The Greek and Albanian workers were intermingled with a few young Brits working in the village for the summer, as well as with a couple of young women workers from the Baltic states of Lithuania and Latvia. David had seen them all around the village over that summer, at work in the bars and restaurants, and also occasionally on the beaches during the afternoon before they started work. He knew most of them by name, as did Alice, although not all of the young Baltic or Albanian women.

While Alice went to get their Tequilas from Pete behind the bar David spotted an empty stool on the other side of the club against an alcove in the far wall and alongside a high table. He made his way over to it after first letting Alice know that was where he was headed. Much to his concern, a minute or so later she appeared in front of him with not two Tequila shots, but four, handing him two.

"Time to get pissed again, I think," she said as she rapidly downed the two shots. He despatched his a little slower. She seemed to be in a good mood now, still trying to live the dream.

When she arrived with the shots he was propped half on and half off the high stool, with one leg resting on the floor and his other foot placed on the lower rung of the stool. After he had downed his two shots he placed the empty glasses on the high table alongside and made as if to get up, asking as he did so if Alice wanted to sit down. She never spoke in response, but much to his surprise instead placed her left hand on his chest and gently pushed him back down on to the stool. She spent a few lingering seconds gazing into his eyes as if she was trying to convey something to him through her actions without bothering to speak and then slowly turned to rest her body against his that was still perched on the stool. He never moved. For the next couple of minutes she remained in the same position while surveying the dancing, talking, and drinking groups of clubbers around them.

Alice's calm, and seemingly comfortable, position was only disturbed by a young Albanian woman, a waitress in one of the Lindos bars, Lucy. She spotted David across the club and made her way over to them. However, she wasn't someone Alice knew at all, and judging by Alice's aggressive over reaction, it was clear she wasn't about to adopt the young woman as any sort of new friend.

"David, I wondered where you'd been? Haven't seen you in our bar for a while."

It was an innocent enough and friendly comment, or so David thought. Straightaway he began to sense something of a change in Alice's relaxed body language. He could literally feel a tension running through her as, still resting her body back on his, she reached behind and took hold of his right hand, placed it across her waist and gripped it tightly. It was like she was marking out her territory to Lucy, her possession perhaps? There was a noticeable change in Alice's actions, now accompanied by something of an aggressive glare at Lucy. The English woman was literally scowling at Lucy, wearing an exceedingly sour look across her face as David tried to reduce the tension and introduce them. Alice though was having none of it.

"Lucy, this is Alice. She's working in a restaurant here for the summer, her fourth season. This is Lucy, Alice. It's her first season working here."

What he tried to say was stilted and clumsy, reflecting the obvious discomfort he sensed over the tension between the two women.

Lucy had clearly picked up Alice's unhappiness and aggression over her approaching David. In an equally clumsy way she simply blurted out to Alice, "Friends, we're just friends that's all." With that she quickly added, "See you around, David," and turned to go back and join her friends across the other side of the club.

What the hell was that about was what he was actually thinking? However, he decided it would be best to let it rest and say nothing about it for now? It appeared at first that Alice wasn't about to say anything about it either. Instead, she

97

remained silent, with her back pressed up against him propped on the stool and firmly gripping his hand across her waist. Was that jealousy, and over a young woman at least fifteen years younger or more than him? That's crazy. He'd never seen that from Alice before. Whatever it was it was certainly an interesting possessive type of reaction. So, should he at least be pleased about that or concerned?

Eventually he couldn't resist. A few minutes later he tenderly turned her around to face him and led her up to asking about it gently, or so he thought. "Another drink, vodka and coke?"

What she said wasn't exactly the answer he was looking for, or expecting though.

She purposefully stepped back half a pace from him and asked straight into his face, "Have you slept with her then?"

"What?"

A frown spread across his face, accompanied by a small chuckle of incredulous disbelief at what she'd asked. The fine line between jealousy and confrontation was looming. The boundaries between jealousy and attraction, as well as those of positive and negative vibes, were being rapidly breached. He had no idea why. What had made Alice's mood change so quickly? Some serious amount of jealousy it seemed, but how had she made the jump from her avowed position of, "Friends, good friends, very good friends," to such a distinct display of possession, jealousy, and concern over who he may have slept with? And why? Did she actually care for him in some way then?

"That's crazy, Alice, of course not-" he started to say.

"Is it, is it really? Crazy, is it, David? Crazy am I? That's good to know, good to know that's what you think of me."

Her voice was raised, and some people nearby were starting to look over at the pair of them. They could hear the start of the argument even above the loud music in the club.

"Hang on, just wait a minute, it's not you that's crazy, Alice. It's just crazy to think that I would sleep with a young woman probably around half my age, or almost anyway I'm guessing.

Just calm down. I could see you were really aggressive towards her, and so could she. But that's stupid."

"Oh, so now I'm stupid as well as crazy, am I?"

She wasn't calming down at all. If anything, she was rapidly boiling over. Something inside her had ignited her anger, but he had no idea what. Not that he knew it, but in fact what had lit the fuse to her anger was that she'd started to expose herself to a man, him, started to reveal her feelings, or at least was on the verge of doing so. Lucy's approach to them, or more accurately David, had simply set off some sort of warning sign inside Alice's mind flagging up all the issues she had over men and trust. She was as angry with herself as she was with Lucy, or him.

He again tried to turn down the heat and cool the situation.

"No, no, you're not stupid. It's about the way you reacted. That's what was stupid, and for no reason. You seriously think I would sleep with someone that young, even if I could? And anyway, I'm confused. I didn't think after what you said on St. Paul's about just being very good friends that you would be bothered about any of that at all, that me sleeping with other women would be of any concern or interest to you. Not that I have. It's not like we have-"

He never got to finish. She quickly stepped closer to him, grabbed a fistful of his polo shirt with her left hand, pulled him into her and kissed him firmly. It was a long, lingering passionate kiss. They could have been anywhere. She clearly wasn't bothered that they were up against the stool in Arches, or that plenty of people had heard them arguing and were now enjoying what appeared to be a clear show of reconciliation.

"You still confused now?" she said as she drew back from the kiss.

"Err ... err ..." He was struggling for words in his totally muddled brain.

She just stood silent, a few inches away from him staring into his face, and with her mischievous grin lighting up the small space between them.

"No ... well, err ... no ... that is, well."

He was babbling like a small child. He took a very visible deep breath and then continued.

"A little, a little confused still, yes I am, Alice."

Was that another deliberate display of possession by her? He hesitated for a few seconds, then took another deep breath followed by a sigh. There was clearly a perplexed, somewhat incredulous edge in his voice as he added while still close and staring intently into her eyes, "Was all that jealousy? Are you jealous? Does that mean we are more than-"

He was interrupted by a man's English voice from behind her. "You okay, Alice? Is he bothering you? I saw you arguing."

David recognised him at once. He was the drunken guy who had given him some grief up at Lindos By Night earlier in the summer, insisting that David had a drink with him. That was David's second week in the village and he was looking for Alice for a late drink, having still not come across her after their initial restaurant meeting. Because of his antagonistic drunken manner David deliberately made a point of remembering his name. He had decided very quickly that particular night that Simon Chapel was clearly someone to avoid.

She turned around. There was a frown and confused look all over her face. After what she'd just done, so obviously kissing David passionately, how could anyone think he was bothering her? But as soon as she saw it was Simon she knew that even a clear display of affection like that wouldn't put him off from getting involved in something that was none of his business, trying to stir up trouble. She had a history with Simon Chapel, although only a very brief one, a very brief regrettable encounter. She was well aware from that, and from other things she'd heard around the village, that he liked confrontation and was never slow to get involved in anything he could that related to it. For that reason she attempted to instantly dismiss his interest in a very low key fashion.

"No, it's okay thanks, Simon. A misunderstanding, that's all, not really an argument, and as I'm sure you've just seen, it's all over now. All sorted thanks."

However, quite deliberately he wasn't choosing to see at all that it was, "All sorted." Alice Palmer might have believed, wished to believe, that her previous encounter with Simon Chapel that summer, very brief as it was, was history, but he clearly didn't want to think so. He wouldn't accept it was, and had tried on a few occasions that summer to revive it, reprise what had happened one night between them. At every opportunity when their paths crossed in a bar or club in the village he would try and engage her in conversation. He definitely wasn't taking the hint at all, even though at one point Alice had made it quite clear to him that what had happened between them was a one off and wasn't going to happen again. She had told him quite forcibly late one night in Jack's Courtyard Bar that there was no chance whatsoever of that. David had no idea about any of that, of course.

No sooner had Alice finished telling him it was all sorted than Simon was in David's face, glaring at him and completely ignoring what she'd said. The fumes emanating from his mouth as he spoke, along with the slight swaying in his stance, gave away the fact that he was obviously quite drunk. Whether it was simply the alcohol, or his character, or a mixture of the two perhaps, it was plain that he was looking for trouble. He patently visibly and verbally wasn't a happy man.

"You bothering her pal?"

He almost spat it out in David's face.

David said nothing. He just grinned back in his face, deciding that was the best way of dealing with the situation. In any case, over Simon's shoulder he noticed Pete, the barman, signalling across to Chris, the large well-built Arches employee operating the inner sound vacuum door exit and entrance at that point. He was attracting Chris' attention and pointing over to where Simon was confronting David.

However, Alice was getting angry.

"Simon, for fuck's sake, I told you it's sorted. Just piss off will you!"

That didn't quite have the effect Alice intended.

"Okay, Alice, don't worry, I get it. He's obviously got you scared of him. Just come over to the bar with us," Simon responded.

With that he grabbed her around the waist with his right arm, assuming she would just easily walk over to the bar with him and join a group of people he had been drinking with. She attempted to wriggle out of his grasp as she shouted, "Fucking get off me, Simon."

Simultaneously David grabbed hold of his wrist and attempted to pull Simon's arm from around her waist, which did actually result in Alice getting free, but also resulted in Simon turning around and grabbing David by the throat. There was the briefest of scuffles before the large muscled arms of Chris grabbed hold of the pair of them and pulled them apart.

"You, go home, Simon. You're too drunk to be in here. You know we don't have any trouble in here," he told him in a low firm voice.

Simon tried to speak, "But-"

Chris wasn't taking no for an answer though.

His voice was slightly raised, but equally as firm, as he interrupted with, "Out now, Simon, or I'll put you out, and you really don't want that do you? I can tell you that if I have to do that it'll be a long time before you're allowed in here again. It won't be any time during the rest of this summer for sure."

Simon Chapel clearly didn't want to be put out of the club by Chris, or banned for the rest of the season. So, he sheepishly made his way towards the exit.

"You two okay," Chris asked David and Alice.

"Yep, thanks, Chris," Alice told him. "It wasn't David's-"

She started to explain, but Chris interrupted.

"It's okay, Alice. I saw what happened. Pete tipped me off. It's one advantage of him being so tall behind that bar." He grinned and winked at David as he added, "I could see from a few minutes before that you two were obviously getting on well."

David smiled back at him, and then also told him thanks, before Chris went back to his place on the door.

Chris had barely left them when David said, "What a bloody crazy night. First Lucy and now bloody Simon Chapel. What was all that about with Lucy? And why is he so bothered about you, and just what's it got to do with him, you and me?"

She just shrugged her shoulders and replied, "That's Lindos for you. It's crazy here sometimes."

She clearly wasn't about to explain the truth of what it was about with Simon Chapel. Little did David Alexander know it at the time, but that was a good sign. She obviously didn't want to damage her developing relationship with him, whatever it actually was by now of course.

She just quickly added, "He was obviously very drunk. Just ignore it, ignore him, David. He's a prick. Everyone in Lindos knows he gets like that. He likes to wind people up, thinks it's clever. I'll get us some more drinks and let's go outside in the courtyard with them for a bit. I certainly need one now."

She got them both another vodka and coke and they made their way through the soundproof exit doors, accompanied by another knowing grin from Chris on the inner door, and then headed for the well-worn wooden bench seat up against the club wall in the courtyard.

For a few minutes they sat on the bench sipping at their drinks without exchanging a word. Despite the late hour it was still a very warm, airless, sticky August night. The contrast with the inside of the club with its full on air conditioning was stark. Alice gazed straight ahead across the dimly lit courtyard at the high stone wall and the few bushes growing high in front of it. The dull light was supplemented only by the bright moon and the multitude of stars in the clear dark sky above. He glanced sideways at her a couple of times but she never moved, never looked back at him. He felt she knew that he was looking, but she never acknowledged it.

He had no way of knowing but, in fact, while they sat there in silence she was going over and over in her head what had just happened inside the club; what was behind the confrontation with Simon Chapel, but most of all her reaction to Lucy. She was as confused as David over why she reacted the way she did to her. What did that mean? Was it jealousy? If so, what did that mean about how she felt about David? Did she care for him, at the very least in some small way? It was certainly a spontaneous reaction, something she was prone to do on many other things. That was in her character, but she'd decided it wasn't any longer when it came to men, or so she thought. She'd been determined not to let herself feel and react that way about a man again after what her ex-husband did to her. No more jealousy or spontaneity, not even in any small way. She needed to think it through and try to understand what was happening between her and David, most of all decide what she wanted to happen. She simply didn't know what she wanted. Yes, there were times when she wanted to be with him, in his company, and sometimes wanted more than that. But she had always stopped herself from letting that happen. Then there were other times when she convinced herself it was better to stay alone, and get on enjoying living the dream in Lindos. One thing she thought she was sure of though, was that at this particular time she wasn't about to talk to David about her confusion. She definitely wasn't ready for that conversation at the moment, and perhaps never would be.

As they sat there sipping their drinks in silence a few people sporadically crossed the courtyard heading for the toilets or back into the club, while some others arrived to go in or came out to leave. A couple of those said, "Hi," to Alice as they passed by, tourist customers from the restaurant or workers she knew in the village. Two other women spotted David on the bench as they were leaving and crossing the courtyard towards the arch that led to the alley outside.

"Hi, David," one of them called across in a quite broad West Midlands English accent.

He was still gazing across in silence at the stone wall on the other side of the courtyard, pondering what Alice's similar silence meant and what she could be thinking, when the woman's voice disturbed his deep contemplation and startled him a little.

"Oh, hi Ruth, on your way home now?"

The two women never stopped, but continued towards the exit as she responded, "Yes, had enough now, time for bed."

The second woman added, "Night, David, don't drink too much. Maybe see you on Pallas tomorrow?"

"Maybe, Louise, night," he replied.

He was anticipating Alice's question now. She didn't disappoint him, although thankfully it wasn't the sort of aggressive inquisition he'd face from her after Lucy had said hello to him earlier.

She briefly looked across at the back of the two women as they left through the arch and then turned her head towards him asking in a low calm voice, "Who's that?"

"Just a couple of women I was talking to up at Jack's one night and then saw them in the sea off Pallas the next afternoon."

He chuckled a little before adding, "They were telling me they had their lilos pinched, stolen overnight on Pallas after they left them there, which apparently they do every night. I gather quite a few people leave them there overnight by their sunbeds. Anyway, that's what those two women told me. They were quite annoyed about it too. They are Lindos regulars, according to Jack. He introduced us that night in Courtyard. They know him well apparently, although doesn't everybody?"

"I guess so," she agreed, as he took another sip from his now almost empty glass.

It was starting to look like yet another middle of the night and approaching dawn episode involving the two of them sitting and talking on the bench in the Arches courtyard. At one point the owner, Valasi, appeared from the alley outside and crossed the courtyard towards the outer soundproof entrance door. He knew them both well, of course. Seeing the two of them on the bench he simply smiled as he told them, "I think I'm going to have to start charging you two rent for that bench given the number of times I've seen you there this summer."

It appeared from the tone of her voice that Alice's mood was now much calmer than it had been in the aggressive confrontations inside the club. Even what she asked him next didn't have the same aggressive tone in her voice as was evident when she confronted him about Lucy, even though it was also about women.

105

"Do you have many women friends then? And many here in Lindos?" She made a short glance sideways at him as she asked.

He looked sideways at her, even though she had resumed staring straight ahead.

"Some, yeah, some, of course some of the women workers here in the village, young Brits working here for the summer, although there aren't nearly so many here this summer, because of Brexit looming, I guess. And some of-"

"Yep, god knows what's going to happen to my living the dream here when bloody Brexit actually does finally kick in full on. Who knows how long or even if I will be able to stay living and working here?"

She continued staring into space ahead of her as she told him that with a slight shake of her head. Her facial expression was vacant, as though she was detached from her surroundings and him as she made that comment.

She'd interrupted him, but he took it as a good sign that at least she appeared more willing to open up a bit and talk about herself, to some extent and for that moment. It was not something she'd done, or been prepared to do, in all their long nights in Arches courtyard. She never continued with it, however. That left him unsure whether to carry on with what he was saying in answer to her question about him and women friends. He waited a full long minute. She never said anything more, so he did.

"Some regular tourists that come and go through the season too."

She turned her head back towards him and asked, "What, what tourists?" She'd clearly forgotten what she'd asked, or she simply assumed he had finished telling her.

He wanted to finish it and hopefully probe a little deeper as to why she asked.

"Women, women friends here in Lindos, you asked?"

"Oh, yeah, I thought you'd finished. It wasn't that important. I just wondered."

With that she turned her head away from him again. He decided to take a chance, push her a bit more on it.

"Why? Are you bothered about that, me and women friends?"

"No, it's nothing, I was just curious that's all. Lucy inside tonight, and then those two women just now, I just wondered, that's all."

He turned back to gaze across the courtyard ahead of them. What he was thinking now was what did that mean? What was actually behind her question? She clearly wasn't going to tell him, wasn't prepared to open up that much.

Maybe it was the silence, or the alcohol, the quantity of it, or maybe it was the mention of Brexit and the uncertainty over her living the dream future, but he was starting to detect that what he took as her calm mood just a few minutes before was now giving way to an impression that she was drifting into some sort of melancholy. He'd been about to suggest that he went inside to get them another drink, but thought better of it for the moment. Instead, he decided he would try to lift her out of her seeming looming depression by asking more about her.

"So, what exactly was your job back in England, the one that you became so fed up with that you decided to come and live the dream here?"

That last part of what he asked at least sparked her up.

"You taking the piss?" she snapped back at him as she quickly turned her head towards him and then turned it away after she finished.

"No, I … you just never really said, and I-"

She never let him finish.

"It isn't that interesting, wasn't very interesting, and that's why it was pretty easy to give it up and come here. Just a regular boring office job, computer data processing and programming for a large engineering company, although to be honest there wasn't that much programming. It was mostly data processing day in, day out, five days a week, nine to five stuck in front of a computer screen. Not the most exciting work in the world, but the pay was okay."

Her tone was much calmer once again.

"Although after I split from my ex-husband and eventually got divorced I needed a bit more to live on. That's when I

107

started waitressing part-time, weekends only at first, but then an added night mid-week. I'd done it when I was younger, before I was married. When I started it again after the split I found I liked it, liked interacting with people. I thought I was good at it. I was good at it, and that's when I first started thinking about coming to Lindos to do it for the whole summer. So, I did, and here I am, sat outside a club in the middle of the night with a former university academic and budding novelist. So, there you are, now you know. What I did back home in my job was nowhere near as interesting as yours, lecturing in Russian literature."

While she told him all that she continued all the while to gaze vacantly into the middle distance across the courtyard. It was as if she was actually talking to herself, convincing herself it had all been a very good thing. That was all very introspective, but at least her mood appeared to be much less aggressive. She turned her head to face him once again as she finished, and even offering him one of her intoxicating slight smiles.

She'd done it again. Used her adept skill at turning the conversation away from her and on to him. He unwittingly obliged.

"It wasn't just that."

"Wasn't what? What wasn't, David?"

"Literature, it wasn't just Russian literature, it was also Russian foreign policy."

"But I'm sure you told me the first or second time we met that that it was Russian literature?"

"Probably, but I thought I also said and some other Russian stuff. That included Russian foreign policy. It links together you see. Russian foreign policy today is rooted in Russian literature and history. Unfortunately, not many, if any, western politicians understand that, particularly the arrogant British ones."

He realised he was being pedantic and really beginning to sound like he was giving her a lecture. Not exactly the impression he wanted to convey at that particular time sat outside a club with her in the middle of the night in Lindos. It wasn't the impression he was aiming for at all.

However, her initial response wasn't anywhere near as bad as he'd anticipated.

"Interesting," she started to say. "That all sounds a bit like Intelligence Services and spies stuff. Perhaps that's what you should write about in your novel."

"Hmm … maybe," was all he replied. He absolutely wasn't going to get into that with her at this point, if ever. She was closer than she knew though. But there are some things that are better left unsaid, untold, when related to the Intelligence Services and that community.

From time to time people continued to wander past on their way to and from the toilet. Although, it was getting late, or rather towards early morning and sunrise yet again, and the club clientele was thinning out and the toilet goers were getting fewer. The two of them sat in silence for a few more minutes, gazing once again ahead at the stone wall opposite. It crossed his mind again to suggest another drink, but in all honesty he didn't really need or want one. His mind was back to again trying to guess just what she was thinking. Whether the conversation they'd just had would get her thinking once more about the two of them and their relationship, whatever that was.

In fact, in a way she was, but not quite in the positive way he hoped for. She wasn't letting the academic stuff go, even if the direction she took it in wasn't one he expected at all. He couldn't figure out at first quite where she was going with it, or whether it was good or bad. He soon decided it wasn't exactly good. Her melancholic introspection had returned and now was being totally focused on, and reflected onto whatever it was that was going on between the two of them. Whatever had been going on between them for three months or so that summer.

Suddenly, without turning her head to face him, but instead continuing to stare vacantly ahead, she broke the silence. "That's the problem isn't it though, David. That's the thing about me and you. About anything happening between us, I suppose."

109

He had no idea what she was about to say, but at that point he was at least feeling a little optimistic that she was thinking and talking about a, "me and you," and, "About anything happening between us." He decided it was best to just let her say what she wanted to say, rather than interrupt and ask what is, "the problem". He misread it completely though, and what came next totally punctured his optimism.

She never looked at him, made no eye contact at all as she told him, "Your life is completely different to mine, has been totally different. You inhabited an academic world of universities, mixing with Professors and the like, studying and reading lots of great books, and travelling to different great places like Russia for academic reasons, all those places in Russia you told me you've been to. Meanwhile, my life has been stuck in an office processing boring data, being a waitress back home part-time, and now here every summer working god knows how many hours every day on basic wages and hoping for good tips from the tourists."

"But-"

He started to try to say something to persuade her otherwise, but her pessimism and melancholy had overwhelmed her. At that point she was having none of whatever he tried to say. As she interrupted him she continued to look straight ahead, as if the very last thing she wanted to do, or could bring herself to do, was look him in the eye.

"Face it, David, we've lived in two different worlds, come from two different worlds, and still do. You're writing a novel, and yes you're here for this summer, but then what? Where after that? Me, I'm stuck here, and will be for god knows how many summers and through the quiet empty winters with no tourists. Brexit permitting, of course. Oh, I know, I know, that's my dream that I'm living as I call it, but it's not all like that. You know that as well as I do. Yes, I know there are worse places to be, like back in a boring bloody office in Sheffield, and this was my choice, is my choice, but your choice and your world is …"

Her voice tailed off. She never finished. An odd, unanticipated unhappiness and melancholy had suddenly crept up and overwhelmed her. She had finally voiced part of the turmoil that was churning away inside her over the relationship between the two of them.

He wasn't leaving it at that, however; wasn't giving up that easily. Despite all she'd just told him he still read something positive into it. To him it was plain that she may have been articulating what she saw as impossible barriers between them, barriers to any relationship between them. However, he also read it as possibly a plea, a plea to let him know that she really did want them to overcome those. Yes, she was telling him that she simply saw it as that, impossible. But what if, instead, she was pleading with him to help the two of them overcome them.

He was determined to try. He started with a gamble by taking her left hand in his right hand and turning his body to face her while leaning his shoulder against the back of the bench. Encouragingly she let him keep hold of her hand.

"Look, Alice, yes my world, as you put it, was different to yours while I was wrapped up in all the academic and university crap. But it certainly wasn't that different before that at all, or even here now. My father was a Docker. I grew up in one of the poorest parts of London, in a council flat in the docks. I was lucky enough to eventually get to university, even though it wasn't straight after I left school. So, yes, of course, the surroundings of that part of my life, my university life, were different, but my character and my personality didn't change, believe me. I never forget where I came from, my roots, and the inequalities and the injustices around me where I grew up. Unlike some people, most people from where I grew up, I was lucky enough to get the chance to change my life, go to university and then get a job in that world, if you like. Of course, I appreciated that opportunity. But I'd had enough of that - the university and academic world – as well as some of the bloody awful people around me in that world who I told you about in Jack's the second time we met. I couldn't wait to get out of it, and then come here, and then was really glad to meet you."

111

As he told her that last bit he squeezed her hand gently and then added, "So, here, now, our worlds, as you put it, aren't so different. Well, I mean, I know you have to work and I-"

He stopped as she laughed slightly at his somewhat inaccurate comparison of their different summers. It was a good sign. Her mood had obviously changed again, even though she wasn't exactly buying his, "our worlds aren't so different now," comment. It wasn't a cynical laugh though. It was a much more encouraging, pleasant one.

What he'd just told her - the way he'd so obviously demonstrated from what he'd said that he was determined not to give up on them and whatever was between them – had an effect. It prompted her to open up a little more to him, seeking even more reassurance it seemed. Their conversation was getting much deeper and more personal than at any time previously.

Initially though, there was another silence between them for a minute or so as she once more gazed ahead into the middle distance. She was palpably thinking over what he'd said, what was behind it, what it meant. When she finally broke the silence with a look towards him introspection had returned, and with a lot more distinct emotion in her voice. The soul searching seemed to be overwhelming her once again.

"Why do we chose people we don't actually love do you think?"

It was a strange change of direction and an unexpected, emotionally charged, question. He quickly realised, however, that it was rhetorical, almost more of a statement than a question. She was thinking aloud and never waited for an answer.

"Of course, we think we do at the time, but then when they let us down, cheat on us, we tell ourselves that we didn't actually ever really love them at all, don't we? Isn't that what we do? Or maybe we just realise that then, when they let us down and cheat on us, realise that we never really loved them all along?"

"You mean with your ex-husband? You're talking about your ex-husband?" he asked. She'd never actually told him the details before, only that they'd divorced.

"Yep."

It was a flat, monotone, simple single word confirmation. She had opened up a bit, but she wasn't going to go into any more detail. She wasn't prepared to do that. That was all he was getting, at least on that. Even that limited emotional revelation had an effect on her, however. It was one that he hadn't anticipated at all. As she told him the single word confirmation she returned to staring straight ahead, rather than looking at him. He noticed as she did that two small trickles of tears slowly traced their way down her cheeks. She was obviously in much more emotional turmoil than she was letting on.

"You okay," he asked. "What is-"

"I can't, I can't do this. I can't talk about it," she started to tell him as she wiped the tears away from her cheeks with her index finger. Her voice was cracking with emotion as she continued.

"Trust is a big thing for me, David. It's a difficult thing now after what happened with my ex-husband. It's not easy for me."

He decided it was best to stay silent and let her continue. It had taken a long time, months, to get her to open up to him about her feelings. Even if it wasn't directly about her feelings for him, it was still a step forward from the detached, ice cool, sometimes aggressive responses he'd had from her in the past, previously throughout the summer. It was best to let her speak.

She took a deep breath, then bit her bottom lip for a moment before she added, "I get scared of getting too close to a man again. I don't want to feel that way again, betrayed. I'm confused though, because I don't actually like feeling this way, too scared to trust a man again, too scared to feel like I did initially over my ex-husband when we first met. And that's why sometimes I get aggressive over the simplest, stupidest things. I don't want to feel like this, I really don't."

She took another deep breath as she finished telling him that and then reached to take the final part of her drink. She wrapped her hands around the empty glass and held it there as she once again glanced sideways at him. She was wondering what his reaction would be, what he would say, if anything. Speaking as she had, telling someone what she just had, particularly a man, wasn't something she'd done recently, not since she discovered her husband had been cheating on her and the divorce. Even then it had only been to another woman friend in Sheffield, but plainly not the one cheating on her with her husband.

He waited a few seconds, no more than ten though, and started to try and say something to help, although he didn't really have a clear idea what.

"I ... I think ... I ..."

He faltered and hesitated. The words just wouldn't come out of his mouth. He actually wasn't sure at all what he thought. She was resting her elbows on her knees, her hands still clutched around the empty glass as she turned her head from her leaning forward position to stare into his eyes. What was he going to say? And what would her reaction to it be? She looked as if she wanted him to say something, but with Alice he could never be sure if that really was the case and that she would just get angry whatever he said. Now it was his turn to take a deep breath. As he gazed down at her staring up at him from her bent forward position on the bench he finally continued.

"But that, all that with your ex-husband is in the past, Alice. We all have things in the past, things that have happened to us in the past we wish we could forget, could change maybe. Of course, we think about the past. We can't rub it out from our memory. But we also think about the present, and we think about the future."

Her look had changed to a frown now. Once again he was desperately trying not to sound like some academic prat giving her a lecture.

"We can't change the past though can we? It's fixed. We can only change the present and our future."

He looked down at her. Her frown had disappeared. She was listening intently. He decided that now was the time. He had to go further and take a chance. He'd waited long enough, put it off long enough, so why not?

"Only we can do that, Alice, only we, you and me, can do that, change our present and our future."

It never came out the way he wanted it to; never sounded the way he aimed for. He should have added, 'together', "our future together." Would she understand that was what he meant?

He slumped back against the back of the bench as she sat upright next to him. Her response was as ambiguous though as his comment about, "our future" obviously sounded to her. She went off on another tangent. Or at least, that's what it sounded like to him.

"You know, David, I realise I can tell you things. I know I can tell you things, personal things like this. I do think that I can actually trust you, and I'm sure I won't hear them repeated around the village. I've told you a few things before, not many I know, but a few personal things during this summer since we met, and I've not heard them repeated anywhere by anyone around the village. The village is always full of gossip. That's what villages are like, I guess. And Lindos is a tourist village with Brit ex-pats living here. Some of them love to gossip, believe me. I've heard them lots of times in the bars. But I haven't heard any of the few small things I've told you, and only you, about me turn up in the village gossip."

She turned her head towards his face once again, accompanied by an encouraging ever so slight smile, and added, "I like that about you."

It was a rare compliment from her, a very rare disclosure about what she actually felt. She was opening up, and maybe even letting him in at last. It was a good sign. This was, indeed, a different Alice, and he liked it even more, liked her even more.

However, he wasn't leaving it there. He'd come this far, so why not push it a bit further and take another chance?

"What is it that you want, Alice?" he asked.

For a very brief moment he thought he'd done the right thing and his gamble had paid off.

She sucked her lip for a few seconds and said nothing. Then she twisted the top half of her body towards him and reached over to put her left hand behind his neck, pulled him into her

115

and kissed him firmly once again. It was another long lingering passionate kiss, similar to the one inside the club earlier. They were both unaware whether there were people passing by crossing the courtyard. For those few moments they were oblivious to their surroundings or people nearby once more.

Had she just given him the answer to his question? That was what was going through his mind now.

While he hesitated, unbeknown to him Alice was actually wondering if he was going to return her kiss. She'd tempted him twice now, inside the club earlier and now on the bench. Okay, the first time was interrupted by the prat Simon Chapel, but David had shown no inkling to return her kiss before or after that. She wanted him to, if only for a fleeting moment each time. Then seconds later she didn't want him to. She was confused. Was it a good or a bad confusion? As she'd told him a little earlier, she hadn't felt like this, confused in a good way, and excited, for a long time, not since she first met her ex-husband. That was the one thing she did know however, was sure of, it was exciting. It stirred something inside her that she hadn't felt for quite a while.

Just at that point though, the cautious, questioning, doubting Alice took over her thoughts. Why hadn't he responded? Why hadn't he kissed her back? Was she being completely stupid and laying herself open to be let down again by a man? She decided to pull back a bit, safeguard herself, but test him. Before she could say anything however, he decided to push a bit more.

"I really like you, Alice."

Confusion was written all across her face as she replied firmly, almost instinctively, "I don't want that."

It wasn't the answer he was hoping for.

"What? Don't want what?"

"That, I don't want that, you to like me that much."

He looked away across the courtyard, bewildered. She was one very complicated and mixed up person. What she told him next as she reached up to turn his face towards her and look into his eyes made him think that even more so.

"But, don't stop trying, David."

"What? What does that mean?"

"I know it sounds odd, but I don't want you to stop trying. I really don't. Please don't?"

Now he was thinking was that a good or bad thing? One minute she's kissing me, seconds later she's telling me not to stop trying. Does that mean she's not ready to do anything about it, any relationship between them, now, but sometime in the future maybe? Was that hope?

"You mean don't stop trying to be more than very good friends?"

He took another chance, another leap, hoping for the reply he so wanted to hear. All he got at first was silence while she continued to gaze into his eyes, like she was willing him to do something more. Should he take the plunge and kiss her? Is that what she wanted? Push her on a little towards what he wanted? Make that abundantly clear to her? There would surely be no doubt for her over that then. But what if that was too much? What if that wasn't what she wanted? Wasn't what she was looking for right now? She did say, "Don't stop trying," so maybe that was her way of telling him to wait and she just didn't want anything more between them at the moment, right now.

After what seemed to him an eternity of a long half minute or so, keeping her gaze fixed on him while tilting her head slightly to one side and shrugging her shoulders she simply softly said one word, "Perhaps."

She was clearly moving closer to him, closer to what he wanted to hear, to what he wanted to happen between them. Should he take one more chance to nudge her even closer to that?

He gently took hold of her left hand, continued to stare straight into her eyes, and asked,

"And with benefits?

It was very much the wrong thing to say, giving her a completely wrong impression. She pulled her hand away from him, accompanied with a very firm, "No, not with benefits, just friends, very good friends."

More silence ensued between them as he slumped against the back of the bench once more while she turned back to staring into the middle distance across the now deserted courtyard. He thought he'd blown it again. However, a good three or four minutes later, totally out of the blue, and this time without turning to face him, she added six simple words that gave him more hope once again.

"For now, David, for now, but perhaps more ..."

Her voice faded. He was more confused than ever now.

10

Nelson's uniform, and the first tentative attempt at filling the Cup

A week later something more encouraging happened again. Initially, it seemed that once more she had reverted to her previous careful reluctance and, indeed, now neither of them would take the chance, make the leap. The leap in the dark. Or would they? Leave themselves open, exposed, vulnerable, fearful of being turned down, rejected, having read the signs all wrong?

Who would, should, make the first move? That first tentative sensitive gentle touch or an attempt at another kiss, exposing his or her feelings, exposing themselves to rejection.

Does she want him to kiss her again? But what if he is completely misreading it all? What if, in fact, they are both totally misreading it all? That would be a disaster. She's a good friend, a good friend to party with night after night in Lindos. He wouldn't want to lose that in all the awkwardness that would follow if he'd got it all wrong. In a small village it would be hard to avoid that awkwardness. Perhaps, neither does she want to lose that, that good friendship, at least for now.

Should it all really be this difficult, such agony? Painful even? Neither of them really knowing each other's private intimate inner thoughts. At times as the summer wore on the indecision had thrown him into bouts of deep despondency. He was almost ready to give up on her at those times. He would feel like that for a few days, at most a week, until something she said or did - what he took as a sign - sparked optimism and encouragement within him yet again.

Yes, there had been sex with others in past years for both of them in Lindos before they met. They knew that, or at least suspected it. But not yet with each other. Not even close to that. Every time she'd given even the slightest hint she was close to taking that leap – grabbing hold of his hand, or placing her arm in his in an alley – something had snapped inside her. It was like an electric shutter suddenly descending and she had flicked the switch. She'd run off. Scurried away, without even any explanation. Sometimes without even a goodnight. It was definitely a bit weird between them. Although to him it often felt all one way, feelings for her from him. Most of the time she was very good at concealing what she felt, if anything.

In Arches courtyard that night a week or so earlier he'd sort of tested it, the water, without exactly drowning, although it wasn't really completely the response he had hoped for. He wasn't giving up easily. After all she had told him that night, "Don't stop trying." That was something for him to cling on to at least. Although, maybe it was just the effect of the lingering end of August heat that was driving him on.

On that particular night a week or so later she was clearly drunk. There were a few nights when they were both drunk. But this specific night she was quite visibly much more so than him, more so than usual, if, in fact, he was drunk at all. He didn't feel or look that drunk, certainly not compared to her. Some of her words were slurred and there was a glazed distant look in her eyes as they sat on the sofa-like bench in the courtyard outside the Glow club around four-thirty in the morning. The music was still pumping out in the crowded club. Not that they heard it very clearly through the soundproofed building, just the low background thud and thump of the speakers inside. It was a Thursday night, the last one in August. The first real night of their holiday for many of the tourists who had arrived on the Wednesday changeover day, and there were those who were determined to make their first night a long one. As was the case in Arches, the first night holidaymakers were joined in Glow by the usual mix of Lindos restaurant and bar workers after they'd finished their shifts for the night – Greeks, Albanians and some young Brits working in Lindos for the summer.

He had no idea quite why she was so drunk on that night compared to others that summer. She'd finished work in the restaurant at the usual time of around one-thirty. Gone back to her flat to change and texted him to ask where he was? She knew from habit that at that time he'd be in Jack's Courtyard Bar or Lindos By Night having a late drink, or possibly even already in one of the clubs, although it was still probably too early for those for him. After he replied she came and found him at around two-thirty, still in the Courtyard Bar. Although she wasn't exactly drunk at that point he could see straightaway that she'd obviously had a drink, or two, or more.

"At work, from customers," she told him when he asked. "They offered me a few drinks, and it would have been rude to refuse, don't you think?"

He merely nodded and smiled. At that time she was just clearly pleasantly merry. That would be the best way to describe it. She always drank quickly, and four more quick Vodka and cokes in the Courtyard before they headed for Glow at almost three-thirty pushed her somewhat beyond merry.

As the two of them made their way the short distance to Glow, just a matter of a few yards from one of the exits from the courtyard that gave Jack's bar its name, the last dim light of the long summer day was long gone. Up in the clear night sky above them in the narrow, almost deserted alleyway, the multitude of stars sparkled in gold and silver. The middle of the night silence engulfed them. It was as if neither of them wanted to utter even a word that might disturb or spoil it. As they walked through the small courtyard towards the entrance to the club the flickering of the strobe lights inside pierced through the small window in the entrance door. Inside they weaved their way through the crowded groups of clubbers to the bar and he managed to attract the attention of one of the bar staff to get them a couple more Vodka and cokes. He dared to ask Alice if she wanted a small bottle of water as well, telling her it might be a good idea, but swiftly abandoned that idea when his suggestion was met with merely a scowl.

At that point her speech wasn't as slurred as later, and she was walking straight, all be it holding on to his arm at times, but not really exhibiting any visible signs of the effect of what she'd already had to drink. Despite the crowded club she even managed to dance, dance alone as if nothing else existed, just the music and her. She was feeling good and obviously visibly living the dream again in picturesque Lindos.

It was only the added effect of a couple more quick Vodka and cokes that pushed her completely over the edge into a much more evident drunken condition. That was when he suggested going outside to sit on the sofa bench and get some air, as well as handing her a small bottle of water.

The courtyard outside Glow was much smaller and narrower than the Arches one. It had the same type of stone entrance arch, but the entrance door to the club was only some seven or eight yards from there. The toilets were inside the club, so there wasn't the constant stream of people crossing the courtyard as there was with Arches. The only people doing so were those arriving or leaving the club. There were a couple of reasonably comfortable cushioned sofa-like wooden bench seats, one on each side of the courtyard, with a small low table in front of them. The seats weren't much used though. Each time he ventured to Glow for a late drink David very rarely saw anyone making use of them. He reckoned the people who most used them that summer were Alice and him for some of their late night chats.

By the time they did so on that particular night the darkness of the night was beginning to be challenged by the rising sun and the first small glimmer of daylight it was bringing. As soon as they sat down his eyes fled to her pale complexion, framed and highlighted by her long dark hair either side of her face. The effect of too much alcohol. He picked the bottle up from the small table in front of them, where she'd placed it, passed it to her and urged her to drink some more of the water.

As he did so the woman whom Alice had described to him before as the nearest to a real friend she had in Lindos, her "drinking buddy," Dianne Arnold, emerged through the entrance archway to the club courtyard, with another waitress from the restaurant where she worked.

"Good evening you two. All I seem to do these days, or should I say nights, is come across you two sat on a bench outside a club. People will start to talk. You know what the village is like, Alice."

"Well, there are plenty of people in the village who always find plenty to gossip about, so we thought we'd give them some more."

Alice smiled at her friend as she told her that, although there was a slight abrasive edge in her voice. Dianne just smiled back, but didn't stop and headed for the door to the club with her work colleague.

David had noticed recently that it wasn't only Dianne Arnold who was making that observation about the two of them, Alice and him spending a lot of evening together. Other workers in the village, and some ex-pats, were drawing similar conclusions.

When some people, ex-pats, saw them together drinking late at night in Jack's Courtyard Bar or together in one of the clubs, or sat outside in their courtyards, it was as if they knew, or at least thought they knew, that there was something going on between Alice and David. As Alice had just reminded Dianne, it was a village. It thrived on gossip, and who had the latest. It was like a local news radio station. The Brit ex-pats in particular liked to think that they knew more than they really did. On a couple of occasions, at separate times, two different ex-pats walked past the rear garden of the Lindian House Bar and spotted David and Alice having a late drink. Each time their glance through the open doorway was followed by a slight nod of acknowledgement and a growing grin. When he thought about those occasions later it brought a grin to David's face. It amused him that some of the ex-pat community thought that there was more to their relationship than there actually was.

As he urged Alice to take another drink of the water he thought for a second that might produce an aggressive response. Her eyes looked sideways at him as if she was about to, but he was pleasantly surprised. She took a couple of long drinks from the bottle. He sat in silence focusing on her while she did so. He was wondering just how drunk she was, and why on this particular night she'd chosen to get so drunk? He'd not actually seen her that drunk before during that summer. He knew she liked a drink after work, to help her relax and wind down she said. Most of the restaurant and bar workers did. She was no different in that respect. She obviously must have known when she'd texted him earlier that she'd had a few drinks and that a few more would push her over the edge. However, she'd still wanted to meet up with him. Even then, when she did she continued drinking. She always drank quickly, but tonight she was downing her Vodka and cokes quicker and there were even more of them. At one point in Jack's she'd even insisted they had shots. Jack readily obliged, as he always did. Alice was obviously on a mission to get very drunk, but at that time David had no idea whatsoever why.

As she placed the small bottle of water back onto the table she went off on a complete tangent and asked him something that made him more than smile, literally laugh out loud to himself when he looked back on it the next day. He assumed it was the alcohol that was putting the strange, bizarre thought and question into her head.

She twisted the top half of her body around towards him on the bench, raised her left leg and rested her thigh and knee on the seat. The bottom of her black dress rode up her calf a little, but that didn't seem to bother her. No doubt that was also the disorientating effect of the alcohol. As she stared into his face, trying to overcome the effect of the alcohol on her speech, she asked with a determined, deliberate concentrated tone in her voice, "So, okay, where is the most unusual place you've ever had sex?"

She was playing a game, obviously trying to shock him. She liked to do that, not just to him, but sometimes to everybody and anybody. The slow smile that emerged and stretched across her lips as she finished asking clearly exposed that she was definitely trying to shock him, and what was more enjoying doing so.

He wasn't playing her game though, even though he returned a smile. However, she wasn't giving up. She liked playing games too much.

"No, come on," she added, trying to inject a more serious tone into her voice. "Where, where is it?"

"You serious? Really? You really want to know?" he responded, followed by a grin and a slight shake of the head.

"Yep, definitely, definitely. Come on. Is there nowhere, nowhere unusual?"

She was still smiling, although her speech was now clearly slurred. He continued to grin in response until what she said next, which jolted him somewhat. Is that what she really thinks of him?

"Nowhere, nowhere at all? Are you really that boring, David?"

Now she was taunting him. It wasn't a part of her character that appealed to him at all, especially as at times like that the tone of her voice displayed the element of an aggressive edge. So, he decided to put an end to it by answering her question. Now it was her turn to be on the back foot. It wasn't an answer she was expecting at all.

"Opposite Nelson's uniform in the National Maritime Museum at Greenwich in London on a Sunday afternoon," he blurted out rapidly.

A blank stunned look spread across her face instantly for a long ten seconds or so as she blinked in surprise and then stared into his face. It was eventually only broken by her loud laugh, followed by, "Really?"

Now it was his turn to chuckle as he added, "Yep, really. Well, I was only seventeen and it seemed like fun. Of course, it wouldn't have been if we were caught, but we weren't, and it was."

"And so ... so ... how old was she?" She couldn't resist asking, although hesitating as she struggled to get the words out still looking stunned.

"Twenty, I think. Well, that's what she told me anyway. She just liked the excitement of doing it in public places, so she said."

"Hmm ... she obviously did. Good job Nelson only had one eye then," she joked.

That brought another smile to his lips, before he quickly added, "Then there was the time with her on a bench on the seafront in Sitges, near Barcelona, in the middle of the night. But we nearly got caught that time by some bloody Spanish police."

She removed her thigh and knee from the seat, turned her body to lean forward slightly with her arms resting on her knees and stare blankly across the courtyard, while slowly shaking her head from side to side. Apart from the low hum of the music inside the soundproofed club there was a silence all around them now. There was no one coming into or leaving the club at that point. The air and the night were silent, almost synchronised with her obvious stunned surprise at what he'd told her.

He couldn't resist a grin as he told her, "So, am I still boring do you think?"

Her lips widened as she glanced back at him with another broad pleasing smile. "No, it seems not, not at all, hidden depths obviously, David Alexander."

She shook her head slightly a couple of times more as she continued to lean forward and then added, "Don't expect me to have sex in public places though, exciting or not."

She stared up at him, completely focused. There was an expression of concentration in her deep brown eyes as they lingered on his, motionless for a good few seconds in total silence. He so wanted to kiss her. Was that what she wanted too? Dare he take the chance now or would that ruin everything?

She answered that for him. She reached up and drew him into her with her left hand, and then kissed him tenderly. Once again she'd taken the leap and kissed him, just as she had done in Arches the week before. It was a soft, tender kiss from her warm, moist lips. What he had just told her had obviously excited her. Thank you Admiral.

As their lips parted from that one fleeting moment he could feel his heart beating faster against his chest. His lips were moist from her lips, but as he swallowed nervously the roof of his mouth felt as though it was sealed off by his dry tongue.

Was she testing him yet again? How should he respond? He smiled as their lips parted and she responded with one of her own. Perhaps he had passed her test?

Then she told him again softly, "I mean it, don't expect me to have sex in public places, exciting or not."

He thought that was an encouraging thing for her to say. Did that mean she was intending to have sex with him at some point, hopefully soon, just not in public places? Anyway, that's what he took it to mean, wanted it to mean. However, he quickly discovered that it wasn't about to happen that night.

As she drew back from the kiss she gulped and swallowed a little. Was she going to be sick? Not exactly a very attractive proposition, but at least he was sure that it was the excessive alcohol that had that effect on her and not kissing him.

"Sorry," she told him. "Not about kissing you, but feeling a bit sick."

Pointing to the small bottle on the table he told her again, "Drink some water," and reached to hand it to her.

They sat in silence once more for a few minutes as he took hold of her hand.

"Shall I walk you back to your place now," he eventually suggested.

"I think you'd better. I still feel a bit sick and I really don't want to throw up here."

She held on to his arm tightly as they made their way quite slowly out of the courtyard and along the deserted alley past the now closed Courtyard Bar, then down the few steps to the alley running down towards the also closed, shuttered Pal's Bar.

A few minutes later she was struggling to place the key to her apartment in the door lock. Eventually he took it from her hand and opened it. As they made it into the small apartment she virtually collapsed on him as she gulped once again. He guided her to the toilet, helped her down onto her knees over it and held her hair back off her face while she finally threw up, retching and praying to the porcelain god.

"It must have been something I ate at work at the restaurant tonight," she suggested as she wiped her chin with some toilet paper after she had retched every element of liquid and solids out of her stomach into the toilet three times.

"Yes, of course, that'd be it," he replied, with just the merest trace of a slight smile while desperately trying to suppress allowing himself a slight chuckle. He knew it was actually the number of rapid Vodka and cokes she'd consumed over the past few hours, followed by multiple shots in the Courtyard Bar and Glow, rather than any food at the restaurant that was the culprit for her incapacitation.

"I need to lie down now," she told him as they made their way out of the bathroom into the other room of her studio apartment and its double bed.

As she sat on the edge of it, and then turned her body to lie down on her side, she asked him, "Stay, stay with me, stay here tonight." Her eyes were pleading with him as she surprised him with her request.

"What? But you're-"

"I know, but I won't be sick again, believe me," she interrupted, with an almost pleading look across her screwed up face.

He hesitated for a moment. It was tempting. But he told her, "No, no, not tonight. Not while you're like this. You need to get some rest, and I don't want us to sleep together for the first time while you, we, are drunk. I want it to be when-"

He stopped speaking as he could see that her eyes had closed. She was already asleep. He had no idea if she'd heard the final part of what he had just told her. He assumed she hadn't. He also doubted that she would even remember the next day that she'd asked him to stay with her. Taking care not to wake her he decided it was best not to try and undress her. He simply pulled the thin bed sheet over her and placed a small bottle of water from the fridge onto the bedside table. He looked around for a bowl, found one in the little basic kitchen in one corner of the room, and placed it beside the bed. Then he kissed her gently on her forehead and left.

11

The Acropolis afternoon

Despite her being very drunk that night after Glow, he took what happened as a good sign. He thought they were clearly growing closer. But did she think the same? Would she even remember that she'd asked him to stay?

If she did remember she never mentioned it subsequently when their paths crossed in the days and evenings that followed. Consequently, he decided it was best not to bring it up. She did tell him that she was sorry she was so drunk and had thrown up, thanked him for taking her home, but never mentioned asking him to stay. Perhaps it really was the case that she actually didn't remember that? Or perhaps she simply chose not to, or at least chose not to let on to him that she did. Acting as the perfect gentleman, taking her home and putting her to bed, did seem to gain him some brownie points. By the beginning of September she was much more open with him. From what she said and did she seemed to be continuing to grow closer to him. Just like the searing heat of mid-summer her sometimes aggressive tone was subsiding, giving way to a much calmer and pleasant outlook towards him. What she told him in that first week of September gave him even more cause for optimism, even though it also looked like she was displaying her jealous side once again.

When they'd had that afternoon together on St. Paul's Bay beach in August David mentioned that if she could get a night off they could perhaps go to the Tambakio Restaurant there for dinner. She responded by telling him that getting a night off at that time of year, at the height of the season in August, just wasn't possible. So, instead, he changed his invitation to lunch there, and her response this time was a decidedly lukewarm, "Maybe."

She'd never come back to him on his lunch at Tambakio suggestion. However, after he'd put her to bed drunk she called him the following night before she started work. That was when she apologised and thanked him for taking her home.

He told her, "It was no problem. We've all been there at some point, drunk and thrown up."

With a complete change of subject she asked, "Have you ever been up to the Acropolis?"

"Err ... no, no I haven't."

He thought it was an odd question, and wondered how it was connected to her being drunk. After what she suggested next he determined that, in effect, it wasn't. It was just a new Alice trying to make amends for what had happened the night before.

"Okay, let's go tomorrow afternoon. I've been before, but the views are amazing, so it's worth going again. See you at two at Rainbird."

"Yeah, sure, see you then," he agreed and she rang off.

He got to the Rainbird Bar ten minutes early and was chatting with Nikos when Alice arrived, spot on two. The two men both welcomed her with, "Hi." Then she kissed Nikos on both cheeks, before the Greek told her, "You look well."

David agreed, indeed she did, in her well cut white shorts, red t-shirt and white trainers, even though he never told her.

"Thanks, Nikos, you're too kind, but I feel tired, of course."

"It's September, towards the end of a long season, everyone working here is tired by this time. You know that by now surely. It's your third season, Alice."

"Fourth," she corrected him. "That's true, everyone does seem tired, but I'm not sure I'll ever get used to it."

"Do you two want a drink," Nikos asked.

"Just a couple of small bottles of water to take with us, please. We're going up to the Acropolis. David has never been, and I'm going to show him the views."

"They are amazing, David," Nikos agreed. "But it's going to still be hot up there at this time. I'll get your water."

A minute later he emerged from inside the bar with their water and they left to start their climb up the two hundred and fifty steps to the ruins of the ancient fortress. As they made their way the bright golden yellow sun was bouncing its hot rays off the rough stone steps and the winding dusty slope pathway.

He was glad that he'd opted for a loose short sleeved shirt over his shorts. As they climbed the steps and he started to sweat he undid more and more of the buttons on his shirt, until it was almost flapping open. As Alice noticed him doing that, and the beads of sweat he attempted to wipe off his forehead from time to time, she smiled and told him, "See, all those steps I've been climbing up and down all summer in the restaurant in the evening heat do have some benefit after all."

All he could manage was a nod and a slight smile in return.

Periodically their progress was hampered by strings of donkeys transporting their tourist passengers from the Main Square up to, or down from, the Acropolis. Lindos was famous for its donkeys, or Lindos taxis as many of the donkey owners referred to them, and there were lots of the Lindos taxis. At times they gave some of the alleys a very distinctive pungent odour as they left their deposits. The smell of donkey dung in the Lindian heat was hardly pleasant. A few times Alice pointed some donkey deposits out to him, telling him to quickly readjust his step in order to avoid it.

Lindos had been successfully fortified over the centuries by the Greeks, Romans, Byzantines and the Ottomans, as well as by The Knights of St. John during the period when they were defeated and expelled from Jerusalem. The Acropolis towered over the village and its two bays, Lindos Bay and the even more beautiful St Paul's Bay. Parts of it dated from the fourth century BC. The two bays were divided by the village itself.

It was a popular tourist attraction, particularly with the day trip visitors from other parts of the island, especially Rhodes Town. This particular early September day was no exception. It was crowded, and even in early September, hot and dusty as the sun beat down on the ancient stones. David was glad Alice had bought the water, although he'd almost emptied his small bottle by the time they reached the top. It was true what she said though. The views were amazing, and well worth the climb.

They made their way through the groups of tourists towards one side of the Acropolis which faced towards the open sea and the panoramic views over the two bays, and stood there in silence for a couple of minutes. The only sound was the babble emanating from the tourist groups. Eventually he broke the silence between them.

"Wow! You certainly weren't exaggerating were you," he told her as they surveyed the view.

Initially she never responded. He stood there gazing out towards the open sea and occasionally glancing sideways in her direction. However, she remained motionless, continuing to stare out at the panorama.

"Makes you wonder what they, the ancient Greeks, actually believed when they built all this, don't you think, David," she finally said.

"Erm … yes, I suppose it does."

"I mean, they must have believed there was more to life than just life itself."

She turned her head towards him as she added, "Do you?"

He was learning quickly that she could suddenly have her unexpected, deep reflective philosophical moments.

"I don't think I do, no, not really," he told her as she turned her head back to gaze out at the view.

As he told her that he reached out to take hold of her hand, adding, "I'm just pretty happy with this life at the moment."

She turned her head towards him again and offered him a small soft smile, accompanied by a slight squeeze of his hand.

As she turned away to look out at the view once more she asked, "Seriously though, do you think there's more? Maybe not what the ancient Greeks believed of course, about Gods and the rest, the sun, the sea, the moon and all that. But something, something more than life?"

It was a serious side to her that didn't surface very often, and that he'd seen only very rarely. Despite her sometimes aggressive nature as she attempted to cover up what she obviously thought were her inadequacies in terms of intelligence, he was rapidly discovering that Alice Palmer was a much cleverer and thoughtful woman than she actually gave herself credit for.

"Obviously the ancient Greeks, like most people I guess, needed something to believe in, cling on to, in life, and after life. With them it was, as you said Gods, sun, sea and the rest, and all the myths and stories. That's not for me though. This is it as far as I'm concerned. We only get one go, so best make the best of it. You sound as though you do, believe there's more."

"I don't know. I think so. Maybe? No, I don't know."

With that she switched off the philosophical Alice; put her back in her box, and reverted to her more regular self.

"Phew! It's hot up here. We're not going to find any shade, but let's find some of these old stones to sit down on for a while. I'm sure the ancient Greeks won't mind that if they are with their Gods. Then we should make our way down and have a drink with Nikos before I have to go and get ready for work and a cooling cold shower."

Even a cold shower with her would be great at the best of times was what he was thinking, and definitely now after this heat. But he wasn't about to make a flippant remark like that at the moment. The time was still not right for that. Hopefully it would come, maybe.

It was as they sat on some of the ancient stones they located that she said the thing that indicated her jealousy to him, yet simultaneously gave him yet more cause for optimism.

"How do you get on with your neighbour then," she asked?

The other flat in his courtyard was also rented long term every summer by a woman who had been a Lindos regular visitor for around twenty years, Patricia. Because of that she was well known in the village and from time to time worked in a number of small jobs or projects in and around the village. Throughout the summer they had exchanged a few, "Good mornings," as their paths crossed whilst eating breakfast in the courtyard outside their flats, in addition to a few, "Hellos," when coming across each other in various bars on some evenings. On a few occasions some of those evening acknowledgements had developed into quite long conversations. Patricia and Alice knew each other, although like the majority of Alice's Lindos acquaintances, not well. David and Alice had bumped into Patricia a few times on their late night drinking sessions, mostly in Glow, which she seemed to prefer to Arches.

He never asked of course, but David reckoned Patricia was of a similar age to him. She had short blonde hair, which he wasn't entirely sure was natural, was around five foot eight, and so quite tall, although like most of the other females living in the village for safety she always wore flat soled shoes. Her accent was definitely from south-east England, although he never enquired where. She managed to retain a quite good figure, although the approaching middle-age was bringing its challenges. Her face never really betrayed her age. It was round, but her hair suited it perfectly. She was pretty. That was the way David would describe her if asked, as he did that afternoon at the Acropolis with Alice.

"Patricia? Fine, although I don't see a lot of her to be honest," he started to answer Alice's question about his neighbour.

"We don't often seem to both be in our flats at the same time during the day. I see her in the courtyard sometimes having breakfast, but not that often. She always seems to be out doing one thing or another work-wise. I think she's got quite a few different things on the go in the village in that respect. She's no trouble though, as neighbours go. Why?"

"She just seems very friendly towards you every time we've bumped into her in Jack's or Glow. I think she wants to get into your pants."

That was just another of Alice's typical out of context remarks which surprised him no matter how many times she made them. It drew a laugh from him and an, "I don't think so. I doubt that very much, Alice."

He was still grinning widely as she told him firmly, "Oh, I do, I definitely do. I've seen the way she is around you. The way she looks at you, practically undressing you with her eyes. We women notice that and can read that on someone's face, another woman's anyway."

134

He merely turned towards her and shrugged, not knowing quite what to say in response. He was thinking why does that bother her? Is she trying to tell him something? Her jealous streak was surfacing once again. Should that make him optimistic again?

She was staring straight into his eyes intensely, waiting to see how he responded. It was as if she was trying to decipher what was going on in his brain. She appeared to be delighting in leaving him dangling once more, testing and teasing him. Sometimes she could exhibit jealousy, sometimes instead she just flirted with him in an obvious way, but then stopped abruptly, went so far and then switched off. Then there was nothing. It could all change like the flick of a switch, as if she had multiple identities and would simply choose one that suited her at any given moment. She seemed to love to disorientate people over feelings, particularly him.

Going round and round in circles in his head over it was only making him dizzy. Rather than answering, or at least responding, to her comments about his next door neighbour he decided to change the subject, and get her focused back on them, him and Alice.

"What about that night off and dinner one evening now it's September? The season will be winding down in a few more weeks."

She frowned at his renewed suggestion and shook her head slightly. She was still reluctant. Perhaps she simply couldn't afford to take the night off. She wouldn't be paid for it. There was no such thing as holiday pay for days off in the Lindos bars and restaurants. Or maybe she knew it would be difficult to get a night off from her boss and leave the restaurant short staffed. Besides that, as David had found out throughout that summer, Alice Palmer was a woman who never really relaxed. Work drove her on. She never stopped, even for more than the odd – very odd, very few – days on the beautiful Lindos beaches while she was living the dream. Perhaps she just didn't know how to truly relax and let go.

He didn't wait for her to tell him no once again. Anticipating it from the shake of her head he added, "Okay, well what about another afternoon, or even a day together. Let's go to Rhodes Town. That'll be somewhere different and you can still be back by five or just after for work at six-thirty? And, I know I should have been, what with all the history, but I've never been."

At least she would be walking around and wouldn't get restless laying on one of the beaches, he thought.

"Yes, it's sometimes a little easier to get a night off towards the middle of September, David.

He was surprised. Was she actually still considering it? It didn't look at first as though she would.

"God knows I need it after the long hot summer of working seven days a week non-stop for the best part of four months, as well as all the late night partying on top. Most of us restaurant and bar workers are totally knackered by September from the long hours, as well as the heat."

She hesitated for a few seconds as though she was mulling it over in her mind.

Finally, she told him firmly, "No, no, it just isn't possible. I need the money and my boss would never let me anyway."

He felt encouraged that she'd actually considered it, and seemed to want to go to dinner with him. He was disappointed, of course, that ultimately she'd decided she couldn't, but what she told him next after another short hesitation compensated.

"But Rhodes Town? Why not? I've only been once a couple of years ago in October at the end of the season. We can make a day of it, as long as I'm back in good time to get ready for work. What about the day after next? How though? On the bus?"

He smiled at the fact that she agreed and then replied, "Sure, the day after next, but no, not the bus, I'll hire a car for the day. That'll be easier, and that way we'll be certain of getting you back for work. What about at eleven up at Krana, by the Ice Bar?"

"Fine," she returned his smile with a pleasant one of her own followed by, "Right, let's get out of this heat and get that drink at the Rainbird."

At one point, just over halfway down, Alice almost lost her footing on a piece of stone that had broken off from one of the steps through years of wear from tourist feet. David managed to grab her arm before she fell, telling her, "Careful, you okay?"

"Thanks, I'm fine, no problem, just a piece of loose stone on the step. Maybe they should get this old place repaired," she joked.

"That's Lindos for you, dodgy steps and slopes everywhere if you're not careful. I heard that a few years ago, three I think, a guy slipped on one of the paths leading from the top alley in the village, cracked his head open and died. It was the middle of the summer and late at night I was told, although apparently it had been raining and made the path slippery."

She turned her head slightly in his direction and frowned but never commented. It was as if she hadn't heard him.

"You must have been here that summer," he asked?

"Err ... yes, I would have been if it was three summers ago. That was my first summer. I never heard about it though. Not that I would expect to really or if I did I probably wouldn't have taken much notice, which is probably why I don't recall it, if it was then, that summer, I mean, my first."

Odd, he thought. In a small village like Lindos news travels fast and wide, especially someone dying from an accident like that. She seemed a bit shaken by him bringing it up, reacting in an almost over defensive way. In the end he put it down to her being a bit shaken up by the fall she nearly just had.

12

Rhodes Town and a revelation

They arrived in Rhodes Town just before twelve, at the height of the midday sun. It was always very busy and full of tourists throughout the summer season. Even by early September the tourist crowds hadn't significantly diminished. The two very large cruise ship moored in the port contributed their fair share of one, two or three day tourists. The numerous, hardly small, ferries which shuttled past them regularly to one or other of the Greek Islands were dwarfed in comparison.

Alice had opted for plain white shorts once again, although this time given the anticipated heat in Rhodes Town she plumped for a loose fitting white short sleeved shirt outside her shorts and open necked down to just reveal the start of her cleavage. Her white trainers, sensible for walking the streets of Rhodes Old Town, were again employed. For David it was also shorts, dark blue, black trainers and a light blue t-shirt. Once they started to walk in the town he wished he'd also chosen a loose fitting short sleeved shirt in the heat, rather than the t-shirt.

In the car on the way they chatted aimlessly about Lindos, Rhodes Town, and occasionally her about her work in the restaurant. She always had some quite strong views and recommendations about what could be done better there, mostly kept to herself though and generally not shared with her boss. On the odd occasions she did it usually deteriorated into a bit of a confrontation and an argument. However, she felt safe sharing them with David.

They'd almost reached Rhodes Town before she turned the conversation on to him. He was wondering where it would be best to try and park when she asked, "So, why not stay in England to write? I know it's obviously nicer here, but does that really help with writing? Isn't it too easy to be distracted here and go off to the beach, or go out drinking half the night and lose part of the next day?"

He laughed, which drew a frown from her and a quizzical "What? What's funny?"

"Go out drinking half the night and lose part of the next day, Alice? I think you've played your part in that, and if only it had been half the night. A lot of the times it was more like till daybreak."

She stared straight ahead through the car windscreen for a few seconds in silence, then let out a small chuckle before she told him, "Well, yes, maybe, but it does take two you know. You can't blame me for every night."

He chose not to respond. He realised she was joking, or at least he hoped she was. Instead, he responded to her original question.

"Well, the more you travel the more ideas you hear, the more things you see and are exposed to. Sometimes you can use them, somehow. Not all of them though of course, but some, in your, my, writing. You become more open to ideas, as well as the exchange of stories and thoughts the more you travel."

She chuckled once again. "Maybe, but I still think it's because you prefer the sun here, and the late night drinking."

She was looking sideways at him. Studying him. He could feel it, her eyes penetrating. He quickly turned his head away from the road towards her very briefly and smiled. This was a much more relaxed Alice Palmer. Maybe it was the effect of getting her out of Lindos, even if only for half a day, but he liked it, liked this Alice. Things were going well.

The most famous image of Rhodes is that of the bronze statue, the Colossus, one of the Seven Wonders of the World, built to commemorate the Rhodian triumph after the siege of Dimitrious the Besieger in 305 BC. It took twelve years to complete. Although the most popular image of the thirty-one metre tall statue is one straddled across the entrance of the harbour with the ships passing beneath it, it is more probable that it stood on dry land somewhere close to where the Grand Master Palace is now. Regardless of where it stood, it did not stand there long because it fell in the earthquake of 266 BC.

David obviously wasn't aware of the debate over where it actually stood as he commented about it as they drove along the harbour side searching for a parking space.

"Shame the Colossus is no longer there over the harbour. No doubt it would have been very imposing, quite a sight to see."

"Did you know that it was built by someone from Lindos? He was known as Chares of Lindos apparently," Alice asked. "Well, it was designed by him at least. I doubt that he actually built it hand by hand, so to speak. And sorry to burst your bubble, David, or maybe it is better described as a fantasy, but there's some doubt that it ever stood over the harbour. It seems it's more likely it was actually where the Grand Master Palace is now."

He was impressed. Yet more of Alice Palmer's hidden depths.

After he simply replied, "Oh, right," Alice added, "We should obviously go and see that, the Palace of the Grand Master, as well as the Street of the Knights. It was all constructed and inhabited by the Knights of St. John between the fourteenth and sixteenth century, after the Crusaders were defeated and driven out of Jerusalem and the Holy Land. Interesting, don't you think? I do like a bit of history. It fascinates me. It's the most beautiful and interesting part of the Old Town for me, the most important street of the medieval town. The street is completely restored or preserved beautifully, and is lined by the buildings where the holy warriors spent their time in prayer or military practice. It stretches up a slight hill to the Grand Master's Palace at the top"

"Sure, we can go and have a look and then get a nice lunch somewhere after," he suggested.

He found a place in a car park near the entrance through the Old Town Wall leading to Hippocrates Square. They were lucky. The car park was almost full. It was virtually in the centre of the busy city. As soon as they parked and left the cooling effect of the car's air-conditioning behind them, and emerged into the bright sunlight, they felt the full effect of the midday sun. Just before they parked David noticed that the outside temperature displayed on the car's dashboard was thirty-two degrees. Without any cooling breeze from the sea, and in a city, it felt even higher, especially within the walls of the Old Town.

Rhodes Old Town is surrounded by medieval walls with seven entrances, known as gates. To enter any of these gates is to enter another world. In 2019 it was a world of tourist shops, restaurants, cafes and museums, more like a Turkish bazaar than any Greek city, but anyone with imagination couldn't help but be touched by the history of the place where a handful of Knights were the last Christian holdouts in a part of the world that had become completely dominated by Muslims, in particular the Ottoman Turks.

When Rhodes finally fell after a siege that exhausted both defenders and besiegers the remaining Knights were offered safe passage and on January 1st of 1523 left Rhodes along with 5000 of the Christian inhabitants of the island who chose to leave rather than live under the Sultan. In the defence of the city 2000 Christians had died. The Turks had lost 50,000 trying to take it. The medieval city was divided into three parts: the northern part included the Acropolis of the Knights and the Palace of the Grand Master, while the southern part included Hora, where the commoners lived. The Jewish Quarter is the third section and the least developed commercially in terms of tourism. It is mostly residential, although Hora is also residential, mixed with bars, restaurants, cafes and shops.

As they entered the city through the Gate of Navarhou and weaved their way through the tourist crowds the remains of the 3rd century temple of Aphrodite was ahead of them, surrounded by a couple of large groups of what looked like Japanese tourists attentively listening to their guide and furiously taking photo after photo of the ruins. Behind it was the Lodge of the Knights of Aiberne, built in 1507. The building housed the office of the Governor of Rhodes.

When they reached the bottom of the Street of the Knights Alice told him, "Apparently the Knights were divided into seven languages according to their birthplace, including English, French, German, and Italian. Each of them was responsible for a specific section of the fortifications and the street has a Palace or Inn for each language."

He looked sideways at her.

"What? What are you looking at me like that for?" she asked.

"Nothing, it's good, it's like having my own personal guide," he replied, with a bit of a patronising grin.

"I told you I like a bit of history, and I have been here before remember? Also, I did some reading up on it online last winter here. It was one way to get through the endless boredom and the multiple coffees in the Red Rose, and use their Wi-Fi of course. Which was just as well as besides the Ice Bar up at Krana it was the only bar open."

They made their way slowly up the cobbled slight slope of the Street of the Knights. The sandstone coloured high walls of the imposing medieval buildings on either side reflected the bright sunlight, only occasionally offering them some intermittent shade. The mixture of light and shade added to the atmospheric historical mood the street conveyed.

She appeared much more relaxed than he'd seen her be all summer. He hoped it was because she was spending time with him, and not just that she was away from Lindos and thoughts of work. The nearest he'd seen her be this calm previously during that summer was the afternoon they spent on St. Paul's beach in August.

Halfway up the street she added to his reading of that when she asked about what he was like when he was younger. She'd obviously abandoned her usual practice of steering clear of too much talk about personal stuff.

"So, that stuff you told me before, about you, your female friend, and Nelson's uniform, does that mean you were a bit of a wild, rebellious teenager then, David?"

She had turned her head towards him briefly, and he was sure he detected a slight glint in her eyes after she finished asking him that. Perhaps she wasn't being that serious and really was feeling at ease with life.

"Bad patterns, I think that are what they are called, shape our characters through our life, affect and shape our relationships with others."

As soon as the words came out of his mouth he realised he sounded a lot more serious than he wanted to.

Her eyes widened. "Really? So, were you a bit of a rebel then? Has that shaped your character now, as well as your relationships?"

This was straying on to dodgy territory, he thought.

"No, I don't think I was that much of a rebel. Like most teenagers I did some crazy things occasionally, but who didn't? I just generally wanted people to like me, I think. On the whole that's how I think today. I don't want to piss people off just for the sake of it, try not to at least. Sometimes that means I don't tell them things, or express an opinion about things. That's not always so easy of course, like all that crap I told you about with the two corrupt Professors when I was working at the uni. I couldn't ignore that, or keep that to myself. But now I find I generally try keep things and an opinion to myself. I suppose I try to be a person who I think people will like."

Hearing that last comment provoked doubts in Alice's mind. Was he simply trying to be a person she'd like, or was he truly being more sincere?

She never got a chance to remark on that and ask him. Although she wasn't sure she wanted to do so at the moment anyway. Asking him such a direct, blunt, question might send him a signal that she really was more concerned about how sincere he was and their possible relationship. She wasn't ready to do that, for now at least.

"What about you, your patterns?" he asked.

She chuckled to herself slightly then told him, "I guess you must know by now that I just say what I think, whatever and to whoever. I say what I think, what I'm thinking, before I think about the consequences of it sometimes. I suppose it's a sort of impulsive behaviour, impulsive reaction. That's me though, and sometimes I piss people off easily doing it. But in doing that I suppose I can say that you always get what you see with me, and I'm not slow in telling people what I don't like. Not that it has always done me a lot of good though."

She shrugged her shoulders as she finished.

He wasn't sure that you did, "always get what you see," with her. He was sure there was more to Alice Palmer than that. He'd discovered some of what lay hidden beneath the surface through their conversation about Russian writers late that night in the Courtyard Bar the second time they met, as well as all the stuff that she'd told him earlier about Rhodes Old Town, the Street of the Knights and the Colossus.

As he was mulling that over in his mind she slipped again, just as she had done on their way down from the Lindos Acropolis two days earlier. This time it was on one of the Street's shiny cobbles worn that way by the thousands of tourists walking over them. She grabbed his arm to prevent falling completely.

"You okay," he asked.

"Yep, I'm fine, just a shiny slippery cobblestone. No problem."

"I guess some of the old streets and alleys here can be just as slippery in places as some of those in Lindos, what with all the tourists traipsing over them over the years. I told you about that guy in Lindos a few summers ago who slipped and cracked his head open," he reminded her.

"Hmm … yes you did."

They carried on in silence for a few more yards as she continued to hold on to his arm. Then she told him, "I need some coffee now."

"It doesn't look like the Knights of St. John got round to building a café in this street," he replied.

"Maybe somewhere at the top by the Palace of the Grand Master. We're nearly there," she suggested.

What she added next surprised him.

"I've got something important I want to tell you. I'll do it over coffee though. I need that first."

More intrigue from Alice Palmer. What could she be about to tell him that was so important?

However, she didn't need to wait until they reached the top of the street for her coffee. Three-quarters of the way up the street at the entrance to a small archway there was a little sign off to the left with an arrow and 'Café' written on it. Through the archway they found a pleasant small courtyard with a nice looking café. It was busy. All except one of the dozen tables in the shady courtyard were occupied by what looked like tourists. It was surrounded on three sides by the old medieval stone high walls, giving plenty of shade from the hot sun.

As soon as they sat down at the table he started to ask her what she wanted to tell him that was so important. He couldn't wait.

"Let's wait for the waitress and order the coffees first. I don't want to be telling you what I want to tell you when a waitress appears and might overhear what I want to say. I'm going to have a cappuccino, and I need some water."

"Okay, if that's what you want, wait I mean, not the cappuccino."

He was getting increasingly intrigued over what it was she was going to tell him, especially something that was obviously so secret, or at least shouldn't be overheard by a waitress.

The young waitress appeared at their table and took their order. He decided to also have a cappuccino and the water. However, while they waited for their drinks instead of starting to tell him what was so intriguing she asked something that to him seemed completely unconnected, or at least not nearly as important as she had implied.

"Why do you write? What made you start?"

He was a bit perplexed. Had she changed her mind about telling him whatever was so important?

"Is that it? I don't follow you, Alice. How is why I write and what made me start so important?"

She reached across the table to squeeze his hand reassuringly.

"No, no, it isn't that. I'll tell you in a minute, after the waitress brings the drinks. Honestly I will. It's as I said just now, I don't want to get halfway through telling you and get interrupted by the waitress with our drinks and have her overhearing what I'm saying."

He nodded and told her, "Okay," once more.

"But I do want to know the answer to my questions. I'm interested. So, why do you write?"

"Well," he reached up to rub his chin for a moment, then continued. "I guess a writer writes because they believe they have something to say, a story to tell, I suppose. I know that once you start you can't stop. Anyway that's the way I feel. You must write, have to write, and keep on doing it, despite the loneliness at times, despite the piles of rejection letters – or sometimes just slips of paper – in response to the synopsis of the story you want to write that you've submitted to loads of agents and publishers."

"You have a story to tell then?" she asked.

"I hope so. Although a lot of the agents and publishers I sent the synopsis of it to didn't think so. Luckily one does, a publisher I mean, and they put me in touch with an agent they use."

"And that's led you to do what you're doing in Lindos this summer."

"Trying to, but I've been a little distracted, Alice."

He grinned across the table at her and added, "But if writers do not write their soul will starve."

"That's a bit deep. Is that what you believe?"

He let out a very slight chortle. "Maybe, but I can't claim it for myself. It's from James Joyce, I think."

"Irish wasn't he?" she asked.

"Yes."

"Hmm … they are everywhere …"

Odd thing to say, he thought. Her voice tailed off as the waitress appeared with their cappuccinos and two small bottles of water.

He put one spoonful of sugar in his cappuccino and took a sip. There was a low murmur of conversations in various languages from the other tables around them.

"Much as I am always happy to talk about my writing, are you going to say now what is so important that you need to tell me?"

She put her cup down and leaned forward across the table slightly.

In a low voice she told him, "That guy you said slipped and banged his head and died three summers ago in Lindos. He didn't, he didn't slip. It wasn't an accident, and it hadn't been raining. The path wasn't wet."

His eyes widened as he asked, although not in the same low tone of voice, "How do you know that?"

She looked around them to check if anyone had heard him, then told him, "Lower your voice, David. This is serious. I don't want everyone in this café to hear."

He stared across the table at her as she momentarily sat back, visibly took a deep breath, and then leaned forward again to answer his question and continue. She was almost whispering.

"I saw it happen that night. It wasn't an accident. It was murder. The police decided it was an accident. That's what I heard in the village that they thought it was. But I saw it, so I knew it wasn't."

"What happened, what did you see? Did you see the murderer?" he asked quietly.

"It was a woman. I was going along the back alley, just a bit along from Jack's, and I heard a bit of what sounded like a stifled scream coming from the alley just ahead of me, the one to the left going down towards the centre of the village. It was dark. Always is up there at that time of night. I stopped walking and tentatively peeked around the corner down the alley. As I said it was dark, but I saw the outline of a man who was attacking the woman. He had his arm around her neck from behind her, and they both had their back to where I was hiding. At first I thought he was some sort of sex attacker, but that's not the sort of thing that happens here though."

David stared across the table with an incredulous look on his face and a half open mouth. Alice stopped for a few seconds to

147

take a quick sip from her bottle of water. Her throat was dry from the nervousness over what she was telling him.

"The woman managed to fight him off and he lost his footing and fell backwards onto the rough path. That was when I saw that he'd had a gun. It dropped out of his hand as his head hit the ground with some force. He was moaning a lot and, from what I could make out in the dark, his head was cut, on the back I think. I thought that might be it, and that the woman would simply run away. But she didn't. He was obviously dazed. She picked up the gun, pointed it at his temple and told him to get up. She said something to him. I couldn't really catch it all, couldn't hear all that she said, make it out, but I heard him call her 'an Irish bitch'. I was frozen, unable to move. I didn't know what to do. So, I just shrunk back into the darkness around the corner. Then I heard him groan again and when I peeked around the corner he was doubled over on his knees and she was beating him furiously around the back of his head with the handle of the gun. As she did so she was saying something. I couldn't hear properly from where I was, but it was something about this being a message for someone. I thought at one point I heard her say, 'bastards', and 'MI6', but I couldn't be sure. I did make out that she had an Irish accent though."

"Blimey!" What did you do then? Did you go to the police?" David asked.

"I waited. I still didn't know what to do. I was sure the man was dead. As I said before it's very dark up there at that time. I was praying that the woman would go on down the alley towards the centre of the village, and that she wouldn't decide the best way to get away was to come up to the top alley."

"You were lucky she didn't."

"But she did, though I was lucky. She must have taken a couple of minutes or so to check that there was no blood on her clothes before she left the body, and to set it up like it was an accident. I heard a couple of thuds, like bone hitting something hard, the wall I guess, from what I heard a couple of days later in the village about blood on a wall. She must have somehow manoeuvred his dead body and cracked the back of his head against the wall to make it look like he'd fallen and hit it there.

When I heard those thuds I decided I had to get away, or at least find a better place to hide. I crept ten yards or so back along the top alley towards Jack's to an even darker doorway and hid there, hoping that if she did come up to the top alley she wouldn't come along in that direction, but go the other way. Literally a few seconds after I made it to there I heard her footsteps going off along the top alley, thankfully in the opposite direction."

"So, that's when you went to the police? But why did they still think it was an accident after you told them what you saw?"

"No, I didn't." She looked sheepish as she told him that and then looked across at him out of the top of her deep dark brown eyes with her head slightly bowed.

"Of course I heard in the village over the next few days that the police were investigating, but I didn't want to get involved. I couldn't afford to, David."

An incredulous look fixed across his face once again.

"Why on earth not?"

"It's complicated. I didn't want to get involved with the police here then. As I said, I couldn't afford to."

He was shaking his head slowly from side to side. Then he told her, "But that's crazy, Alice. It makes no sense. Why, why couldn't you 'afford to'? For god's sake what do you mean by that?"

He was still whispering, but there was an undeniable insistence and agitation in his voice.

"Look, David, after a few days everything calmed down in the village. I found out, and I know it was only village gossip, but I heard the police had investigated and finally concluded it was an accident, unfortunate, but an accident. That's what everyone in the village took it as it seems. And that's obviously what you've heard since. So, what would have been the point of me going to the police about what I saw and just causing myself problems?"

Now the firmness was fully evident in her voice, even though she too was still whispering.

149

This was turning out to be one of the most eventful cappuccinos he'd ever had.

"But a man was murdered," he told her even more forcibly. "I'm sorry, Alice, but I just don't understand why you couldn't go to the police, 'couldn't afford to', as you put it. What could possibly be so important, more important to you, than a man's murder? It doesn't make sense. What problems could going to the police and telling them what you saw have possibly caused you?"

"Okay, okay, David, I'll bloody tell you, but you have to promise me not to repeat any of this to anyone, what I've already told you, and what I'm about to tell you. Not anyone."

She was glaring across the table at him now with a fixed stare and steeliness in her eyes as she told him that.

He wasn't sure at all he could do that, agree not to tell anyone. This was about a murder. Okay, it was three years ago, but if any of this somehow came out he'd certainly be facing serious charges about withholding evidence, as would she. Besides which he had his own reasons for not wanting to get mixed up in that sort of thing, especially if she was right about hearing the woman refer to MI6. He wasn't about to tell Alice that, and why, at the moment though, if ever.

He never actually told her that he agreed not to repeat to anyone what she was telling him, but she didn't wait for that. She just assumed he did.

She took another sip of her cappuccino. Then fixed an intense stare across the table at him again, accompanied by a pained frown, and told him simply in an even lower whisper, "I stabbed a guy."

"What?" he blurted out back at her. This time he'd raised his voice.

"David," she glared across at him once more, as she reminded him to keep his voice down simply by indicating through placing the index finger of her right hand on her lips.

Their trip to Rhodes was rapidly becoming more and more eventful, he thought, and he wasn't meaning the history of the place. He'd definitely never had a discussion over a cappuccino like this before.

He was shaking his head again. Then he stopped abruptly. He'd gathered his senses a little as he asked, back in almost a whisper, "Here? In Lindos, I mean?"

Her head was bowed and she was looking out of the top of her eyes across the table at him. "No, of course not, back in Sheffield."

"Oh, that's okay then." He had a sarcastic half-grin on his lips as he finished telling her that, and was once more shaking his head.

She wasn't exactly impressed by his sarcasm. Despite still almost whispering she sounded agitated now. "It's not sodding funny, David. It was in his leg with a bloody fork, and he bloody deserved it."

"What? A fork?"

He was thinking this was getting more and more bizarre. They were sitting in a beautiful pleasant courtyard café in one of the most famous places from the medieval world on a hot sunny September day and he was hearing about a bizarre set of events from the woman opposite him who he liked a lot. A murder in Lindos she'd witnessed, but not reported, and now the fact that back in the U.K. she'd stabbed someone, in the leg with a fork. Bizarre! He recalled that about a month or more ago he was convinced Alice Palmer was not a person to let anyone in, open up to them about how she felt or about herself in general. Now he was beginning to understand why. Now he was getting the full on opposite of her not letting anyone in; the turbo charged version. He wasn't sure if that was good or bad.

She was merely staring across the table at him in silence for a moment or two while biting her bottom lip slightly. The look across her face told him she was not best pleased with his reactions.

He took a deep breath, tilted his head slightly to one side, and told her while trying to sound more serious and sympathetic, "Okay, Alice, tell me what happened with the guy and the fork, and why that stopped you going to the police in Lindos to report what you saw. I can't make out how it's connected, but I'm intrigued."

151

She sat back, took another sip of her cappuccino, and started to explain.

"As I told you before, I was working as a waitress in a restaurant in Sheffield part-time three nights a week, mostly over weekends. At the end of the summer of 2015 I decided I was going to come to Lindos for the whole of the summer the following year. So, I wanted to get some extra money on top of what I was getting in my regular job to have enough to quit that and do what I planned. I thought I could get some work in the village too, in a restaurant or a bar, but I wanted some money behind me as insurance in case it took a while to find a job in Lindos."

He sat in silence looking across at her, wondering what she was about to tell him.

"It was all going well, and with tips and what they were paying me I was managing to save quite a bit. Basically, I was saving everything I got from the restaurant waitressing job. The run up to Christmas was particularly busy with quite a few party groups from local businesses, and the tips from those were always great. Christmas coming and parties makes people generous, I guess, especially when they've had a few drinks. In fact, by then I'd already saved more than enough, or at least I worked out it was more than enough for what I wanted to do the following summer. So much so that I thought about giving up the restaurant job then. I wish I had now."

Her voice tailed off and she reached for the final sip of her cappuccino. As she placed her cup back down on the saucer on the table she glanced over at him before she continued. She was wondering just what his overall reaction would be to all this, what was going through his mind?

"Anyway, I didn't, didn't give it up. On the last Saturday night before Christmas we had a group of a dozen people from a local office in the restaurant, all on one table. There were five women and seven guys. There were two of us serving them, me and another much younger waitress, Sarah. She was nineteen, a student, who also only worked weekends to get some money to help her at Sheffield Uni. Some of the group were getting quite pissed, especially a couple of the guys, who looked like they were about my age. The five women all looked a lot younger, early twenties I reckon. Secretaries and general admin staff perhaps? But clearly not any of the men's wives, if they were married. That was obvious as the evening wore on and they got through their meal, as well as quite a few bottles of wine and Prosecco. There was a lot of groping of the women going on, and then as we were serving them their desserts the guy who was clearly the most pissed put his arm around Sarah's waist and tried to pull her onto his lap. She let out a loud, 'No,' and pulled away. Obviously she was upset, so I told him quite calmly, 'Please don't do that, sir.' I found Sarah in the kitchen a bit shaken and talking to the boss. I explained to him what had happened and he asked me if I could just finish serving the group for the rest of the evening by myself. I told him, 'Sure, no problem'. We'd almost done serving them anyway. A couple of the more pissed guys had been making some quite crude remarks to me and Sarah throughout the evening. It looked like they'd had more than a few drinks prior to arriving at the restaurant. But we just laughed the remarks off. I can give as good as I get, as you have no doubt seen by now. So, a few crude remarks were no skin off my nose."

At least that last remark brought a temporary small smile to her face as he nodded slightly in agreement.

"Instead of backing off though the guy who was the most pissed, who had put his arm around Sarah's waist, got more arsey when I was serving the last of the desserts to the rest of the group. He started taking the piss, trying to be cocky, and going on about me, 'Only being a bloody waitress,' and how I should, 'Know my place.' I took a deep breath and told myself to ignore him. A couple of the women on the table told him to, 'Pipe down,' and to, 'behave'. That only seemed to make him angrier and more obnoxious. Then as I leaned over to pick up one of the finished empty desert plates from the table in front of the woman next to him he grabbed my arse and made an oink, oink sound, like a pig. I didn't wait to ask him what he meant by that. I saw red, grabbed the fork from the desert plate I was holding and stabbed him with it in the thigh as hard as I could."

David's eyes widened in disbelief at what he'd just heard.

Meanwhile opposite him the woman who only a few weeks before he thought couldn't open up and let anyone in to know her was chuckling to herself quite loudly. Her shoulders were vibrating with the force of it.

"He squealed like a bloody skewered pig. Well, he did between screaming obscenities at me and telling me I was 'a fucking bitch'," she added between her chuckles. "There was blood everywhere, as you can imagine."

She reached for her small bottle of water and took a drink as he asked, "So, what happened then?"

She replaced the cap on her bottle and told him, "The police got called and I got charged with assault. They said it could have been with a deadly weapon, but they weren't sure a desert fork was one."

She let out another small laugh as she finished telling him that.

He asked, "And?"

"After Christmas it went to court and I pleaded guilty. My solicitor said I didn't really have much option. There were plenty of witnesses. Although the solicitor said the court would take some of the provocation into account to some extent, plus what the guy had done to Sarah. Also, if I pleaded guilty I was likely to only get put on probation because of that and because it was my first offence."

She added, in a quite matter of fact fashion, "I lost my job at the restaurant, of course." She was tilting her head to one side slightly and grinning again as she told him, "Not exactly good for business for a restaurant, I suppose, having a waitress stab one of the customers."

Sarcastically she added, "I didn't even get a tip from that group."

"No, I guess not, not exactly a good advertisement for the restaurant service, Alice. Although it sounds like the guy was a complete prat and had it coming to him."

What he was actually thinking as he told her that was that Alice Palmer was clearly not a woman to mess with. Hidden depths indeed and he wasn't just referring to her love of

Russian literature which she'd told him about in the Courtyard Bar the second time they met.

"Yep, he was, believe me, a total prat, and I definitely don't regret what I did. As for losing the job, as I said earlier I was thinking of giving it up before Christmas because I already had enough for my planned Lindos summer. I probably only hung on for the expected bigger tips in the run up to Christmas. That didn't happen though."

She took another swig from her bottle of water. As she did so she noticed he was frowning, but it wasn't for the reason she thought. It wasn't actually because of what she'd just told him. There was another reason. He was bemused.

Now it was his turn to lean forward slightly across the table and whisper, "But I still don't see what all that has got to do with you not telling the police here what you saw in Lindos that night when the woman killed the guy? I don't understand what the connection is?"

She hesitated for a few seconds and bit her bottom lip again. There was a firm, intense edge to her voice as she told him, "Look, David, I was on probation. I wasn't supposed to leave the country was I. That was part of the terms of my probation. Therefore, I could hardly turn up at Lindos police station and tell the Greek police what I saw. I was afraid that somehow they'd contact the police in the U.K. to check up on me, even if only for background to see if I was a credible witness. Also, I didn't have the necessary foreign workers' tax papers and the rest that I should have had and needed to have to work here anyway. That would have been the first thing they'd ask. I've got them now though, got them last summer. Don't ask how. So, going to the police was impossible after what happened in the restaurant back home."

He nodded. "Hmm ... right, oh yes, I can see that now."

He may have been nodding and agreeing with her logic, but some entirely different questions were going through his mind now about Alice Palmer. Was it possible that her aggressive nature that sometimes surfaced in her voice also did so in her actions? How did he feel about that possibility? This was a whole new conundrum he now faced over how he felt about

155

her. There was him thinking that the important thing she wanted to tell him, needed to tell him, was about the two of them and their possible relationship. This was very far from that.

However, she hadn't finished. There was more.

"But then I saw her again, the woman, the murderer, two nights later with a guy in Jack's. I went in for a late drink after work as usual and there she was. I know it was dark in the back alley that night of the murder, and I couldn't be completely sure it was the same woman, but I think it could have been. I overheard her and the guy talking in the bar. She had an Irish accent, but he was English. From what I heard in the alley I think the guy she murdered was also English."

David's mouth was gaping wide open yet again. When she finished he asked, "Do you think that if it was her there was any chance she recognised you in Jack's?"

"I don't think so. I can't be sure, but I don't think she could have seen me that night in the alley. I'm pretty sure she couldn't have."

She hesitated, before adding, "I hope not anyway. It was dark and when I saw her do what she did she had her back to me. I was ten yards or more away from her, peeking around the corner in the gloom. I don't know though. I couldn't, can't be sure. I must admit I was a bit worried for a week or so after in case she'd seen me and would come after me. But then, after a couple of days, and that night in Jack's, I never saw her around in the village again, or for the rest of the summer. I did ask Jack about her a few nights after I saw her in his place with the guy. I tried to sound as casual as possible about it while I was chatting with him late on. Just dropped it into the conversation. He said she'd been here trying to trace her birth father apparently, who she thought was Greek, but never knew who he was. Her mother worked in Lindos for a couple of summers in the seventies. Jack arranged for her to meet his mother and grandmother a couple of times to hear from them about those times. He did confirm that she was Irish, and he said she'd been here earlier that summer in 2016 with some friends, but that was her first time. So, she wasn't exactly a regular Lindos visitor, but I must admit I do worry occasionally that she did see me and might just turn up here again at some point if she thought for some reason I might suddenly decide to go to the police."

"But that was over three years ago," he tried to reassure her and reached across the table to take hold of her hand as he did so. "Surely if she had seen you that night she would have done something about it at the time, or even, if she recognised you, soon after she saw you that night in Jack's."

"I know you're right, and she would surely have done something about it by now, but I do still worry that ..."

Her voice tailed off and a worried look spread over her face.

"Worry that what? What is it?" he asked.

She put one of her index fingers onto her lips, shook her head slightly from side to side slowly, and then told him abruptly, "Let's pay the bill and get out of here."

The relaxed appearance she'd radiated earlier when they arrived in Rhodes Town had suddenly drained out of her for some reason. Tension had returned, fully evident in her voice and across her face.

"But what, what is-"

He tried again, but this time she interrupted him.

"I'll tell you outside," she whispered. She didn't even wait for the waitress to appear, but just left the money on the table with the bill she had given them when she brought their drinks. Then she told him, "Let's go," and tucked her arm tightly into his.

Once again he was bemused. There was obviously never a dull moment with Alice Palmer. Was it a good sign that she took his arm, or was it just that something had obviously spooked her? Something had definitely suddenly made her very twitchy.

They quickly made their way out of the café and the alley in total silence, him wondering exactly what was going on. He couldn't wait any longer. As they walked arm in arm further up the slight slope of the cobbled Street of the Knights towards the Palace of the Grand Master he started to say, "So, what is-"

Once again though she stopped him, this time putting her index finger to his lips as they kept walking. They were almost at the top of the street and near the Palace when she spotted another small alley off to their left. While still grasping her arm in his she told him, "In here, quick."

She guided him ten yards or so down the narrow deserted alley, then stopped, removed her arm from his and pushed him against the wall. She stared up into his eyes intently. For the briefest of moments it crossed his mind that she was going to kiss him. Far from it.

"Didn't you hear it?" she asked.

"Hear what?"

"The accent."

"What accent?"

He was thinking that this was getting more and more bizarre. So much for a lovely relaxing sunny September afternoon in Rhodes Town together.

Alice was now very agitated and obviously visibly nervous. He had never seen her like this before. He repeated his question, hoping it would calm her down.

"What accent? What are you talking about, Alice?"

He was getting agitated too, at her strange, unexplained behaviour.

"The woman sat two tables over from us in the café with her back to us, with the guy. Her accent was Irish."

He tried desperately, but he just couldn't stifle an incredulous slight laugh. It didn't help her disposition at all. She scowled at him. She definitely wasn't happy at his reaction at all. She almost barked out at him, "The woman, David, the woman that I saw in the alley in Lindos, the killer, was-"

But he didn't let her finish. He knew precisely where she was going with what she was about to say. He interrupted,

"Jesus, Alice, yes, the killer was Irish and there was a woman customer in the café who was also Irish. So what? There must be hundreds, if not thousands, of Irish tourists on Rhodes. So what makes you think that was the woman? Did you recognise her? Could you have recognised her? You said you only saw the woman in the alley that night from the back, and you only just saw the woman in the café a few minutes ago from the back. Perhaps you're being a little bit paranoid don't you think?"

As he finished telling her that he wrapped his arms around her shoulders and drew her in close to him. Then he brushed one side of her hair off of her face, pulled her in even closer so that she was pressed right up against him with the wall behind. It was all a bit blurry and just seeming to happen between them. Maybe fear does that to some people. It certainly seemed to do that to her, remove all her defences and release her inhibitions, all her doubts. They shared a long soft kiss.

As their lips parted she told him, "Sorry, I was just being-"

Now it was his index finger that was being placed on her lips to stop her speaking. Her eyes were sparkling with a concoction of fear and pleasure as he told her, "Stop it. Let's forget all about all that; what you saw, what you did back in that restaurant in Sheffield. We all have secrets, Alice. Some are easier to live with than others though."

Her face displayed a quizzical look.

"Really? What are yours then?" she immediately asked as she drew her body away slightly from the ring of his arms around her shoulders.

He never answered her question directly. Instead he suggested, "Let's go and see the Palace. Then we'll find a nice secluded table outside a restaurant and perhaps I'll tell you all about it over lunch. The telling needs wine."

It was her turn to be confused now. What could his secret possibly be that it needed a, "secluded table?"

A few minutes later they made their way into the Palace.

The Palace of the Grandmaster is the single most impressive site in Rhodes, if not all of the Dodecanese Islands. It was originally built on the foundations of the ancient Temple of the Sun God, Helios. In medieval times the Palace was the residence of the Governor of Rhodes and the administrative centre.

It is enormous, with one hundred and fifty-eight rooms. However, only twenty-four are open to visitors. So their tour wasn't going to take anywhere near as long as it would have if all one hundred and fifty-eight had been open. On the first floor

159

they viewed the official rooms, as well as the private quarters of the Grand Master. On the ground floor Alice insisted they visit the Grand Reception Hall, the impressive ballroom, as well as the elegant music room. She had been before. She appeared more at ease again and was enjoying being David's unofficial tour guide, insisting they see the Medusa mosaic. Finally, she took great pleasure in informing him that the Palace belonged to the Greek State now, but in the past at times it had served as a holiday residence for the King of Italy, Victor Emmanuel the Third and for Mussolini.

"See, told you I liked history," she commented, accompanied by one of her lovely, more relaxed smiles.

They didn't really linger in any part of the Palace and were only just over an hour going around it. It was already gone two by the time they entered it after their traumas earlier, well, Alice's revelations and traumas. They wanted to have a nice long lunch, even if it was a late lunch, before heading back to Lindos in good time for her work.

A couple of times as they were going around the Palace she reached for and squeezed his hand, telling him the first time, "Thank you for bringing me, suggesting this, persuading me." There was what appeared to him to be a deep caring look in her eyes. The new Alice Palmer had re-surfaced, hopefully the real one.

After they left the Palace they made their way back down the Street of the Knights and found a busy, nice tree-shaded restaurant in Great Alexander Square. Once the waiter had delivered their menus David told her, "I'd love to share a nice bottle of cold white wine with lunch, but I've got to drive us back to Lindos and you've got to work later, so I guess it'll have to be a glass each."

She looked across at him and agreed, "Very sensible. Good job one of us is."

They did just that and ordered a glass each, with some calamari and salad for him and moussaka, also with a small salad, for her.

While they waited for their food she looked across the table into his eyes and asked, "Come on then, David, I've told you mine, so what are these secrets of yours? You said earlier we all have secrets. Everyone has, has things they keep just to themselves, things about themselves, and their past and present that only they know." She tilted her head slightly to one side and raised her eyebrows as she finished.

"I did, yes, and I suppose that's true, we do all have secrets of some sort. Is mine a secret though? Of sorts, I suppose. We simply don't always admit it though, even to ourselves. Most people do that. Keep it, them, their secrets about themselves, firmly locked up deep inside. You said you had, about the woman and the murder, and stabbing that guy in the restaurant back home. I suppose I do to. We're no different, you and me, from everyone else in that respect, even if we think we are, convince ourselves that we-"

The look on her face across the table had now turned to frustration. Alice Palmer wasn't the most patient of people at the best of times. David's frustrating prevarication was pushing that to her limit. Eventually she'd had enough and interrupted.

"David, for god's sake spare me the philosophy in this lovely Rhodes sunshine and just bloody tell me."

"Okay, okay," he took a deep breath and started to tell her. "You said earlier that you thought you heard the Irish woman who murdered that guy in Lindos mention MI6 in the alley that night and-"

"So, what about it? I could have been wrong, but I thought I did. What's that got to do with your secrets?" She interrupted him again.

"Just let me finish, Alice. It's nothing bad, really it isn't, just a coincidence related to MI6, and not actually connected obviously, but I thought I should tell you after what you shared with me. And anyway, if the guy was from MI6 they'll almost certainly know, or at least assume, it wasn't an accident. They'll know who the murderer was too, most likely have a pretty good idea anyway. They'll have dealt with her, the Irish woman, by now as it was three years ago."

"Dealt with?"

161

"Yes, disposed of her, killed her. So I really wouldn't worry about overhearing a female Irish accent, on Rhodes or anywhere."

"You think so?"

She rubbed the back of her neck with her left hand as though she was feeling tension building up there. "But what's all that got to do with your secrets?" she asked again, growing impatient. "And how would you know all that about MI6?"

"I'm not entirely sure I should tell you, whether I'm allowed to. I've not signed the Official Secrets Act or anything, but …"

He was hesitating again. Across the table her frustration was surfacing rapidly, and mention of the Official Secrets Act was definitely making her nervous over what he was about to tell her. What the bloody hell could be so difficult to just tell her. After all, eventually she'd just found it easy enough to tell him that she'd seen a murder and that she'd stabbed a guy with a f-ing fork.

"But what, David? Unless you think you're going to be arrested and carted off for treason just bloody tell me, and then we can forget all about it and get on with our nice lunch. And you better be quick about it, the waiter will be back with our food soon."

He nodded slightly before telling her, "Okay." Then he hesitated for a few seconds again, and took a deep breath, before he blurted out, "As I said, it's just a coincidence, related to MI6 too. They tried to recruit me. MI6. They tried to recruit me because of my Russian academic expertise, Russian foreign policy stuff."

"As a spy?" she exclaimed.

Now it was his turn to tell her to keep her voice down.

Alice was left hanging in frustrating curiosity as the waiter appeared at that point with their food and glasses of wine.

"No, no, not really recruit me, not permanently," he told her after the waiter left their table. "They simply wanted me to help them with something at an academic conference I was going to in Moscow."

"What was it they wanted you to help them with?" she asked.

"They wanted me to contact a Russian academic at the conference and talk to her. I guessed that they wanted her to defect, leave Russia, come to the U.K. and share any of the secrets she had access to about Russia's foreign policy intentions. She was known in academic circles internationally as a very clever woman. Officially she was just an academic expert on Russian foreign policy in the Far East, especially China, Japan, Vietnam, and North and South Korea. I knew that, of course, but I reckoned there was more to her, shall we say, activities, than that. I had no way of knowing, and really didn't want to, but I assumed that as MI6 wanted me to contact her at the conference and tell her some sort of coded message she must have had some connection with the FSB, the Russian Secret Service. Presumably they, the FSB, used her academic knowledge on certain projects they had in play, which would have meant she had access to a lot of information on those and Russian foreign policy intentions and MI6 wanted that."

"Foreign policy intentions about what? I'm interested, and curious, David."

"Oh no, no, I definitely don't think I should tell you anything more on that, Alice."

His voice got a lot more strident. "You really don't need to know. Not that I really know much more to be honest. A lot of what I've just told you about MI6 and her possible defection was, is, just me speculating. As I said, I didn't know, and didn't want to know. Call it an educated guess, and there's not really much more to tell. I just wanted to tell you that, to show you we all have secrets."

"So, you didn't do anything else for them, MI6, and you don't work for them now?"

"No, of course not, that's all. That's all they wanted me to do and I did it. Put them in touch with the Russian woman. Set up the contact between her and MI6, and that was it, pass some contact details on to her from them. It meant only having the briefest of conversations with her at the conference. The contact details message had to be verbal, nothing could be written down. I've heard nothing from MI6 since, thankfully, and would prefer not to. I don't even know what happened to her,

163

whether she actually defected or not. As I said before, I never signed the Official Secrets Act or anything like that, but I'm not sure I should even have told you all that I have, but anyway, I thought, wanted to-"

"What happened after, after you did that?" she interrupted.

"As I said, no idea. I didn't want to get any more involved. That was the deal when they asked me to do what they wanted me to do at the conference and contact the woman."

What Alice asked him next stunned him. She leaned forward across the table, stared intensely into his eyes and asked, "And did you sleep with her? Did what they wanted you to do mean you needed to sleep with her?"

He shook his head vigorously. "What? No, of course not. I know that's how people think spies operate, from the movies, but it wasn't like that, and as I said I wasn't a spy anyway. We just had a very brief conversation that consisted of me telling her the contact details."

"Was she attractive though? How old?"

He was thinking this definitely wasn't supposed to go like this at all. It was supposed to demonstrate to her that he was prepared to share one of his secrets with her, as she had done with hers. However, it looked like spikey Alice was back and her jealous side was rapidly surfacing again. He should have been flattered by the jealousy to some extent, and seen it as a good sign perhaps, but he didn't see it like that at all at this point. He thought he was making headway with her. It felt like they were going backwards again though.

"What? Are you being stupid again, Alice?"

At least she didn't react angrily at him suggesting she was stupid in the way that she had that night in Arches over Lucy. She just ignored what he'd said and repeated the same questions.

"So, was she, was she attractive? How old was she?"

"Bloody hell, Alice." He was raising his voice once again. That provoked her to wave one of her hands up and down in front of him across the table, signalling to lower his voice.

Almost in a whisper, but with anger ringing in his voice, he told her, "Around my age at the time, mid-thirties I'd guess,

164

and yes, she was attractive, in a typical European Russian sort of way. But I had one conversation with her at the conference, quite a brief one at the coffee service during a mid-morning break. She knew someone was going to contact her from the British Secret Services, so she was expecting it, as well as the contact information I was going to relay to her. It all had to look innocent, like two academics chatting while waiting for their coffee. It took no more than a minute. My MI6 contact gave me some code words I had to use and said she would know what they meant about contacts. There were agents from the Russian Secret Service watching everyone in the conference, as well as outside it. And again, no I didn't shag her. I didn't want to. That's not why I was there. I was actually there for the bloody academic conference. Contacting her for MI6 was not the main reason I was there, and actually it only arose when they approached me after I'd already arranged to go."

He tried to lighten the mood a little as he finished by telling her with a smile, "I think you watch far too many James Bond movies, Alice."

She allowed herself the slightest of slow smiles, but she wasn't finished asking her questions.

"What was her name?"

He laughed slightly. "I can't tell you that, Alice." He added firmly, "No way. That really would be a dodgy thing to do. If anything came out on it, and her, I'd be in deep trouble with MI6. Besides which, if she did defect, they, MI6, would have furnished her with what's called a 'legend', a new identity and a whole new personal history around that identity. So, her name now wouldn't be the same anyway as it was back then at the conference."

She nodded, signifying she understood that, then asked, "When was it?"

"Err … erm …"

He was genuinely trying to remember, work that out.

"It must have been end of the summer five years ago, about this time of year, slightly earlier, early September. That's when most of the academic conferences take place, then and in the Easter break."

"Quite a while ago then. And you haven't seen her since, or know what happened to her?"

"No, I told you, I never even spoke to her after that day over the coffee break in the conference. As I said before, I assume she was going to defect, get out of Russia, and that she had some information useful to MI6. The Russian Secret Service is known to recruit academics. They become their sort of useful eyes and ears in their universities, and in the academic world internationally. To be fair, so do the British Secret Services and many others worldwide, especially the Americans. But I didn't know, and I really didn't want to know if that's what happened to her. That was the deal I did with them and they haven't bothered me since, thank god. It was all a bit hairy, although not as hairy as your secret sounds, of course."

As he told her that he reached across the table to give one of her hands what he hoped she would see as a reassuring squeeze.

She smiled back across at him and then took another bite of her moussaka. She finished that mouthful, bowed her head slightly, looked sheepishly across at him out of the top of her eyes, and told him, "I'm sorry, David. I told you before it's very difficult for me to trust anyone because of what I saw that night in Lindos, as well as because of what my shit of an ex-husband did cheating on me with my best friend. It's a really big thing for me to share all that with you, trust you. Sorry I reacted the way I did."

13

End of September elation

It had gone on and on throughout the whole summer; the sparring game between them. But by September there were at last some signs that she was now more ready to take the chance, make the leap, the leap in the dark, and go beyond being simply, "Friends, very good friends." Certainly that increasingly appeared to be the case as the end of September approached, then beyond that the final lingering month of the season, October. Occasionally obvious bouts of jealousy from her would rear its ugly head, but he took even those as positive signs.

It may have been a completely misguided impression, but his reluctance to go to bed with her the night she was very drunk and threw up - not taking advantage of her even though she had asked him to stay - had actually done his pursuit of her no harm. Doing the honourable thing had clearly gained him some brownie points. She even went so far as to tell him one time later that she liked that about him, and that she reckoned it definitely wasn't the way some of the other Brit ex-pat men who she knew in Lindos would act.

Their trip to Rhodes Town, with its revelations of their secrets, only seemed to add to all that. She was definitely much friendlier. Also, she was turning up to meet him, or texting him to find out where he was drinking late at night, much more regularly, three or four times a week soon became virtually every night.

Things between them had definitely moved on throughout that summer. To David, it seemed as though she now felt she could trust him much more. Perhaps she really was ready to explore taking things further with him? So, who would, should, make the first move? Who would make that first tentative, sensitive, gentle touch? Who would make the attempt at something more than the previous kisses between them and truly expose his or her feelings? Although also, of course, simultaneously exposing themself to rejection.

On many occasions there had been times when he wondered if she wanted him to kiss her. He didn't realise it, but she was also wondering if he wanted her to kiss him? In fact, for Alice, the few times they'd kissed had been on her initiative, fleetingly exposing her feelings, not his.

However, in the background of both their minds there was always the persistent element of doubt of what if they were both totally misreading and misunderstanding it all? That would be a disaster. By now they were indeed in her words, "Good friends, very good friends." Both were a good friend for each of them to party with night after night in Lindos. Neither of them would want to lose that in all the awkwardness that was bound to follow if they had misread the situation over what either of them really wanted. It would be very difficult to avoid that in a small tourist village.

However, should it all really be this difficult? Painful even? Neither of them really knowing each other's private intimate inner thoughts. As the summer wore on the indecision threw David into bouts of deep despondency at times. He was almost ready to give up on her at those times. He would feel like that for a few days, at most a week, until something she said or did sparked optimism and encouragement within him once again. Then on the night that clicked over the dying of the September days into the start of October it all changed. He thought for the better.

It started as a good Lindos day. It felt like a good day for him. He hadn't had a late night and the final late September Rhodian sun was beating down outside as he opened the shutters to his bedroom just before nine that morning. The overbearing heat and humidity of August had long gone, disappeared almost overnight as that month faded into September. Now September was about to do the same into October and the morning felt fresher, pleasant. He could even feel a slight breeze outside as he pushed the shutters open fully.

168

Such a good mood would help his writing, which he would get on with straight after a shower and some breakfast. Why wouldn't his mood be good in such a lovely paradise?

Within twenty minutes he was seated in front of his laptop and Beethoven's Violin Concerto was playing agreeably in the background, assisting his creative thoughts he hoped. Indeed, his writing did actually flow well. A good morning's writing, an afternoon on the beach in the sun with a couple of swims, followed by a Lindos Monday night out as a reward for his work, was what he had planned

In effect, he thought it would be just another regular Monday night in Lindos. Monday nights were usually quite busy in the village, even at the end of September. For those people leaving for home early on one of the changeover days, Wednesday morning, Monday night was their last real chance to have a good long night in the bars, and maybe one of the clubs.

Alice texted him as she finished work on that Monday night to find out where he was for what was now becoming their regular late night drink. Instead of the Courtyard Bar though, he was up at Lindos By Night chatting with Angelos, one of the young Greeks who worked up there on some nights. Both David and Alice knew him well. When she turned up three-quarters of an hour later she'd obviously been back to her flat to shower and change out of her work clothes. Even though it was approaching two o'clock, and almost at the end of a long and tiring season, she still looked stunning and fresh, at least to David, She'd changed into a simple short black sleeveless dress with a loose wide red leather belt and her Lindos regulation flat sandals. Angelos raised his eyebrows in David's direction as she appeared, no doubt in reaction to Alice's broad sparkling smile. It was the young Greek's turn to smile as she reached to put her left arm on David's shoulder and kiss him quickly on the lips. David's pleasant surprise reaction was clearly in evidence all over his face as Angelos asked, "Vodka and coke, Alice?"

"Sure, just the one and then let's go to Glow, David. It sounded busy as I came by just now."

As they'd done quite a few times that summer, once they'd got their drinks inside Glow they went outside to sit in the small courtyard to talk. This time, however, not for long. And this time that wasn't because she scuttled off suddenly to her flat and her bed. Within seconds of them sitting down on the wooden sofa-like bench with its plump soft cushions she placed her vodka and coke down on the table ahead of them, twisted her body to face him, and then placed her left hand on the side of his cheek and kissed him full on the lips firmly.

He was pleasantly surprised. He thought he'd perceived some degree of change in her attitude towards him since their trip to Rhodes Town, but he never expected her to be so forthright, so direct, as she was that night. He'd only rarely experienced that with her a couple of times all summer.

As she pulled back from kissing him there was a distinct show of obvious pleasure and affection on her face this time. Unlike on that night the last time, she wasn't drunk. Her eyes were sparkling and there was a rich, distinct, smile across her lips. He didn't hesitate. He seized the moment and took the leap, grabbed her by the upper arm and tugged her back into him. The fingers of his left hand gently compressed the soft skin of her bare upper arm. He kissed her again. This time a long lingering kiss as he removed his left hand from her arm and ran his fingers through her hair. As their lips parted once again her eyes flicked up to stare into his. Now there was no hint of any growing anger on her face, no tightening of her jaw, only affection, signified by mutual small grins of satisfaction between them. After a long minute staring into each other's face she broke the silence.

"Make a suggestion, David," she told him softly, her brown eyes fixed on his, almost pleading for him to make the right suggestion. The one she'd now finally decided she wanted to hear from him.

"Oh, err ..." he stuttered.

Why was he getting tongue-tied now for god's sake? For some crazy reason he was looking bemused. His mind was a muddle of tangled thoughts over the surprise at what was happening, incredibly seeming incapable of fully understanding what she meant. She didn't wait. Instead she helped him.

"Your place, let's go to your place now."

The tone of her voice was strong, determined, committed.

This time he didn't hesitate. The fog in his mind had evaporated. He took her hand and stood up as he told her simply, "Okay, yes."

They had barely touched their drinks, but that didn't seem to matter one bit to either of them. As they left the courtyard she released her hand from his and instead tucked her arm into his, giving him a reassuring small squeeze of his arm as she did so. That felt good, finally. Arm in arm they walked along the short alley and down the steps outside one end of the Courtyard Bar, then on through the almost deserted main alleyway of the centre of the village towards his flat. It was approaching three o'clock. Most of the late night revellers were in one of the clubs by then. The very few people they came across were those outside Nikos pizza place waiting for their pizza or sat on the small low walls around the square munching on the slices they already had. Above them the clear night sky with its array of bright stars and the striking full moon over the Acropolis seemed to be guiding them towards his flat as she clung tightly on to his arm.

When they reached the door of the courtyard to his flat he got another surprise. As he reached into his pocket for the key she removed her arm from within his and reached up behind his head to draw him into her for another lingering soft kiss. He gazed into her eyes happily once again as she finished kissing him and she told him softly, "Well, yes, ok, I guess I do like you."

Before he could respond, as she had done a few times before, she placed the index finger of her right hand on his lips and added, "Don't, don't say anything, David. Just take it for what it is."

It was a simple remark, but the intensity of its effect on him was marked, even though he wasn't completely sure what it really meant, or more accurately, how much it meant. He wanted to ask her, but clearly this wasn't the time, as she'd made plain by placing her finger on his lips. At least it was the first time she'd actually gone as far as telling him how she felt about him with some passion and feeling behind it, rather than the sanitised, lacking feeling, "Friends, very good friends."

Minutes later she was pulling her dress over her head by the side of his bed to reveal her black bra and panties, while he was also tugging his polo shirt off over his head, kicking off his deck shoes and unfastening his shorts.

She lay back on the bed, unfastened her bra and removed her panties, then beckoned him on to her. He'd waited a long time to see her like this, and in his bed, or at least on top of it. He thought it would never happen, but now it was. He took a moment to dwell on how good her body was, how good it looked to him. After the long dance of the summer between them he thought there might be, but there was no awkwardness whatsoever. He could still sense some apprehension from her though. Not something he could point to, just a small, slight feeling he was getting. Maybe it was just him overthinking, as usual.

He kissed her and stroked her hair as he lay on top of her. She could feel his excitement growing against her immediately. As he moved his hand to stroke her full breasts she whispered, "Kiss me."

He moved his head up towards her lips and kissed her once more. Her lips were wet and her eyes were sparkling more than he'd ever seen them before. This wasn't a woman taking a chance, making a leap not knowing what she wanted or what would happen after. This was a woman enjoying what was happening, wanting what was happening.

As their lips parted once more she told him, "Not just there, David. Kiss me down there."

She didn't need to point. He knew what she meant, where she meant. He slowly slid his body down hers, planting a couple of gentle kisses on her flat stomach as he did so. She placed her left hand gently on the top of his head, grasped a little of his hair, and guided his face to where she wanted his lips to be, ached for them to be. As they arrived at her desired destination he quickly discovered that she was already quite wet. Within seconds she was letting out small moans and whimpers of anticipated satisfaction. Barely a few minutes later they grew to a shriek, followed by a few more low moans, this time not anticipated ones but instead the fulfilled type of contented satisfaction.

He pulled himself back up onto the pillow beside her. The two of them lay there silently and motionless for a couple of minutes more. The symbol of the excitement she had produced in him was still firm and visible to her. He knew what he wanted to do now; climb on top of her again. She took the initiative for him though. She rolled over on top of him and sat up astride with her knees either side of his hips. Then she reached down with her right hand to guide him gently inside her and sink herself onto him..

He looked up at her and smiled slightly, but she didn't return it. Instead, across her face was a concentrated determination as she began to rock back and forth on him, slowly at first. He fought to keep control of himself. It wasn't easy. His face began to screw up with the effort to make it last as long as he could. He'd waited so long, all summer. He didn't want it to end quickly.

She sat there astride him rocking for a few moments. She seemed to be composing herself, retaining her self-control, and totally enjoying the expectancy of what was about to happen, as well as what had already happened.

"Wait, don't, not yet," she said quickly from above him, feeling his excitement growing.

She angled herself forward slightly above him as her rhythmic rocking began to get more intense and faster. As it did her long hair swayed from side to side, and occasionally right across her face, leading her to throw her head back forcibly to remove it whilst once again beginning to emit low moans of exertion and anticipated impending satisfaction.

At one point he reached up to fondle her breasts with his right hand and then attempt to pull her face down towards him to kiss her. But she thrust her left arm out to push his hand away and then planted the palm of her left hand firmly on his chest to pin him down to the bed.

173

Clearly there was only one thing in her mind now. Not just producing his satisfaction, but another for her, a simultaneous one for them both. Her face was screwing up more and more in concentrated desire, bordering on a look of pain, and the motion of her lower body on his was becoming frantic. Seconds later her lips widened as her mouth opened, her face creased up even more, and her whole body shuddered hard and long in uncontrolled pleasure. As she did so she let out a small gasp, followed by another loud shriek of ecstasy. Another few gasps and soft, "Oh," sounds and her rocking body slowed to a gentle stop, accompanied by panting deep breaths. All that had the effect she obviously desired on him and he exploded inside her, accompanied by his own groans, gasps and expressions of ecstasy, although nowhere near as loud or appealing as those she had just shared with him.

He smiled up at her, one of complete contentment. As she responded with her own she stretched her hand down to stroke his cheek. He took hold of it to kiss her finger tips. She stayed there sat astride him, looking down into his eyes for a good half minute and then collapsed forward onto her hands and kissed him passionately while she could feel he was still very much part of her, so very obviously still connected to that most sensitive part of her body. Eventually she manoeuvred herself off him to lie down alongside with a deep satisfied sigh, her flushed face close to him on the pillow as a few traces of small beads of sweat lingered above her breasts and on her neck.

Her eyes flickered closed for a few seconds almost as soon as her head hit the pillow. Drowsiness and the lateness of the night, or more accurately the approaching early morning, as well as from their exertions, were overtaking her. She fought against it. She didn't want to just drift straight off to sleep. Now, more than ever, more than ever before, she felt she needed to talk to him. When she opened her eyes he was staring at her. There was clear joy in his eyes and across his face.

He had no idea what had brought about her sudden change, her decision to at last go to bed with him. However, he wasn't going to dwell on that. Instead, he was trying to decide if what he'd just done with Alice was just like he thought it would be?

174

As he imagined it would be when he thought about it in the Rainbird Bar on that late afternoon on his way back from Pallas Beach in August. He'd wondered then if sex with her would be as aggressive as her character and responses sometimes were in everyday life. It hadn't been. There were times just now when she had been a little aggressive, like when she brushed his arm away from her and then pinned him down with her hand on his chest. But that was relatively mild compared to some of the aggression he'd seen her display verbally in some situations that summer, particularly that night in Arches towards Simon Chapel, and Lucy for that matter. He was smiling to himself inside, if that was possible, while the thought crossed his mind that the little bit of aggression Alice had just displayed while they had sex was definitely nowhere near as much as, or as serious as, stabbing a guy in the leg with a fork.

Even if she had been aggressive a few times, sex with Alice had been good, in fact more than good. Not fantastic, not mind blowing, but he wasn't about to tell her that, even though there were no forks nearby. Anyway, he reckoned that was down to them both being a little apprehensive, nervous perhaps? After all it had been a long time coming between them, although he hoped it wouldn't be the last time. But at least it was warm, gave him a warm, contented glow inside, and it felt natural and right between them now.

However, rather than complete satisfaction that they had at last had sex he was filled with the strange feeling of sorrowful pleasure. He knew he should be very happy, ecstatic, but for some reason he was overcome with a sort of emotional pain. Perhaps it was the worry after all that time - the whole summer of waiting for it to happen - that made him scared, fearful it would all go wrong after sex between them? Or maybe it was the worry that something might happen to cause it to all go wrong, go sour? He decided that the best thing to do to put all that out of his head was to push things along, push things further, try to be sure. He couldn't have been more wrong.

As they both slumped, satisfied, warm, drowsy and misty eyed he turned his head towards her on the pillow and told her softly, "I think I love you. I know it's crazy but I think I have from that very first time I saw you."

Her reaction wasn't exactly the one he was hoping for.

"Woah, hang on." She immediately threw off her drowsiness and sat up straight. Her voice was raised and she was now clearly in one of her agitated states again as she stared straight ahead, determined not to look him in the eye.

Sensing his mistake he attempted to instantly repair the situation. "No, no, I don't think I'm in love with you. I just love you, love being with you. We have good times here, don't we?"

She calmed down slightly. Biting her bottom lip momentarily she waited for what seemed like an eternity to David and then merely told him, "I see."

It was as though she was now clinically calculating the consequences of the change in the relationship between them, and she wasn't at all sure she liked it or felt comfortable with it. He did though. He liked the change a lot. However, whether she did actually truly, "see," and believe his attempted explanation, bothered him. As did her agitated reaction to his initial comment.

They lay there, drifting back into a warm drowsy silence once again, one of her legs draped over his. After a few more minutes he turned his head to kiss her gently on the forehead, and then reached beyond her with his right hand to try to turn off the bedside light. She stirred slightly and reached up with her left hand to grasp his hand and prevent him doing so.

"Leave it, please," she told him softly. "I'm not a lover of the dark. I prefer to sleep with a small light on.

14

A visitor from the past

The calm silence of the centre of the village outside his flat felt reassuring when they woke up together that morning. Even the small shafts of bright sunlight breaking through the bedroom's shutters seemed to offer a comforting new beginning. After all the previous parrying back and forth between them over more than four months it all felt more settled. This was what he really wanted during all those many late night meetings and drinking sessions which sometimes stretched into early mornings, as well as all those accompanying talks between them in the courtyards outside the two clubs. Now it had finally happened. He woke up happy. He hoped she felt the same as he looked at her drowsy face and ruffled hair alongside him while she dozed in his bed.

Resolving his dilemma over Alice, or at least hoping and thinking he had, also provoked another feeling inside him. Feeling calmer now had conjured up for the first time in a few weeks a feeling that he wanted to write. He'd hit a bit of a block for some reason. Ideas for his novel were buzzing around in his head now though as he continued to watch her sleeping. Perhaps what they had finally done had the effect of clearing his writer's block?

After that first time they slept together he hoped it would be a different start to a different closer relationship. When it happened again two nights later he was even more convinced that was what it would be.

His certainty over that was not even shaken when she made a point of emphasising to him while they lay together in his bed after the second time, "It, this, is just for the rest of the season, till the season ends. You do realise that, David, don't you?"

177

Even then he was sure from the way she'd reacted to what had happened between them on those two nights that wouldn't be the case. Despite that, after a slight hesitation he agreed, "Err … hmm … yeah, okay, of course, just till the end of the season."

Alice Palmer was, indeed, a riddle, wrapped in a mystery, inside an enigma. David knew from his academic work that Churchill had said that about Russia, but he was sure it could equally be applied to Alice. She could change in an instant and was entirely unpredictable, as she'd demonstrated perfectly with what she told him about, "just for the rest of the season," after the second time that they slept together.

The sex between them had been even better the second time. That's what he thought. However, shortly after that, a matter of a few days, something changed within Alice Palmer. Her previous contradictory and indecisive ways returned. All the positive signs on those two nights they slept together disappeared, vanished, and were superseded by nothing, just nothing. Her text messages to meet after work stopped, and she never replied to his. She never even bothered to reply with a reason for not meeting up with him later, as they had done for much of the summer. Their late night meetings and drinking sessions became less and less frequent, only happening by chance if she came into the bar that he was drinking in late. She gave nothing away to him, nothing about how she felt, or about what had happened between them. She simply ignored it, erased it from her memory it seemed. Even her previous comment that sex between them would only be till the end of the season had clearly lost its meaning, lost any intent on her part.

His confusion returned. He was back where he started, and even more bewildered. The elation of finally getting to bed with her rapidly drained out of him. In the end he tried to be relaxed about it, although he couldn't help being not just confused but also a little angry.

When their paths did cross in one of the bars late at night over the following week he noticed what looked like a sadness to her, a sadness in her eyes. Perhaps it was merely tiredness, the effect of the long season, but the spark had definitely gone.

Even the sometime aggressive edge to her character had disappeared. It was as if something had died inside her; a fire had been extinguished. He began to wonder if it was simply because there was a large barrier within her over a fear of a lack of trust. The trust she had told him before was so important for her, especially where men were concerned. It was as though she'd been ground down inside through being let down before, betrayed. All ability to trust anybody had been removed, replaced by a lingering fear of ever over-committing again and being let down once again.

For a while he thought it might just be him. Something he'd done that she didn't like, betrayed her trust over what had happened between them, sleeping together. But he hadn't told a soul about it. No one in the village knew about it from him, even though he was sure some people in the village assumed they were sleeping together simply from the amount of time they were seen in each other's company on their late night drinking sessions. He went over and over it in his mind for days, and nights. Whenever they happened to be in the same place, the same late bar at the same time over that next week, if he tried to ask what had happened, what was the problem, she simply told him coldly, "Nothing," and refused to talk about it any further when he pressed her. It was all very strange, but for the time being he decided to leave it. Maybe over time she would change yet again and go back to the Alice Palmer of their trip to Rhodes and their two nights of sex.

It was the end of the second week of October. Although most of the days were still warm and sunny there was slightly more of a chill in the evening air, and one day that week there was a storm. Storms in Lindos never lasted very long, but within a matter of fifteen minutes or so the storm lasted it would be enough for torrents of water to be rushing down the village slopes, sometimes six inches deep.

It was the time of year when the bars, restaurants, and shops were beginning to wind down for the fast approaching end of another season. Many of the Brit young workers in the restaurants and bars had taken their weary selves back to the U.K. after the long summer season of endless seven day weeks of seven or more hours working and then partying at the clubs long into the night. Some of the owners were making plans for the winter, a break for a couple of weeks or possibly longer somewhere that would still be hot or warm. The village had taken on an air of calmness resulting from a mixture of tiredness from the long season and expectancy of the coming rest in the months ahead.

With the end of the season approaching, and the time when he'd have to leave for the U.K., David knew that he wouldn't have many more Lindos nights to enjoy. Just over a week had passed since the second time he and Alice had slept together. He decided that with what had changed between them since then the only thing to do was make the best of the nights that he had left, try and forget about his confusion over her, and have a good drinking night in the village.

It started out as just another Friday night in Lindos, an end of the second week of October night now, but still a warm twenty-four degrees according to the temperature display on the wall outside the Symposio restaurant. After he got back to his flat just after six-thirty from his swim and pleasant lazy afternoon on Pallas Beach he cooked some food. Calling it cooked would be stretching it. It wasn't exactly cooked. It was pitta breads, taramasalata, and black olives, all of which he'd bought in the supermarket near his flat on his way back from the beach, along with the ingredients to make an accompanying small Greek salad with feta. Hardly cooking, but perfect for a warm Greek evening. It was ready in minutes and consumed al fresco in the courtyard outside his flat with the view of the lights of the looming Acropolis peering through the rapidly fading light of the Rhodian night sky. That was definitely one of the things he was going to miss after he left for the U.K., eating outside in the courtyard in the warm night air with the stunning view of the illuminated Acropolis.

While he ate he pondered which of the village's bars to frequent later. He decided he'd start at the Lindian House, just around the corner from his flat, and at the start of the slight hill up to one end of the top of the village. Then maybe wander up to that end of the village to see Stavros in the Atmosphere Bar.

One or two Mythos beers in there and then a stroll along the top road to the Lindos Ice Bar at the top of the other end of the village at Krana. The exercise would do him good between beers, and help them go down. Also, he hadn't been to those bars for a while, so it'd be a nice change. Then he'd make his way back down into the village for the rest of his pleasant Lindos Friday night in a few more of his regular bars. His evening changed considerably later though, as did the subsequent effect on his Lindos summer.

After a quick shower and shave he pulled on pair of clean white shorts, a light blue Harmont and Blaine polo shirt, and a pair of navy canvas slip on plimsolls. As he planned, he began with a beer at the Lindian House Bar. It had an inside bar, a garden outside with a number of high-backed wicker chairs and tables which was reached through that inner bar, and an upper roof terrace with more tables and chairs. The inner bar with the entrance had an area for dancing, some stools at the bar which ran all along one side, and some short padded benches on the opposite wall, as well as a couple of small low tables. The DJ area and console was in one corner opposite the bar. The inner bar also displayed a magnificent wooden Lindian carved ceiling. The outside garden area at the back was busy. Many of the tables were occupied by couples or groups, presumably having a first drink after an early evening meal. The inner bar at the front though was almost empty. There were only a couple of quite young women – David reckoned they were probably only in their late teens - sat on stools at one end of the bar, obviously being chatted up by one of the two young Greek barmen. He picked up straight away that they were English when he heard one of them speak in conversation with the barman. In Lindos bar time it was still relatively early and that part of the Lindian House didn't really get very busy until later. While his fellow barman did his best with the two young women the other guy served David his beer and contented himself with chatting with him. At one point halfway through his beer David nodded in the direction of the two women and told the young Greek who had served him, "Don't let me delay or distract you."

That drew a smile from him, followed by, "No, don't worry about that, I'll leave it to Giorgos for a bit. He's good at it, better than me." The last part was accompanied by a wink.

Fifteen minutes later, his first bottle of Mythos of the evening consumed, David made his way out of the Lindian House to start his walk up the slope to his next port of call for the evening. The climb up the slight hill to the Atmosphere Bar at the top of one end of the village was always a warm one, even in the evening, and especially at the height of the summer in July or August. Luckily the real summer heat of those months had passed. Although it was still warm, there was a slight breeze once he rounded the corner by the alley leading to the police station and the hill was no longer sheltered from the breeze by buildings on either side.

The bar was near the top of the village by Lindos Reception, where tourists staying in the village were dropped off and picked up by their airport coach transfers. It was only a couple of minutes' walk at most, but uphill most of the way.

Atmosphere was busy. Most of the tables outside were full, with customers pleasantly drinking a range of cocktails, spirits and beers while chatting, listening to the music, and enjoying yet another impressive view of the illuminated atmospheric Acropolis. There were also a few people inside at the bar. The owner, Stavros, was being his usual perfect convivial host and was engaged in conversation while standing by one of the outside tables at which two middle-aged couples were sat. Like many of the bars and restaurants in the village the Atmosphere had its fair share of regular returning tourists, particularly Brits, always pleased to see Stavros and be greeted by him as old friends. Many of them were. Quite a lot of them returned for a second, or even a third visit of the season as it was beginning to wind down in October. As with some of the other bars and cafés in the village the Atmosphere was famed amongst many regular Brit tourists for its cooked breakfasts.

As David stepped onto the outside terrace Stavros spotted him and immediately came over to give him a hug of welcome, asking how he was followed by a questioning, "Mythos?"

"Yes, please, I always need one after that hill," David replied and the two men went into the bar for the owner to get David's beer.

The interior furnishings of the Atmosphere Bar were quite modern, with sporadic subtle light purple lighting around the bar, and the obligatory large television on one wall and the music console in one corner. Most of the customers preferred the outside tables on the terrace area. However, inside there were a couple of guys sat on the stools at the bar chatting to the barmaid behind the bar, which stretched along the back wall opposite the wide entrance doors. Once again, as soon as he overheard their conversation David recognised the two guys were English, although not as young as the two women in the Lindian House. He reckoned the guys were probably in their early thirties.

While David drank his beer at the inside bar Stavros alternated between going outside to talk to some of his customers there and returning inside to chat with him. Mostly their conversation was about the season, how it had been, and what, if anything, Stavros and his family had planned for the winter. He was married to an English woman, Clare. Having met her on a number of occasions as she usually ran the bar during the day, David asked after her.

"She's fine, all fine," Stavros told him, adding, "Tired, of course, but then we all usually are at this time of the season. How much longer are you staying?"

"A couple more weeks, I think. Then I have to go back to England. Back next spring for another season, I hope."

Stavros looked surprised as he then asked, "What about Alice? Is she staying for the winter again or going back to England this time. Only I saw you in Glow with her a few times this summer and I thought maybe …?"

His voice tailed off and a grin spread across his face.

"Ermm … staying I think."

He was a bit taken aback by the fact that Stavros had noticed they had been in each other's company a lot that summer, and seemed to be making an assumption, although not with any malice to it of course. Lindos was a village. Stavros knew Alice from her summers working there. Most people in the village knew what others got up to. Perhaps that was what freaked Alice out and changed her mood towards him after they'd slept together?

"Anyway I assume she is. I haven't really asked her," David continued.

"Maybe she will still be here when you come back next spring then?" the bar owner told him.

"Maybe," he agreed, as Stavros noticed a man in a couple sat at one of the outside tables signalling for their bill and turned to go out to them.

David finished his beer once again and decided it was a good time to move on to the Lindos Ice Bar for his next one. He said goodbye to Stavros outside and made his way towards the top road with its panorama of the village below and the sparkling lights of its buildings. The five minute walk in the warm night air took him past the Lindos View Hotel and then to Krana Square, with its supermarket, kiosk for bus tickets at the main bus stop, and the Ice Bar.

The bar got its name from the small area in one part of it in which the walls, bar, sculptures and seats were made entirely of ice, with the temperature well below freezing. Outside that area the rest of the bar was the normal temperature with its inside and outside range of tables and chairs. Like Atmosphere its décor was quite modern. Situated up the hill just outside the village it tended to be frequented by tourists from the nearby hotels and self-catering complexes in and around the area known as Krana. It served good food, which helped it attract tourists from those. David was particularly partial to its fine fish and chips dish when he tired of Greek food at times and missed the English cuisine. This particular night the bar had its fair share of customers, although it was by no means full. It was also one of the only two bars in and around the village which remained open during the out of season winter months, which made it popular with locals during that time.

The first faces David saw as he made his way inside and towards the stools at the short bar against the back wall were those of Sophie and John, two young Brit workers he knew who

184

worked in Lindos for the summer season and also stayed the whole year round. Sophie was a blonde not long out of her teens, but had worked in and around Lindos in various bars for the past two summers. Similarly, this wasn't John's first summer working there, although he was a few years older.

"Hello stranger, it's been a while since we saw you up here," John commented as David sat himself down on one of the bar stools.

"You come for our world famous fish and chips?" Sophie added, with a grin.

"Not tonight, I've already eaten thanks. Just a bottle of Mythos will be fine."

As he started on his third beer of the evening Alice popped into his mind. For some reason he couldn't resist any longer and muttered quietly to himself, "Sod it, just one more try." He took out his phone from the pocket of his shorts and wrote, "Meet later?" then pressed send.

He didn't expect her to reply straightaway. She was no doubt busy working. It may have been October and approaching the end of the season, but the restaurants were still pretty busy. It was approaching ten o'clock. She would still have been fully occupied serving customers, and the restaurant wouldn't start winding down until gone eleven. Hopefully she'd reply then, when she had more time. That was usually around the time she'd replied earlier in the summer, or sent a similar text to him saying, "Meet later?"

By ten-thirty he'd finished his Ice Bar beer, declined another when offered it by Sophie, and decided it was time to make his way down to the Main Square and into some of the by now getting busy bars in the village. There was another clear starlit night above as he made his way down the winding hill, occasionally glimpsing the impressive view of Lindos Bay through the trees off to his left. As he strolled down some couples passed him intermittently, making their way back up to their accommodation in Krana, no doubt after a dinner in the village. A couple of the distinctive black and cream Lindos taxis passed him, also going up the hill out of the village with their passengers. One of them offered him a toot of acknowledgment. Obviously it was one of the drivers he knew. He'd used plenty of the Lindos taxis during his previous visits, as well as during that summer, although he couldn't really make out just who the driver was of this one. It was too dark and passed him too quickly, accelerating up the hill.

As he reached the Main Square there were another four taxis to his left waiting hopefully at the Taxi Rank for fares to take tourists who didn't want to face the hill up to their Krana accommodation, or even further afield to some of the hotels outside the village like Lindos Memories and Lindos Mare.

Crossing the square towards the main alley through the village an older couple stopped him to ask the way to the Courtyard Bar. Just like the comments a couple made to him one afternoon earlier that summer on his way to Pallas Beach the man told him as he asked for directions, "The alleyways and the whitewashed buildings all look the same, and there's no street signs. It's our first night here and it's very confusing. Friends of ours who have been here many times recommended the Courtyard Bar. They said turn right by the Donkey station in the Main Square, but we can't see any donkeys."

David pointed to the corner of the square at the start of the main alleyway through the village and the slope going off it.

"It's over there, but there are no donkeys there at this time of night, of course. I think that's where your friends may have confused you, that, and the fact that, as you said, there are no street signs or names. It's where the donkey owners usually congregate with their donkeys during the day for tourist rides down to Pallas Beach or up to the Acropolis. You go up the slope alongside it and the Courtyard Bar upper terrace is about thirty yards along on the left. You can go in through the entrance to the upper terrace and the steps will take you to the bar downstairs."

The man thanked him as he pointed them in the direction of the slope once they had all crossed the square.

It's true, David thought to himself, the myriad of similar looking alleyways with their alike multiple white buildings could be confusing the first few times in Lindos. It was easy to lose yourself. Perhaps that was some sort of ironic symbolism for his confusion once again over Alice Palmer and her myriad of moods.

He glanced at his watch. It was coming up to eleven. Hopefully she'd reply soon. In the meantime he'd head for Pal's Bar for another beer. He was sure that would be busy. It wasn't very large so it didn't take that many people to make it look busy, and there were always a few groups stood in the alley outside drinking. Plus, the music was good, and to his taste.

As he anticipated Pal's was busy. As well as the crowded bar inside there were two separate groups of half-a- dozen people or so outside drinking in the alley, as well as another ten or more sat at the various small tables outside. As he made his way inside he was greeted by the song 'Never knew love like this before' blasting out from the large speakers. Music to his taste, indeed. The bar was owned by a Greek, Toni, and his English wife, Sarah. It was a bar he'd frequented many times that summer and on his previous Lindos visits, and he knew them both well. Like many of the Lindos bars it had its regular constantly returning patrons, regular Lindos visitors over many years. Most of the clientele were in their thirties or older, although it sometimes attracted younger groups being the first bar they came across after leaving the Main Square. Whether it was younger or older customers, Sarah was good at gauging the music they would like.

One of the barmen, Stelios, spotted him and handed him a bottle of Mythos beer over the bar as he made his way towards the music console at the far end of the small bar to say hello to Sarah busy pumping out the music. After a quick peck on her cheek he asked, "Love this song, but never know who sings it."

"Stephanie Mills," she told him in his ear over the loud music.

Then he turned to make his way through the buzzing crowd that was a mixture of women trying to find space to dance and others, mostly men, probably husbands and boyfriends, content to just stand, drink and watch. He emerged into the alley outside and found himself a spot leaning against the wall by the place opposite that sold Crepes. At that point he couldn't resist

187

checking his phone again. Nothing, there was nothing from her, no text. Perhaps he'd been overly optimistic in thinking the restaurant would be winding down by eleven and it'd be easier for her to find time to reply to his text. It was just after quarter past. Maybe she'd have more time in three-quarters of an hour or so and reply then?

Just as he finished checking a voice in front of him bellowed, "Malaka! Who you checking for a message from then? A woman I bet."

He recognised the English voice, as well as the insult, instantly, and looked up from the phone to see his friend Jason clutching a bottle of beer. Jason had spent a few previous summers working in the village as a DJ in various bars. David met him two years ago when Jason was playing the music in the Lindian House. They'd spent quite a few subsequent long Lindos nights in Arches or Glow consuming far too much alcohol and far too many shots between them during David's couple of two week holidays that summer.

Jason was a tall, well over six foot, good looking, fair haired guy in his mid-thirties. As a DJ in Lindos over those summers he attracted his fair share of younger women tourists, and not only Brits. Jason was based just outside London. David kept in touch with him sporadically after that summer they met and a couple of times they had a beer or two in London. He didn't know Jason was going to be in Lindos at any time this summer though.

"You just arrived? Didn't know you were coming. How long you here for? Haven't seen you here so far this summer."

David rattled the questions off at him.

"An hour ago, got here an hour ago, so straight out for one of these."

He held up his bottle of Mythos.

"Just for a sneaky week at the end of the season. Couldn't get away before at any time this summer. Too busy with work and the new music company I've set up. But decided on the spur of the moment that I needed a break, a week here at least. Only booked it three days ago, but sometimes I think that's the best way. How long you been here?"

"All summer, came out early May," David told him.

"Any good? Has it been busy?"

"Well you know what it's like here in July and August. Very busy, a lot of the Italians came as usual, and it was bloody hot and humid as always. But, yep, interesting, yep that's the way I'd probably describe my summer here. It's had its moments," David told his friend with a slight shake of the head and a small ironic smile.

"Well, come on, is it?" Jason pressed him.

"Is it what?"

"A woman, of course, is it a text from a woman you were checking your phone for?"

"Err ... no, no, where you staying?"

David lied, then changed the subject. He really didn't want to get into the story and the ups and downs of his summer with Alice right now.

"One of Mike's places the other side of the Amphitheatre Square from Café Melia and Gatto Bianco. It's fine. Last minute and all that, but because it's almost the end of the season his places aren't full."

Mike was Greek and one of the regular Lindos DJs, usually playing in Lindos By Night every night and then Arches Club on some nights. He had a few studio apartments in the courtyard of his own place which he rented out. Jason had known him for a few years and they shared a common interest as DJs in music and its production.

Mike was playing up at Lindos By Night that night and as he finished his beer Jason told David, "I'm off up LBN. Told Mike I'd pop up and see him after I arrived. He left the key to the studio in the door for me, so I haven't seen him yet. You coming?"

"I promised Ledi in Antika I'd go in for one tonight, so I'll catch you later somewhere no doubt."

"Arches then? First night and all that for me, so got to go in there later," Jason told him.

"Yep, Arches no doubt, of course, your first night."

As Jason left up the alley towards the steps by the Courtyard Bar David reached for his phone once again. Still there was nothing from her. For a few seconds he wondered whether to send her another text. But why would that make any difference. If she'd seen the first one she hadn't bothered to reply. So, why would she bother to reply to the second one? It was approaching midnight. She must be finishing work at the restaurant soon, so if she hadn't had a chance to read his text before she surely would soon. Maybe he would go to Arches to meet Jason later, and maybe she'd turn up there anyway. Before that though, he'd go to the Antika Bar in the centre of the village for another beer. As he'd passed it on his way back from the beach earlier he'd promised the head barman there, Ledi, that he'd come in for a drink that night.

It was only a very short walk from Pal's through the main alley to Antika. The village was still busy. Even at approaching midnight groups of people were making their way from one bar to another. It wasn't mid-August type busy, when the alleyways could be full with tourists, but the bars still had their fill of a good number of them in early October. It was the time of year that many of the Lindos tourist regulars preferred, along with mid-May in early summer. The temperature was still very pleasant well into October.

Antika was a large trendier bar, in a traditional old stone building. It had various levels. A large area close to the entrance led to five broad steps the width of the building up to the bar area, which in turn had a further stone staircase at the far end that led to another area with tables and chairs outside at the back of the building. To the right of the bar was another stone staircase that led up to a roof terrace with more tables and chairs. The bar tended to be popular with younger tourists and Greek locals and usually got busier after eleven, especially in high season. However, this particular night wasn't high season and there were only a dozen or so customer in the bar, with what looked like another three couples sat outside at the back.

As David approached the bar Ledi looked up from the cocktail he was preparing to give him a nod of acknowledgement, then continued making the drink. He looked tired from the toll of a long season of working on St. Paul's Beach during the day and then running the Antika Bar to past one in the morning for his employer in both places, Panagiotis. Ledi was very good at his job though, or jobs, and got on very well with the tourist customers on the beach and in the bar. He'd looked after David and Alice very well when they spent that summer afternoon together down on Pallas Beach in August. Working with him behind the bar was a young, good looking, slim Greek woman with long dark black hair, and there were two equally young looking attractive waitresses circulating between the bar and the various tables inside the bar and outside on the terraces. They were also Greek.

After Ledi nodded he reached down beneath the bar for a bottle of Alfa Greek beer and placed it on the counter in front of David, knowing from his many previous visits to the bar just what he wanted to drink. Although David never turned his head to look, for some reason he could feel the woman standing a couple of feet away along the bar to his right glaring at him. He assumed it was because she was waiting to be served before David had arrived at the bar and was a bit put out at him being served first. He was about to apologise to her and explain that as a regular Ledi already knew what he wanted to drink when she pre-empted that by asking the barman what was a good cocktail that he could recommend.

Now David did turn his head towards her and before Ledi could answer interjected with, "They are all good when he makes them."

The woman turned her head towards him, fixed a stare on his face for a few seconds, and then told him a simple, "Thank you." Her lingering eyes suggested there was more to it than that.

David replied, "You're welcome," accompanied by a small acknowledging smile.

As he turned his head back to look straight ahead at the back wall of the bar he was thinking why had she stared straight at his face for so long? He was wracking his brain to try and recall if he'd met her before. Then it came to him. He was stunned. She was the Russian academic at the Moscow conference who MI6 got him to pass their contact details onto so that she could defect.

He wasn't at all sure if she'd recognised him. Maybe though that was why he could feel her eyes glaring at him a few minutes before, and not because Ledi served him before her? If she did recognise him she never said anything and they both stood at the bar in silence with only the sound of the music in the bar between them while Ledi made her cocktail.

He couldn't decide what to do, should he say something to her or not? After a couple of minutes, however, he decided to go ahead and ask as diplomatically as possible if she was the same woman, or rather if they'd met before.

He turned his head towards her. His voice betrayed his hesitancy as he asked, "Erm ... Excuse me, but didn't we meet at a conference years ago? I ... err ... I think I ... err ... helped you with something, Well sort of anyway. It's Alexandra isn't it?"

There was a blank, expressionless, cold look across her face. She didn't respond immediately, didn't even turn her head towards him, but continued to stare at the back wall behind the bar. For a very brief moment he thought that he'd made a big mistake and it wasn't the same woman at all.

She was biting the inside of her lip for a few seconds more until she told him quietly, "Please, it's Sophia Orlova now, for obvious reasons, as I'm sure you understand. Alexandra Ivanova is no more."

"Of course," he told her, relieved that he hadn't got the wrong woman, but realising that was her new identity. He was somewhat surprised that she'd revealed it to him so readily. Almost whispering he added, "You obviously got out."

"Yes, thanks in part to you and the initial contact." She replied also in a very low voice, adding an encouraging smile as she finished. He was very surprised when she continued with, "I should thank you properly. Maybe dinner one night while I'm here?"

"Oh, err ... no ... err ... no that's really not necessary."

"I see. At least a drink then," she insisted.

"Well I've only just got this beer. Maybe I'll have another in a while, thanks."

"It's the least I can do after the way you helped me. It's David isn't it?"

"You remembered that from just one conversation we had. I think it was five years ago. That's impressive."

"I never forget a name, or a face, and that one conversation did turn out to be quite important in my life after all."

Another smile from her followed as she finished telling him that. As Ledi handed her the cocktail, telling her with a cheeky grin that it was called 'Sex on the Beach', David was thinking that this was interesting. Not what he expected, and not at all a usual occurrence on his many night's out in Lindos.

When Alice asked him that afternoon in Rhodes Town he deliberately avoided going into much detail for obvious reasons, but Alexandra, or Sophia, as she was now known, was attractive, very attractive. Her face exhibited all the characteristics of the classical elegance of many women of the Russian aristocracy of the nineteenth century. Indeed, she could easily have been one of Tolstoy's heroines such as Anna Karenina. She was slim and tall, almost six foot, even in the flat sandals she was wearing that night. She had kept her figure well in her late thirties. She spoke good English, which she had obviously polished in her academic career having learned it previously at school in Russia as a second language.

That evening she wore a simple sleeveless knee length cream dress with a wide red belt at the waist, all of which accentuated her fine tan nicely. Her hair had been a dark brown and cut to shoulder length when they met at the conference. Now it was blonde, obviously dyed, as well as cut very short, in what he'd heard called by women a pixie style. It was no doubt part of the change of her identity provided by MI6.

As she sucked on the straw of her cocktail David told her, "I never really got the chance to have a proper conversation with you at the conference, for obvious reasons. I knew a little bit about you, your work speciality, from your academic publications, but not anything more. To be honest, given what I was being asked to do I guess I thought it best not to linger too long or try to have a proper, longer conversation."

193

"No, that wouldn't have been a good idea, for either of us. We, us Russians, were being watched and monitored all the time at the conference. The State Security Services were terrified that what did eventually happen with me would do. And they were right. It did. I think they thought there might be more who did what I did. There wasn't though."

"Hmm … that must have been tricky, but-"

She didn't let him finish what she assumed would be more questions about her defection.

"I'd rather not talk about it anymore, and certainly not here," she told him firmly. "It's all in the past, my past life, another life altogether."

"Of course, I understand, of course it is."

There was a silence while he reached to take another swig of his beer. Then he changed the subject.

"So, where are you from in Russia originally? I know from your academic publications you were at Moscow State University, but are you from Moscow?"

"No, St. Petersburg."

"Beautiful city, the Venice of the north I believe it's called. I loved it. Out of all the cities I've visited in Russia it's my favourite, much more than Moscow I'm afraid," he told her.

"I agree. I much prefer it to Moscow. You've been then, to Petersburg and other places in my country?"

"A few times, I was lucky enough to go a few times for my work at the university back in England, to conferences and for academic research. St. Petersburg three times, Moscow a couple of times, Smolensk, which I also really liked, as well as a couple of places in the Northern Caucuses, Nalchik and Vladikavkaz."

She raised her eyebrows, looking surprised as she told him, "Northern Caucuses, Nalchik and Vladikavkaz? They aren't places I'd expect an English academic to have visited at all. Why did-"

"Now it's my turn to say, don't ask, Alexandra."

"Sophia, please," she corrected him, with an irritated edge to her voice while she quickly looked around to ensure no one had overheard him use her former name.

"Sorry, yes, of course," he apologised. "Let's just say my visits to the Northern Caucuses were also for my academic research work. It also took me to Tbilisi and Minsk, in Georgia and Belarus. They used to be part of the Soviet Union before it collapsed of course."

"And Vladikavkaz used to be called Orzhonikidze before 1990, after one of the leading Bolsheviks in the 1917 revolution. Like Stalin he was Georgian though, not Russian. For a while after the revolution he was in the Cheka, the Secret Police. But I'm sure you know all that, David?"

She was staring into his face quite intently as she told him that, very intrigued as to why he had visited those places in the Northern Caucuses that were so off the beaten track, off the tourist track anyway.

"Yes, I do know all that. "

He nodded slightly, although he was somewhat uneasy that she seemed so sure he would, especially about Comrade Orzhonikidze and the Cheka.

A frown had spread across her face and she was looking at him out of the top of her eyes as she sucked on the straw of her cocktail while taking another drink. While she was pondering whether to ignore his, "don't ask," comment and go ahead and ask more about it, his visits to those places, he deliberately changed the subject.

"I presume you're here on holiday? Where do you live now though, when you're not on holiday? Or shouldn't I ask, it being part of your new identity I guess? Maybe you'd prefer not to tell me where Sophia Orlova lives now? Would that be safer?"

He was rattling off questions to her somewhat nervously, like the magazine of a machine gun, in an effort to get her away from the subject of his visits to Russia.

"Oh, okay."

She was taken a little by surprise by his change of direction.

"But yes, I am here on holiday, just for ten days. But there's no problem telling you where Sophia Orlova lives now."

She appeared more at ease as she darted a slight smile across her bright red lips in his direction.

"In Athens, I have a flat there and work as a translator."

As she finished telling him that she reached to squeeze his forearm gently with her hand and added temptingly, "You should come to visit sometime."

Now it was his turn to be put a little out of his comfort zone. He didn't respond to her invitation. He was thinking that sometimes there is a time to just stay silent. While he was preoccupied with her unexpected invitation she took the opportunity to return to the subject of his visits to her homeland. They were engaging in some sort of shadow boxing, dancing around subjects they each were trying to avoid talking about, or at least avoid disclosing much information about to each other.

She was good at it, but then so was he. That's what he thought at that point. However, his complacency was quickly dismantled, briefly shown to be misplaced. She'd had no problem disclosing her new identity to him, seemed only too happy to do so, as well as where she was living now. But he was thinking was it all really just bait, a ploy to get him to talk about his Russian visits and connection? And how much of a coincidence was it that she just happened to turn up in Antika that night and end up next to him at the bar?

Increasing doubts and questions were momentarily racing through his mind. His previous dealings with MI6 had taught him to be suspicious of almost everything, and everyone, initially. Or perhaps all that had simply made him unnecessarily paranoid. That was what he was trying to convince himself when she threw in a curve ball of a question that rapidly pushed him straight back into his realm of paranoia and suspicion. It was her very clever way of gently leading him back to questions about his Russian visits.

She let go of his arm after a couple of seconds and picked up her cocktail once again to finish it. After she placed the empty glass on the bar and nodded to Ledi for another she turned to face David to ask quite bluntly, "So why did they choose you?"

"Choose me for what?"

"To pass on those contact details to me at the conference. Why you?"

She lowered her voice to almost a whisper and added, "Why did MI6 choose you?"

He was definitely detecting an element of suspicion in her voice now, particularly her whispered tone.

The surprise clearly evident across his face, along with his hesitation in answering, gave her the opportunity to throw another probing question at him.

"Had you worked for them before? Did you work for them before?"

"I ... err ... no ... I, that is-"

She didn't let him finish, not that he really had any idea what he was going to say. He'd heard about Russian interrogation techniques, read about them in his work, but never about them taking place in a trendy bar in Lindos. He'd had some grim drunken nights in Antika in the past, but he was sure the sort of Russian interrogation he believed was happening to him now usually took place in much grimmer surroundings. This certainly felt like it had now developed into an interrogation however, rather than just a couple of coincidental acquaintances chatting over a drink. He wasn't sure quite how he'd got into this situation. He may well have just been being completely paranoid, but one thing he was sure of was that Alexandra Ivanova, or Sophia Orlova, or whoever she called herself, was bloody good at what she was doing. He was becoming increasingly convinced it was deliberate. She was bloody clever, and she seemed convinced that there was more to David Alexander than met the eye. Her next comment only added to his conclusion, and fuelled his suspicion even more.

"After all, you did say you'd been to all those places in Russia. Nalchik and Vladikavkaz are hardly regular places on the tourist trail are they?"

She'd made the leap from his MI6 contact, and passing the contact information on to her at the conference, to a link with his Russian visits to the unusual places for tourists of the cities of Nalchik and Vladikavkaz. She was clearly inferring there was some sort of connection between the two, and that he had a much greater and closer connection with MI6 than he was prepared to disclose. Her questions were certainly heavily laden with suspicion now. He tried to stay calm, skip over it, and make light of it at the same time.

He took a final swig of his beer, ignored the part of her comment about his visits to Russian cities that were not, "on the tourist trail," and then told her, "My academic background and expertise on Russia. I guess that's why they chose me, approached me, as well as partly I suppose because I'd been there quite a few times. Plus, I had actually been invited to the conference, which was a sort of requirement and an advantage in choosing to approach me. There was obviously no point in trying to get someone to do what they wanted at the conference and pass the contact details on to you who wasn't actually going to be there and hadn't been invited, was there?"

He finished telling her that with an ironic smile, hoping it would lighten the mood. However, in his head he was thinking something much more serious. This was a woman who knows how to play people. She'd obviously been well trained in that. The question going through his brain now was by whom? Was it by MI6 after she'd defected or by the Russian Security Services before that, or maybe both? Whichever it was, he decided it was time to leave, before she could start probing further and throwing any more awkward questions at him.

Before he could say anything, however, she placed her hand on his forearm once again, telling him, "Excuse me for a moment. I need to go to the toilet."

He pointed her in the direction of the toilet entrance over in the far corner by the top of the steps, thinking that he was, for now at least, off the hook of any more of her awkward questions. While she disappeared he took the chance to check his phone. Meanwhile, Ledi took the chance to give him a little knowing smile of appreciation over the fact that it appeared to him that David was clearly getting on well with her.

But nothing, there was still nothing from Alice, no reply to his earlier text. He decided he would finish his beer with Sophia and just go off to his bed for a relatively early night. The music would be ending in Antika soon at one o'clock anyway, in line with the local by-law, and he didn't have any enthusiasm at all now for a club tonight, even though Jason would probably be in one or both of them. The lack of response from Alice had left him feeling very flat and more confused than ever.

When Sophia returned he told her it was good to meet her again, that he was glad everything worked out so well for her and that he could help, but that he was off to bed now.

She seemed surprised, but squeezed his arm once more and told him, "That's a pity. Perhaps we will meet again while I'm here."

She kissed him on one cheek while she placed her left hand tenderly on his other cheek, and then whispered softly in his ear, "I hope so. I would like that very much."

As she drew her head back he could almost feel the stare of her penetrating steel grey eyes drilling down deep into his soul.

He gulped hard and then partly nodded as he barely spluttered out, "Yes, maybe. Well ... err ... goodnight."

He was left in no doubt as to what she wanted. He felt extremely virtuous as he made his way back to his flat. He'd resisted temptation well. It had definitely been a strange night, even for Lindos. Certainly an unexpected one. Not one he'd anticipated at all when he'd left the beach that afternoon. Mostly he was extremely intrigued as to just what was behind the last part of it with Sophia.

15

An invitation

"Why do we always go crazy on the first night? Bloody stupid!"

David looked up from his Giorgos full English breakfast into the bright glare of the mid-day sun to see a very worse for wear looking Jason slumping into the chair across the table from him. He couldn't hold back a small grin.

"You look rough. Too many shots?"

Jason turned his head towards the open doorway into the café bar and through his badly needed sunglasses indicated to the owner, Tsamis, standing just inside that he wanted exactly the same as David, a cooked breakfast and coffee, as well as a bottle of water.

"Arches or Glow?" David added.

"Both, and yep, far too many shots." He sighed deeply before he went on. "You know what Michalis is like in Glow and Pete behind the bar in Arches. Shot after shot. They never take no for an answer."

"You could actually refuse some of them you know."

Jason looked over the top of his sunglasses at him across the table, but didn't have the will to reply to that.

"Nothing but water in my flat too when I woke up half-an-hour ago. Of course I got here too late last night to get anything sensible from the supermarket, like coffee and milk."

At that point Tsamis appeared with his coffee and water. He couldn't resist telling Jason, "You look like you need this. Welcome back."

"I need some of this as well, for energy," Jason said as he stirred a couple of sachets of sugar into his mug of coffee. "Anyway, what happened to you last night? No sign of you in Glow or Arches."

"Got distracted in Antika. Long story, mate," which David wasn't about to go into for obvious reasons.

"Connected to what you've been up to here all summer no doubt?"

"Not really, no, just an old acquaintance from a few years back, but not here."

"So, what have you been up to all summer here then? Plenty of stories, I'm guessing."

Tsamis appeared with Jason's breakfast and as he started to tuck into it David told him, "Writing, trying to anyway, trying to write a novel."

"Trying to?"

"Yeah, well you know what it's like here, Jason, late nights into early mornings and drinking."

"Sure do. All melted into a bit of a blur day after day and night after night during those summers I was working here."

As they got on with their breakfasts Giorgos was beginning to get busy with the lunchtime trade of a range of nationalities, some Brits, but also a smattering of Germans and French day trippers from Rhodes Town. Even though it was the second weekend of October the village was still buzzing with day tourists enjoying the warm autumn sunshine while they browsed the many small shops or headed towards Pallas Beach or the Main Beach. Much to David's surprise the Brit, German and French nationalities passing by or enjoying their lunch in Giorgos were added to by a Russian he knew.

He'd finished his breakfast and Jason was halfway through his when Sophia appeared on her way to Pallas Beach.

"Hello, are the breakfasts good here?" she stopped to ask having spotted him.

"Very, the English ones are at least," he confirmed. "On your way to the beach?"

"Yes, I like to swim in the bay. The water is so clear, and still very warm."

He nodded and then pointed to Jason to introduce them. She looked relieved when he used the right name.

"This is Sophia. I met her a few years ago. She's from Athens."

Jason nodded, saying, "Hi," as he turned back towards David, bit the inside of his mouth and nodded again slightly to him in approval.

"I heard there is a good Italian restaurant in the village. Is it?" she asked.

"Is it what?"

"Good, is it good?"

"Oh, yes, sorry, yes it is, very good, Gatto Bianco, across the square from the remains of the ancient Amphitheatre. Do you like Italian food?"

Jason kept his head down finishing his breakfast while the conversation between David and his Russian friend went on. He couldn't resist raising his head to give a small smile across the table at David at his last question. He could see very well where this was going, at least where Sophia wanted it to go, the direction she was gently nudging it in, and David was falling for it. It was an obvious invitation, an open goal, and he couldn't resist.

"I love it," she responded, followed by precisely what Jason had read was coming, even if he wasn't entirely sure David had. "Will you join me tonight, around eight-thirty? I said I owed you a dinner, remember."

Standing behind him, Sophia couldn't see it but now Jason was grinning broadly across the table at David and his eyes were widening with every second.

"Oh ... err ... tonight? Well, I was going to have dinner with Jason tonight, so-"

"That's ok, mate, we can have dinner another night, no problem," Jason interrupted.

She didn't wait for David's confirmation. She told him, "Good, I'll see you at the restaurant at eight-thirty then. Nice to meet you, Jason, Bye, see you later, David." With that she turned to head off down the alley in the direction of Pallas Beach.

Jason chuckled as he told David, "So, that was what, or I should say who, distracted you in Antika last night. Very nice."

"Yes, mate, she was, but as I said before, it's a long story."

"She seems keen though. What's the problem? You seemed hesitant."

"Like I said, it's a long story and I can't really go into it."

Jason frowned. "Sounds a bit cloak and dagger. And why does she owe you a dinner?"

"It is just a bit cloak and dagger, better you don't know. Can we just leave it at that?"

"Ok, sure, but Athens you said. She doesn't sound Greek. Doesn't look Greek."

"She's not, she's Russian. Moved to Athens years ago apparently. Anyway, looks like I'm going to be eating Italian food tonight. No doubt Valassios will be pleased to see me, and her, I'm sure. Catch you for a drink or two later in Glow or Arches no doubt, or more."

Jason was smiling broadly as he replied, "I won't bank on it. I think she has something different in mind rather than a late drink and clubbing, mate."

"Maybe, but I don't, and don't ask me why," David replied firmly.

Jason simply raised his eyebrows slightly, grinned across at David, then said, "We'll see."

David was right. The Gatto Bianco owner, Valassios, was pleased to see him when he turned up just before eight-thirty. He always was, and was even more pleased when Sophia turned up five minutes later looking stunning dressed in a very smart, not inexpensive, low cut, short bright red dress and a thin silver necklace. The bright colour of the dress showed off her nice tan to perfection.

Valassios showed them to a nice table on the roof terrace overlooking the Amphitheatre Square, and of course with the obligatory fine view of the illuminated Acropolis looming over the village.

They ordered some Italian white wine and a pasta seafood dish each with a salad. David wasn't exactly comfortable being with her, but he reckoned it was only dinner, and was determined it was only going to be that, dinner. Dinner with another woman, even one as lovely as Sophia, wasn't in his plans at all. His mind was too preoccupied with what the hell

203

had happened with Alice, what had possibly gone wrong. Even when Sophia reached across the table a couple of times to take his hand and one time ask where his flat was in the village he was very restrained, only telling her it was in the centre and disclosed no more detail. In fact, it was only just around the corner from the restaurant, literally no more than thirty metres away. He certainly wasn't going to tell her that, however. He knew full well what was in her mind, and was determined to avoid it, avoid sleeping with her.

After they'd finished their meal and the wine Valassios brought them a Lemoncello Italian liqueur each. As David sipped on his Sophia told him, "I didn't ask how long you're here for?"

"I've been here all summer, trying to write a novel. I gave up my position at the university because I'd decided to come here to write. But I'm only here now for another week or so as I have to go back to England for some meetings about the novel with my agent and publisher. What about you? How much longer are you here for?"

"I've been here for eight days, but only two more days then back to Athens for work."

"Funny really, all the times I've been here to Lindos but I've never been to Athens. Through the airport on connecting flights to here once, but not the city at all."

As soon as the words came out of his mouth he knew that it could be a mistake.

She took her chance and responded instantly with, "You should come soon. Come on your way home, when you go back to England from here."

"Oh, I ... err ... I-"

He was stuck for just what to say, how to decline politely, but she didn't let him and was insistent.

"Come, please, just come for a few days on your way home. I will be your guide. I'd love to be. I'm very good," She added jokingly, followed by a bright smile and an ironic, "And I'm very cheap."

At that time, lovely as Sophia was, and as much as he would have liked to see Athens, the Acropolis and the Parthenon, all he could simply do was smile and nod his head slightly. He knew that would definitely not be a good idea in terms of his pursuit of Alice Palmer. It was bad enough him having to leave Lindos and go back to England soon, but Alice definitely wouldn't understand that at all, him claiming he was stopping off there on his way home simply because he wanted to see Athens as a tourist. Certainly not with a lovely woman as his guide, the very woman she got so uptight about when he told her about MI6 getting him to contact her at the Moscow conference. Not that he was intending to tell Alice any of that in relation to visiting Athens and that it was the same woman, of course. Besides anything else that wouldn't be very clever security-wise in any case for Sophia in her new identity.

It was another of those times to say nothing, or as little as possible and be non-committal.

After his very slight nod of the head he merely told her, "I'll see. I'll have to check a few things."

He was deliberately vague, but she appeared to accept that, much to his relief.

A couple of nights later, however, his view on a stopover in Athens to see her on his way home changed dramatically.

16

Deflation

As she'd told David one early morning in August over pizza in the little square by Bar 404 after a long night with a fair bit to drink, Alice Palmer never really had any true friends in Lindos, not as far as she was concerned. Something stopped her from letting anyone get that close to her, male or female. No doubt it was because of what happened in her past with her ex-husband and her then best friend, and she wasn't going to make that mistake again and leave herself vulnerable. The nearest to a best friend she had in Lindos was Dianne Arnold. Like Alice, she worked in one of the Lindos restaurants. She was a tall woman in her early forties and was from Manchester originally. Her well-groomed shoulder length light brown hair framed her long attractive face perfectly. When she wasn't wearing the required restaurant dark t-shirt with its logo and a knee length black skirt at work she always paraded an impressive wardrobe. She was always immaculately dressed in the bars and clubs after work, whether in a blouse and skirt or a smart dress. Unlike Alice, one night a week she had a night off.

Alice introduced him to Dianne in Glow one night earlier that summer. The two women, if not best friends, were at least drinking partners after work on quite a few regular occasions. Usually they would often meet up in Jack's Courtyard Bar or the bottom bar at Lindos By Night after work for a late drink and then eventually around three move on, sometimes with other summer season workers, for a few more in the clubs. Three, sometimes four times a week that would be their usual routine. More than a few summer nights drifted by in a blur for the pair of them. Also like Alice, Dianne had been a regular Lindos one or two week holiday visitor over many years from her teens and had decided to come and live and work in the village for the summer six years before. She enjoyed that summer of 2013 so much that she decided to stay permanently and now lived there all year round.

Dianne had never been married. However, in Lindos she was never short of male admirers, whether they were tourists staying in the village for one or two weeks, Brit ex-pat men who lived there, or male Greek locals. Whenever David saw her in the clubs and bars after that initial night they were introduced she always seemed to be getting plenty of attention from men. She was always very friendly towards him too when their paths crossed in Arches or Glow, he thought even more so on Dianne's night off from work when Alice wasn't around. Their paths seemed to cross increasingly as the summer wore on. Initially he put that down to the fact that it was a village after all, and a very small one at that. But in mid-October that summer, less than two weeks before he was due to leave to return to England, something happened one night that made him doubt whether constantly bumping into Dianne on her night off when Alice wasn't around, and ending up drinking with her late in one of the clubs, was merely an innocent coincidence.

Two nights on from the night he'd had dinner with Sophia he went to Glow late on after his usual couple of late beers in the Courtyard Bar. There had been no sign of Alice in the Courtyard. He'd had no message from her for quite a few days now. The Courtyard owner, Jack Constantino, told him that he reckoned she hadn't been in there for the best part of a week.

When he got in Glow he spotted Dianne with a group of three women and two Greek men at the far end of the bar. Even from a quick glance from a distance he could see from her facial expression that she was already quite pissed. He thought about going over to her straightaway, but hesitated for a while, and instead made his way to the middle of the bar to get a beer. As soon as he turned away from the bar Dianne spotted him and waived him over to her group. She gave him a peck on the cheek and introduced him to the rest of her company. One of the guys was her boss at the restaurant in which she worked, and he guessed a couple of the women were waitresses there.

However, he didn't really catch all their names over the loud music.

He leaned in to say in Dianne's ear, "I haven't seen Alice around for a few nights."

It was more of a question really. He was hoping it would prompt her to tell him something about what had happened to her, whether she'd seen her.

Instead, she simply replied, "No, I've not seen her either."

She was slurring her words, so David guessed his distant assessment of her pissed state was accurate.

He decided that he would only have the one beer and then probably push off to bed. Glow was fairly busy for October, but he wasn't really in the mood for a long night of drinking. He was about to say goodnight to Dianne and her group when out of the corner of his eye he saw Simon Chapel stumble through the entrance door to the club. There was no doubting David's immediate assumption of how drunk he was. Within a matter of minutes there was even more confirmation of that when Simon started shouting at the top of his voice at a couple of young English guys at the other end of the bar. David never saw what started it. He hadn't seen the two young guys in the village at any time previously that summer, so he assumed that they must be tourists. The shouting deteriorated into Simon pushing one of the guys and the other one stepping between them as a bit of a scuffle broke out. He was clearly just trying to stop it getting worse, but Simon wasn't having any of it. Fortunately though, Simon Chapel's reputation in the bars and clubs of the village was well known, and a couple of well-built local Greek guys intervened. One of them was the guy who worked on the door of Glow. At least Simon still had some of his faculties that were not drenched in alcohol and he knew better than to try and object physically as the Greek guys marched him out of the club, at one point almost lifting him off the ground from either side as he continued to shout what seemed to David like obscenities in the direction of the two young English guys. Thankfully though, over the loud music of the club it wasn't exactly clear what they were.

By the time Simon Chapel had been despatched from the club most of the clientele had seen what had happened, including all Dianne's group.

"That guy's a total arsehole," David told her as he shook his head.

He wasn't sure she actually heard what he said over the loud music as she simply smiled slightly, or perhaps it was because she was pissed. It was the sort of small smile that indicates, "I didn't really hear what you said that much, but I think I agree."

This time David leaned in to speak directly into her ear as he told her, "He was a right arsehole to Alice and me in Arches one night in August. And the very first time I came across him earlier in the summer up at LBN he was pissed and was just as stroppy to me. All I did was ask the guys behind the bar if Alice had been in. I didn't know him from Adam, so don't know why he took such a dislike to me. He's bad news."

Dianne drew her head back from his face, stared at him for a few seconds while biting her lip, and then leaned forward again to say into David's ear, "Alice slept with him early in the summer. That's probably why, David, probably why he doesn't like you."

He was totally shocked, hoping that he'd miss-heard her, or maybe she was just pretty pissed and didn't realise what she was saying.

His jaw dropped a little for a moment. Then he told her, "Come outside into the courtyard a minute. I want to be sure I heard you right."

When they got outside she repeated it, word for word. He was still stunned, thinking was that why Alice kept telling him earlier in the summer she only wanted to be, "Just friends, good friends"? As he and Dianne sat on the bench in Glow's courtyard – the very bench where Alice had kissed him before they slept together for the first time - he was shaking his head, distraught and confused. A concoction of emotions of despair and anger swept over him. All he could say was, "No, no, not her and that arsehole, surely not."

A whole range of different thoughts and questions were instantly rushing through his mind. Was it true? Or was it simply Dianne trying to put him off Alice? Did Dianne even want him for herself? Was that it? She'd made some pretty blunt suggestions to him to that effect on a previous night when he'd seen her in Arches. She'd had too much to drink that night too. He just brushed them off though, putting them down to her over consumption of alcohol on that particular night.

As angst invaded every part of his body Dianne appeared to want to try and remedy the situation over the way she'd betrayed her friend.

"It was only one time, David. Alice told me it was only the one time. She said she realised it was a big mistake straightaway and it has never happened since, which is why I guess Simon has been so stroppy, especially with you. He's obviously seen you around with Alice a lot this summer and that's pissed him off. You should just forget about it though."

However, he couldn't simply do that. So many of the stories and rumours about Simon Chapel he'd heard in the village over that summer were rapidly resurfacing in his mind, rushing into his head. There were plenty of them. None of them were good or exactly complimentary. One of them was particularly juicy. That also came from Dianne one night too, earlier in the summer. Two women she was serving one night in the restaurant in which Dianne worked told her they were in Lindos on holiday visiting the boyfriend of one of them, who was working in the village for the summer. When Dianne asked who it was the boyfriend turned out to be Simon Chapel. Just like Alice, Dianne was also good at her job as a waitress. She could always engage the customers in pleasant conversation, hoping by doing so to encourage them to come back another time. This conversation though exposed her to a little more information than she bargained for or anticipated. It was far more surprising than the innocent conversations she had with most tourist diners.

David dismissed most of the rumours that he heard that summer about Simon Chapel and women in the village – women tourists, workers and locals – as meaningless unfounded gossip. None of those he'd heard included Alice however, until now.

Following Dianne's revelation he sat slumped on the bench for a minute or so while she rapidly tried to repair the damage, if that was truly what she wanted to do. He couldn't quite figure out how to react.

Finally he asked, quite aggressively, "When was it? When did she sleep with him? You told me once about serving a woman here on holiday who said she was his girlfriend. Was it before then?"

Dianne was trying desperately to sober up at little.

"It was … erm …," she hesitated for a few seconds.

"It was quite early in the summer. I can't remember exactly, late May, early June maybe. I knew when I served his girlfriend in the restaurant that evening that Alice had already slept with him. She told me about it a couple of nights before, I think. I don't know exactly how long before that it was though, that they'd slept together I mean."

Dianne tried to gloss over it by suggesting to him, "Let's go back inside and join the others. Get another drink."

However, he definitely wasn't in the mood to socialise now. All he wanted to do was to get out of there, go back to his flat and try and think through what had just been revealed. He certainly didn't want to risk running into Alice now in one of the clubs. He had no idea how he would react. All he knew was that this wasn't the best time for any instant reaction. He abruptly said, "Goodnight," once again to Dianne and left to head for his bed. Not that he thought he'd be able to sleep much.

Throughout that summer David had experienced some unexplained mildly provoked confrontations with Simon Chapel. Or he thought that they were only mildly provoked until tonight. There was a simmering undercurrent of obvious mutual dislike. Now he had a much better idea why.

As he reached his flat he tried to forget about that prat. He was determined not to waste his energy or thoughts on him. It was Alice Palmer, and what to do about her, that should be occupying his mind right now. Should he let her know what Dianne had told him, confront her or not? He certainly wasn't going to confront Simon and ask him if it was true. He'd probably only lie anyway and revel in David's discomfort. That wouldn't achieve anything, other than Simon Chapel knowing he'd got under his skin.

He reverted to trying to dismiss it all. Dianne was drunk. Perhaps she didn't intend to tell him what she did, but just mindlessly reacted instantly, blurting it out. Or what if she did simply have an ulterior motive and was trying to put him off Alice so she could get him into bed with her? When he thought about it that way he reckoned that Dianne was hardly going to tell Alice that she'd told him about her and Simon. And anyway, she was so drunk that by the next day she probably wouldn't even remember telling him.

He didn't get much sleep that night. He couldn't decide whether it was best to talk to Alice about it or whether that would simply damage their, what appeared increasingly fragile, relationship, or friendship, or whatever it really was. Even that conundrum merely provoked more questions than answers in his mind. If he did try to talk to her about it, what if it turned out not to be true? What if it was Dianne making mischief for her own reasons? That would simply drag up the whole trust thing, something very important for Alice.

Two days drifted by and he never saw her around in the village at all. Which was just as well as he still really had no idea how he would play it if he did see her. Then something else happened late on the second night which added to his confusion even more. He was going into Arches with Jason, around two o'clock, when he saw Alice and a guy deep in conversation sat on the wooden bench at one side of the club courtyard. The guy, who looked as if he was in his early forties, was grasping her hand. They were sitting very close and to David it looked as if they were staring into each other's eyes while the guy was telling her something. It appeared an intense conversation. David assumed he was English. When they got inside the club he told Jason that he thought he should go outside to see her. His friend persuaded him that wasn't a good idea at all, especially as the both of them, Jason and him, had quite a few drinks by then and David wasn't exactly thinking straight.

However, while he and Jason were up at LBN having a late drink the next night, much to his surprise, Alice turned up, around two o'clock. She was alone. He hadn't seen her in any of their usual bars for late night drinks over the past couple of weeks and now he had, two nights running.

Even more surprising was that as soon as she came into the bottom bar at LBN and spotted the two of them she came straight over to say, "Hello," and give him a kiss on the cheek. It was as if the past couple of weeks had not happened. She seemed chirpy and pleased to see him as he introduced her to Jason, who was now looking very confused after what David had told him about the silence recently between the two of them. Immediately after she ordered a drink she asked if they were going to come to Glow with her. David nodded slightly, still surprised and bemused, adding "Expect so," while Jason shrugged his shoulders behind her at his friend in continuing bewilderment.

After an initial sip of her Vodka and coke David took her to one side of the bar to ask as subtly as he could about the guy he saw her with in Arches courtyard. The frown across her forehead suggested she had no idea why he was asking that, but she clearly wasn't even bothered enough to ask.

"He's here for three weeks, well one more week I think. He and three other guys chartered a yacht for a month. They are moored in the bay for a few weeks and been in the restaurant a few times. I bumped into them in Glow and Arches later on a couple of nights. They were very generous with the tips and drinks for me and the other waitress at the restaurant. They invited us back to the yacht one night, but we both declined. We didn't think that was exactly a very clever thing to do, if you get my drift."

As she finished explaining she looked up at him out of the top of her eyes and then added, "Why? Why are you so interested in him?"

He shrugged off her question with, "No reason, just curious. Thought maybe he was someone from your past, even connected to your probation thing?"

There was a clear hint of anger in her voice now. "No, and I told you never to mention that. Have you told Jason?"

"No, of course not. I've not told anyone. Sorry, I won't mention it again."

He'd clearly touched a nerve and now was in full retreat. He decided that this definitely wasn't a good time to bring up what Dianne had told him about Alice and Simon Chapel. That would have to wait for a more opportune moment.

Alice appeared to calm down very quickly and, never one to dwell very long over a Vodka and coke, within ten minutes she was urging that the three of them get off to Glow.

That was hardly the end of David's concern over the mystery yacht man. When he, Jason and Alice got into Glow he was there with his three mates from the yacht. Alice never spotted him at first. He was deep in conversation with one of the other guys from the yacht at the other end of the bar. David had half recognised him and guided the three of them to the opposite end of the bar to order some drinks. Just as their drinks arrived however, the guy from the yacht appeared behind them to tap Alice on her shoulder.

As she turned around to face him he simply said, "Hi, you just finished work, bit late?"

"No, been up top LBN, Lindos By Night, for one first."

As David and Jason turned around from the bar she added, "This is my friend, David, and his friend, Jason."

The guy nodded slightly, but never said anything. It clearly wasn't them he was interested in speaking to. David and Jason nodded back in recognition. Then the guy deliberately managed to wedge himself at the bar between David and Alice, which prompted Jason to glance at David and raise his eyebrows. He was clearly picking up what the guy was up to as far as Alice was concerned. David always told himself that he tried to avoid doing jealousy. In this case, however, it was becoming increasingly difficult not to. It soon became a lot more so as he heard the guy ask Alice bluntly, "Is he your man? Your boyfriend? Are you together?"

He rattled the questions off like he didn't actually want to leave a gap for her to answer, leave a pause, a chance to answer, just in case it turned out to not be the one he was clearly hoping for.

David thought he detected a slight grin across her lips as he tried to not only hear her response, but also detect the expression on her face as his eyes flashed sideways without turning his head towards where she was standing. What he heard was not her answer he was hoping for.

"No, none of those," she said quite firmly.

"What then?" the guy asked.

"Friends, good friends, we're very good friends," she told the guy, equally firmly.

There was that bloody phrase, back again. One that had haunted him the whole summer. He froze. She obviously assumed he couldn't hear the conversation above the loud music, but not only David, also Jason, had made out enough of it to understand what was going on, particularly the last part and her emphasised, "very good friends," comment. Hearing that stunned David a little after what they'd been through all that summer, what had happened between them not that long ago. Stunned him more than a little, in fact, that they were back to that as far as she was concerned. And there was no equivocation in her reply whatsoever. She was making it very clear to the guy, and seemingly deliberately so. Perhaps that's what stunned him the most and left him numb. She appeared very clear and determined about it once again.

David merely stared straight in front of him to behind the bar, turning all that he'd heard over in his mind, but saying nothing. What did what he'd just heard mean for him, for him and her?

Jason, meanwhile, had once again raised his eyebrows in surprise at what he was overhearing and now decided that the only thing to do for his friend having heard that was to order some shots and get drunk. He waived over to Giannis behind the bar and ordered Tequila shots for David and himself, telling his friend, "Might as well get drunk, mate."

Alice's reply to his questions certainly never deterred the yacht guy one bit. Why would they? That clearly didn't appear to be her intention at all. On the contrary, he took it as encouragement and took his chance to once again invite her to their yacht.

"You really should come out to our yacht in the bay tomorrow for lunch. I could collect you from the little beach in our small dinghy. There are just the four of us guys on the boat, plus the cook. You can bring some women friends if you like."

David continued to try desperately not to show that he could overhear their conversation, and yet equally desperately try to hear Alice's reply. She never said yes, but she never said no. In fact, her response was a typical non-committal Alice Palmer one, avoiding any commitment.

"Okay, I'll see. Let me check with a couple of friends."

The guy obviously thought she meant women friends, as he'd suggested. Maybe she did. However, David was grimly clinging to the chance that she meant checking with him, as a "friend, very good friend."

While he was optimistically turning that over in his mind Jason whispered in his ear. "Deluded mate, I can see what you're thinking. It's written all over your face. Don't even start to think for one minute she means you," Then he ordered two more Tequila shots for them.

Meanwhile, the yacht guy took a business card from out of the top pocket of his short sleeved white linen shirt and handed it to Alice.

"Here's my number. Text me in the morning and we'll sort it. See you tomorrow I hope."

She took it, but said nothing. She picked up her drink from on the bar and turned back to join David and Jason as the guy went back to join his three mates from the yacht at the other end of the bar.

Was her saying nothing in response to the guy giving her his business card a brush off? Or was it just her typical non-committal response which David had seen so often that summer, experienced and been on the receiving end of? Or maybe it was simply the fact that she was well aware David was nearby, and could possibly overhear her conversation with the guy, so would hear her accept his invitation to lunch on the yacht if she did so then?

He was confused about all of that. However, his confusion over whether she would accept the invitation was cleared up the next day. He was on Pallas Beach just before mid-day enjoying the warmth of the mid-October sun after a swim in the still warm clear sea in the bay. He was drifting into a nap when he heard a man's English voice raised in annoyance down at the front and over towards one end of the beach. He was cursing as he repeatedly unsuccessfully tried to get an outboard motor to fire up on a small inflatable dinghy. When David sat up on his sunbed and looked over he recognised it was the guy from the yacht. That brought a smile to his lips, along with the fact that there was no sign of Alice and her women friends going for lunch on the yacht. Obviously she had declined the invitation. The only accompaniment the guy had was what looked like a couple of carrier bags of stuff from the supermarket at the back of the beach. David's smile broadened when the guy was forced to give up on the outboard motor and begin to slowly row the dinghy with great difficulty and effort across the bay to the yacht anchored on the far side of it.

Initially he'd doubted if what Dianne had told him about Alice and Simon Chapel was true. Admittedly, if true, he was shocked by it, but he couldn't bring himself to believe it was. The fact was that he simply didn't want to. However, he faced the dilemma over Alice's concern about trust if he raised it with her and it wasn't true. If Dianne did have some ulterior motive in terms of prising him away from Alice so as to try to get him into bed with her that would definitely do it, demonstrating to Alice that he didn't trust her. Even if not resulting in getting him into bed with Dianne, as she may have wanted, it would succeed in respect of prising him away from Alice by driving her away from him. He was very sure of that second part.

Now though there was more than just what Dianne had told him to be confused over. There was all the stuff with the yacht guy. The way Alice had appeared to encourage his interest, as well as the way she had been so adamant in telling him that David and her were just, "Friends, good friends, very good friends." After everything that had gone on between them that summer it felt like he was back at square one.

Despite what he saw that afternoon on Pallas Beach with the yacht guy, and the fact that Alice had obviously not taken up his lunch invitation, when he started to go over it all he was gutted. Not only what Dianne had told him about Alice and Simon Chapel, as well as all the stuff with the yacht guy, plus some other things that summer, particularly Alice's propensity to disappear for days on end and not reply to his texts. That quickly turned to anger. It was only a very short leap from there to what would eventually turn out in future to be a not very clever decision. But yes, why not, he would go to Athens on his way home, see Sophia, and take up her tour guide offer. After all, what did he have to lose now?

When he got back to his flat from the beach around six he called her.

"Hi, Sophia? It's David."

She sounded a little surprised as she replied, "Oh, hi, are you still in Lindos?"

"Yes, that's what I was calling you about. Well, sort of, it's connected anyway."

He sounded confused and was rambling. He stopped talking for a second, took a deep breath, and told her, "Listen, it turns out I am going to be in Athens for a few days on my way home. Three days I think, at the end of next week, from Friday, the twenty-fifth."

That was greeted with silence at the other end of the line. She never said anything. He was expecting, hoping, that she would respond quite positively, but initially all he got was silence. He decided to just plough on.

"So, if you're around, and your offer to be my guide still stands, I'd love to meet up for you to show me the Acropolis and the Parthenon, as well as the rest of the interesting things."

"The rest of the interesting things," ouch, that was clumsy to say the least was what was racing through his brain while he waited for her reply. Maybe he'd totally misread her invitation?

He needn't have worried.

"Sure, yes, of course, that'd be great. Good, I'll look forward to it."

She sounded much more enthusiastic now. He was reassured and his confidence returned.

"Okay, I'll check some flights as I'll have to make some changes, and I'll check out some hotels online and let you know. It'll definitely be Friday the twenty-fifth though."

Was he sounding a little bit over keen? He took another deep breath and then continued. "I'll try and get an early flight from Rhodes to Athens, so maybe we can meet around lunchtime and you can show me the Acropolis that afternoon?"

"Sure, that would work for me. I'll get Friday off from work. That won't be a problem."

Now she was sounding much more relaxed about meeting him. Perhaps she was merely a little surprised to hear from him so soon before. He decided to take a chance and push it a little further.

"I'm sure you know a few good restaurants, so perhaps I could repay you for being my guide by taking you to dinner on Friday evening?"

"Yes, I'd like that. Thank you. When you've booked it text me which hotel and I'll meet you there around eleven-thirty that Friday morning, if that fits with your flight from Rhodes. There are a few good ones in Plaka, quite near my flat, but I'm sure you can find some online."

"Okay, I'll have a look online tomorrow and let you know." Interesting that she wanted him to book a hotel near her flat he was thinking.

"Great, see you at the end of next week then, David."

With that she rang off. No sooner had the line gone dead than he was already beginning to wonder if in anger he'd actually done the right thing.

219

17

Stay

His doubt over whether he'd done the right thing in anger by calling Sophia and arranging to see her in Athens on his way home didn't linger very long. Within half an hour of ending his call with her he'd showered and gone to nearby Yannis Bar for a small beer with his laptop in order to use their wifi. He changed his flight from Rhodes to London on the following Friday, the twenty-fifth to one from Athens to London on Monday the twenty-eighth, and then booked an early morning seven o'clock flight from Rhodes to Athens on the twenty-fifth. Finally, he booked a hotel for three nights, the Electra Palace, in the centre of the Plaka in Athens.

Quickly it was all sorted, done, and he was going to Athens on his way home to see Sophia. In his mind that was all settled. His mind was clearer and he felt a sense of relief. As he sat outside Café Melia in the Amphitheatre Square just around the corner from his flat the next morning having a croissant and cappuccino for breakfast in the sunshine he felt much calmer and more relaxed. Whether it was in a moment's anger or not, he'd made his decision. At least now he wasn't in such a state of turmoil over it all with Alice. He'd go and see Athens with Sophia. He'd never been and always wanted to go. So, why not take the opportunity, and Sophia's company would be a bonus.

It was only just ten on a Saturday morning, the 19th of October. The morning air was already nice and warm, even that late in the season. Café Melia was a popular stopping off place for tourists on their way to the beach at St. Paul's Bay, whether for coffee or a cold drink, or even for one of the selection of filled baguettes and fine Greek feta cheese pies to take to the beach for their lunch. At this time of the season there weren't so many tourists heading for St. Paul's and the café wasn't anywhere near as busy as it was in the height of the season in July and August.

The square in front of the café was also a regular spot for taxis or smaller airport transfer vehicles to drop off their arriving tourists or pick up departing ones. That Saturday morning it was only a few departing tourist couples that David watched as he sat outside sipping his cappuccino. It was still too early for any arrivals, although at this time of year they would have been fewer anyway.

He'd almost finished his cappuccino and was about to abandon people watching to go back to his flat and do some more writing, when much to his surprise Alice appeared from around one of the corners of the square heading towards the café. He'd deliberately gone to Melia rather than his usual breakfast haunt of Giorgos in order to avoid the possibility of bumping in to her. Giorgos was also her regular breakfast place. Having sorted out in his head that he was going to Athens to see Sophia he didn't want any confusion creeping back into his mind over Alice. So, he chose Melia for breakfast instead. She spotted him straightaway and headed straight for his table.

"What's the chances of this? Hasn't happened much this summer, if at all," she told him as she sat down in the chair across the table from him.

"Chances of what?"

"You and me both having breakfast this early on a Saturday morning. Usually we'd both still be in bed after a long Friday night's alcohol consumption, wouldn't we?"

"I see what you mean. You obviously didn't have a late night either then?"

"No, I had a couple of late drinks in the restaurant with some customers and then went straight to bed after I finished work. Too knackered, always am at this end of the season. All that early season enthusiasm and energy seems a long time ago now."

At that point the waitress appeared from inside the café and took her order for a coffee, while David ordered another cappuccino, having abandoned for the moment going back to his flat to write. His earlier decision to avoid bumping into

Alice in the village that morning had obviously also been discarded, although initially not from choice.

"No Giorgos breakfast for you this morning then?" she asked.

"No, didn't want another full fried breakfast, just a croissant and a cappuccino."

She was making small talk, which he thought was strange. All that summer he'd never seen her do that, talk for the sake of it. As far as he was concerned Alice Palmer didn't do small talk. Maybe there was something more to it. He didn't have to wait long to find out that there was.

Her forehead creased in concentration as without any lead up to it in the conversation she surprisingly asked with determination clearly evident in her voice, "Stay, stay here for the winter. I am. With me, stay here with me?"

It was forced. The way she asked was as if she had been choking on it for a few days and didn't know how to say it. It sounded like a plea. Because it was. In the end she just blurted it out. She didn't know how else to do it. It wasn't something she was used to doing at all. It was, to say the least, unfamiliar to her. For once she was making herself vulnerable. Exposing herself to him, giving him the choice, when all summer it had been her making the choices.

There was no disguising his complete surprise. It was written all over his face. Not that Alice had any idea of course, but her surprise suggestion had created a real quandary inside his head. It was a dilemma over Athens and Sophia on the one hand, and staying in Lindos with Alice on the other. He thought he'd resolved that, not least because up until now Alice Palmer had shown no inclination whatsoever that she wanted him to stay for the winter. Now, however, she was really putting him on the spot.

He simply couldn't think quickly enough to decide in that instant what he wanted to do. He settled for referring to the practicalities, some of the things that he knew he had to do that winter.

"I can't."

"Why not? Why can't you?"

222

There was a frown across her face. It was mostly a reaction to her own unexpected willingness to expose herself to possible rejection, rather than over the rejection in his answer. He wasn't the only one who was surprised. Exposing herself in that way, opening herself up, was something she usually determinedly avoided.

He turned to look at her as he explained as gently as possible, "I'd like to. Of course I would, but I've got things I have to do back in the U.K. I have to be in London at the end of this month, as well as in November, for publishers meetings, meetings with the publisher's editor and my agent, about the novel. When I meet the editor there are bound to be changes they'll want me to make and will need to talk to them about. There always are apparently, so my agent told me. I'd love to stay but all those things need to be done face to face unfortunately."

He wasn't exactly being completely honest. At best he was being economical with the truth. Yes, he did have to be in London to see his publisher and his agent, but there was also Athens and Sophia and he certainly wasn't going to tell her he'd arranged to stop over there for three days on his way home.

Alice's body language changed as her defence mechanism kicked back in.

"Ok, sure, no problem," she told him simply in a very matter of fact, quite cold detached manner. Her voice portrayed a concoction of disappointment and self-anger over exposing herself emotionally so much. Now she was shutting down once again, not even making eye contact with him.

There was nothing but silence between them for a few minutes. Sensing the awkwardness, and her disappointment, he tried to repair the damage. He was wrestling with his conscience. He really had no clear idea what he wanted to do himself now, but he decided to ask her bluntly, "Do you really want me to stay?"

She looked up at him across the table and shook her head slightly.

"No … yes … I don't know now. I thought I did, but-"

223

"What does that mean, Alice?"

"I told you, I don't know." She shook her head once again and part of her hair tumbled down over one side of her face.

She took a couple of deep breaths, bordering on sighs, as they sat in silence again for a half-a-minute or so. Then she told him in a firm determined voice, "Yes, yes, you should go, of course you should if that's what you want."

He'd never seen her like this before, openly confused. The Alice Palmer he'd seen all summer had always put on a very clear face of knowing exactly what she wanted to do, and did it.

He decided to try to retrieve the situation a little by telling her, "I have to see my kids too you know, Christmas and all that. I haven't seen them all summer, obviously."

There was no reaction from her to that at all. No sign of one on her face whatsoever. He tried to go further.

"Look, maybe I could come back in early March. I was planning to come for all of next summer again at the start of May, but I could come a bit earlier. I could do that."

He looked towards her, searching for encouragement on her face. There was none. She was back in her defensive shell.

"Sure, whatever suits you best," she told him in a cold non-committal tone.

He was desperate for her to provide him with some greater, more definite encouragement; even provide him with more of a reason for not leaving. Not by simply asking him to stay in a very confused way, one minute saying she wanted him to stay and the next saying no she didn't, and being unable to bring herself to admit to him why she wanted him to stay with her. She just couldn't bring herself to tell him how she really felt about him and what she really wanted. Perhaps she actually didn't know herself, but maybe it was more than that. Perhaps it was a step that she simply couldn't bring herself to take, one that would again expose herself and her feelings too much. Whatever the reason was she couldn't bring herself to do that.

Inside him there remained some degree of lingering anger over what Dianne had told him about Alice sleeping with Simon Chapel. However, he couldn't bring himself to confront her about it. Instead he bottled it up inside, unable to decide what to do. Soon he would be leaving for the U.K., now via Athens. Perhaps there was no point in having a massive confrontation at this point before he left, and then having to dwell on that, let if fester between them over the winter. Of course, not confronting her would also mean it would fester within him over the winter anyway, but he decided that was a better choice than a big bust up just before he left. As he'd told Alice that afternoon in August as they walked up the Street of the Knights in Rhodes Town when she asked what he was like when he was younger and now, it was in his character that he never wanted to piss people off just for the sake of it, tried not to at least. Sometimes that meant he didn't tell them things, or express an opinion about things when he knew he should. Sometimes he simply ran away rather than face confrontation. He was doing that very thing now over what he'd heard about her and Simon Chapel.

So, he left and went to Athens on the following Friday, the twenty-fifth. There was no big goodbye between them, merely a, "See you in March and let's keep in touch over the winter," from him to her over a final late night beer in the Courtyard Bar.

"Sure, see you in March," she replied, followed by a kiss on the cheek as he left the bar to go back to his flat and his early morning start for the taxi to Rhodes Airport.

18

Athens

David's early seven o'clock flight from Rhodes to Athens took just over half-an-hour. He jumped in a taxi from the airport and was attempting to check-in at his hotel just after nine. There was some doubt whether his room was ready that early, but after a half-an-hour wait and a coffee, which the receptionist kindly arranged, it was.

His meeting with Sophia in the hotel lobby wasn't until eleven-thirty so he decided he'd try and grab a nap for an hour or so before then. When he texted the name of his hotel, the Electra Palace in centre of Plaka, she'd replied, "Yes, I know it. It's very nice, 5 stars and only a couple of streets away from my place."

Once again she mentioned about being near to her flat, which he again thought was interesting.

Even at almost the end of October the city felt hot, certainly hotter and more stifling than the still warm Lindos with its closer and more open proximity to the sea. According to the weather app on his phone the Athens temperature was twenty-four degrees. Pleasant, but in the city it felt hotter. Because of that, and that he expected to be climbing up to the Acropolis and the Parthenon looming over the city that afternoon with Sophia, he decided shorts would be fine, along with a cool cotton light blue short-sleeved shirt and his trainers.

At twenty past eleven he made his way to the lift and down to the hotel lobby to wait for her. While he did so he found an empty seat on one of the long couches in the reception area with a view of the entrance.

Eleven-thirty came and went. It was almost a quarter to twelve and he was now beginning to wonder if she'd changed her mind and wasn't coming. What a pain that would be, and

226

what a wasted journey to Athens, when he could have already been in London, or even placated Alice a little more by staying a few more days in Lindos.

His anxiety melted away as he spotted her stepping out of the revolving entrance doors. She looked good, very good, even better than he recalled her looking that night in Antika a few weeks earlier. She was wearing a sleeveless plain light grey dress with a loose wide black leather belt just below her slim waist. The dress was very short, highlighting perfectly her fine tanned legs all the way down to the flat light grey leather sandals. As she entered the lobby and spotted David she removed her large sun glasses and placed them into her small canvass shoulder bag, while simultaneously smiling across at him.

"Welcome to Athens for your first time," she told him, then bent down to kiss him on the cheek. "But maybe not your last?" she added.

"That depends if I like it, I guess," was all he could think to reply.

"Well, many people here call it the ugly city, but I love it. Maybe you will. Let's go and see."

As they made their way the short walk from the hotel through the Plaka towards the bottom of the hill to the Acropolis she asked if his hotel room was okay.

"Yes, its fine, more than fine actually, very good, and a great view of the city and the Acropolis."

On the way up the hill she threw in an occasional comment, information about the historic sites they passed and the Acropolis and Parthenon they were approaching. There were quite a few tourists around on their way up, as well as at the top, but nowhere near the crowds he'd anticipated. That was obviously down to the time of year.

They wandered around the various parts of the site at the top, taking in the Acropolis and the Parthenon mainly. After half-an-hour up there Sophia suggested they make their way back down and find somewhere nice for lunch, to which he readily agreed. A cold drink or a beer would be welcome now he was thinking. She told him she knew a very nice place for lunch.

Almost at the bottom of the hill she took him to a tucked away, very traditional looking Greek restaurant called To Kafeneio. It had nicely shaded tables underneath some trees and its own small vineyard. She'd made a good choice. It was a very pleasant place to stop for an early afternoon, but late, lunch. It was not directly on the tourist trail from the Acropolis and the menu was only in Greek. For that reason Sophia suggested he let her order, telling him she would just order some small Greek mezza which they could share, as well as something to drink and some water.

"I love it here. I come here quite a lot. The food is very good, and I like the setting," she told him.

"That'll be fine, the food I mean, and yes, it's very relaxing considering we are right in the centre of the city," he agreed.

After no more than ten minutes the waiter reappeared with a tray laden with small dishes of black olives, humus, tzatziki, pitta breads and a Greek salad.

"This looks good," David commented. He was waiting for the waiter to reappear with their bottles of water, which he was now gasping for. He was more than a little surprised when he did appear with their water, but also with an ice bucket in which there sat a fair sized bottle of Ouzo.

"Wow! This, now?" he said somewhat incredulously. He glanced at his watch as he added, "It's just gone two in the afternoon. If we drink all that I don't think I'll be able to stand, let alone make it back to my hotel and out for dinner tonight."

She laughed. "We don't have to drink all of it, David. That's not the idea, just a couple of glasses each with the ice and the water. You are in Athens, remember. It's good. It'll make you even more relaxed."

She reached across the table to squeeze his hand as she added, "Just relax and enjoy the surroundings, as well as the company of course. Don't worry I won't let you get too drunk for dinner tonight." She ended with another quick smile across the table.

He struggled through two glasses laden with plenty of ice and water, accompanied by a few good helpings of the pitta and the other dishes.

Sophia insisted on paying for their lunch. It wasn't something David usually agreed to, but as she reasoned that she had been the one who ordered it and insisted, he eventually agreed, telling her he insisted on paying for dinner that evening then.

"Of course, David, if you want. I've booked a nice restaurant by the sea that I know."

He didn't know Athens at all, so he couldn't figure out where that could be, but if it was as nice as the place where they'd had lunch it would be fine. And, as she'd suggested, he was certainly enjoying the company, which was, indeed, very good.

They wandered around the Plaka for part of the rest of the afternoon. At one point they went into the Acropolis Museum for an hour. Periodically she tucked her arm in his. It appeared to be going well. A very pleasant way to spend a Friday afternoon. Some people might well refer to Athens as the ugly city, but his company, his unofficial guide, was far from that.

They arranged to meet in his hotel lobby that evening at eight-thirty. Once more he was there ten minutes earlier and seated on the same couch in his light beige chinos, plain white short-sleeved shirt and smart boat shoes. He wasn't sure at all what sort of clothes might be required in the restaurant she'd booked. He didn't think to ask, although the clothes he had taken to Lindos for the summer never included any formal trousers or shoes, let alone a tie. Apart from the pair of chinos, all he had taken was shorts.

Sophia turned up looking immaculate, stunning in fact, in a simple, but effective, outfit. She carried herself as though she knew that very well. She was wearing a knee length halter neck black dress with a thin silver chain around her neck and black sandals, this time with a heel. Her small black leather bag hung nicely on her bare shoulder.

This time she greeted him with a small kiss on the lips and then she asked him to get one of the receptionists to call a taxi to take them to the restaurant in Piraeus. The taxi ride took around twenty-five minutes, during which she again tucked her arm in his a couple of times as she pointed out some of the significant sites they passed on the way.

Their table in the restaurant had a great view over Piraeus Harbour and the twinkling lights of some of the moored boats. It was all very nice was what he was thinking, and Sophia appeared quite relaxed in his company. However, his feeling that it was all very nice quickly changed when he looked at the menu and saw the prices. Sophia had told him that they specialised in fish and she wanted to have some with a nice bottle of white wine. The cheapest of which he saw on the menu was 120 euros. He swallowed hard, bit the bullet so to speak, and they ordered some fresh fish each along with the nice bottle of white wine she wanted. Even though he did order the cheapest, he had to admit that it was very nice, although not necessarily 120 euros nice.

Over dinner they chatted generally. She asked how Lindos was when he left. Was the village getting ready for the end of the season, the bar and restaurant owners? Were there a lot less tourists around? He replied, "Yes," to all of those, but didn't expand on his replies much at all.

They'd finished their main meal and were waiting for the arrival of the coffees they had ordered when her questions took on a much more serious focus. He was more than a little surprised when she asked, "What did you think of the Soviet Union collapsing? Did you expect it?"

She was suddenly asking him academic questions. Not what he'd expected or anticipated talking about over an expensive dinner in a beautiful setting overlooking Piraeus Harbour with a good looking woman. He'd certainly never had that type of conversation before with her. Unfortunately, he got far too academic with his answer, almost like he was giving her a lecture. With anyone else that would have been a disaster. However, she appeared to enjoy it and actually seemed very interested in what he told her. Perhaps that was simply the result of a mixture of her academic analytical training and her Russian character.

He told her what happened in the Soviet Union, what is happening there now, has similarities with what happens to all Empires throughout time, including now also the American Empire.

"I think the best description and analysis I've seen was in a documentary a few years ago, about five or six years ago I think, called 'The Four Horsemen'. It's about how Empires end. Not in the way traditionally believed, with barbarians at the gates. Overstretched Empires are brought down from within, which is what happened to the Romans, Britain, the Soviet Union, and is now gradually with the United States."

He stopped momentarily to take a drink of his water. As he placed his glass back on the table and looked across at her he said, "Sorry that was beginning to sound like a bit of a lecture."

However, she encouraged him. "No, it's interesting, please go on,"

"Empires actually don't begin or end on a certain date, but they do end over a long period of time," he continued. "The U.S.A and the west have not yet come to terms with its fading global supremacy. At the end of every Empire, going back to the Ancient Greeks and the Romans, under the guise of renewal tribes, armies and organisations appear. They develop, and then devour the heritage of the former superpower, often from within. The life cycle of Empires runs from the early pioneers to the final conspicuous consumers who become a burden on the state. According to the analysis in that documentary six ages define the lifespan of an Empire. Firstly, there is the age of pioneers, followed by the age of conquests and then the age of commerce. That is followed by the age of affluence and then the age of intellect. Finally, there is the age of decadence, the time of what is referred to as 'bread and circuses', mindless entertainment to occupy and distract the masses while the basics of life – food, shelter, health – decline. The common features of the age of decadence are an undisciplined and over-extended state military, a conspicuous display of wealth by a minority, a massive disparity between rich and poor, an increasing desire to live off a swollen enlarged state, and strangely, an obsession with sex. The most notorious trait of all in the age of decadence is the debasement of the currency. Take the case of the United States. In 1945 the global purchasing power of one U.S dollar was around sixty cents. In 2008 it was something like five cents. In the case of the Romans their currency became almost worthless and Roman Senators, the rulers, became only interested in the end in how much wealth they could personally accumulate. Meanwhile the ordinary Roman people were distracted by 'bread and circuses', grand Gladiatorial events in venues like the Colosseum. The equivalent today of those 'bread and circuses' in the U.S.A. are television programmes, sports personalities, movie stars, all providing the distraction of mindless entertainment while exhibiting a conspicuous display of vast wealth. Again, strangely, there was one other group, one other profession, which was respected and revered as the Greek, the Roman, the Ottoman, and the Spanish Empires declined. Those Empires all made celebrities of their chefs. All of those groups – the sports personalities, the entertainment stars, even the chefs, and the modern day equivalent of the Roman Senators accumulating their vast wealth - all exhibited a never ending desire for the best clothes, the best and highest rated entertainment. The equivalent of those today would be the best movies and television shows, as well as the largest most selective houses, the most opulent forms of transport – today cars and even private jets. They are all modern day equivalents of what the ruling and well off Romans desired and accumulated. All of that then and now took place, and is taking place, when what was and is needed is moral direction to save society and the Empire, the American Empire based on the currency, the dollar, and military might. The problem for the U.S.A today is that its financial moral authority evaporated with the American financial crash of 2008. A lot of those similarities also happened in the collapse of the Soviet Empire with its privileged rulers in the Soviet Communist Party and their elite accumulation of private wealth."

"What about Gorbachev though? He did try to change it didn't he, or don't you think so?" she asked.

"Yes, I suppose he did, try I mean, but the problem was that all he did was substitute PR slogans, public relations words, for any meaningful solutions, fine sounding words like perestroika and glasnost. In a way they were intended to impress the western politicians, but there was nothing behind them, no substance. In many respects that was exactly, is exactly even today, what happens in many countries in the west, like Britain and the U.S. Gorbachev and the new Soviet leadership after 1985 had no real substantial policy solutions behind the slogans, no policy solutions to the country's economic and social problems. In historical terms though, Sophia, the collapse of the Soviet Empire was relatively quick, around ten years from its war in Afghanistan in the early 1980s. That's unusual for the collapse of Empires. America's historical decline won't be so swift. It could happen over a hundred years or more."

"That long, really, you think so?" she asked.

He smiled and then told her, "On a visit to Paris in the 1970s the Chinese Communist leader, Zhou Enlai, was asked, by a journalist I think, what he thought about the French Revolution of 1789. He replied that it was too early to say."

She was staring across the table at him quite intensely throughout all of his long answer to her question of what he thought about the collapse of the Soviet Union. Her face was expressionless, although at least looking as though she was interested in what he was saying. He got carried away however, and as he finished was wondering if he'd sounded really boring, and far too serious. His last comment about the Chinese Communist leader did bring a small smile to her lips though.

"Sorry," he started to say once again. "I get a bit carried away with it all sometimes. Get swept up into the academic mode."

She reached across to squeeze his hand again and told him, "No, no, don't worry it was fascinating, very interesting for me. It's good to hear someone's view on it all. I don't get much, in fact not anything, of that sort of conversation here now."

He thought she might be being a bit too flattering in suggesting it was fascinating, particularly given the surroundings in which the two of them found themselves.

"Oh good, I just thought-"

She took his hand again and stared across into his eyes as she interrupted, sparing his obvious embarrassment and trying to lighten the mood by changing the subject.

"Let's just get the bill and ask them to get us a taxi."

He nodded as he told her, "Sure, but I'm paying this time remember, I promised."

The bill was considerably more than he'd anticipated when he made that offer earlier that afternoon, and it wasn't simply the wine that made it so. The fish was also very expensive.

As they waited outside the restaurant for the taxi in the cool night air she suggested, "Why don't you come back to my place for a nightcap? It's only a few streets away from your hotel, just a few minutes' walk. So, we can take the taxi to my place and you can walk back to the hotel later, if you want."

"Oh, okay, yes a nightcap would be good," he gladly immediately agreed. Her final comment of, "if you want," registered with him again as interesting.

Just over half-an-hour later the taxi pulled up outside a neoclassical apartment block. He'd recognised his hotel as they passed it in the taxi. As she'd told him, her apartment was only a couple of streets away from it. It was on the top floor, the third. As she unlocked the door to the apartment he told her the building looked very nice and that the location was great.

"I think it is about sixty years old, but the apartments were all renovated and modernised just before I moved in apparently. And yes, the location is great, as is the view. Let me show you."

She walked across the lounge to open the curtains and a pair of floor to ceiling large sliding glass doors to reveal a large terrace with wonderful views over the city, including the illuminated Acropolis.

David was thinking that this certainly wasn't some cheap apartment, and in the historic centre of the city, definitely not a cheap part of Athens. She had obviously been treated well by MI6. The floor in the lounge was real wood. It was expensively furnished with modern bright furniture.

She turned around to face him on the terrace and asked, "Now that nightcap. Would you like some wine?"

"That'll be fine," he replied, as he followed her into an equally modern, bright, expensive looking extensive kitchen.

After she poured them both a glass of cold white wine they returned to sit on the large leather couch in the lounge. However, the wine was barely touched by either of them. Within ten minutes, after a few minutes of meaningless chit chat, David's tour of the apartment was complete as they adjourned at her suggestion to her bedroom. Seconds more and they were both naked on her king size bed exploring each other's body.

He knew he shouldn't compare, but for some reason he wasn't prepared to acknowledge to himself that having had sex with Sophia he definitely didn't feel the same as he had after he'd slept with Alice that first time. Was it guilt?

Sophia on the other hand appeared to be more than satisfied from what they'd just done as she lay drowsily with her head on the pillow next to him.

There was a silence between them for a time that was drifting into becoming an awkward one. David was actually wondering how long he should lay there before suggesting he would leave when she asked him another surprising question.

"Do you actually know why they, MI6, wanted me to defect? What they wanted me for?"

As she asked him she continued to lay flat on her back and stare dispassionately up at the bedroom ceiling.

He turned his head slightly to look at her and could see that something was troubling her greatly.

"No, nothing, they told me nothing, I was just to be the messenger and give you the contact details for them. To be honest, Sophia, I didn't want to know."

"Nothing at all?" she asked once again, remaining motionless alongside him and still focused on the ceiling.

"No, nothing at all, other than it was you I was to contact and what to tell you. They actually told me, insisted, that I didn't engage in any other further conversation with you, I just assumed from what I knew about you academically that it was something to do with information which MI6 knew you had access to from the Russian Security Services, information on Russian foreign policy intentions in the Far East, particularly China and North Korea, which would be of use to them."

"So, you knew who I was then?"

"Only from some academic articles of yours I'd read, a couple that were of interest to me because of my lecturing at the university. I didn't know much more about you though, other than that you were a Professor in the International Relations department at the St. Petersburg State University. That was in those academic journal articles of yours I read. When MI6 wanted me to pass on the contact message to you I assumed you must be someone important to be a Professor at the oldest, and one of the largest universities in Russia. I knew that much about your university, but that was the limit of what I knew about you personally. I really didn't want to know anything more, as I said I just guessed that you must have had some connection with the Russian Secret Services for MI6 to be interested in you."

She turned on her right side to face him. Still resting her head on the pillow she asked, "So, you thought I was a spy?"

She allowed the barest of smiles to creep across her lips as she finished asking him that, signifying to him that she was teasing him to some degree.

He decided to play along, although he had a much more serious look on his face. "Were you?"

She ignored his question, but went back to his previous assumption as to why MI6 were interested in her and getting her to defect. She lifted her head up off the pillow and rested it on her right hand for support with her elbow and upper arm now on the pillow.

"To some extent, you're right, it was to do with information that I had access to from the Russian Secret Services on Russian government foreign policy intentions in the Far East, particularly China and North Korea. That was certainly part of the reason MI6 were interested in me and wanted me to defect."

She was staring into his eyes, watching closely for his reaction to what she was about to tell him to see if it would shock him. Her voice now was cold and calculating, almost detached.

"But it was also because I could give them, MI6, information on people, the names of people in the U.K. and the Far East, mainly Russians, but some others, all Russian spies who they could try to turn to spy for them, or, of course, kill."

He gulped hard. He had no idea that what he did for MI6 was part of that, would lead to that. He felt sick and his head was starting to spin with it all. This was a lot more than what he had told Alice in Rhodes Town that afternoon. He certainly wouldn't be telling her any of what he'd just heard, including how and where he'd heard it; in Sophia's bed. Indeed, there was a lot more in his past about him and MI6 that he could have told Alice on that August afternoon in Rhodes Town but avoided doing so. He could add what Sophia had just told him to that.

Sophia could see he was shocked at what she'd done that he'd contributed to. But she carried on, with an even more dispassionate tone in her voice.

"As soon as they got me out of Russia and into one of their 'Safe Houses' just outside London I gave them a list of names. In return they gave me a new life, a new identity, all necessary documents, even a new birth certificate in my new name, U.K. passport, and a whole new family history. They referred to it as a legend, making me a completely new and different person, whose family managed get out of Russia just after the collapse of the Soviet Union, when the new me, Sophia, was very young, just twelve. Alexandra Ivanova instantly became Sophia Orlova, and that's me today."

When she told him it though, he did try to quickly calculate from it just how old she actually was. He knew the Soviet Union collapsed in 1991, at the end of December. Consequently, she must have been born in 1979 or 1980, which would make her forty or thirty-nine now. Or at least, that's how old the new Sophia Orlova would be. He knew that at MI6 they would probably have stuck as close to her real age as possible. So, the previous Alexandra Ivanova would have most likely been the same age.

He had no idea why his brain was so concerned with that particular meaningless diversion from the much more serious and worrying things he had just been told. He wasn't sure at all that he really wanted to know all that she'd just told him. She was revealing a lot about her new identity and how MI6 had arranged it, much more than he needed to know or was comfortable with. She appeared determined to do so, however, as if she needed to. He was thinking that actually made him vulnerable in all sorts of ways.

"Of course, they gave me quite a lot of money, which enabled me to buy this flat, as well as have enough left to live quite comfortably here in Athens," she continued. "I still wanted to work though. What I had left after I bought the flat wasn't enough to last forever. So, I set about learning Greek. The Greek alphabet is quite similar to the Russian one. There are not many similarities apart from that, but I'm a fast learner, and I had my English of course, which is pretty good, I think."

"It is," was all he manged to squeeze out of what was now his very dry mouth. She was rambling on, appearing to be determined to tell him as much about her new identity and new life as possible.

"I was lucky. I got a job quite quickly as a translator for a Greek company here in Athens that had business connections in Russia, which was perfect. I even made some new friends at work, Greeks. It was one of them who suggested when I was looking for a holiday that I should go to Rhodes. I did some research on the internet, liked the look of Lindos very much, so decided to go, and of course, met you. So, here we are."

As she finished she lay back down with her head on the pillow.

"How do you feel about all that," he asked?

"Well, I saw that there were a few Russian tourists in Lindos, so that made me a little nervous at times in case by chance someone might recognise me, just like you did I suppose."

She looked up at him and saw he had a confused frown.

"Oh, sorry, you mean you and me here? I thought you meant Lindos. We don't really know each-"

"No, not me and you here," he interrupted. "I meant how you feel now about what you did, what you gave to MI6 that resulted in people possibly, probably being killed."

She pulled herself up to sit with her back against the bed headboard.

"I did what I had to do, David."

It was another cold statement, devoid of any hint of contrition whatsoever.

He felt very uncomfortable now. What on earth had he bloody done? Not just that evening in Athens with such a hard-hearted, seemingly emotionless, woman, but also for MI6 back at that conference when he passed their message on to her. And what had he done coming to Athens at all and deceiving Alice, just because he was so angry with her over what he'd heard from Dianne that Alice had done with bloody Simon Chapel earlier that summer.

He'd been bloody stupid, again.

Part Three

19

March 2020

Alice Palmer stayed in Lindos for the winter. David went back to UK via his regretful short diversion in Athens. They kept in touch quite regularly with texts between them, as well as the occasional Skype and Facetime when she could find a place open with a Wi-Fi connection in the village. Basically, that amounted to the Red Rose bar in the centre or the Lindos Ice Bar up the hill in Krana.

Through the winter he tried to put his guilt over Athens behind him, concentrating on meetings with his publisher and editor, and making changes to the first draft of his novel. His guilt re-surfaced over Alice's reply after texting her to wish her a Happy Christmas in Lindos. She texted back, "Happy Christmas to you too. When are you coming back? I miss you. X."

He had no further contact with Sophia after he left Athens following those three days at the end of October. He wasn't to know it at the time, but she would have an impact on his following year in an unanticipated manner, and in more than one way. So, his winter didn't turn out to be quite what he expected and planned. At least, not the final part of it in February 2020, just before he returned to Lindos in early March as he'd promised Alice.

There weren't that many people around in the village at that time, early March, certainly hardly any tourists. A few of the bar and restaurant owners, along with some of the shopkeepers, were starting to get their properties ready for the start of the upcoming summer season following their winter hibernation.

David arrived back at the start of the first week of March, on Monday the 2nd. He didn't actually meet up with Alice until the Friday evening of that week. They exchanged a few texts when he got back and he suggested they meet up. But she put him off, and kept doing so until that Friday evening.

All evening there seemed to be an underlying tension. At first Alice had seemed pleased to see him. Although there was no indication at all that they would sleep together. It appeared that she wasn't pleased enough to see him for that.

They went for a drink in one of the only two bars that were still open at that time, the Lindos Ice Bar. Quite a few of the locals from in and around the village were there. For many of them it had been their regular drinking spot throughout the winter months; a place to meet and play cards or just chat. Alice and David knew quite a few of them from their visits and summers in the village. Over a fair few drinks they caught up from some on how the winter had been. The bar seemed to stay open for as long as anyone was prepared to carry on buying drinks and consuming them.

They didn't actually meet up and make it into the bar that night until around ten, but David was surprised when he glanced at his watch and saw it was approaching three o'clock. He'd had enough drink by then and decided it was time to make for his bed. It was not only because he'd had enough drink though, it was because for the past hour he was gradually sensing a growing whiff of hostility from Alice. Something was wrong. He had no idea what. Unusually for her she hadn't mentioned what it was, and he decided that for now he wasn't going to ask. He'd pick his moment. Their first meeting after his winter away didn't seem the best time for it.

"I think I'm going to head off to bed," he told her. "It's nearly three, and pretty soon before I know it we'll be heading for another of those Lindos long nights where we watch the sun come up."

"Okay, good idea, I'll come with you."

He raised his eyebrows. His facial expression hinted he'd misunderstood her meaning.

"You can get that out of your head, David. I meant leave with you, not what you're thinking, not your bed."

She knew precisely what she meant, and was very firm in putting him straight. "I'll walk down the hill with you into the village. That's all."

When they got to the Main Square at the bottom of the hill she suggested, "Let's sit on the bench over there looking out over the bay for a bit. I'm not actually very sleepy, and I haven't had that much to drink. It's not as though I've been doing much during the day here at this time of year, not like in the summer. Even if I go to bed now I won't sleep."

He was surprised at her suggestion. It felt like she'd been avoiding meeting him all week since he'd got back, and at best she'd not been over friendly all evening with him. Something was obviously churning over in her mind. From her comment minutes before as they left the bar he thought she would leave him to go straight off to her bed and do one of her disappearing acts of early on in the previous summer.

He agreed and they headed towards the bench at the far side of the square. The sky was clear above them, with a myriad of stars shining brightly. The temperature had dropped somewhat through the night, however. It was cooler now. Having spent some winters in Lindos since she first came to work there Alice was used to the lower evening temperatures outside the summer months and was sensibly wearing a black long sleeved jumper and a pair of jeans. Unfortunately, David hadn't experienced them and was feeling a little chilly in his shorts and polo shirt. Nevertheless, he agreed straightaway to her idea of sitting on the bench for a while. He thought it might give her a chance to say what was bothering her.

For a full couple of minutes they sat there in silence. She appeared content to just stare out over the darkness of the bay with its few twinkling lights from the boats moored within it. Eventually he tried to prompt her into telling him what was bothering her.

"You seem preoccupied. You have all evening, as if something is bothering you? To be honest you don't seem very happy, not living the dream anymore like you were last summer? Did something happen here during the winter to upset you?"

She said nothing, just briefly turned her head to glance sideways at him sat on the bench beside her and then turned back to gaze out over the bay.

"So, I'm wondering-"

She broke her silence by interrupting him sharply, "Happy? What's that then, David?"

"Well, I guess-"

He had no idea what he was actually going to say, but she didn't let him finish anyway.

"Come on, happy, what's happy mean? You're supposed to be the bloody educated one. You tell me."

"Erm ... well ... I suppose that depends really."

He was hesitating, floundering and wondering how far to take it as she seemed so agitated. She said nothing though.

"I guess it's whatever makes you happy, Alice. Why do you think it is so difficult for you to be happy? That's what it seems to me is the case quite a lot of the time, was the case a lot of the time last summer."

She turned her head to glance at him briefly once again. Even though he only fleetingly saw her face it was clear there was a look of contempt spread over it. He had no idea what it was that was bothering her, except that from the way she looked at him, even briefly, he was rapidly getting the idea it was something to do with him. Whatever it was she appeared determined to remain silent, at least for now.

He tried to get philosophical in reply to her question about what happy meant. For some bizarre reason he momentarily thought it would lighten the mood. He was hoping that it might either divert her attention away from what was bothering her, particularly if it was about him or something he'd done, or at least prompt her to open up and tell him about it. It did eventually, but not in the way he liked at all.

He started to tell her, "Okay, so you reckon I'm the educated one. Well ... yes ... well how about this. A French philosopher, Rousseau, wrote that at the very moment we feel we've achieved happiness, we actually stop being happy. We can do without happiness as long as we want to. But even if happiness fails to come, hope that eventually it will come still persists, and that hope lasts for as long as the passion behind it, the passion for happiness. So, that feeling, the passion for happiness, is enough in itself. Even the anxiety that hope for happiness inflicts on us is a pleasure that we allow and endure in order to compensate for reality. Indeed, sometimes that feels even better. We embrace it and enjoy it, because while we have hope of happiness we aren't burdened by actual commitment. So, we enjoy less what we actually achieve in reality in terms of happiness than that we hope for, the happiness we hope for, search for. And we are only really happy during the time before actually achieving what we think of as being happy, the time while we have hope in searching for happiness, or before achieving what we think will be happiness. Maybe that is you, Alice? Maybe that is the reality of your living the dream in Lindos? Perhaps, that is your hope of happiness in living the dream here? Searching for happiness here is your living the dream."

He was telling her that and talking about her, but he knew he could just have easily have applied it to himself. She was his unfulfilled passion, and his hope of happiness. That was what he thought about her. That was the hope at the time that actually made him happy. Even though they'd slept together twice, all through the previous summer he'd worried that to take the leap and tell her how he truly felt might destroy that hope through the possibility of a negative response from her. His hope that she might respond differently, more positively, and share his feelings, served to prolong his happiness, even though it could ultimately be unfulfilled. All the while that he never made that leap his dreams, his hope, were a substitute for the danger of any possible cold unhappy reality of rejection from her. Was that enough for him though? Could he survive, continue, with his dreams, his hope, even if testing it could destroy those, destroy his happiness of not knowing, as well as his perpetual hope? Was it simply a never ending form of mental pleasure, yet simultaneously mental torment? In many ways effective, but unreal, lacking any form of reality, lacking any actual substance within the comfort of fantasy and its personal satisfaction for him? However, lingering in the back, or maybe now much more in the front of his mind, was the knowledge that despite all the purity of his attempted philosophical reasoning there was one quite large problem, a stain on all that reasoning, the fact that he'd gone to Athens and slept with Sophia. He was in an interminable agony of hell, not just over his hope and constant indecision over Alice, but also through his guilt over what he'd stupidly done with Sophia.

She shook her head slightly.

"That's all a bit deep, David. But if I understand it right, you think that me being happy is all bound up with my hope of living the dream here then, and it's really that ongoing hope which actually makes me happy?"

She had turned the whole of the upper part of her body towards him on the bench as she asked that. From her body language he sensed that there was still a large amount of aggression wound up inside her. So much so that she didn't wait for his answer, but ploughed on with a philosophical analogy of her own. Not from a French philosopher however, but a Greek.

"Have you ever heard of a Pythagoras Cup?"

"No, what's that?" He looked confused over what appeared was her going off at a tangent.

"It's a cup, a goblet if you like, designed by the Greek philosopher, Pythagoras, not a bloody French one."

"Right," he nodded, not sure at all where she was going with this. It was becoming an increasingly bizarre conversation for the two of them to be having sat on a bench in Lindos Main Square at coming up to four in the morning in early March. There was a ring of hidden anger in her voice, so he decided to go along with it.

"It's not easy to explain how it works. It's better to see a drawing," she began to explain.

245

He still had no idea where she was going with it, but he let her go on, simply nodding as if he was actually perfectly clear what she meant.

"A Pythagoras cup looks like a normal drinking cup or a goblet, except that the bowl has a central column in it and a line marked a short distance below the rim. The central column in the bowl is positioned directly over the stem of the cup and over a hole at the bottom of the stem. A small open pipe runs from that hole almost to the top of the central column, where there is an open chamber. The chamber is connected by a second pipe to the bottom of the central column, where a hole in the column exposes the pipe to the contents of the bowl of the cup. When the cup is filled, liquid rises through the second pipe up to the chamber at the top of the central column. As long as the level of the liquid does not rise beyond the level of the chamber, the cup functions as normal. If the level rises further, however, the liquid spills through the chamber into the first pipe and out of the bottom. Gravity then creates a siphon through the central column, causing the entire contents of the cup to be emptied through the hole at the bottom of the stem."

"I see, but-" he said, although if he was honest, at that time of the morning or middle of the night, and without some sort of diagram, he didn't really see, not clearly anyway, or why she was telling him this. She didn't let him finish.

"The point is, David, overfill the cup beyond the line, for instance with wine, and the wine will drain out of the bottom of the beaker. The philosophy of the cup is about morality and greed. Don't want or seek more and more than you have, because if you do in the end you'll end up with the accidental disaster of nothing."

As she finished she purposefully looked him straight in the eyes. Clearly she was attempting to subtly drive at something. He was getting increasingly worried that in an obtuse way the thing she was driving at was about him. The guilt inside him over Sophia and Athens was forcing its way to the front of his mind. He had to tread carefully.

Tentatively he asked, "Is that what you think about everything?"

"Yes, I guess I do, that's about it."

Her voice was clear and firm.

"I'm happy with what I have here in Lindos and I don't need any more than that."

She stopped for a few seconds and glared into his face. Then in a deliberate, very calm explicit manner added, "And that includes anything more between you and me."

Her last comment was intentionally pointed. For some time the greatest barrier to one element of Alice Palmer's possible happiness had actually been her very anxiety over the fear of a relationship and all that came with it, of being let down again when she trusted a man. More than ever that was true now.

He merely sat in silence, disappointment deep inside over what she'd just told him. She turned away from him and back to looking straight out across the bay as the first slight glimmer of shrouded daylight was invading the night sky. She didn't want to look at him, but she guessed he wouldn't be very happy with what she'd just told him. After a few seconds she relented and tried to soften what she'd told him a little.

"Look, what we had last summer was special, a special very good friendship, David."

He turned his head towards her.

"Really special, but I thought it was more, hoped it was more. You must have known that, Alice?"

She didn't reply, but continued to gaze ahead into space. After a few minutes of agonising silence she said, "No, I don't think I did know that, not clearly. I was never sure. You never said as such, did you? And after that first time you never even appeared to want sex with me. I know, I know that we did sleep together again, that second time a few days later, but after that something happened and you never pushed it, never seemed to want to as much as I did. Anyway, that's what it seemed like to me. I don't like to put myself on the line and be let down, so …"

Her voice tailed off, like the fading darkness all around them.

"But I did want to, Alice, of course I did. I wanted to, but then some things happened that put doubt in my mind again about how you felt."

He should have stopped there. He made the mistake of carrying on.

"And I heard and saw things, things I didn't like."

There was surprise all over her face as she turned back to face him.

"Things, what things?"

"Things, like with that guy, the one from the yacht. I was put off, felt let down, I suppose, when I saw the way you were with him that night in Glow. What I heard you tell him about you and me made me wonder why I should try to go any further with what we had between us and trust you?"

There was anger in her voice and she was glaring into his face. "What? Let down? With the guy from the yacht? For your information I never slept with him. I have no idea why you would think I did. Anyway, I don't see why I should be so defensive about it even if I did. We all have secrets, don't we, David?"

"What do you mean by that?"

As soon as that came out of his mouth he knew that could be another mistake. He was pretty sure he knew what she meant, but was at a loss over how she knew it.

She didn't answer. Instead, she turned back to gaze out across the bay while slightly biting the inside of her cheek. It looked like she was contemplating whether to continue along the path of recrimination that she'd taken.

She never got the chance to as he tried to keep the focus on her, what she'd done the previous summer, and finally get off his chest what had bugged him for months. Unfortunately, it proved to be 'the straw that broke the camel's back' for Alice. He took a deep breath and turned his head to look at her as she continued staring out across the bay.

"There was also Simon Chapel though wasn't there? Dianne told me last September about that, you and him."

She never moved. Her head was motionless, still staring ahead, out across the bay. She said nothing for a long minute as

248

the initial small flickers of the rising sun started to light up the horizon. Her anger was rising, just like the morning sun, and was infused with confusion now.

He waited, anxious for her response. Eventually, she turned her head back to stare straight in his face once again. Her face was contorted by a frown, betraying her anger as she aggressively rattled off questions. "Why didn't you say before? Why didn't you tell me you knew about that before, last October before you left? Why bloody wait till now if Dianne told you last September, David?"

"I ... err ... I ... I suppose-"

He was struggling. He was desperately searching for the right words to explain why he hadn't confronted her about it before. To some extent he simply couldn't bring himself to believe it. What was more, he was worried it would frighten her off if it wasn't true, causing her to think he didn't trust her. Even raising it with her would send that signal. He'd been over and over those things in his head many times since Dianne told him. Now it was out there though, that he knew about it. However, much worse was to follow.

She continued to stare straight into his face as she interrupted him with aggression, bordering on venom, oozing from her lips.

"I've been told you had something going on after you left here last October, on your way home, something with a Russian woman who lives in Athens, who you met while she was on holiday here."

He was worried that might be coming from the remark she made earlier, but he was nonetheless stunned, mystified over how she found out.

"Who told you that?"

She ignored his question for the moment, and instead snapped back at him.

"It's true then?"

"Why are you so bothered about her? That's in the past, last year before us."

He attempted to wriggle out of answering her question directly. He lied. He knew he'd already slept with Alice when he met Sophia in Antika that night at the end of September.

Now she did answer his question about who told her. The anger had drained out of her voice. She turned her head away from him once again, back to the view of the beautiful pale rising sunlight over the bay. She leaned forward, rested her forearms on her knees, and spoke slowly and calmly.

"Dianne told me two weeks ago. One of the women she worked with in the Village House restaurant last summer, Marianthi, told her. She's from Athens. The Russian woman - Marianthi told Dianne her name was Sophia - got friendly with her when she was here on holiday and ate in the restaurant a few times. They stayed friends when the woman went back to Athens after her holiday and Marianthi went home there for the winter. The Russian woman told Marianthi that an Englishman, David, a writer, who she met here on her holiday, and who'd been staying in the village all summer, stayed over for the weekend in Athens to see her on his way back to England last October. Marianthi stayed in touch with Dianne because she wants to come back to work in the Village House again this summer. She'd seen you with me and Dianne a few times in the clubs through the summer. You even met her once in Glow with me when she was there with Dianne. So, she knew it was you that this Sophia woman was talking about, and she told Dianne about you staying in Athens with her on your way home. Of course, Dianne couldn't wait to tell me."

As she finished telling him that she turned her head and glanced up briefly at him, and then turned her head back away once more to gaze into the distance. A resigned look of disconsolate disappointment was etched all over her face.

When Dianne Arnold told her about David and Athens, and Sophia, Alice's emotions swung between devastation and disappointment on the one hand, and feeling justified and relieved on the other. Deep down she knew she always expected it, to be let down by a man. What she found difficult to comprehend however, was why she felt so hurt this time. Why did it seem so serious and matter so much to her? That was something she didn't want to acknowledge at all, wasn't prepared to. All those emotions had been swept away though, crowded out by anger now that she'd met and confronted him.

What else could he do but own up to his stupidity? He sighed and then took a deep breath.

"She lived in Athens, and yes, she was on holiday here. I went to Athens on my way back home last October to see her after she left here. It was stupid, a stupid thing to do, Alice."

Even then, however, he didn't go so far as to tell her that Sophia was also the woman from the Moscow conference five years ago who he'd told her about that afternoon in Rhodes Town. He conveniently convinced himself that was information about Sophia's new identity that he simply could never share with anyone.

Alice looked calmer, from what he could make out anyway. She continued in silence not to look at him. Perhaps she'd accepted what he'd told her, and at least they'd moved away from talking about her and Simon Chapel.

In fact, she was running through things from last year in her mind, the sequence of events and what he'd just said about their relationship, or good friendship as Alice preferred to refer to it. In effect, she was focusing on the timing of when they first slept together and what he referred to as, "us".

She sat up on the bench and told him, "Hmm, I'm not sure what you thought that "us" was that you just referred to, or even if there was an "us" at all?"

She looked pensive as she continued to stare into the distance through the emerging light. It didn't take very long for her to realise that he'd just lied. Her anger returned. She turned back to face him again and asked aggressively once more, "Did you sleep with her in Athens or here?"

Before he could answer, or even try to answer, she continued, her anger growing once more by the second.

"Actually, no, no, that doesn't matter. Don't bother lying, David. Dianne said Marianthi told her that the woman was here at the start of October, so whether it was then or later in Athens doesn't matter as neither of those would have been bloody,

'Before us'. Either of them, whenever, was after we bloody slept together here last summer."

He hesitated, knowing she was right, but not wanting to acknowledge his mistake again, his stupid angry knee-jerk jealous response to what he'd heard about her and Simon Chapel. He was struggling again with what to say, but she never waited for his reply. She was in full flow, turbo charged with anger, and now desperate to find out what, if anything, his past in Lindos held that she didn't know about, that he hadn't told her. He was a little surprised by the direction her questions took next, and even more so by the fact that she was so obviously bothered about it. Her trust in him had clearly completely collapsed.

"Dianne said she remembers you here in 2018 for a few weeks in June and early September. I don't remember you, but Dianne did."

He was wracking his brains, trying to fathom out if there was possibly anything from that summer that Dianne Arnold may have revealed to Alice which he would have preferred her not to. He was sure there was nothing.

"I don't remember seeing you either. I think I would have done, but it was only a few weeks," he interjected with something that he hoped she would take as a compliment. She ignored it.

"And were there others you slept with here two years ago while you were here?"

"Others? I … err-"

"Other women, tourists or workers, did you meet any other women here too that summer, particularly summer season workers?"

He rubbed the back of his neck with his left hand. This wasn't the end to the evening he'd hoped for, the first evening they'd met since he returned. His intention to head off to his bed when he'd said he was leaving the Ice Bar earlier seemed a very distant one.

He removed his hand from the back of his neck and shook his head slightly.

"No, no, not really," he told her in a soft voice, hoping that would help calm her down again.

All around them there was the silence of the first minutes of the light of a new day dawning. The only exception breaking it was their voices, particularly Alice's raised in anger at times. It should have been a beautiful silent time gazing out at the stunning, calm dawn panorama of Lindos Bay. It was far from that. The conflict between them didn't fit the surroundings at all. Alice Palmer was anything but calm. Her anger was showing no sign whatsoever of subsiding. Clearly what she'd heard about him and Sophia in Athens had been festering inside her for a while. If, as she'd said, Dianne Arnold had told her about it two weeks previously that was obviously why she had avoided meeting David during that first week he'd been back.

"Not really? What does that mean, David? How do you not really sleep with someone?" She was antagonistically mocking him. "Either you did or you didn't? Who was it? A tourist or a worker here, someone still working here?"

She was rattling off the questions like a machine gun, spitting them out from close up. now straight into his face.

"It means what I said, no I didn't. Obviously I met a few women here then. Had a few conversations, went for some dinners and drinks, and yes, I guess there was some flirting."

He rubbed his chin with two fingers of his right hand as he looked away from her briefly before continuing.

"In LBN or the Lindian House, or outside Pal's, anyone of those at different times maybe. I can't remember exactly, but no, I never slept with anyone. I think I'd remember that. In any case this is crazy, Alice. Why should I have to explain myself for some things that happened almost two years ago, before I even knew you, or more accurately, some things that didn't happen?"

She never responded, merely gave him a sceptical glance. Could she believe him about anything now after Sophia and his Athens visit?

There were a few more awkward moments of silence before he asked, "So, what about you? If we're going to get skeletons out of the cupboard what about Simon Chapel, not exactly

253

someone with a great reputation here? You skirted over that just now. That's why he was such a prat in Arches that night last summer wasn't it, because you'd slept with him?"

"Well, so what? What's your bloody problem? I thought you didn't do jealousy? It was once, bloody once. I was pissed and it was a mistake, a big, big mistake. He just sodding kept coming back every time he got pissed, wanting more. I told him to piss off every time after that one time. A bloody one night mistake, that's all it was."

She was shouting at him again. He waited a few seconds as they both sat in silence again. He was thinking it was interesting that she was so defensive about it; so bothered over what David thought about it, how upset he'd been over it.

He tried to calm things down, lighten things a little.

"Seems Dianne's had a busy late summer and winter telling me about you and Simon Chapel, as well as you about me in Athens."

She ignored that and went back to staring out across the bay in silence.

Unfortunately though, he couldn't leave it at that. He made what turned out to be another stupid remark in response to something she'd just said. Now it was his turn to display an edge of annoyance in his voice.

"Hmm ... jealousy, that's an interesting comment from you, but you're right I did tell you last summer that I didn't do jealousy. Have I got something to be jealous about though? Like over you and the guy from the yacht?"

Her face quickly grew bright crimson with anger as she turned to shout straight into his, "I told you nothing fucking happened. I never bloody slept with him."

She stopped for a second or two, glared at him with her face full of contempt, and added, "Oh, what's the point, fuck off, just fuck off, David!"

He didn't though. He couldn't bring himself to leave it at that.

"But, I just-"

"Look," she interrupted, "if you must know he has a few restaurants in places across England and he told me that if I

254

ever went back there and wanted a job to let him know. That's why he gave me his sodding business card that night in Glow. Okay, yes, he also wanted me to go for lunch on their yacht as well, but I bloody didn't, and was never going to. Credit me with more sense than that at least. That's all. I never even phoned or texted him. Haven't heard from him since. Why would I?"

She pounded every word of that out to him, like she was hammering in an obstinate resistant nail. His response was only one of silence, together with a slight nod of the head to hopefully show he understood and believed her.

They'd shared quite a few Lindos sunrises the previous summer after long nights of drinking, clubbing and talking, often finished off wearily in the bright sunlight of the new dawn with a slice of pizza from Nikos by the tree in the little square in the centre of the village. This though had been a completely different experience of a Lindos sunrise. Instead of the calm, relaxed but tired conversations between them of the previous summer's sunrises, this time they'd argued over each other's indiscretions, sometimes loudly, on the bench in the Main Square against the background of the atmospheric pale Lindos March sunrise.

The silent tension between them now was palpable. It was so thick in the night air it would have needed a very sharp knife to cut through it. The interminable silences were becoming excruciatingly long as they both continued to stare ahead into the distance of the gradually lightening bay.

However, Alice wasn't finished. He misread her silence once again, assuming that she'd calmed down and still wanted to try to work something out between them. He thought he would try to push that along by apologising for doubting her about sleeping with the yacht guy. He was wrong.

"Sorry again," he started to say, "I just thought, wrongly obviously, that with the guy from the yacht-"

She didn't let him finish. She had obviously still been dwelling on him and Athens. It was festering inside her and then burst out. She screamed at him loudly again, "Don't be a fucking hypocritical dick! You were angry over what Dianne told you about me and Simon bloody Chapel, a bloody one night stand, a fucking meaningless one night stand. But instead of talking to me about it you scurried off like some spoilt brat to Athens to fuck the Russian. So, what was it some sort of revenge fuck? Good was it? Hope it was worth it? Was it? Was it?"

Small traces of single tears trickled down both her cheeks, the result of a mixture of anger and disappointment. David sat there not having any idea what to say, how to answer? It was now becoming increasingly obvious to him that she cared about what he'd done, about him, a lot more than he thought back then, back in October when he'd stupidly decided to go to Athens to see Sophia. She wouldn't let on back then, wouldn't go so far as to tell him that, how much she cared about him. Although he did recall that unexpected moment outside Café Melia a few days before he left when she asked him to stay in Lindos with her for the winter. However, when he replied he couldn't she didn't appear that bothered. He clearly misread that as well. That was Alice Palmer though. Once she'd taken a chance in exposing her feelings, even the smallest one, she would retreat into her defensive shell again if she didn't get the response she'd hoped for. After that she would get angry with herself for laying herself open to rejection.

He stammered, as he struggled to answer her question, his voice virtually echoing with a plea to her for some sort of leniency, some sort of understanding.

"No ... no ... it wasn't ... it wasn't good. It really wasn't. But okay, yes, I guess it was some sort of meaningless revenge fuck. I thought-"

She didn't allow him to finish. "That's just it though, David, isn't it. You never thought at all did you? Your dick did your thinking for you!"

Her anger wasn't dissipating one iota.

He sighed heavily. All he could do was respond quietly with, "I guess so."

He returned to staring out across the bay in silence for a few seconds before trying to finish telling her in a low, regretful voice what he previously attempted to say.

"Look, Alice, I just thought that you and me ... well, that there was no future in anything between you and me. You didn't seem interested in anything serious. That's how it seemed to me. Every time it looked as though that was what was developing you ran away, not just physically, but emotionally. To me it seemed like you were scared of something, scared to commit. Perhaps that was because of what happened to you in the past, with your ex-husband, and I can understand that? I don't know, but that's what it seemed like to me, that it was pointless, hopeless. I tried, god knows I tried, all summer, and I tried to tell you a few times how I felt, but you seemed frightened of any sort of meaningful commitment, even avoided talking about it. I know it's not an excuse, but I'm just telling you how I felt, what I thought was or wasn't happening between us, that's all."

She turned her head towards him once again, wiped away the traces of the tears on her cheeks with her hand, and told him, "It was good last summer. It was good between us, wasn't it? You know it was."

Her voice was breaking up with emotion as she continued. "Those couple of times, the sex, it was good. I know it was. You know it was. It was special. Don't get me wrong, it was. But it was always me who initiated it, and in fact I felt I was getting mixed messages from you because you seemed so reluctant. It was, wasn't it, the sex? Good, I mean?"

It seemed she was calmly seeking some sort of reassurance. However, she didn't wait for him to answer. He would have only agreed anyway.

He thought he detected the faintest reconciliatory slight smile from her as she told him, "At times we've all made mistakes, I suppose. Me with Simon was just one of those. A one night stand, that's all. We've all had those here. Maybe you too, but I don't care about those now. I know I asked you earlier if you had, but I was angry that's all. Even if you had I wouldn't care now, shouldn't care now. That was in the past, before we even knew each other. It's about trust, trust since we first met, and you know that's a big thing with me."

257

She stopped speaking for a few seconds and wiped away some the last remaining traces of her tears.

She sighed heavily, a resigned sigh, before telling him, "I guess I knew it was a mistake to go any further with what we had between us, to go any further than being just very good friends. I was afraid of precisely this, that somehow everything would eventually be spoilt, messed up. I should have stuck to my 'friends, very good friends' thing and known that taking a chance and wanting more would end in a disaster."

He wasn't as resigned to that as she was, however. He wasn't prepared to give up on them that easily.

"But why should it be like that? You made a mistake and-"

He just made another bloody mistake right there. He shouldn't have started with her mistake.

She glared at him again, causing him to stop what he was saying. He could see that anger was again growing in her eyes.

In response he quickly changed what he was trying to say, going to say. "Okay, I made a mistake. It was a stupid thing for me to do and I regret it, but-"

He'd dug a hole for himself once again, opened it up again, and was firmly back in it. Just a few moments ago he'd almost clambered out of it.

"I just don't understand why you didn't ask me about it before, that one night, me with Simon?" she interrupted. "Why now? He's not even here anymore. What did you think ... I mean why-"

He took a deep breath and interrupted her confusion.

"Anyone can have sex with anybody if they want, Alice. We're all grown-ups. Well, most of us are I like to think. That can happen here in a holiday village as much as anywhere, if not more so. I sometimes think Lindos is perfectly set up for it, what with all the tourists coming and going every week or two. It's perfect. No need or expectation of ongoing commitment once the one or two week holiday is over. I just happen to think there's more to life, and particularly relationships, than that. Eventually people need a little more, don't you think? More than a few screws over a couple of weeks?"

258

He didn't let her answer. Perhaps he didn't really want her to.

"For me, sex with anybody, lots of people, I mean lots of women, and yes there have been a few for me over time, doesn't come close at all to, can't compare to, connecting with one special person. I've come to realise all that over the years. Yes, of course the sex with that one special person should be good too, but I hope, happen to think, it is precisely that, bloody good, because there is more that connects me to them. And it was with you, was bloody good. Anyway, that's what I thought."

He paused for a few seconds while she continued to sit in silence alongside him, just offering him a very brief sideways glance for one moment. Her face was emotionless now.

He continued, "Perhaps that's sort of old fashioned these days. Who knows? I hope not. But that's the way I felt about you and me, through most of last summer. I know there was that time when you were drunk, very drunk, and I'd had a few drinks too, but wasn't anywhere near as drunk as you, and you wanted us to go to bed for sex, or at least wanted me to stay over with you. But, if you remember, maybe you were too drunk to remember, but I told you at the time, "No, not like that, not while you're so drunk." I wanted us to both be sober. That might seem crazy to you, and I remember you weren't very happy about it, but that's how I felt and what I wanted. So ..."

His voice tailed off. She nodded silently. A dark veil descended over her face, a mixture of confusion and disappointment. The brightness now of the early morning sun wasn't being mirrored in Alice Palmer's mood. She was totally despondent, and a long way from living the dream.

He should have simply remained silent now and given her some time to think about what had happened, what he'd just said. He certainly shouldn't have told her what he said next. God knows why he felt compelled to. What definitely wasn't the right thing to do at that moment was to appear to pick holes in her character. Alice Palmer didn't respond well to that sort of thing at the best of times. And this was certainly not one of

259

those, quite the contrary. He'd just laid bare to her his feelings about what happened between them last summer. He should have left it at that and waited for her response; given her time and wait to see what she said. But it wasn't in David Alexander's nature to leave things hanging. He always had to try and get things straight and sorted, had to push things, very often too hard and too much. This time it had disastrous consequences for what he really wanted. Yet again he got it all wrong.

Maybe it was her continuing silence over what he'd just told her that prompted him to unwisely tell her, "You know, Alice, you listen, but you don't process the words."

Her expression changed immediately. Unfortunately he was clearly oblivious to it and ploughed on regardless.

"You choose not to, because of the barrier you put up, seem to need to put up, between you and people who like you, even love you."

The last two words weren't words you used easily with Alice Palmer, let alone going on about barriers in her character. The crimson raging glare returned as she turned her head towards him. She looked as if she could have stabbed him there and then, with a fork or whatever was to hand. Luckily for him none were. All he got was the sharp edge of her tongue.

"Fuck off, David, just fuck off," she told him again. "I don't need some sort of amateur psychoanalysis session from you thank you. Just take bloody responsibility for what you did, what you did in Athens. There, is that enough words for you that I've processed?"

He was stunned. He'd messed up in a big way, and he didn't just mean in going to Athens. He'd tried to make things better between them. At one point he thought he had. But now he'd just made it worse again.

They sat in silence for a long half-minute. He thought it best to say nothing for now. He had no idea what was going through her mind or what would come next. He soon found out.

People were crossing the square now behind them. Locals on their way to open up their shops and cafes as the morning wore on. Some of them looked over on hearing Alice's raised voice again.

"And by the way, while you're weighing up what we both did and trying to equal them out, balance them out, or whatever way you want to put it, our mistakes, I bloody slept with Simon on that one disastrous night early in the season last summer, which was months before we slept together, had sex together, you and me. At that time you and me were just friends, very good friends, remember? I should have kept it that way."

She jabbed her index finger into his shoulder as she went on, "According to Marianthi you stayed with the Russian woman for three nights in Athens in October, which was after we'd slept together, had sex together a few weeks before, and not bloody 'before us', as you put it earlier. So, what was that, three night's sex? And after, not 'before us'? Not very equal or fucking balanced is it?"

"I-"

He tried to say something. He hadn't the faintest idea what it was going to be, but he never got the chance. She was determined not to let him say anything more.

"So, it is all about trust, David."

She had lowered her voice and at least was no longer shouting at him as she added that last sentence. However, the anger was clearly still charging through her body, as well as her mind.

She stood up, leaned down to glare directly into his face yet again, and then told him, "Pythagoras got it bloody right with his sodding cup."

With that she stormed off towards the alley in the corner at the far side of the square.

He knew that it was all about trust for Alice. She'd made that pretty plain to him at various times the previous summer. Now she knew he'd betrayed her trust, at the very point at the end of last summer when it appeared - from what she'd just told him earlier on that eventful evening and early morning - she was starting to be prepared to take things further with him. That was why she'd asked him last October to stay in Lindos with

261

her for the winter. That was obvious to him now. If only it had been so obvious to him last October.

She'd even trusted him enough to share her secret with him of being on probation in the U.K. and not being supposed to leave the country, as well as about the murder she saw in the Lindos top alley one night back in the summer of 2016.

Of course, on that same August afternoon in Rhodes Town he'd shared his secret with her about passing MI6 contact details onto a Russian woman at a conference in Moscow so she could defect. Although, he'd convinced himself that for obvious reasons concerning Sophia's security and her new identity he hadn't shared with Alice the fact that the woman at the conference and the Sophia he'd slept with in Athens were the same person. He told himself he couldn't, daren't, even if he'd wanted to.

A few weeks before he returned to Lindos though, he'd been instructed to do something that amounted to a much greater and darker secret than that; one which he definitely couldn't share with Alice.

After that night, or more accurately early morning, on the bench in the square she avoided him, wouldn't even talk to him on the phone or return his texts. Every time he called it went to voicemail. He left a couple of messages saying he really needed to talk to her, but she obviously ignored them. The restaurant she worked in hadn't opened for the season yet so he couldn't go and see her there, and somehow even in such a small village he never bumped into her. He went round to her apartment a couple of times and banged on the door, calling out her name, but there was no answer. He had no idea if she was in there or not and was simply refusing to answer the door to him. He asked a few of the locals in the village if they'd seen her, including the woman he got to know quite well who ran one of the supermarkets near his flat which he used regularly and that he knew Alice used, but no one said they had seen her. He started to think that perhaps she'd left Lindos?

He despaired. How could he have been so stupid as to do what he did by going to Athens? If she was still in the village then surely in a few weeks as the season started he would see her. The restaurant where she worked would be opening up, and if nothing else he could go and find her there.

Then David Alexander's world, and everyone's world, got much, much worse, changed dramatically. His despair and frustration over Alice paled into insignificance in comparison. On the twenty-third of March the Greek government announced a full national lockdown in response to the Coronavirus pandemic that had spread to Greece, including to the island.

20

Lockdown

At first after the twenty-third of March there was nothing, only the short trip to one of the small supermarkets in the village that were allowed to open in order to get what he needed while wearing a mask and with social distancing. The village was deserted, a collection of deserted white walled alleyways and boarded up shops, restaurants and bars. Even with the warmth of the spring sunshine it felt bleak and desolate, reminiscent of an English seaside town in the depth of winter, and yet somehow managing to seem even sadder than that because of the warm sunshine. It was a time of year in the village that should have been full of optimistic expectancy and anticipation of the coming summer tourist season. Normally there would have been plenty of busy activity as the shopkeepers, as well as the bar and restaurant owners, prepared their properties for the forthcoming season due to start in early to mid-April, depending on the calendar of the Greek Orthodox Easter. The outer and inner walls of some of the shops, bars and restaurants would be being given a new coat of paint and any exposed woodwork spruced up. With lockdown they all remained closed following their usual winter shutdown. The village was quiet, calm and mostly deserted. With the government lockdown announcement there was to be no start of the 2020 tourist season in Lindos or anywhere in Greece at the usual time.

The Coronavirus, Covid-19, originated in China before Christmas. David had seen some reports on it in the news before he left the U.K. to return to Lindos at the start of March. Nobody in the U.K. appeared to be taking it that seriously. There was certainly no indication of the pandemic that was to quickly sweep the globe, resulting in millions of deaths.

The first case in Greece was confirmed on the 26th of February 2020 when a 38-year-old woman from Thessaloniki, who had recently visited northern Italy, was confirmed to be infected. Subsequent confirmed cases in late February and early March also related to people who had travelled to Italy, as well as a group of pilgrims who had travelled to Israel and Egypt. The first death from the virus in Greece was a 66-year-old man, who died on the 12th of March.

Following the confirmation of the first three cases in Greece all carnival events in the country were cancelled at the end of February. Health and state authorities issued precautionary guidelines and recommendations, while measures up to early March were taken locally and included the closure of schools and the suspension of cultural events in the affected areas. On the 10th of March, with eighty-nine confirmed cases, but as yet no deaths in the country, the Greek government decided to suspend the operation of educational institutions of all levels nationwide. Then, on the 13th of March the government closed down all cafes, bars, museums, shopping centres, sports facilities and restaurants in the country. On the 16th of March, all retail shops were also closed and all services in all areas of religious worship of any religion were suspended.

The countrywide complete lockdown announced to take effect from the 23rd of March placed restrictions on all non-essential movement throughout the country. From that date movement outside your place of residence was only permitted for things such as going to or from a workplace, going to a pharmacy or a doctor, going to a food store such as a supermarket, or exercising locally, including taking a dog for a walk. Even in those cases people leaving their homes were required to carry their police ID or passport, as well as a signed confirmation in which the purpose or category of travel was stated. The police were empowered to enforce the restrictions and could issue fines for each offence. The regulations were to be reviewed on a couple of dates in April.

For David, isolated in his flat with no internet connection, and consequently without even access to U.K. radio or press for news, it took a couple of days to fully obtain details of the extent of the lockdown regulations in Greece. The woman serving in the little supermarket he used regularly near his flat told him initially about the lockdown. The Greek government actually announced it on Sunday 22nd of March, to come into effect from the next day. By chance he happened to go into the supermarket early that evening to get some milk. That was when the woman told him about it, although she didn't have all the details. Consequently, he had to call his eldest son and ask him to find the details of the Greek lockdown regulations on the internet and then text the gist of them to him. That was just one of the unforeseen difficulties of finding himself in a countrywide lockdown situation in a foreign country and with no access to the internet.

Most of the Brit summer season workers in the village hadn't arrived at the time the lockdown was imposed. Now they weren't likely to any time soon. They weren't allowed to under the regulations, and also weren't allowed to travel anyway through restrictions introduced by the U.K. government shortly after. Only a handful was around, those like Alice who had stayed in Lindos through the winter.

Both David and Alice found themselves stuck in Lindos at the start of the Greek lockdown with nothing open except two of the small supermarkets, but none of the bars. The Greek government acted swiftly in imposing full lockdown measures and that appeared to initially pay off. The number of cases and deaths in Greece was relatively low compared to other countries in Europe such as Italy initially, and later the U.K. It wasn't easy to get access to accurate information without the internet, but again the woman serving in the supermarket told David that cases on Rhodes were very low. She said there had only been four at that time, shortly after the lockdown started. How accurate that was he had no idea or way of checking. Being an island, however, it seemed logical that it would be easier to control the spread of the virus, as was the case on most of the other Greek islands. At that time there weren't that many tourists arriving on Rhodes as the season hadn't started, and now with the restrictions there wouldn't be any. Consequently, that source of any possible spread of the virus had seemingly been averted.

It was quickly clear that no one had any idea just when the 2020 summer season might begin in Lindos and across Greece, as well as most of southern Europe, if it ever would. The virus was in control of the holiday calendar now, and politicians and governments, including the Greek one, were battling to stay ahead of its effect. When the masses of summer tourists might be allowed to arrive was really anyone's guess. The island of Rhodes may not have been too badly affected in terms of the number of cases of the virus, but cases in the countries from where most of the tourists to the island came from were soon increasing rapidly, especially Britain. Also, on the Greek mainland the number of cases quickly began to grow, particularly in Athens.

Occasionally on his way to the supermarket in the first couple of weeks of the lockdown David came across one of the bar or restaurant owners in the village as they were going to, or coming from, their premises to check all was okay with them. When he engaged them briefly in conversation while social distancing they all told him the same thing; that they had no idea when the season might get underway. They were all downbeat and full of pessimism, with no expectations whatsoever that it might actually ever do so. All of them were resigned to the sad anticipation that the 2020 season would be a write off. Aside from those brief encounters and conversations the only sound in the village he experienced was ones of echoing emptiness.

Usually at this time in the four years Alice Palmer had been living and working in Lindos she would be starting work at the restaurant. Not serving customers yet, but helping the owner and his wife get things ready and set up for the coming season, and for when the first tourists would start to arrive in early to mid-April. This year the restaurant wouldn't be opening in April and nobody really quite knew when it would. Consequently, there was no work for her, and that meant she wasn't getting paid. Through the winter months from November until March she usually lived on her savings from the summer season. She was careful, and budgeted that way through the summer. Even though her wages were hardly excessive, she lived on some of that during those busy months and saved her tips as extra for the winter when there was no work. Because she was good at her job, always chatty and friendly in the restaurant, the customers, the tourists, liked her, and gave her some good tips, helping her through the winter. In addition, there were hardly any bars open in which to go and drink and spend money in Lindos in the winter, and certainly no clubs open for long late nights and early mornings. There was only the Red Rose Bar in the centre of the village, where some of the locals mostly congregated during the day and evenings to play cards or backgammon, as well as the Lindos Ice Bar up at the top of one of the hills out of the village. The winter clientele there was also mostly local Greeks in the evenings, with some Brit ex-pats occasionally who had stayed for the winter, or those who now lived in or near the village. This year the characteristics of the quieter winter period had been extended by the lockdown, and enhanced somewhat. Not even those two bars were allowed to be open during lockdown.

At times in the first week or two of the lockdown it felt as though the village itself was sad, as though its feelings were hurt from missing the usual hordes of tourists. As exercising outside was allowed as long as it was near where you lived, to relieve the boredom and get some fresh air Alice walked down to the Main Beach on a few days, then slowly along it a couple of times, sometimes more. It was odd, strange, with no one there except her. In summer it would usually be filled with multiple sun beds, parasols and lots of tourists, as well as multitudes of tourists having lunch or a late breakfast in the restaurants and cafes at the back of the beach. Now there was no one, and the restaurants and cafes were all sporting their winter shutters. With no idea about an end in sight to the pandemic, strolling along the empty beach clutching her flat espadrilles in hand and occasionally dipping her feet into the chilling sea she wondered if there would be anyone at all that summer on the Lindos beaches. How would Lindos, its tourist businesses, and its people survive?

As she walked on the Main Beach on one day in those first couple of weeks even the usually calm clear sea in Lindos Bay appeared agitated, as if it was in sympathy with the village and its people over the unknown and unpredictable turmoil looming over it and them in the coming months. The waves appeared angry, rhythmically crashing onto the deserted beach as she watched the dark foreboding storm clouds of that particular day gathering overhead. It was a forlorn vision in such a usually beautiful and happy place. Perhaps one that reflected the impending turmoil about to engulf not only Lindos and its residents - including the bars, restaurants and shop owners - but the whole of Greece and far beyond? Initially, that's how the scene before her on registered with her. Or did the angry waves and the uncertainty of the gathering dark storm clouds overhead merely also represent the turmoil and doubt within her over her supposed relationship with David? Although, she did feel that her anger over what he'd done in Athens had actually subsided somewhat. It had been a few weeks since their argument on the bench in the square. Meanwhile she had avoided any contact with him. She dwelt on that for almost an hour as she meandered back and forth along the deserted beach. The surroundings of the usually vibrant, hot Lindos beach were abandoned and empty. It seemed a far cry from living the dream now. Despite that it was somehow still beautiful in its stark, dramatic emptiness, framed by the rough sea in the bay and the dark clouds overhead. There were plenty of worse places to be in the world right now, and plenty other things to be angry about rather than what David Alexander had done the previous October.

Perhaps the visits to the Main Beach with its quiet emptiness, as well as the loneliness of the lockdown, mellowed her in terms of her anger with him, but after a couple of weeks she decided she needed a friend. She needed someone to talk to, even if only on the phone, someone to get some support from through the lockdown and its accompanying boredom. That turned out to be David. In reality, he was virtually the only option. Who else could she turn to? Anyway, that's what she convinced herself. In fact, there were one or two others, including Dianne Arnold. She knew Dianne would be supportive, but she also guessed she would press Alice about David, going over and over what she knew about his Athens visit. She decided she couldn't face that right now, not with anyone except him.

He was surprised when she called. After leaving plenty of voice messages and sending numerous texts in the weeks after their argument, as well as before and after the start of the lockdown, all with no response, he'd almost given up. He began to think she must have left the village. Everyone he'd asked before the lockdown said they hadn't seen her.

At first when she called her voice was tentative, simply asking how he was, how he was surviving the lockdown. He asked her the same after he told her he was okay and was trying to use the time for some editing he had to do to the second draft of his novel. She said that she obviously had no work as the restaurant hadn't even begun to prepare for the season when the lockdown was imposed. Then she told him about her walks to the Main Beach and how strange it all felt down there.

He noticed quite quickly that she seemed determined to avoid any conversation about their argument on the bench in the Main Square. He was relieved, and certainly wasn't going to raise it.

Basically, they both realised that in the circumstances they only had each other. Not physically because of the lockdown, but in terms of communication verbally by phone. Even Skype or FaceTime between them wasn't possible as neither of them had an internet connection or access to Wi-Fi in their accommodation, and of course none of the bars and cafes that had it were open. The lockdown was draining, physically tiring, tedious in an empty small tourist village like Lindos. It had to be so, of course, but the usual winter emptiness of the place in terms of people and tourists had been stretched by another few months at least. The spring sunshine brought only some slight relief. For David, and he hoped for her, it was additionally emotionally frustrating not being able to meet inside, not being supposed to even touch each other.

After six weeks of lockdown, starting from the 4th of May Greece began to gradually lift some restrictions on movement and to restart business activity.

After that date they did meet a few times, always outside. Neither of them was really completely sure of the rules of lockdown, so they initially agreed that any meeting or contact should be minimal, as that was what they at least believed was allowed. Usually they went for a walk down to one or other of the deserted beaches, Pallas, the Main beach or St. Paul's. Initially it seemed there was still some lingering tension between them just below the surface over their indiscretions the previous summer and autumn. Just like the Main Beach on Alice's walks during the full lockdown all of the beaches looked odd without their large numbers of sunbeds and umbrellas and the multitudes of tourists. They sat on the sand and talked for an hour or more, usually about what they had heard about the news from the U.K. or what they had heard from locals occasionally in the village about the situation on Rhodes or in Greece generally. They studiously avoided any talk of their argument and previous indiscretions. Always when they were walking or sitting on the beach they kept socially distanced, one-and-a-half or two metres apart roughly. Although, he desperately wanted to touch her, grab hold of her hand, hug her and kiss her.

One day on St. Paul's while they were talking about, and recalling, the August afternoon they had spent down there together the previous summer, as well as how much they laughed at the nearby Russian tourist guy's tight swim shorts, she reached over to take David's hand. He knew that because of the Covid regulations and social distancing strictly he shouldn't, but he took it and squeezed it as they exchanged a smile. He simply couldn't resist doing so any longer.

"I'm glad you're here," she told him. "I know we shouldn't do anything more, but I just wanted to touch you, hold your hand if nothing else is possible. I'm happy you came back. I really don't know what I would have done if you hadn't, if I had been here alone through all this craziness, the lockdown and the pandemic."

He watched her closely, never taking his eyes off her, as she told him that with her eyes firmly fixed on his face. He could hear the concoction of emotions of agony, frustration, yet also happiness in her voice, and see it plainly on her face and in her eyes.

He nodded slightly and allowed a small smile of satisfaction to grow across his lips as he replied, "Me too, I'm glad I came back, and that I'm here with you."

She squeezed his hand as he told her that, and then let out a small chuckle.

"What's funny," he asked?

"Oh, silly really, but according to all the books and movies a woman is supposed to come to a Greek island to meet a Greek man, not an English one. Clearly I never read the script."

He smiled as he replied simply, "Clearly."

What he was actually thinking was if that was an optimistic sign? Maybe all the anger of the previous summer and autumn was behind them, paled into insignificance by the effects of the pandemic and the events in the wider world.

They sat in silence for half-an-hour, grasping hands and gazing out into the empty bay with two small fishing boats anchored in the shallow water bobbing up and down very slightly with the movement of the sea. Moored at the jetty below the small picturesque Greek Orthodox chapel was a slightly larger tourist boat, originally moored for the winter, but obviously remaining there because of the lockdown.

Despite all the craziness and sadness that was happening in the pandemic stricken wider world, for those few hours of that peaceful St. Paul's bay afternoon in the early May pale sunlight all was silent and calm around them. The only low sound was the crystal clear sea lapping gently on the shore at the edge of the beach. Stretched out before them was the view of the high rocks on either side of the entrance to the bay from the open sea with a few birds swooping between those and the water of the bay below. For a few moments, those few hours together, they were completely detached from the madness of the pandemic, cocooned from it within their own company, as well as by the beauty and solitude of the deserted St. Paul's bay. The panorama of the beautiful bay and the tranquillity all around them felt light years away from the Covid pandemic madness and tragedy engulfing the world.

It wasn't only David and Alice, and any relationship they may have had, that suffered during the weeks and months of the various stages of the lockdown. They were starved of company of course, deprived of being drinking buddies and possibly more, but so were many people in the village. Most of all though David felt starved of her, her company, her smile, even her defensive aggression. Despite the long days of continuous sunshine for most of the lockdown he felt they were in a constant cloak of frustrating darkness as far as their relationship was concerned. It was a darkness that felt never ending; a bleak unremitting darkness in a beautiful picturesque place, Lindos. The lockdown meant he was further away than ever from resolving their relationship; getting the time and opportunity to explore how she really felt about him.

His writing, or rather his editing based on his editor's suggestions, along with books and reading, were his only brief glimmer of light, his only refuge from the frustration of initially not being able to see her. There were half-a-dozen paperbacks that had been abandoned and left in the flat that he was renting by tourists from previous summers. There was nothing greatly interesting amongst them, except for a dog-eared paperback copy of Dickens' 'A Tale of Two Cities', which he'd already read, but now re-read. It began with the line, "It was the best of times, it was the worst of times ..." With the Covid pandemic this certainly didn't feel at all like anything resembling, "the best of times," though.

His lockdown consisted of writing, reading, and talking to Alice on the phone often after she made that initial call to him. His only other very brief conversations through those lockdown months were through their obligatory Covid masks with the woman working in the nearby small supermarket as he shopped for provisions. So, the initial few weeks of the full lockdown only became bearable for him in his small flat through his writing and reading. Then his frustration at not being able to see Alice was alleviated a little through their telephone conversations after she called him. Finally, after the 4th of May, he got to see her again.

21

End of lockdown

Although some lockdown restrictions on movement and business activity were removed from the 4th of May the changes were limited. All commercial flights to and from Italy, Spain, Turkey, the United Kingdom and the Netherlands remained suspended until the 1st of June. Therefore, in early June there were still no tourists. However, there was a more optimistic atmosphere in the village as the shop, bar and restaurant owners began to prepare their premises for an anticipated opening for tourists returning in a few weeks, or maybe a month. Restrictions on entry to Greece for international travellers were finally lifted in mid-June and entry restrictions on British tourists were set to expire on the 15th of July. Passengers arriving from countries with high infection rates were required to take a test and agree to a two week quarantine. Passengers from lower risk countries were to be tested at random at arrival airports having registered on a Greek government website prior to arrival, including with an address for their stay in Greece, but did not face a mandatory quarantine period. Masks and social distancing whilst travelling, however, as well as in shops, including supermarkets, were mandatory.

Slowly the village came to life. Some shops opened up first, then gradually a few bars, cafes and restaurants as some of the tourists started to appear by the middle of June, although not yet from the U.K. As some of the cafes opened David and Alice met for coffee at Giorgos and Café Melia, in addition their walks to the beaches.

One afternoon in the middle of June when they were at St. Paul's Alice informed him she was supposed to be starting work back at the restaurant the next week. He was puzzled when she added that she wasn't sure about it now, whether she wanted to. She seemed vague and uncertain about it. There was no sign at all of the spark of her living the dream that had often been so visible in the past.

Before he could ask her why she wasn't sure she went on to talk about their walks to St. Paul's together during the earlier part of lockdown, how deserted it was and peaceful. How they talked about what a different world it was with all the madness of the pandemic going on. Then completely out of the blue she asked if he ever found out the truth about why MI6 wanted the Russian woman from the Moscow conference to defect.

"That afternoon in Rhodes Town you said that you thought there was more to her activities than just some academic expertise that they wanted, MI6. Did you ever find out what that was?"

He was sure that Alice had no idea that it was the same woman who she knew he'd visited in Athens, Sophia, but he really didn't want to take a chance of opening up that can of worms again just in case he made some mistake revealing that she was.

He simply shrugged his shoulders and told her, "No, I thought it best that I didn't know anyway."

Her questions and conversation appeared to be zigzagging all over the place now. Why was she digging around in all that again? Her next question suggested she appeared obsessed with it, especially his comments about MI6. Perhaps she still had concerns about the Irish woman she saw commit the murder and wanted reassuring?

"Yeah, I guess so." She waited a few seconds, then added, "When I told you that afternoon in Rhodes Town about seeing the Irish woman kill that guy and that I heard something between them about MI6 you told me I shouldn't worry about the woman finding out I'd witnessed it and coming back to kill me because MI6 would have killed her by now."

"Did I actually say that? I can't remember exactly what I said now."

"Yes, I'm sure that's what you told me. How come you know so much about MI6 David, so much as to be able to make a comment like that?"

She looked at him with suspicion written all over her face.

"Why would you think I do? Even if I did say that, and I really can't remember I did, it was just an assumption, I suppose. I don't really know. How could I? I was just trying to put you at ease I guess, help your peace of mind that's all."

Despite his attempt to dismiss it and make light of it, seeds of doubt were still swirling around in her mind. She simply wasn't totally convinced by his explanation by any means. Was this another secret of his? Were there yet more secrets that he wasn't telling her; more things that would undermine her trust in him?

During the next couple of times that they met for coffee he could sense that her unease at his explanation over his MI6 comment hadn't gone away. She became more insular and detached, even while they chatted over some of the more mundane daily occurrences in the village as it started to emerge from the lockdown.

He decided he would tell her a little more, needed to, but not in such a public place as one of the cafes or even one of the beaches, that were now starting to get more tourists using them. He suggested that they go for a walk up to the monument on the hill above the northern end of Lindos Main Beach one morning, before the sun got too hot. There wouldn't be many people around up there, if any. The monument was a stone shrine dedicated to Ioanni Zigdi, a Greek politician who was born in Lindos in 1913. He told Alice that he'd never been up there, but always wanted to as he'd heard it had great views over the Main Beach and the village, and it was only a short walk up the hill.

"Why not, I've never been either. It'll make a change from St. Paul's and the Main Beach," she agreed.

Although it wasn't yet noon when they got up there it was still quite hot under the mid-June sun. They sat for a while drinking from their small bottles of water while looking at the stunning panorama of the village and Main Beach below. His assumption was correct. There was no one else around, just the two of them. For a while they chatted about the beautiful view

277

and being lucky to be in Lindos. He waited and then picked his moment.

"You know you asked about me and MI6, how I knew so much about them. Well, to be honest, there is more. There is a little more I can tell you, a little more I think I should tell you, want to tell you."

She turned away from looking at the view to face him. Her face was blank, expressionless. She said nothing. Silently she was thinking she knew that there must be more. Perhaps he was about to redeem himself, and her trust in him.

"After I did what they wanted and passed their contact details onto the Russian woman at the conference MI6 did try to formally recruit me to their Russian Department, Russian Desk they called it. They said it was because of my academic Russian background and all that stuff, my expertise on Russia. But I turned them down, told them no. It definitely wasn't something I wanted to get into. I never signed anything, nothing like the Official Secrets Act or anything. The guy from MI6 who approached me to pass the contact details on to the woman at the conference only asked me verbally. He said it was off the record and asked if I would be interested in working for them officially at Thames House, MI6 headquarters in London.

When I told him no he said that was okay and that the conversation had never happened as far as he and MI6 were concerned. I'm actually not clear, or sure, if I should be telling you this, Alice, Official Secrets Act and all that, even though I never signed anything. It never got that far, just the one brief conversation. That's why I never told you all of it before."

She wasn't sure whether to be relieved over what he'd finally told her, or disappointed and angry that he hadn't told her before. Somewhere deep in the back of her mind she couldn't help wondering if there was even more he wasn't telling her, which there was, of course.

Her face betrayed her confusion.

"I see, and is there more, David?"

"More?"

"Yes, what I asked you about before at St. Paul's. Do you actually know more about what happened to the Russian woman who defected?"

He did. He knew quite a lot about what happened to Sophia, of course, but he wasn't about to tell her all of it. He hesitated slightly as he began to tell her. He was figuring out just how much he could tell her, how much he should tell her. Above all he wanted to make sure she never connected the woman at the conference as being the same woman as Sophia.

"Yes ... err ... well, yes and no really. I don't know what happened to her after she defected. They, at MI6, wouldn't have let on to anyone about that as I guess they would have given her a new identity and a new life. Not that I was in any position to, but it would have been pointless asking, plus I wasn't really bothered. Why should I have been? She was nothing to me. I was just asked, told, to deliver a message to her with the contact details so she could defect."

Was he being a bit too defensive on that last point, protesting a little too much he wondered? Alice simply stared at him, listening in silence. He ploughed on, hoping what he was going to tell her next would distract her from dwelling too much, if at all, on the new identity stuff.

"I did have that conversation with the guy from MI6 after she defected though. It was the same conversation in which he asked me to go and work in their Russian department. I don't know if he should have told me, but I asked him why they wanted the Russian woman to defect. Was it because of her academic stuff or more? I didn't expect him to tell me. I was surprised when he did."

"And what was it for?"

He bit his top lip and his face contorted slightly into a frown.

"She gave MI6 a list of names. Apparently some of them were in the Russian Secret Service who she knew would defect. Some of them were in Russia, but some were spies in the U.K. My MI6 contact guy told me that the ones in Russia would be worked on and encouraged to, helped to defect. But he also said that some of the ones in the U.K. already, the spies who they knew would never defect, would likely be eliminated."

He looked her straight in the eyes as he added, "Killed."

He could see straightaway she was shocked. Her mouth was half open and it was all over her face. She thought he might have been holding something back from her, but she had no idea it would be something like that.

He tried to respond instantly to her obvious shock by telling her how he felt about it; his obvious remorse.

Still staring straight into her eyes he added, "It haunts me, believe me it does, being responsible, even indirectly, for people being assassinated. I don't feel good about it, Alice. How could I? You're the only person I've ever told about it. It's a secret that I've had to carry within myself ever since, a dark secret that I know I probably shouldn't even be telling you. But you asked, and I wanted to be honest with you. By telling you that I want you to know that you can trust me."

She reached to take his hand, told him, "Thank you for telling me," and then kissed him tenderly on the lips.

Even now though, he knew that he wasn't telling her the whole truth, and not simply the fact that the Russian woman at the conference and Sophia in Athens was the same person. He had an even darker secret deep inside him than that, in addition to what he had just told her about MI6. He knew he couldn't tell her that. He daren't.

22

Middle of July

By mid-July the British tourists started to arrive. The lockdown in the U.K. had been eased and travel restrictions to and from some countries lifted. The same regulations were still in force at Greek airports in terms of random testing and registering on the Greek government website prior to arrival in the country. The requirements of masks to be worn in shops were also still in operation, as well as by staff in bars and restaurants and on public transport, plus on flights and in the airports.

The village was much busier. It wasn't the same level or number of tourists as was usual in the middle of July, but most of the bars and restaurants had opened and were doing a reasonable trade. Alice's restaurant opened at the end of June and she was back to doing her long shifts. Although with less tourists around compared to previous years she was finishing nearer to midnight than her one o'clock finishes of previous summers. She was, however, back to meeting up with David regularly after work. The clubs had not opened after the lockdown ended, so their late nights were restricted to late drinks in Jack Constantiono's Courtyard Bar or, less often, the Lindos By Night Bar. It also meant there were far fewer late nights that turned into early mornings for the two of them.

The only very late night stretching into early morning option was on Friday and Saturday nights at the open air club, Arches Plus, on the road down towards the Main Beach. That stayed open until six-thirty or even seven in the morning. Because it was the only club open in the village, as well as on that part of the island, it was always very busy. As both David and Alice knew the owner, Valasi, well from their Lindos stays, and from frequenting his other club in the centre of the village, Arches, they had no problem getting in.

They'd met up a few times during the day for coffee or for a late breakfast at the usual places in the village during the first couple of weeks of July, as well as for late night drinks. Alice seemed more at ease with him again after their walk up to the memorial above the Main Beach and his revelations. David thought things were going well once more, and the trials and tribulations over his Athens diversion were well behind them. However, he was still wrestling with a dilemma over her in his mind, one he couldn't share with her.

On the second weekend of July, on Friday the 10th, his feeling that things were once more going well between them was considerably enhanced, or so he thought initially. They met at the Courtyard after she'd been back to her flat to change after work. Around two-thirty Alice suggested they move on down to Arches Plus, to which he agreed. On the walk down there they could hear the music blasting out from the open air club and she reached over to take his hand while smiling broadly.

Soon they were inside and getting their first drinks at one of the bars. It was crowded, very crowded, seemingly even more so than usual. Perhaps it was because of the increase in the Brit tourists as the summer season was finally beginning to open up.

As was her way, Alice finished her Vodka and coke quickly. He was still only halfway through his however, as he noticed her scanning the crowd for familiar faces, people from the village she knew, mostly Greeks.

"You ready for another," he asked over the booming music. "Are you looking for someone?"

"What? No, not someone, just looking to see if there is more space anywhere."

"Doesn't look like it. I've not seen it this packed so far this season. Well, since it was allowed to open up after lockdown anyway."

He was about to ask again if she was ready for another drink when she surprised him by saying, "Let's go."

"What? Now? It's still early really."

"Yes, let's go, let's go, it's too crowded. I don't feel comfortable here when it's this crowded, especially with all the Covid shit," she told him loudly over the music.

He took another swig from his glass, placed it on the bar, and told her, "Okay." As he did so he took her hand and led her through the crowded club.

"Phew! That's better. How can it be so bloody hot in there when it's open air," she said as they emerged outside.

The view of the bay across the road was magical, sparsely lit up by the small lights twinkling on the few boats moored in the bay.

"It is a warm night, and it is July, Alice, plus it's more crowded in there than I've ever seen it. Probably because I guess there aren't that many clubs open on the island."

She was still clutching his hand as he suggested, "Pizza?"

She never answered. Instead, she told him, "It's always a beautiful view isn't it," and started to walk across the road towards the low iron railing opposite, still clinging on to his hand and taking him with her."

"Yes, stunning," he agreed as they reached the railing. "Don't usually see it like this though do we, lit up in places in the middle of the night by the lights from the boats moored in the bay."

She let out a small chuckle.

"Yes, it's usually the sun coming up and daylight by the time you're ready to leave, David."

She was teasing him. A good sign, he thought. So, he reached to put his arm around her shoulder and hold her close to him.

He thought he'd misread the situation again, however, when she pulled away slightly, shrugging off his arm after a minute in silence while they stared out across the bay.

"I'm not ready for this yet, David. I don't want this right now," she told him quite firmly.

In a few seconds the romantic moment had evaporated. Or so he thought.

Another long half-minute passed as they both stood gazing out in silence at the picturesque sight of the bay before them.

He was bewildered, frozen, although not from the air around them at all, and wondering quite what to do next. Suggest pizza again, or just say goodnight and go off to bed. A few seconds later he was even more bewildered. But that was the conundrum that was Alice Palmer. He should have known that by now.

She turned her face towards him. As she looked at him her eyes were darting and studying every part of his face. It was as if she was an artist checking out his features and searching for inspiration. She obviously found it.

She reached up to put her left hand behind the back of his neck, pulled his head down into hers and kissed him with a warm, soft, gentle, lingering kiss.

"But I … ," he started to say as she pulled back from the kiss and they parted.

Alice stopped him by placing her index finger to his lips while gazing into his eyes enticingly.

After a few seconds she removed her finger and he tried to speak once again.

"You just said …"

She stopped him again by kissing him once more.

This time as she drew back from the kiss she told him, "Sometimes life just happens, David, and you just have to let it. Don't over analyse it. Just go with the moment."

He was speechless. All he could do was nod in agreement. This was one confusing woman indeed. Beautiful as far as he was concerned, inside and out, but bloody confusing.

So, life did "just happen" again for the two of them that night. For the first time since the previous summer they slept together, had sex. Made love? Perhaps that was the way it could be described. He thought so, although he knew that there were other complications and barriers to that now because of the instructions he'd been given before he came back. It couldn't be that straightforward. Whether she shared his view that what they'd done was make love that night, and not simply had sex, was another matter.

23

Leaving

The following afternoon they went to the beach for a few hours. This time it was Pallas Beach. She left his flat around ten that morning and then called him at one to suggest a late breakfast at Giorgos, followed by a few hours on the beach. He was tired, but readily agreed. Going to the beach together wasn't something she'd often suggested throughout the previous summer. In fact, he could only recall it happening a couple of times.

All seemed well between them, and after a couple of nice swims to wake him up, followed by a short doze on the sunbed, she left him at five-thirty to go off to get ready for work.

As she left she told him, "See you later after work. I'll text you to find out where you are, but I think I can guess which bar you'll be in."

"Maybe I'll surprise you," he responded.

"No, you won't, you'll be in Jack's, as usual," she said with a smile as she left to make her way up the hill from Pallas.

She was right. He was in Jack Constantiono's Courtyard Bar. Despite what she'd told him she didn't even bother to text, just went back to her flat to shower and change into a pair of tight bright green shorts and a loose white t-shirt before going to the bar.

When she arrived Jack was telling David that the rumour he'd heard was that the Greek government might introduce a midnight curfew on all bars and restaurants in the country sometime in the next few weeks if the Covid situation didn't improve, or in fact, continued to deteriorate.

"Bloody great, we've only just started to pick up on the tourist trade in the restaurant," Alice chipped in.

"Well, I guess it'll mean you'll finish earlier," David suggested.

"Not really, will be pretty much the same by the time we've cleared up, and where the bloody hell will we be able to get a drink after that? All the bars will be closed by then."

Alice didn't look happy at all at that news as she reached to take the first drink of her Vodka and coke. What Jack told the two of them next made her even more unhappy.

"Oddest thing, you probably wouldn't remember her, Alice, probably never met her, but there was an Irish woman here four summers ago who was trying to trace her Greek father. She had no idea who he was, but her mother worked here for a couple of summers in the seventies and that's when she got pregnant with the woman."

Alice quickly placed her drink down on the bar as a look of concern spread across her face. David was too busy focusing on Jack and his story to notice her changed expression, and Jack was too engrossed telling it to notice the change.

"No, can't recall meeting any woman here doing that," she interjected with a quiet tone in her voice.

"Anyway, it's a long story," Jack continued. "I introduced her to my mother and grandmother who were able to help her about some things in and around the village at that time when her mother worked here."

David had begun to link the dots together, particularly as he glanced at the concerned look on Alice's face.

"So, what's odd about that, Jack?" he asked.

"Well, I haven't heard anything at all from her since that summer, not a word since she left. I thought that maybe she'd let me know how she got on with the rest of what she was trying to find out about her family, particularly the Greek side and the village, especially after my mother and grandmother helped her so much. They even asked me a couple of times if I'd heard from her. And she never actually said when she was leaving, just left out of the blue without even saying goodbye to anyone here from what I can gather. Then yesterday I got a text message from her, asking how I was, how the village was, and that she must come back someday soon."

286

David knew exactly what Alice was thinking as he quickly glanced sideways at her face. Simultaneously she did the same and as their eyes met concern was clear on both their faces.

Jack never noticed. As David said, "Yes, I suppose that is odd," he obviously merely assumed it was his story that had created the changed expression on both their faces.

They finished their drinks and left together. As soon as they got outside the bar Alice stopped walking, turned to face him, and said quietly, "It's her, isn't it. I know it's her."

She was distraught as she added, "I knew it, I knew she'd come back, looking for me."

He never really actually believed what he said next, but he thought it was the only way to calm her down.

"You really don't know that. How do you know it's the same woman you saw?"

"She was bloody Irish, David."

Her voice was raised now. She wasn't calming down at all. A couple of people outside Pal's Bar at the bottom of the alley finishing their last drinks, as well as a couple sat at the small table munching their crepes from the crepe shop opposite, heard her and turned to look up the alley at them.

"Just calm down," he told her as he placed both his hands on her shoulders. "Even if they are, were, both Irish it doesn't mean the woman Jack is talking about and the woman you saw kill the guy in the back alley are the same woman. There are plenty of Irish tourists in Lindos all the time."

"But it was the same summer, 2016, David. That's a hell of a coincidence don't you think?"

"Yes, the same summer, but how many Irish female tourists do you think were here through that summer, Alice, bloody hundreds, maybe even a lot more? And you don't even know if the woman, the killer, saw you anyway. Even if she did, why would she wait four years to come back to find you? Why now?"

She hesitated for a few seconds and took a deep breath.

As she did he added, "It can't be the same woman. It really can't. That wouldn't make sense would it, to wait this long?"

She nodded slightly. "Maybe, maybe you're right, but you know from what I told you, from what happened that afternoon in Rhodes Town when I overheard an Irish accent, that I get nervous about it, paranoid."

There was a worrying frown all over her face. He put his arms around her shoulder and pulled her into him for what he hoped would be a reassuring hug. They stood there at the top of the alley like that for a long half-minute.

She moved away slightly as he told her, "Look, if it makes you feel better, safer, why don't you come back to my place for tonight? We don't have to do anything, just sleep, and I'm sure you'll feel better in the morning."

"I ... I ... err ... ," she hesitated, obviously thinking things through and still dwelling on what Jack had just told her.

A few seconds later she told him firmly, "No, no, not tonight, David. I think I need to be alone to think all this through."

"Are you sure?"

She nodded slightly once again, then replied, "Yes ... err ... yes, I am. I don't think I'm in the mood to be with anyone right now. I need to think it through and decide what to do next."

"What do you mean-"

He started to ask, but he never got to finish his question. She was back into her disappearing act mode of last summer.

"I'll tell you tomorrow, text you or call you in the morning and we can meet for breakfast. I'll tell you then, after I've figured all this out in my head."

She quickly kissed him on the cheek, told him, "Goodnight," and rushed off down the alley.

Just another eventful Lindos night with Alice Palmer, he thought, as he wandered through the main alleyway of the village heading towards his flat and his bed. It was still quite early for a Lindos night, just approaching two. So, as he reached the small square by Bar404 and Yannis Bar he debated in his head for a very brief few seconds whether to go up the alleyway and into the Arches Club for one more drink. He was tempted. He certainly never felt tired after the short naps he'd had on the beach that afternoon. Would he be able to sleep now anyway, especially with the turmoil he'd just had with Alice swirling around in his head. In the end he decided not to, even if it turned out that he couldn't sleep once he got in his bed. Besides which, she said she'd call or text him in the morning to meet for breakfast. No doubt she'd have plenty to say about what Jack had told them, and what she intended to do, what she meant by her "what to do next" comment. He reckoned he was going to need a clear head for that conversation, as well as a good night's sleep.

He did manage to get off to sleep surprisingly quickly considering, and he woke up at nine the next morning. He shaved and showered, and her text suggesting breakfast at Giorgos came through just after ten. He was hoping that when he got there she would be more relaxed after a good night's sleep about what they'd heard from Jack Constantino. However, when he arrived she was already there with her coffee looking like the worried frown had remained with her all night. He ordered a cappuccino from Tsamis, as well as a couple of croissants.

"No breakfast for you?" he asked her.

"Only coffee, can't face anything else at the moment."

"Did you sleep ok? Manage to put all that stuff Jack was on about out of your head?"

She looked sceptical as she glanced silently across the table at him for a few seconds out of the top of her eyes.

"Hardly, how could you expect me to after that?" she eventually told him.

"I suppose so, but look it's probably nothing, just-"

He was trying to reassure her once again, but never got to finish.

"I'm leaving, leaving Lindos," she blurted out.

David slumped back in his chair, stunned. That was the last thing he'd expected to hear from her.

She reached for her coffee as he asked with an air of desperation in his voice, "What? When? But I thought after Friday night that we had a connection again."

She simply shrugged as she placed her coffee cup down on the table, but said nothing in response.

"Leaving, but where to, home?"

"No, I can't go there obviously, because of skipping the probation. Another island, maybe one of the smaller ones."

He leaned forward to rest his arms on the table and tried to push her for more detail, "Which one?"

But she wouldn't budge, not least because she didn't know. It seemed like a spur of the moment thing and that she hadn't thought it through that much, even though perhaps she'd been dwelling on it all night.

"I haven't decided yet." Then the unpredictable, surprising Alice Palmer resurfaced.

"Come with me, David."

Her eyes clearly told him that she meant it as she stared anxiously across the small table waiting for his response. He didn't respond to that directly though.

"Why now? Just because of what Jack told us last night?"

He knew the answer to that was yes, but she didn't admit to it.

She tried to sound as matter of fact as possible. "Time to move on, I've actually grown tired of supposedly living the dream here now. I've been here living and working for almost four seasons. Want to try somewhere new."

"Really?"

He raised his eyebrows. He knew that wasn't true, or at least not the real reason. She knew it too.

She took another drink to finish her coffee and then lifted the empty cup in Tsamis' direction standing in the doorway to signal that she'd like another. "And one of those please, Tsamis," she added as she pointed to David's croissants.

Now it was David who was frowning as he once again slumped back in his chair at her lack of the real answer. Eventually she did admit what he guessed.

"Okay, David, yes, perhaps it is a bit because of what Jack told us last night. I know it might just be a coincidence, like you said, and not the same woman, but I'm tired of worrying, always looking over my shoulder in case that bloody woman shows up. I know that she might not have, probably didn't see me that night. But all the time I'm here I keep thinking she knows where to find me if she did see me, which is why I want to go somewhere new, somewhere different. At least I'll feel safer and be less worried there."

"So, where," he asked again.

"I'm not exactly sure. I told you, perhaps one of the smaller islands, more remote. Just come with me and we'll decide together, just go and decide when we get to the ferry port at Rhodes Town."

She was leaning forward across the table and anxiously almost pleading with him. He'd never seen or heard her do that before. Her voice was bordering on a whisper now.

He stayed silent, not responding at all as Tsamis arrived with her second coffee and the croissant. He was facing a real dilemma. One that he couldn't tell her about, daren't, or even start to explain. Besides which this was all too much of a shock, all too quick, too much to take in. She hadn't prepared the ground at all. Was this merely typical Alice Palmer? Always running away?

She took a bite of her croissant and then a swig of the coffee before telling him, "But if you won't come with me I'm not going to tell you where I'm going, not that I know that right now to be honest, David, or let you know where I end up. I don't want anyone to know. I'll feel safer that way."

He sat there in a daze, shattered. Despite the bright hot Lindos sunshine his mind was a hazy fog. Just a couple of nights ago they'd slept together and he thought everything was good between them again, a new beginning, but now this. Deep down he knew this was always a possibility, that it might come eventually and he would then have to face up to the fact that there was no way he could be with her or go with her. However, he never anticipated it would arise so soon. For reasons known only to him he daren't go with her, for the safety of them both.

"I can't, I can't come with you. I have to go back to London for my novel," he replied.

He knew that was only partly true, and certainly wasn't the main reason. Despite his immense disappointment, one small part of him could only be relieved that she was leaving. He knew that there was something he would have to do eventually

291

if she remained in Lindos. Something he was being forced to do, instructed and expected to do. He'd put it off at first when he returned in early March. Then lockdown enabled him to put it off longer. The people who gave him his instructions at the end of February back in London reluctantly accepted that. They had to. They had no choice because of the lockdown. Anyway, that's what he told them. He'd wracked his brains over how to get out of it, out of doing what they wanted. Now, thankfully, by leaving Alice had provided him with an option, a way out, what seemed to be a solution to his dilemma, even if it wasn't ultimately what he wanted and it meant he couldn't be with her. As much as he really wanted to he couldn't go with her, or even tell her the real reason that he daren't.

The cold, defensive and indifferent part of her character resurfaced as she replied, "I see, okay, of course. I'm gonna leave the day after tomorrow then. That'll give me time to sort a few things here, with the restaurant and my landlord and that."

"Oh, that soon, I-"

He never got to finish.

"Right, I need to pay Tsamis for this inside and then it looks like I've got plenty to do, to sort before work tonight. I'll text you and we can meet later tonight or sometime tomorrow."

She took a quick slurp of her coffee, went inside to pay, and she was gone.

He checked the usual places for her late that night but there was no sign of her. No one in the Courtyard Bar or Lindos By Night had seen her. The next morning in his flat he got a text from her at eleven suggesting they meet at five that afternoon before she started her final night working in the restaurant at six-thirty. He replied, suggesting Café Melia, and she agreed.

It was an awkward meeting. Initially she displayed no emotion at all. He knew deep down that she had to leave. It was for the best. However, it didn't prevent him from being sad, disappointed. For the first few minutes as they ordered coffees the conversation was stilted, forced. Clearly neither of them knew quite what to say. It appeared obvious that they both wanted to avoid re-opening the whole conversation about wanting him to leave with her, or indeed, why she wanted to leave at all, felt she had to.

After their drinks arrived she asked unexpectedly, "So, is the great novel finished then?"

He was taken by surprise by her question.

"Err ... oh, yes, almost ... err ... Yes, just a few very brief final touches and then it will be. Then I'll have to go back to London to finalise a few last things with my publisher, like cover design and the rest. Hopefully it'll be published by September."

"That's good then." She flashed a quick smile across at him and a small nod.

Meaningless small talk wasn't what he wanted, or expected. He wanted to talk about them, whatever was between them. He tried to bring the conversation around to that tactfully, or so he thought.

"Perhaps we could meet up later in the summer, on whichever Greek island you end up on? That would be good. I'd really like that. I'll be heading back this way, Greece I mean, late September for a month anyway, I think."

She ignored his suggestion. Instead, she asked, "So, what's it about, this novel? I think you said last summer it was about relationships."

He hesitated for a few moments, took a sip of his coffee, and then looked straight across the table into her eyes as he answered, "It's ... err ... us ... it's about us."

That took her by surprise, although she was trying not to let it show.

"Oh, I see, and is there a happy ending?"

As she asked that he thought he detected a slight tone of regret in her voice.

"Don't know. You tell me, Alice."

She didn't answer, just reached to take another sip of her coffee as she looked across at him out of the top of her eyes.

"You know the ancient Greek, Homer, wrote that life is a never ending odyssey," he started to tell her as she placed her coffee back on the table. "He wrote that it's a search for adventure, for new experiences, and for meaning. Are we, whatever it is that is between us, never ending, or just a fleeting new experience do you think? You tell me what you think the meaning is of whatever is between us?"

As he finished speaking he stared hopefully across into her eyes once more. It wasn't as simple as all that for Alice however, and he knew deep inside that in reality it couldn't be as simple as that for him either. There was a large barrier that prevented something between them being anything other than a fleeting new experience. It was a real dilemma for him. He was searching over and over for a way to overcome it, and had been for weeks. But he was still at a complete loss how to, and he certainly couldn't tell her what it was. That wouldn't solve anything anyway. He was simply desperately trying to finally find out how she felt about him now, and about any relationship between them. He had to finally know. Perhaps it would help him find a solution.

"I don't know, David," she told him.

She looked away to stare into the far distance across the square, shook her head slightly from side to side, and then took a deep breath before she continued.

"I really don't, don't know. I can't get some of the things that happened last year between us out of my head, what you did in October. Sometimes I try to convince myself I can, like when I asked you to come with me, leave here with me. Sometimes I try to believe that over time I will, but I can't just dismiss and forget it all quite that easily after what happened to me in the past with my ex-husband. Unfortunately the bad things are as much a part of what is between us now as the good times. I, we, can't just remove them from our memory can we? That's just not possible."

"But-"

He tried to interrupt. He thought they were questions and she was asking him to help resolve her dilemma, the things that troubled her. She wasn't. She hadn't finished explaining what was troubling her about what might be between them.

She briefly looked back towards him then turned away again to stare straight ahead. She appeared determined not to make any eye contact with him as she continued.

"Trust is big thing for me, David. You know that. I've told you that plenty of times. Lies destroy trust. They actually prevent people from really knowing us, knowing who we are and being able to understand us. If you can't understand someone, the truth about who they really are, how can you help them, support them, really love them?"

As she turned her head to look back into his face traces of two small tears were running down her cheeks.

"And I know you lied to me, David. I didn't want to believe that you did when Dianne told me about it all, you and Sophia in Athens. Believe me, I didn't. But part of me knew it was true because that's what I always expect now, expect to be let down. And you did let me down. Oh, I know you can say that you never actually directly lied about Athens, but you did only say you were flying home. There was no mention of Athens, let alone her of course. So, for me that's a lie by omission. Whatever, even so it was a lie, and destroyed what trust I had in you. When you came back in March I thought I could get over it, put it behind me. I tried, believe me I tried, struggled with it all through lockdown. Yes, I was glad, happy even, that you were here for me then. I told you that, and you told me the same. But most of all what you did, and your lie over Athens, not only destroyed the trust between us it also made me question whether I actually knew and understood you at all at a difficult time like now when who knows what is going to happen here for the rest of the season with this bloody virus still swirling around the world"

As she finished she reached up with her index finger to try to wipe away the small traces of tears from her cheek.

He didn't know quite what to say, how to respond. He'd never heard her talk to him as openly as that, about her feelings and the two of them. He knew that trust was a big thing for her. She'd told him that quite a few times. He had to admit to himself that he hadn't been exactly honest about a number of things. However, there was one more thing, a big thing, probably the largest, that he simply could never be honest with her about. It was at the very heart of the comment she'd just made about trust, loving someone, and knowing the truth about who someone really is. Instead, he attempted to hint at it without actually telling her.

"Secrets and lies are a dangerous thing, Alice. We all think we want to know them, find out all about them. But if you've kept one to yourself for so long you soon come to understand that by doing so that may help you learn something about somebody else, but ultimately you also discover something about yourself. And that's not usually good. That's the side effect, I guess."

She misunderstood and clearly thought he was talking about her, when, in fact he was talking about himself.

"What are you on about?" She looked completely bemused, but he'd gone as far as he could.

"You'll see, maybe in time it will all become clear, Alice. But if you don't let go of your past it'll strangle your future."

As he finished he took her hand and leaned across to kiss her gently on the cheek.

The next day she was gone. He had no idea where. Since she told him she was leaving he hadn't asked again, so she never told him exactly where. She never even saw him that day to say goodbye.

Now, for him, it was in the past. The recent past, but nevertheless in the past. It had to be. Was it a lost opportunity, a lingering, never forgotten, endless regret, or nevertheless despite that an enjoyable, happy time? One and a half enjoyable Lindos summers, on the whole. Only time and looking back would perhaps tell David Alexander which. One thing he knew for now though, if you have any chance of happiness grab it with both hands, no matter what obstacles are in your way. Overcome them somehow and don't let happiness escape through missed opportunity.

On the other hand, perhaps Pythagoras was right and it is actually about the morality of the Pythagoras cup. Sometimes in life it is better to not want or seek more and more than you have because if you do you may end up with nothing in the end.

In their relationship Alice settled for that in the end, and understood that. Maybe it wasn't only in the end though. Maybe she knew that, and settled for that all through those one and a half Lindos summers. David Alexander clearly didn't. Contented with a little, yet always wishing for more. That summed up his situation, how he felt about Alice Palmer. But as with so many times in his past, he managed to balls it up. This time however, he knew that unfortunately he didn't really have much choice.

24

His insurmountable secret

The morning after she left he walked up to the memorial overlooking the Main Beach again. He needed to make a call and it had to be somewhere there was likely to be no one around. In his flat there was always the chance that someone from the other one in the courtyard could overhear. He couldn't take that chance.

He retrieved the burner phone taped to the underside of the draw of one of the bedside tables in his flat and made his way quickly through the village and up the hill. As when he was up there with Alice before there was no one else around.

He pressed the speed dial memory number one and a voice answered immediately, "Is this phone safe?"

"You tell me. It's the one you gave me before I came back. So, unless you've-"

The voice on other end of the line interrupted with, "Okay, okay, is it done?"

"Yes, it's done. All clear here now. No sign of any suspicion. Your informant was right. There was a witness to what happened to your man here in the summer of 2016. Don't ask how I discovered that, or even to give you the name because I'm not going to."

David had known that was the case, that there was a witness, since last August the previous summer when Alice confided in him about it during their afternoon in Rhodes Town, but he'd sat on it and kept it to himself all through the winter. In any case, he had no idea at that time that MI6 would be interested to know.

"We don't need or want to know how," the voice told him. "Just that it's done, as instructed, as we agreed. Okay, and?"

"As I said, it's done. The witness has been dealt with, been removed, left us you could say," David responded firmly. He thought that would be enough and he could get off the phone and get on with his life. But it wasn't. The voice wanted clarification and more confirmation.

"Dealt with, as in no longer around, disposed of, if I get what you mean, and there's no mess to clear up from the disposal?"

David hesitated momentarily and the voice at the other end of the line simply said, "You still bloody there?"

"Yes, yes, that's right, no longer around, and no mess for you to deal with. I've already done what needed to be done," David eventually responded.

He was becoming agitated. He just wanted to get away from all of it and try to put it all behind him. He took a deep breath and tried to calm himself before continuing.

"And I've never picked up any indication, or heard anything here, to suggest that anyone thinks that what happened in 2016 was anything other than an accident, including it seems the local Greek police. So, there's no sign that anyone has any idea there was a witness, other than the witness themselves of course, and I've dealt with that now."

"Good, the Irish woman assassin was dealt with back in 2016, shortly after the event. Now you've taken care of the witness all the loose ends are tied up very neatly," the voice told him. There was a moment's silence and then the voice added coldly, "That's the way we like things, all neat and tidy."

"So, the Irish woman is dead?"

Surprise was obvious in David's voice as he asked that. He'd tried to convince Alice that MI6 would have taken care of her that way after she was spooked over the text Jack told them a few nights ago he received, The text from the Irish woman who Jack said had been in the village in 2016 trying to trace her birth father. Alice was sure she was the killer who she saw in the Lindos top alley that summer. However, the voice at the other end of the phone was as equivocal in answering as David had just been.

"Yes, she's been dealt with."

David wanted more though. He pushed.

"Dealt with as in dead? When? Where?"

"You don't need to know any more than I've just told you, old boy. You know better than to ask that."

David was left dangling. Had the Irish woman been killed, or was the voice at the other end of the line simply using the same evasive language as David just had. If she had been killed then Alice would be safe, from her at least. Perhaps then he would be able to find her later that summer on whatever Greek island she'd run off to, tell her that for sure, and be with her. Although even if he could find her later that summer, persuading her of that wouldn't be easy. He knew that. After all, he could never tell her that he knew it was the case, that the woman had been killed, because he'd got that from MI6. He'd face that particular dilemma when he came to it, if he could find her. Besides which, he was very unlikely to be able to find out for sure if MI6 had actually killed the Irish woman. They never gave that sort of information out easily, and they certainly wouldn't trust him with it. They only gave him information that they believed he needed to know in order to get him to do whatever they wanted for them, like passing on contact details to Sophia at the Moscow conference, or finding out something in Lindos for them from 2016.

Indeed, when MI6 unexpectedly contacted him towards the end of February, before he came back to Lindos, it all sounded like a simple enough request.

"Just try and find out if what our informant says is true, that there was a witness. Another of our sources told us last October that you were there, that you'd been there for the whole summer, and was a regular Lindos visitor. So, you must know a few people there you can tap up casually about it to see if they know anything. See what the locals think happened, if everyone thought it was an accident, and if by any chance there is any talk or rumours at all of a witness."

It was the same voice over the phone as the one now. They made it all sound very innocent, very straightforward, just an information gathering exercise. It was the 'need to know' principle. Just give as little information as was needed. There

300

was no mention of assassinating any witness. David Alexander was far from being some kind of trained MI6 killer now anyway, so why would there be. That was all in his past life and he'd put all that behind him. He was a different person now. They'd recruited his help in making contact at the Moscow conference with Alexandra Ivanova, who he subsequently knew as Sophia,. As far as he was concerned that was to be it in terms of helping them again; just innocently pass on some contact details to help her defect. However, they never really let go. Once they've got you then you're always an asset as far as they are concerned, a resource to be used when necessary or useful. What the MI6 voice told him in their call in February caused him to briefly wonder whether Sophia was their other source who had reported he was in Lindos last October. After all that was when she was there, supposedly on holiday. Was she still working for them? Perhaps bumping into her that night in Antika wasn't the coincidence it seemed.

When he initially met Alice Palmer that first night in the restaurant he obviously had no idea at all that there had even been a witness to what happened in a Lindos back alley in the summer of 2016, let alone that she would turn out to be the possible witness MI6 had been tipped off about. In fact, he'd only heard a few bits of local gossip about it on one of his two week holidays a couple of years before, and those portrayed it as an accident, put down to the uneven path in that part of the village.

At the time he came back to Lindos in early March he was still wrestling with the dilemma of whether he should tell MI6 what he knew. As far as his contact was concerned he couldn't try and find out what they wanted to know until he returned to the village. That bought him a little time to try and decide what to do, what was best. What he did know was that whatever he decided it should be what was best for Alice. He realised that eventually they might pressurise him to tell them who it was, the name of their witness, but at that stage they had only instructed him to find out if there was one, and who it was, nothing more. He'd decided he would try and avoid giving them Alice's name, or even that the witness was a woman.

After he'd been back just over three weeks, shortly after the Greek government declared a complete lockdown because of the Covid virus, he called his MI6 contact to report that he'd confirmed that there was witness. He figured that as it was a full lockdown nothing could happen anyway. It wouldn't be possible, whatever action they wanted.

He was shocked when his contact instructed him firmly to, "Dispose of the witness, or else."

They informed him in no uncertain terms that if he didn't they'd send someone to, "Dispose of the two of them," him, as well as the witness. He'd been very careful at all times to do what he'd decided and not name Alice, or even that the witness was a woman. His controller never even bothered to ask. It seemed he didn't need to know, or didn't want to. So, David was at a loss to see how they could send someone to dispose of the two of them. Him, yes, obviously, but Alice, how would they know?

Initially he tried to convince his contact that there was no point in killing the witness. It had been over three years and surely if the witness was going to say or do anything they would have done it by now. The only response he got down the phone line was a very firm, "Just bloody do it, or else."

When he pressed and asked what reason they could possibly have for killing a witness to the murder of one of their own operatives all he got in response was an emotionless, cold, statement.

"The fewer people who know who works for us, what they do, and why, the better, and safer for our existing operatives. And that includes people like the Greek police and others poking around trying to find out why an undercover IRA assassin would have killed one of our operatives back in that summer of 2016. An IRA assassin who had infiltrated our security services over a number of years. I'm sure you can understand that it's not exactly good publicity, old boy, for anything to come out publicly from whatever source - the Greek police, this witness, or you for that matter - to the effect that the British Security Services had been infiltrated for almost twenty years by an IRA operative and assassin, and very successfully. That just wouldn't do, would it? Make us look like a bunch of fools. No, the Section Head and the top brass think it's better to have everything of that mess cleared up, cleaned up, rather than something sneaking out later, or someone opening their mouth publicly later and the whole embarrassing episode coming out. Some of the oiks and cretins in the British media would have a field day over that wouldn't they, not to mention some of our so-called friends at MI5. So, just do it, just do what we require you to do, old chap. then we can all rest easy can't we."

David tried one more time and pleaded with the MI6 voice. He was in agony.

"I did five years of killing for you while I lived two different lives. Can't you just leave me alone? Can't you just leave this? It's bloody pointless. I came out here to get away from all that and get on with my life."

His MI6 contact wouldn't relent, however. He responded firmly, "We gave you a whole new life when you finished with the Service, a new identity, a legend. We looked after you, old boy. That's what you wanted, wanted to finish, and we did that for you. Don't ever forget that. You still owe us for that. Now you have to do this one small thing for us and it's quits. Just this one thing and it's over, for good. That'll really be the end of it all."

That was the only time David got an explanation as to why MI6 wanted Alice killed. He knew never to ask again. It would have been no use. Now, as far as they were concerned by mid-summer of 2020 he'd done what they required.

Once again he was deliberately being economical with the truth though. He'd done that a few times with Alice through the past two summers. However, this time he felt he had good reason. As he stood on that hill overlooking Lindos Main Beach in the bright, warm sunshine he knew exactly what the voice at the other end of the line meant by, "disposed of", that he had killed the witness, Alice. However, there was no way he could bring himself to do that after the two summers, or at least one and a half, that they'd spent in each other's company. He'd fallen well and truly in love with her over that time. Yes, he'd stupidly acted like a spoilt brat by running off to spend time in Athens with Sophia because of what he'd heard from Dianne about Alice and Simon Chapel. He regretted that more than he could ever show her or convince her. He desperately wanted to leave with her for another Greek island. She obviously wanted him to from what she'd told him in those last few days they were together. She'd even asked him to. But to do so would only mean MI6 continuing to look for her, as well as him, the two of them if they were together. He'd resigned himself to the fact that this way was best, safest for her, even if it meant he couldn't be with her now or possibly ever. He knew now that he daren't try to overfill their particular Pythagoras Cup by seeking more between them than was possible or safe. Seeking to live a life together would only produce the lingering continuous threat of the Hades of death for them both.

"Yes, all the loose ends are tied up, and that's the end of it all for me. I'm done with you lot now, for good. I mean it this time," David told the voice firmly at the other end of the line. All he wanted to do now was to try to forget about it all, get down from the hill onto the beach and take a refreshing, soothing swim in the clear sea of Lindos Bay Just get on with his new life in the picturesque beautiful village, for now at least.

"Of course you are, old boy, done, if you say so," the voice told him. Then with a clearly evident heavy dose of menacing smug mockery it added, "By the way, Alexandra, or should I say Sophia, says, "Hi." I never told you before, had no need to, but we saw that you had a good time with her in Athens last October. She told us she certainly enjoyed it."

David was stunned. Before he could say anything in response the line went dead.

Printed in Great Britain
by Amazon